W9-BQX-937

A DANCE THROUGH TIME

Lynn Kurland

JOVE BOOKS, NEW YORK

This is a work of fiction. Names, characters, places, and incidents are either the product of the author's imagination or are used fictitiously, and any resemblance to actual persons, living or dead, business establishments, events, or locales is entirely coincidental.

A DANCE THROUGH TIME

A Jove Book / published by arrangement with
the author

PRINTING HISTORY
Jove edition / December 1996

The Penguin Putnam Inc. World Wide Web site address is
http://www.penguinputnam.com

ISBN: 0-515-11927-X

A JOVE BOOK®
Jove Books are published by
The Berkley Publishing Group, a division of Penguin Putnam Inc.,
375 Hudson Street, New York, New York 10014.
JOVE and the "J" design are trademarks
belonging to Penguin Putnam Inc.

PRINTED IN THE UNITED STATES OF AMERICA

15   14   13   12   11   10   9   8

To my Grandad,
who gave me unconditional love
and taught me how to balance my checkbook,
gifts without which I would truly be lost.

The author gratefully acknowledges the timely advice and gruesome descriptions of L. Kirk Lorimer, D.P.M., in regards to all things medical.

Come to me in dreams, and then
One saith, *I shall be well again,*
For then the night will more than pay
The hopeless longing of the day.

Nay, come not *thou* in dreams, my sweet,
With shadowy robes, and silent feet,
And with the voice, and with the eyes
That greet me in a soft surprise.

Last night, last night, in dreams we met,
And how, to-day, shall I forget,
Or how, remembering, restrain
Mine incommunicable pain?

Nay, where thy land and people are,
Dwell thou remote, apart, afar,
Nor mingle with the shapes that sweep
The melancholy ways of Sleep.

But if, perchance, the shadows break,
If dreams depart, and men awake,
If face to face at length we see,
Be thine the voice to welcome me.

Andrew Lang
1844–1912

Chapter 1

"COME TO ME."

His deep voice echoed in the stillness of the great hall. He held out his hands, waiting.

She looked at the man standing before her, a warrior tall and powerfully fashioned. The firelight from the huge hearth played over the rugged features of his face, glinted off his long, dark hair, turned his eyes to a deep, fiery green. His gaze locked with hers, warming her, imprisoning her.

She walked to him, slowly. She reached out and put her hands in his. There were calluses on his skin, hard places where the sword had left its imprint. He ran his thumbs over her palms, caressing her hands before he took them and slipped them up around his neck. She caught her breath as his arms came around her and pulled her hard against him.

"Och, but you're a bonny thing, my Elizabeth," he said, in a husky voice.

He lowered his head and covered her lips with his own. He plundered her mouth, ravaging it with kisses that made her knees buckle. She clung to him as waves of desire crashed over her, leaving her weak.

A ringing began, intruding on the sounds of wood crackling in the hearth and the harsh rasp of the man's breathing. She ignored the bell-like noise, but it continued, persistent.

She turned to see what it was, then felt herself falling. She looked back at the man in disbelief.

"Nay, do not leave me," he said, clutching her more tightly to him.

She stared up at him, mute, unable to stop the feeling of plunging into nothingness. She slid through his arms and felt a sharp pain . . .

Elizabeth Smith winced as her elbow connected with a solid wood floor. She opened her eyes and blinked a time or two.

Then she lay back and let out an anguished groan. Falling out of bed was *not* how that dream was supposed to end.

And that ringing had been the phone. She reached up and groped for the receiver on her nightstand. This had better be some kind of emergency, or she was going to kill whoever had ruined the best kiss of her life.

"Hello?" she croaked.

"Yeah, is this Eddie's Breakfast Pizza?"

Elizabeth lifted her chin and peered up at her clock, squinting to make sense of the glowing numbers. Good grief, it was only nine A.M.

"Wrong number, buddy," she mumbled and hung up the phone. She had been snatched from possibly the most perfect dream of her life for some idiot wanting pizza for breakfast?

Hopefully it wasn't an omen.

She lay back on the floor and stared up at the ceiling, still wrapped in the remains of her dream. She could almost feel the man's arms around her, hear his rich voice washing over her, taste his lips on hers. Her name from his lips had been a caress, a possessive touch that branded her his. If he only could have been real! No more putting up with men who could take her or leave her. *There* was a man who would be more interested in her than TV or sports. How distressed he had sounded when she had started to slip away from him! Of course she'd found him in a dream. Somehow, it just figured.

Well, there was nothing she could do about it. She groaned as she forced herself to sit up and face reality.

It was enough to make her want to go back to bed.

Her apartment, furnished as it was in early starving writer, was a sty. It was a minuscule Manhattan garret, and every available surface was covered with a stack of something. Her table, which served both as a place to eat and a place to write, was piled high with research books, drafts of her novel and a collection of soda cans. Dishes were piled in her sink. Clothes were strewn from one end of the place to another. It was a complete disaster, one she had put off dealing with for weeks.

Well, there was no sense in postponing the inevitable any longer. She hauled herself to her feet, then walked purposefully across three feet of floor to her table. To fortify herself, she took a gulp from the cola can she'd opened the night before, then sat and reached for the notebook that contained her list of things to do.

Finish cover letter for manuscript. She paused. Writing a novel was hard enough. Pitching it in three paragraphs or less was murder. Maybe she'd give herself another day to come up with something brilliant. She crossed the item off her list with a quick swipe of her pen.

Exercise. Oh, definitely not. She squelched the small stab of guilt over crossing off that reminder.

Clean apartment was number three. She was fairly certain there were no unpaid bills lurking anywhere, so maybe there wasn't much sense in wasting time getting organized. She was sure she still had some clean underwear in her drawer, so what was the point in straightening up when the place would just get messy again anyway? Especially since she had much better things to do with her time this morning—mainly fantasize about that man from her dream. She tossed her notebook onto a handy pile of research materials, then sat back, ready to give her imagination free rein.

She closed her eyes and struggled to bring back his image. Tall, dark-haired, green-eyed. The feel of his arms around her was something she was certain she would never forget.

She opened her eyes suddenly, wondering why it hadn't occurred to her before. She would write a book about him. If she couldn't have him in the flesh, she could certainly have him in print. It made perfect sense, being that her passion was romance. Reading about it, writing about it, thinking about it: it didn't make a difference to her which way it came. As long as there was a love story and a happy ending involved, she was all for it.

It had all started innocently enough. She'd begun by rewriting in her head endings to all the great tragedies. After she'd seen Romeo and Juliet settled in a quaint little Italian villa with five kids, she'd moved on to tampering with Ophelia's head and Hamlet's timing. Somehow, all of that had led her to thinking perhaps she should start from scratch with her own characters.

Her first attempt had wound up as kitchen shelf liner. But the manuscript sitting on her table was different. She had agonized for months over it, putting her whole soul into the fashioning of the characters. And now it was finally finished and ready to mail except for her letter of introduction. She paused and stared at it thoughtfully. Maybe she really should finish it up before she started on anything else.

Come to me.

Elizabeth froze. Her apartment was too small for anyone to have sneaked in without her knowing as much, unless they'd done it sometime during the night. Maybe they had, and they were just waiting for her to notice before they did her in. She took a deep breath. She might as well know now. She turned in her seat slowly, fully expecting to come face-to-face with the business end of a lethal weapon.

She came face to face with a month's worth of dirty laundry.

She shook her head, as if by so doing she could clear up her sudden hearing problem. Her apartment was empty, but she had heard a voice, just as surely as she was sitting there.

Come to me. Wasn't that what the man from her dream had first said to her?

Chills went down her spine, and her skin erupted into gooseflesh. Either she was losing her mind, or somebody was trying to tell her something. Maybe that incredibly sexy man was calling to her. Did he really want his book written? She nodded to herself. That had to be it. She had a vivid imagination. Her characters were taking on a life of their own and demanding their due. That happened to other people. It could happen to her.

Make haste, Elizabeth.

She squeaked in spite of herself. All right, either she was hearing things, or her apartment was haunted. Whatever the case, it was obviously a sign; she had no qualms about taking it as such. If the man wanted his book written right away, who was she to say no?

She jumped up and began shuffling through her piles of papers. Last week her fiancé had happened upon a few books he thought she might find useful. Though he was helpful and accommodating, he wasn't exactly thrilled by her choice of careers. But since he wasn't exactly her fiancé, he really didn't have the right to say much about what she did.

Stanley Berkowitz worked at the New York Public Library. She'd been loitering in the reading room one day, poring over a lithograph of King Duncan's dining table when Stanley had seen her. He'd recommended more books to her, then, as time went on, smuggled others out to her. He'd wooed her with research materials and Godiva chocolate. How could she have resisted two of her favorite things? When he'd presented her with a proposal and a diamond, she'd said yes to both. So he wasn't her dream man. He was nice. There was a lot to be said for nice.

Or so she'd thought until last night. She'd begun to feel concerned that Stanley hadn't exactly committed to a wedding date. Pushing him about it over chicken marsala had revealed he wasn't all that interested in getting married any time soon, but he was interested in maintaining an engagement because it got his mother off his back. How she'd held onto her composure through chocolate decadence pie was beyond her. She'd accepted Stanley's latest book offerings, but she hadn't accepted his offer to come in. It was all she could do not to club him over the head with the biography of Robert the Bruce he'd handed her. That man from her dream certainly wouldn't have been so blasé about her, no sir. No phoney engagement for him.

Elizabeth sat down with a thump. She was losing it. How would she know what that man would or wouldn't do? She was taking her dreams way too seriously. It was a bad thing to start. Who knew where it could lead?

Elizabeth, now!

Like that, she nodded to herself. Not only was she starting to hallucinate in broad daylight; her hallucinations were starting to order her around. It was a very bad sign.

"All right," she said out loud. "Keep your pants on. I'm working on it."

She searched through the stacks, flinging papers, magazines, paper plates and red pens onto the floor, looking for those books Stanley had brought her the week before. They were on Scotland. Though her current novel was set in England, that wasn't where her passion lay. Aye, 'twas Scotland that fascinated her. She dreamed of Scottish moors and fields of heather, of gloomy keeps with fierce lairds—ruthless warriors the size of linebackers who wielded swords against their enemies and wooed their ladies with sweet words and gentle kisses. It wasn't that she didn't already have linebackers. She did, in the persons of her five brothers. There were times she was sure she'd scream if she had to sit through another college fourth-and-goal story. But that was where big ended and the rest of her current situation began.

She had come to New York, sure the city would inspire her to write wonderful books. She'd found inspiration, but she hadn't run into any ruthless warriors who had demanded she allow them to woo her. She had, however, been approached by that balding librarian who wanted to use her ring finger.

Elizabeth, by all the saints . . .

The hair on the back of her neck stood up without permission. Okay, so her hero was getting really impatient. She lifted up a collection of newspapers and hit the mother lode. She shoved the rest of the table-top contents onto the floor, then spread out the books in front of her and looked over the titles: *Rulers of Scotland; Scotland: An Historical Perspective; Fact or Fiction: Scotland's Turbulent Past; Life in a Medieval Hall; Scottish Lairds and Their Clans.* She picked up the one on medieval life and glanced through it.

The keep was definitely the place to be. At least a body got clothes and a meal now and then. Bathing, though, didn't seem to have been a priority. Elizabeth could only speculate as to the smell of not only the keep, but the unwashed bodies inside. Living on savings and the small amount she could bring herself to accept from her parents was tough, but at least she had her own bed, free from bugs and secure from men with rape on their minds. Nope, medieval life was not for her. She pitied the women who'd had to endure it.

The book on Scottish rulers caught her eye. She flipped through the centuries, from Kenneth MacAlpin to James IV. Robert Bruce? He had ruled from 1306 to 1329. For some reason, the dates appealed to her. Yes, this time period would surely suit the man from her dream. Now all that remained was to find a clan for him to rule over. Of course he would be a laird; a man of her warrior's stature would find himself nowhere if not at the head of a company of equally fierce warriors.

She reached for the volume on Scottish clans. It fell open to a page on the Clan MacLeod. A chill went through her, as if Fate had come up behind her and blown softly on the back of her neck. She devoured all she could about the clan, their history, their wars and their enemies.

At the end of the chapter was a pen and ink plate of a forest. The familiarity of the place struck her like a blow. It looked so real she was half afraid to touch it, for fear some elf would reach out, snag her hand and pull her into his magical world.

Ridiculous. She resisted the urge to look over her shoulder and make sure there weren't a dozen bogeymen there, winking at her from the shadowy corners of her apartment—along with her very vocal dreamboat, of course. No, the forest looked familiar because she had seen it in another book. Goodness knows she had read enough about Scotland.

But that didn't explain away the whispers of magic in the air. Maybe it was her grandfather's fault. He had filled her head full of tales of Scottish enchantments from the time she was small and somehow, in the back of her mind, she almost believed them. That and the gift of his Gaelic language was his legacy to her. Perhaps weaving a bit of enchantment into her story in his honor wasn't such a bad idea. Even though nothing magical ever happened to her, there was no reason her heroine couldn't enjoy a different fate.

All right. Now that she had found a time and place, she needed to immerse herself in what she'd learned and seen and let her imagination run away with her. Maybe she should get dressed and go for a walk to get her creative juices flowing.

Aye, come to me, my love.

Elizabeth jumped as if she'd been stuck with a pin. She had the insane desire to get dressed in the bathroom so whoever insisted on talking to her wouldn't watch.

She shook her head. Ridiculous. There was no one in her apartment. Maybe all that was calling to her was that emergency box of truffles under the couch.

Well, whatever it was, it was something she definitely needed to get away from. She yanked on a pair of jeans, an oversized blue sweater, tennis shoes, and a leather jacket she had recently appropriated from her brother's wardrobe. Alex was a big mucky-muck corporate attorney, making far more than even *he* could spend on clothes. Elizabeth made herself at home in his closet as often as possible.

She checked her pockets for her key and sundries, then ran from her apartment. She wasn't afraid to be there by herself, just because her characters were talking out loud to her. No, not at all. She just needed some fresh air. Yes, that was it. A nice walk to Gramercy Park where she could plot her story in peace.

She pulled her collar up around her ears as she walked down the street. The chilly fall wind whipped her hair around her face and scattered leaves in front of her. There was a tingle in the air, as if the world held its breath, waiting for something magical to happen. Not that she believed in magic. She was a practical girl with her feet planted firmly on the ground. Which was, no doubt, why she spent most of her time writing about men who existed only in her imagination.

By the time she reached the park, she was ready not for a plot line, but a bagel and something hot to drink. She was also starting to feel a little silly. She had a *very* vivid imagination. That coupled with Stanley's bombshell the night before had just sent her for a loop. Dream lovers were not loitering in her apartment, commanding her to come find them. She could go home any time and feel perfectly safe and perfectly foolish.

Well, maybe later. There was no sense in wasting fresh air. She nodded to herself in agreement. A half an hour meditating on a park bench, then a nice breakfast and cup of hot chocolate with whipped cream on top. Maybe she'd also look up that number for Eddie's Breakfast Pizza.

First things first. She looked around, noted the mothers with small children and the apparent lack of thugs, then made her way to her favorite bench. It was unoccupied, in the sun, and free of bird droppings. Elizabeth smiled. Life didn't get much better than that.

She stretched out and closed her eyes. The bench back blocked the wind, and the sun was warm on her face. This was the life. Much more comfortable than a musty-smelling castle. Her hero might have had to put up with it, but she didn't. Nothing like fresh autumn air to really make you glad you're in the twentieth century.

As she relaxed, the image of the forest she'd seen came back to her, filling even the edges of her mental vision. It just seemed so real. Where in the world had she seen it? She'd read countless books on Scotland, but surely she would have remembered such a beautiful place. It was probably even more beautiful in person. She needed to get herself to Scotland. What did heather really smell like? And who was to say she wouldn't run into some handsome Highlander with a horse at his disposal and lots of time on his hands? She could imagine worse ways to see the countryside.

Now, if she'd just been able to run into that man from her dream, she would have been truly content. What a tour guide he would have made!

A shiver went through her. She pulled her coat closer around her. The bench back was supposed to be blocking that chill. Maybe the wind had changed. She turned her face to one side, then brushed away the annoying blade of grass that tickled her ear.

Grass?

She sat up, her heart thudding against her ribs. She looked around her slowly, her eyes noting every clump of weeds, every scrap of bark on the trees and forest floor, every pile of molding leaves. Realization dawned, then reverberated through her, as if she'd been a gong struck by an enormously angry orchestra member. She trembled from her heart out to the ends of her fingers and toes. Her surroundings looked frighteningly familiar, and there was a simple reason for it. It was the same forest she'd been looking at in the book.

Only now she was *in* it.

She lay back down, willing herself to feel the hard wood of the bench beneath her back. She was dreaming. Or she was delirious. Yes, that was it. Twenty-four years of sneaking cola drinks for breakfast had finally taken its toll, and she had been tossed into a sugar-induced hallucination. No more soda for breakfast. She crossed her heart as she made that vow. That box of truffles was definitely going into the Dumpster. No more peanut butter and jelly either. Who knew what sorts of terrible things peanuts could do to a person's mental state? And pizza? She'd never touch the stuff again.

Unfortunately, all her solemn vowing didn't help her ignore the mounds and dips of the uneven forest floor beneath her back and legs.

She took a deep breath and opened her eyes again. The sky was just growing light. Well, yes, that was sky. She had seen sky before and knew what it looked like. She sat up and reached out to touch the grass. It was stiff and resilient under her fingers. She plucked a blade of grass and bit into it. It tasted real enough. She rose unsteadily to her feet, turned and put a shaking hand on the tree. The bark was rough under her fingers.

She looked down at herself, hoping she would see she had sprouted wings or something else that would convince her she was dreaming. She still had on the same jeans she had put on that morning, the same pair of shoes, the same baggy blue wool sweater and Alex's leather jacket.

But no wings. No shiny monster scales. No pointy toes.

She checked her pockets. She had her house key, her driver's license and her American Express card. Her dad always told her never to leave home without it and, since he paid the bill at the end of the month, she followed his advice religiously. But she had no hard cash. Not even a tissue in case she became hysterical. She tried not to think about that appealing alternative. Well, at least she had warm clothes. That was a plus. She could have lost her mind with her shoes off.

But that was where the pluses ended and the minuses began.

She slowly pressed her forehead against the tree, putting her hands on the bark in an effort to regain her balance. All right, so she had a fantastic imagination and it was currently running away with her. Soon she would wake up in the park and feel very stupid for having panicked. Right?

Right. She was dreaming. Wow, what an imagination she had. She envisioned a self-help book in her future entitled *Sugar and Historical Research—Never Take Them Together.*

After another deep breath, she pushed away from the tree and looked around. And as this was just a sucrose-induced delusion, what did it matter what she did? She would simply put one foot in front of the other and walk until she was tired. At least she wasn't hearing voices anymore. It wasn't a bad trade-off.

The early morning sun spilled down into the woods, the beams separating into soft threads of light as they fell through the trees. The air was cold and crisp. Elizabeth rubbed her arms as she walked. Strange. She had never had such a discernible sense of temperature in a dream. Maybe she should add last night's bedtime helping of Deep Chocolate–Chocolate Chip ice cream with hot fudge sauce over it to her list of Forbidden Sweets. She definitely didn't want a repeat of her current situation.

She walked until the trees began to thin on her right. She paused. Well, she was where she was. No sense in not having a good look around.

A beautiful meadow opened up before her. She stared at it for several minutes in pure enjoyment. Delicious, flowery smells wafted past her on a current of air that was sharp and clean. She lifted her eyes to the far side of the flat expanse and saw another forest of tall trees, equally as beautiful as the forest behind her. Then she looked to her left.

She almost fell over in shock.

Rising up from the meadow, at the base of a craggy mountain, was a castle. Not an elegant French castle like Versailles, nor a comfortable English castle like Buckingham Palace, but a medieval castle. And it wasn't the remains of a hall that sat so sternly on the face of the land; it was a hall in perfect condition.

Smoke rose from the towers in thin streams, and distinguish-
able figures moved about in the village outside the castle walls.

The ground began to buck under her feet, and she realized
belatedly that she was trying to faint. She sat down with a
thump and put her hands on her head to stop it from spinning.
Fantasy was fine, but this was going too far.

The earth continued to tremble. Elizabeth looked up in time
to see two horsemen bearing down on her. Dream or no dream,
there was no sense in being trampled. She jumped up and ran
for her life.

Seconds later she felt the ground come up to meet her.
Abruptly. A heavy body pinned her facedown in the grass. She
lost her breath, unable even to gasp at the pain of the lumpy
field digging into her hips and chest. *Good lord, I am going to
die,* she thought with a sudden flare of panic. Twenty-four years
seemed too short a time to live, but who was she to argue with
Fate?

The weight was suddenly gone, but she was far too stunned
to move. She got help. She was hauled to her feet, and a rough
hand grabbed her by the hair and pulled her head back. If she'd
had any breath left, she would have cried out at the pain, then
gasped in surprise at what she saw.

A man no taller than she stood disconcertingly close to her,
wearing the grimmest expression she had ever seen. His hair
was reddish blond and hung down past his shoulders. While
there was a tiny bit of hair braided on each side of his head, the
rest was a tangled, matted mess. He was not handsome, and his
angry expression made him appear positively gruesome.

As he looked at her, his expression changed. This new expression alarmed her even more than the first.

"Och, but you're a fetching wench," he rumbled.

He yanked her against him and crushed her lips under his.
Elizabeth choked at the foulness of his breath. The man shoved
her to the ground and fell on top of her. He fumbled with her
clothes, then swore in surprise when he encountered her jeans.
Before Elizabeth could open her mouth to beg for mercy, he
had rolled off her and drawn his knife. She sat up and backed
away, but not swiftly enough to evade the hand that grabbed her
jacket.

"Stay where you are, wench."

"Enough, Nolan!" another voice called from behind him.

"Go to the devil, Angus," the first man snarled. "I'll cut her clothes from her an' have her just the same."

"Jamie willna like it," the other said firmly. "Put away your blade and leave her to me. I'll take her to Jamie and he can decide her fate. Better that he give her to you than you take her and risk his wrath."

Elizabeth's breath came out as a half sob when the knife disappeared.

"You're a comely wench," the man called Nolan said. "Where're you from? Where'd you find these garments?" He tugged at her coat.

Elizabeth could only look at him, too shocked to speak. Good grief, this was no hallucination!

Nolan suddenly heaved himself to his feet and spat in disgust.

"Take her, Angus. I canna abide foreign wenches, no matter how comely they be. Though I'll have a go at her after Jamie's done."

Elizabeth put her face in her hands and shuddered. Nolan's curses receded, and she felt the ground tremble beneath her as he rode away. The sound of a knee popping and the feel of a callused hand under her chin made her pulse race all over again. She lifted her gaze warily.

"What's your name, little one?" the man asked.

She swallowed, and almost choked on the fear lodged in her throat. "Elizabeth," she managed.

"A fine name, lass," he said with a smile, the skin around his eyes crinkling as he did so. He had a tooth or two missing and looked to be about fifty years old, though that was a guess at best. All she knew was his eyes were kind and his expression was gentle. Instinctively, she knew she had found an ally.

"Who are you?" she asked.

He smiled again. "Angus, my lady. Come, and I'll take you to the MacLeod."

The MacLeod? Elizabeth felt her trembles begin again. Angus helped her to her feet, then took her arm.

" 'Tis not safe for a young lass to be out wandering so. Have you lost your lord?"

"Ah," she stalled, "I have no lord."

"How did you come here?"

"I wish I knew."

He looked at her appraisingly but commenced walking toward the castle, his hand firmly under her elbow. His horse followed like an obedient dog. Elizabeth felt terribly conspicuous as they passed through the village, even though Angus had obviously chosen a back route. The villagers who looked at her crossed themselves. She didn't want to speculate on the reasons why.

Angus led her through a set of heavy wooden doors and into a dark cavern. Ah, the Great Hall. Elizabeth took one look and started to wheeze. Rushes were strewn over the floor. Dogs lay near the enormous hearth that dominated the room. Wooden tables were set up around the hall, and torches hung along the walls in heavy metal brackets. The very smell of the place was blinding.

"Here, lass," Angus said softly. "Take your seat and rest for a bit."

Elizabeth sank down gratefully onto a hard, wooden chair near the fire, then accepted a metal goblet. She sniffed at the contents. Wine? Angus put his hand around hers and tipped the cup toward her.

"Drink, child. It will soothe your nerves. I'll be back to fetch you soon."

Elizabeth heard Angus walk away, but she didn't look up. She could feel other pairs of eyes staring at her. She focused on the cup in her hands and the chilled wine sliding over her tongue and down her throat. There was absolutely no way she was going to look up and see who might be giving her the once-over. She pulled her feet up into the chair with her and tried to hide her jean-covered knees under her brother's coat. *Concentrate on the fire,* she told herself, turning toward the hearth and paying attention only to the heat that whispered against her face. With any luck, whoever was running this place would be a kindly old elf who would take her back to the forest and show her the way out of her hallucination.

As if in answer to her prayer, the front door opened.

And closed with a resounding bang.

"Someone fetch me ale!" a voice thundered. "Angus!"

Elizabeth prayed the creator of such a bellow would overlook her. She sat perfectly still in hopes that she would blend in with the furniture.

A heavy tread came her way and she held her breath. Bruising hands grasped her arms and hauled her to her feet. She looked straight ahead, finding that the top of her head came to the man's chest, right at the collarbone. She tilted her head back and looked up at his face. She sucked in her breath and dropped her cup. If her captor hadn't had hold of her arms, she would have collapsed in a heap at his feet.

It was the man from her dream.

Now she was *sure* she was hallucinating. The being standing a hand's breadth away from her was tall and built like her brothers. His dark hair was thick, hanging well past his shoulders. The firelight flickered over his finely chiseled features, highlighting his cheekbones, his firm lips and his unyielding jaw. Though his face was beautifully sculpted, his eyes were what drew her gaze. They were still the color of pine, framed by long sooty lashes. His eyelashes would have been the envy of any woman.

His mouth had gone slack, and an expression of amazement sat squarely on his features. He stared at her for several moments, his mouth twitching, as if he struggled to speak.

"Who *are* you?" he asked, finally.

What a voice he had. Dark, warm, rich. She had the insane desire to curl up in his arms and ask him to tell her a very long story, something that would require him to talk for hours on end. She stared up at him, unable to speak.

And he was staring at her as if he'd just seen a ghost.

"Your name," he said, that look of astonishment still plastered to his face. "I think I asked your name."

"Elizabeth," she whispered.

The man looked even more startled.

"Elizabeth?" he echoed.

She nodded. "Elizabeth Smith."

He continued to stare at her for what seemed an eternity.

Elizabeth could only stare back, speechless. It was the same man. His accent was the same. The way he said her name was the same. His eyes, those beautiful green eyes, were just exactly how she'd dreamed them. She could have looked into them forever.

She looked at his mouth and saw it was moving. She shook her head to clear the attack of the giddies she'd just had.

"I'm sorry," she said, "I wasn't listening. What did you say?"

"I said, you sound English and we've no use for English here," he said, with a frown, "except as serfs."

"Huh?" Elizabeth said, snapping back to reality.

"Serfs," the man repeated, his frown deepening. "If that."

It was then she realized he too had shaken off whatever trance had held him initially. His look of astonishment had been replaced by one of displeasure.

"But, I'm not English," she protested quickly. Good grief, that was the last thing she needed—to be mistaken for serf material. "I'm American."

"American?" he repeated. "What is american?"

"United States? Below Canada?" She frowned at his blank expression. Good grief, what kind of backwoods delusion was this anyway? "We won our freedom from England two hundred years ago?"

He grunted, obviously dismissing her answer. "Be that as it may, still you trespass on my lands. How did you come here?"

"I'm not exactly sure how I got here," she said, defensively. "I didn't ask to get dumped into this dream."

"Your accent is passing strange," he rumbled. "Who *are* you? Damn you, girl, are you a Fergusson?" He shook her. "Speak the truth, if you're capable of it."

Gorgeous though he might have been, the man had just pushed one of her buttons. Elizabeth stiffened in spite of herself at the arrogant tone of his voice. It was the same tone her brothers tended to use when verbalizing their doubts about her intelligence and/or common sense.

"Who are *you*?" she retorted, sticking her chin out.

Mouthing off to a man twice her size wasn't very diplomatic, nor was it exceptionally wise, but she had grown up in a houseful of boys and knew how to hold her own. Show them from the beginning that you aren't afraid, unless you never want to live down cowardice.

"I am James MacLeod," the man said, his tone curt.

She looked at him blankly.

"*The* MacLeod!" he shouted. "Damnation but you are an insolent wench. A good beating might serve you well."

Well, his manners had certainly been better in her dream. This wasn't working out at all. He was supposed to be crushing her in his arms and telling her not to leave him. He was *not* supposed to be eyeballing her as a potential slave, nor was he supposed to be planning to do her bodily harm.

What she needed to do was get out of his hall until she could figure out what was going on. Maybe she'd drop him a line from a nice little hotel and suggest they meet over a cappuccino.

Elizabeth shook off his hands with an effort.

"If you'll excuse me, I'll just be going."

"You'll not move—"

All right, so being polite wasn't going to cut it. Elizabeth brushed past him and walked swiftly toward the door. His heavy tread followed her. Fortunately none of her brothers were around to call her chicken for what she was about to do. Without another thought, she left her pride behind and fled.

The rushes weren't cooperative. Not only were they uncooperative; they were wallowing in a layer of slime. Before Elizabeth knew it, her sneakers had become as slick as new dress shoes on carpet and she was out of control.

She felt herself falling, right toward the wooden bench that looked a great deal like the picnic table in her parents' back yard, right through the MacLeod's strong arms, right down into nothingness.

She felt a sharp pain as her head connected with the wood, and her elbow connected with the stone floor beneath the slime . . .

Willingly, she surrendered to the blackness, her last thought a prayer that she would wake up on her comfortable, dirty apartment floor.

Chapter 2

JAMES MACLEOD, LAIRD of the Clan MacLeod, peerless warrior, bastion of strength and courage, felt weaker and more skittish than a newborn colt. There was a woman in his house. There was a woman on his bed. Just what, by the sweet name of St. Michael, was he supposed to do now?

He paced the length of his room one time, two times, finally losing count after twenty. He was a learned man and could count much higher than that, but he found himself completely unequal to the task of determining just how many times he had crossed from the trunk at the far wall to the bed and back.

A woman. There hadn't been a woman in the hall since his mother died in his fourth year. He was now a score and ten years on God's green earth and in all the years since his mother's death, a woman had never crossed the threshold of the MacLeod keep. His father wouldn't tolerate it. After his father had died during Jamie's sixteenth year, Jamie had kept up the tradition. No women past the doors of the hall.

Until today. Angus had brought her in and set her down in *Jamie's* chair as if she belonged there. Damn him anyway, Jamie thought with a black scowl. The old busybody deserved a thrashing on the field and he'd have it, just as soon as Jamie figured out what in hell's name he was going to do with the creature lying atop his blankets.

He stopped at the foot of the bed and looked down at her. By the saints, her beauty stole the very breath from his body. Her dark hair was spread out over the pillow in glorious disarray. It begged to be touched, smoothed, wrapped around his hands and kissed. Ah, then there was her face. Her skin was very fair and her features pleasing, exceedingly so. He remembered the flush in her cheeks when she had denied being English. Aye, she was full of fire when she was irritated.

But that hardly atoned for her other flaws. Jamie folded his arms over his chest and recaptured the frown that had somehow escaped his attention. The woman's clothing was scandalous. Horribly so. He could hardly believe her lord had allowed her to roam about in such a fashion. Her cloak was fine indeed, but it was fashioned strangely. And her hose! Just what was she hoping? To pass herself off as a squire? Not bloody likely with those fetching legs.

She shifted on the bed and Jamie jumped back, startled. He quickly crossed himself. Perhaps she was a witch. She was surely like no Englishwoman he had ever met, and he'd met enough in his travels to last him a lifetime. Her clothes and her beauty were things she had conjured up to tempt him.

There was also the dream to consider. Had she not appeared to him the night before? The vision of her had haunted him from the moment he awoke. Her voice had echoed in his ears; the touch of her lips had lingered on his mouth. Saints, even his poor arms had ached to hold her again.

And had he not known her name was Elizabeth even before she spoke? That alone was enough to turn him gray before his time.

She was a witch. He nodded. 'Twas the only thing that made sense. How else could she have materialized from his very dreams? She was a beautiful witch, but a witch nonetheless. He turned away and walked to the hearth. She would have to be put where she couldn't work her enchantments. The dungeon would serve well enough for now.

And then he would follow the only sensible course he could. He would have her burned.

•   •   •

Elizabeth awoke, her head pounding. What a dream. She could still remember the sight of James MacLeod's hall sitting in the meadow; she could still feel the cool breeze that had teased open her coat and slid icy fingers beneath her sweater. In fact, it was still cold. The furnace was probably on the fritz again. Mr. Perkins would heave his usual long-suffering sigh when she called, then trudge down to the basement to work his miracles.

The only thing that puzzled her was the smell in her apartment. Maybe it was time to look under the couch and dig out the crusted-over paper plates she'd let accumulate during the last draft of her novel. The smell was suffocating. She sat up and rubbed her eyes wearily. The sooner Mr. Perkins was called, the sooner she would have her furnace . . .

After blinking a time or two, she began to shake. She was in a musty-smelling room illuminated by light from the window and fire from the hearth. The mattress she was sitting on was lumpy, and the blankets and furs under her fingers were covered with what looked to be years of living. The conclusion was hard to accept, but there was little use in denying it.

She wasn't dreaming.

A long, deadly looking blade winked in the firelight. She followed the sword up past the hand that held it, up past an enormous chest and massive shoulders to meet the hard eyes of James MacLeod. *The* MacLeod.

"Up, witch," he rumbled, gesturing with his sword for her to rise.

"Witch?" she echoed. Great, first she was a serf and now she was a witch.

She froze. A *witch*?

Elizabeth eased herself up to her feet carefully, her eyes never leaving his face. "If you'll just let me by," she began, her voice shaking as badly as her body, "I'll leave."

His eyes narrowed. "And have you cast your spell on me once my back is turned? I think not."

"I'm not a witch!" Who knew what they did to witches in this place? Elizabeth felt her way to the end of the bed, ignoring the quicksilver fear that raced through her veins at the sight of the long, sharp sword in those enormous paws. James

MacLeod held the sword easily and probably wielded it just as easily. She swallowed convulsively as she imagined just how intense the pain would be when he either slipped the blade between her ribs or used it to sever her head from her neck.

She would run back to the forest. She could make other plans once she was there. Perhaps she could ask someone for directions to the local loony bin, as she was certain she had just lost her mind.

Her captor stepped toward her suddenly and she shrieked. She caught sight of the door and bolted for it. Before her hand reached the latch, a powerful arm grabbed her about the waist, lifting her off the floor.

"Please, let me go," she gasped, her breath coming so hard it hurt her throat. She tried to force her fingers between her coat and his arm. Superglue wouldn't have held his forearm against her middle any tighter. She changed tactics and tried to twist around in his embrace. If she could just get her knee within striking distance . . .

She heard the clatter of metal against wood as he threw his sword aside. Then he bent and dumped her suddenly over his shoulder. He grunted the first time she kneed him in the belly, then merely wrapped his arms around her legs and carried her out into the hallway. Elizabeth pounded on his back as he thumped down a flight of stairs. Good grief, didn't he feel her fists? She sank her teeth into his back right over his kidneys, a move that had always guaranteed her freedom from her brothers in the past. It didn't phase the man carrying her.

After descending another flight of stairs, he stopped and dropped her to her feet. The first thing she noticed was the dampness. Then the darkness. Then the pit in the middle of the floor. Another man pulled up the trapdoor before Elizabeth could find her wits to scream.

"No, please," she gasped, looking up at the MacLeod's unyielding expression.

He took her hands in one of his. Without ceremony, he pushed her toward the gaping hole.

"I'm not a witch!"

He ignored her.

"Please," she begged, "don't put me down there. We can

work this out. Let's just talk, and I'm sure we can come to some kind of understanding. *Please!*"

She clung to him with every limb available. She wrapped her legs around one of his thighs and pleaded, her movements growing more frantic the closer he moved to the pit. With a mighty jerk, he pushed her away and lifted her off the ground, holding her up by her hands. He lowered her down into the hole. Elizabeth caught the edge with her feet, pulling herself back toward him.

"Cease," he commanded. "Saints, think you I take pleasure in this? I only do what I must."

And with that, he pushed her feet away from the lip of the pit and dropped her.

It was a long way down. Elizabeth fell into the soft ground and then pulled her hands up swiftly out of the muck, wincing at the pain in her wrist.

There was no ladder in the pit and no illumination. The trapdoor closed above her with a clang. She jumped to her feet and shuddered violently. She stared up at the ceiling, catching the faint light of a torch. She heard the slow, heavy tread of booted feet recede, and then there was silence.

She wiped her slimy hands on her jeans, then wrapped her arms around herself. She was just a simple writer, trying to write a simple romance novel. Why in the world had she been consigned to hell?

Something slithered over her shoe. She jerked her foot up, slipped in the mushy floor of the pit and lost her balance. She went down into the mud with a heavy slap, then scrambled back up to her feet. Something crawled up her heel; she shrieked and shook her foot violently. She stopped long enough to feel something else wiggle up the front of her other shin.

She began to scream.

"Bring her up," Angus said quietly.

Jamie took his fingers from his ears and glared at his steward. He winced at the sound of the pitiful wails that floated up from the cellar. He was tempted to plug his ears again so he wouldn't have to listen.

"She'll stop screaming soon enough," he said. "I want to wait until she's good and tired before I burn her."

"Now, Jamie," Angus chided, "you know the lass is no witch."

"I say she is," Jamie growled. "You saw how she was dressed. And I've a thing or two to say to you about bringing a woman into this house. You know it isn't allowed."

"Jamie, lad, your father wouldn't allow women in his home because he couldn't bear to have anything about that reminded him of your sweet mother. You've no need to carry on the tradition."

"Women do nothing but whine and complain," Jamie said, disgruntled. "*And* weep. Like the witch. Listen to her wail like a newborn babe."

"You'd be wailing too if you were down in the pit. Have you no idea of the vermin crawling about down there? Bring her up. She's been there the whole of the afternoon."

Jamie turned his face away. "Her fate is to be burned. I hardly care what happens to her before then."

There were several moments of silence, during which time Jamie pointedly ignored the reproachful noises Angus was making.

The hall door banged shut, and a man cursed.

"By the saints, what is that horrible noise?"

Jamie glared at his cousin Ian.

"A witch."

Ian rolled his eyes. "When have we ever had a witch on our land? The poor lamb sounds as if she's screamed herself hoarse. Fetch her up out of that bloody pit, Jamie."

Jamie ignored him. Ian might have been his closest kin and his most trusted ally, but he had no sense when it came to women. Jamie wasn't about to let a bloody romantic tell him what to do with a woman who could easily put his entire clan under a spell. Ian would likely bring her up and wed her. Jamie frowned again. Aye, it was best to keep Elizabeth and Ian as far apart as possible. Somehow the thought of Ian wooing that beautiful woman made Jamie want to grind his teeth.

Angus cleared his throat. "She came out of the forest, Ian."

"All the more reason to burn her," Jamie muttered darkly.

"Saints, Jamie," Ian exclaimed. "Have you lost all sense? You've no idea where she might truly have come from—"

"But I know where she's going, and that's to the fire," Jamie said, standing suddenly. "And if either of you still possesses any wits at all, you'll leave her be. She's mine to deal with."

"See?" Angus said, throwing up his hands. "There's no reasoning with him."

"Aye," Ian agreed. "I can see that well enough. I think I'm for riding the border this afternoon. I can't stomach the thought of watching any of this."

Jamie watched Ian leave, then stared Angus down, daring him to say anything. Angus opened his mouth to speak, but Jamie interrupted him.

"I'll set fire to the wood myself," he promised.

Angus turned and walked away. Jamie turned to stare into the hearth, watching the flames licking at the logs. Flames would soon lick at the long limbs of the witch in his dungeon. Would she magically escape harm, or would the fire blacken and char her fair skin as he had seen it do to others?

The witch's screams had died down to pitiful moans that echoed eerily in the keep. Jamie's heart wrenched inside his chest at the sound, despite his resolve to remain callous.

He cursed and began to pace the length of his great hall. So she could still spin her enchantments while captive. Never in his life had he felt anything but lust for a woman. The thought of actually feeling pity for one infuriated him. He slammed out of the hall and headed for the stables. A long ride would clear his head.

He rode to the edge of the forest, then simply sat and stared into shadows. Now, here was a place to be reckoned with. He'd lived on its border for the whole of his life and had nothing but abhorrence for it. He'd heard the tales in his youth, tales of enchantments and magics. Though he'd never believed them, he'd been unsettled by them just the same. Of course that had been before his younger brother had wandered off into the forest one day and disappeared. Jamie had searched for weeks in spite of his unease at riding under those haunted boughs. He had come home each time empty-handed.

Until one fateful morning. Jamie had been out riding, a few months after Patrick's disappearance, when he had seen his brother standing at the edge of the woods. He had ridden to him immediately, overjoyed. Patrick had felt real enough and had hugged Jamie until he thought his back might break. Then Patrick had babbled on and on about the place he had been, where men did things Jamie could not for the life of him fathom. How was it a man could journey to the moon and back again and live to tell the tale? And the other things: wagons that moved without horses pulling them, strange new weapons of war, healers who could fair bring a man back from the dead— aye, they were nothing more than the ramblings of a madman. Patrick had been driven daft by his wanderings in what he claimed was the future. Jamie could count to 1996, but he certainly couldn't imagine the world lasting that many years.

Patrick had bidden Jamie farewell, saying he had a woman he needed to return to, a future girl who would bear him a child in a few weeks. Jamie had pleaded with him not to go, but Patrick had turned and vanished into the trees. Jamie had been convinced it had been nothing more than a dream.

But now the forest had yielded something else to him, a woman who had been nothing but a dream but was now clothed in flesh. Was she recompense for having lost Patrick? Was she spirit made flesh, or was she a demon? Or was she from the future, that unimaginable place Patrick had been to? Did she perhaps know his brother?

He rubbed the back of his neck, torn. The sensible thing to do would be to pull the girl out of the pit and send her back to the forest, then forget she had ever wandered into his hall. He certainly didn't want a woman in his life, fouling it with her meddlings. The *last* thing he needed was a woman who had materialized from his very dreams. Seeing her, touching her, finding that she was indeed alive did nothing but trouble him. He could ill afford such a distraction.

But it was possible she might know something of Patrick. She had come from the forest. Her clothing was very odd and her accent strange. It could have been a coincidence, but he was desperate enough to believe it might not be. If there were even some slim hope she might know his brother, it was worth keeping her to question her.

He turned his horse back to the keep.

Angus was sitting in the great hall by the fire, nursing a cup of wine when Jamie strode past him.

"Find her proper clothes. I'll wait for you below."

He ignored Angus' exclamation of triumph and stomped across the floor, grimacing at the layer of scum built up under the ancient rushes. Dog piss, spit, rotten bones, table scraps—the thought of what lay beneath his feet had never bothered him before. He cursed as he walked to the stairs. Perhaps the girl was a witch after all; before her arrival he had certainly never cared about the condition of his floors.

There was no noise coming from the pit. He squatted down and strained to catch even the sound of breathing.

"Angus!" he bellowed.

Angus came down the stairs at a dead run, skidding to a halt next to Jamie.

"Is she dead?" he asked, concern written all over his wrinkled face.

"How would I know?" Jamie snapped. "Go down and bring her up."

Angus paled. "Jamie, I feel for the lass, but I'm not about to go get her."

"Coward."

"Call me what you wish, but you'll not goad me into descending into that hellhole."

With a curse, Jamie jerked up the trapdoor and shoved the ladder down into the darkness. He flinched as he felt it sink into something soft; hopefully that something had not been his captive. He snatched a torch off the wall and took a deep breath. Though he had no great love of pits either, it was obvious no one else was about to do this deed in his stead. He descended the ladder carefully, ignoring the chill and the miserable dampness. The torch spluttered and went out. Damn Angus for bringing the wench home! Jamie cast his eyes about, trying to locate the prisoner in question.

Elizabeth was huddled miserably on the floor. Or what

should have been the floor. A shiver went down Jamie's spine when he saw how the ground shifted. Vermin of all kinds and varieties slithered, crawled and oozed in the mud. He stepped down to the last rung of the ladder and reached out, trying to grab hold of Elizabeth's arm. She was too far away.

"Elizabeth, give me your hand."

She didn't respond. She did nothing but sit listlessly in the mud, her eyes unfocused and unseeing.

"Elizabeth!"

Her head snapped up. Merciful saints above, there were creatures in her hair! Jamie thrust his hand out again.

"Come," he commanded.

With a cry, she jumped up and threw herself at him. He caught her to him with one arm and mounted the rungs with speed he would have been proud of, had he been thinking of anything besides the vermin that were crawling off her onto him.

Once they were out of the pit, Jamie thrust her away from him. He didn't recognize half the things she was covered with. Half the things *he* was now covered with. He pulled her away from the gaping hole and pushed her strangely fashioned cloak down her arms.

"Leave us," he barked to Angus and the guard who stood nearby.

"But—" Angus protested.

"Now!"

Jamie waited only until their backs were turned before he pulled at Elizabeth's heavy tunic, a strangely fashioned garment that looked like thick, woven wool. Elizabeth grabbed hold of the hem and struggled to pull it back down. Jamie ignored her struggles and pulled the tunic over her head. Her breasts were covered in some odd, flimsy material, but he ignored that too. He also forced himself to ignore her beautifully fashioned form. He concentrated on her hose and found them to be completely beyond his scope of experience.

"Take them off," he said.

"Oh, no," she moaned. "Now rape?"

Jamie cursed as he pulled off his plaid and dropped it at her feet.

"I've no mind to take you. Cover yourself with that." He waited. When he realized she wasn't going to obey him if he watched, he cursed and turned his back to her.

"Be quick," he growled, steeling himself against the feelings the sound of her soft sniffling created in him. By the saints, he had no use for a bawling woman! "The sooner your clothes are gone, the sooner you'll have a bath."

Several minutes passed during which time he heard every sound she made as clearly as if a dozen maids had been making like sounds. He scratched his chest, suppressing the impulse to bellow for her to hurry so he could be free of what was crawling over his skin.

"I'm finished," she whispered.

Jamie turned around and picked her up in his arms. He ran up the stairs and through his hall, through the back garden, out the gate and straight for the pool near his keep. He didn't care what a sight he made in only his shirt and boots. By St. George's knees, there were vermin in his hair!

The lake was a small affair, fed by mountain streams and usually too frigid to swim in. Jamie gritted his teeth and plunged in, carrying Elizabeth wrapped in his plaid. He didn't even bother to take off his boots.

Leaving her shivering in the shallows, he swam out further and scrubbed himself vigorously, wishing he'd had the time to snatch a bit of soap on his way. Once he had finished, he looked back to find Elizabeth standing in the same place, trembling. He swam back to her and then pulled her out into the deep water. She didn't protest when he stripped away the covering of his plaid, nor did she protest when he dunked her under the water and washed the creatures from her hair. He assumed she was too distraught by what she had just been through to care. Until, that is, he tried to wash the rest of her. The flat of her hand across his cheek shocked him so, he could do nothing but gape at her.

"Don't," she whispered.

"I think I won't," he grumbled, rubbing his cheek in annoyance. Then he noticed the way she held her wrist to her chest as though she tried to protect it from something.

"Let me see," he demanded.

Either she didn't understand, or she was ignoring him. Or she was too frightened to think clearly, he thought grimly. He carefully pried her arm loose and groaned when he saw her swollen wrist.

"You fell on this?"

She nodded, her teeth beginning to chatter.

He took her other hand and began to pull her to shore. "I'll bind it with stiff cloths once we return to the keep."

She struggled to pull away. "I have nothing to wear," she said, crossing her other arm over her breasts. "Once we get out," she added, so softly he came close to missing her words completely.

Jamie sighed in frustration and wondered if his soggy plaid would dry before she died from the chill.

"Jamie," Angus called, "bring her out. I've clothing here for her."

Jamie pulled Elizabeth behind him and glared at Angus, who stood on the shore.

"Leave it there and go back to the keep. You've no need to embarrass the lass by gaping at her. Go on," he shouted when Angus made no move to leave.

Angus shot him a warning look before he turned and trudged back up the path. Jamie vowed to wring the older man's neck at his first opportunity. As if he now planned to rape the girl!

"I'll turn my back," he threw over his shoulder at her. "Follow me out and wrap up in that plaid."

He kept his word and did not watch until she said she was finished. Jamie then waded back into the pond and dove under to retrieve the clothing that had sunk to the bottom. He made a haphazard attempt at washing the garments, then crawled up to shore where he tossed his tunic and plaid over bushes to dry.

He dropped down next to Elizabeth and looked at her closely. She was staring off over the water numbly, still shivering. He pulled her hair from under the blanket and spread it out over her shoulders. Och, but she was a beauty. He tucked a lock of her long, dark hair behind her ear, then pulled his hand away when she flinched at his touch.

What do you expect, dullard? he grumbled to himself. The girl had spent probably the most terrifying afternoon of her life locked in his dungeon and now he wanted her to long for his touch?

And somehow, beyond reason, he wanted that very much.

He let his gaze roam over her face. Her eyes were the most beautiful shade of blue he had ever seen. In fact, they were almost more green than blue. Her nose was slim and well formed; he could still remember how she had looked down that nose at him the day before, when she had demanded to know who he was. There was fire in that soul, and, despite himself, he had been fascinated by it. The women he knew did nothing but cower. Even his bastard son's mother had lacked fire. She had accepted Jamie in her bed in the village, resigned herself to the fact that she would never see the inside of his hall, borne him a son and died. Jamie had the distinct feeling Elizabeth would never have tolerated the like.

"Are you real?"

He jumped slightly and looked at her mouth, realizing she had spoken to him.

"What did you say?"

"I asked if you were real," she repeated, looking at him with troubled aqua eyes. "Or are you a dream?"

Jamie frowned. A dream? Those had been his exact thoughts about her. Could she have dreamed him too? The feelings that had haunted him from daybreak returned in a rush.

Only now, the creator of those feelings was made flesh, and she was sitting a hand's breadth from him.

"Of course I'm real," he managed.

She nodded, a single tear slipping down her cheek. "That's what I was afraid of."

Her accent was the strangest one he had ever heard. There were many foreigners at the Bruce's hall, but never had Jamie met one who spoke as Elizabeth did.

"Where are we?"

Jamie looked at her, startled. "The Highlands, of course." Saints, had her time in his pit made her daft?

She paled. Jamie tensed, certain she was on the verge of swooning. He started to reach for her.

"What's the year?"

Jamie froze, certain he'd heard her amiss. By the saints, she *had* lost her wits.

" 'Tis the same year as it was yesterday," he said, hoping to spark some show of sense.

She only waited, silent.

" 'Tis the Year of Our Lord 1311."

She looked as if he'd just slapped her. Then great tears formed in her eyes. She looked so miserable, he wanted to weep himself. He frowned to drive away the impulse as he awkwardly put his arm around her shoulders.

"There, there, lass," he said, "you've no reason to weep."

That was like a spark to a pile of dry wood. She burst into tears and leaned against him. He spluttered helplessly, but she seemed not to hear him. He looked around for aid, but there was no one there to give it to him.

"Stop it!"

That command did absolutely nothing to quiet her. In fact, it only made matters worse. She reached up and put her arms around his neck, sobbing into his chest. With a sigh of frustration, he patted her back firmly. When her tears did not cease, he tried to comfort her by using a bit more force.

"You're going to break me," she gasped.

"Oh," he said in a small voice. He looked around quickly. If any of his men saw him, he would never live down the action he currently contemplated. Seeing that the glade was empty, he put his other arm under Elizabeth's legs and drew her onto his lap. His son had liked to be rocked when he was a wee bairn. Perhaps that was what Elizabeth wanted.

Her sobs lasted for hours, or so it seemed to him. The grief in her voice wrenched at his heart. Had she lost her family? He thought about that for a goodly time, and then a more disturbing thought occurred to him. Perhaps she had lost more than her wits. She could have lost her husband. He felt up behind his neck, and his fingers encountered a ring on one of her fingers. He felt a deep scowl settle over his features. So she was wed. Or betrothed.

Jamie started to push her away, but then he realized her tears had stopped. He slowly pulled his head back to peek at her. She was asleep. The pang of jealousy he felt toward the man who possessed her came out of nowhere and stuck him sharply in the heart. With an effort, he forced aside the feeling, along with the accompanying desire to keep her in spite of her lord's possession.

He laid her gently on the ground and then retrieved his clothing. He pulled his wet shirt down over his head and then belted his damp plaid around him. Carefully, he picked Elizabeth up in his arms and carried her back to the keep, marveling that she still slept.

He stopped still as he put his foot over the threshold of his hall. If she just didn't look so peaceful and content in his arms . . .

Nay, the tradition was a fine one, and he would continue it. After Elizabeth woke. He carried her through the hall and up the steps to his chamber, ignoring the astonished looks he received from his men. He laid Elizabeth down on his bed and covered her with a blanket. Satisfied that she was comfortable, he made his way down to the cellar to retrieve her clothing. There was no sense in having garments lying about that might mark her as a witch to a less intelligent man.

He returned to his chamber and tossed her things into his trunk. He would clean them later, then give them back to Elizabeth once she was fed, rested and ready to be on her way.

He sat in his great chair before the fire and closed his eyes. Aye, she'd have to go. Women were nothing but trouble, and he needed no trouble in his life.

And then, with complete disregard for the firm decision made by the powerful laird of Clan MacLeod, thoughts of a beautiful girl with aqua eyes assailed Jamie's tired mind and lulled him to a peaceful, contented sleep.

Chapter 3

ELIZABETH WOKE TO darkness. She sat up with a shriek, trembling violently. Then she realized where she *wasn't*, and she lay back down with a shuddering sigh. She fought the memories that assailed her, memories of things crawling under her sweater, up the legs of her jeans, into her hair. It was over. Jamie had come for her.

She stared up at the ceiling, ruthlessly shoving aside the urge to weep. Tears wouldn't help her. Though she was tempted to pretend she was still dreaming, she knew she couldn't. The Highlands? 1311? She wanted to laugh, but she had the feeling it would sound rather shrill, and then she just might continue right over the edge into full-blown hysterics. Medieval Scotland? Much as she wanted to deny it, she couldn't. The evidence just kept stacking up.

First off, she was lying under a scratchy sheet, a heavy woolen blanket and some kind of animal skin. That certainly wasn't the nice Laura Ashley bed set her mother had sent her last Christmas.

Then there was the smell in the room. She was the first to admit that during writing fits her unrinsed dishes stacked up until they reeked, but this wasn't the same kind of smell at all. This was stale, sweaty and a bit on the outhousey side. The MacLeod really should hire a maid.

That didn't begin to address the rushes on the floor in the hall, nor James MacLeod's long, sharp sword. Was it possible? Had she truly been sucked back in time thanks to that book about the Clan MacLeod?

She shifted on the bed, grimacing in pain as she did so. Her head hurt from where she had smacked it on the table, and her wrist sent shooting pains up her arm every time she moved it. No matter how vivid she believed her imagination to be, it wasn't vivid enough to give her aches of this magnitude.

So what to do now? Her options were extraordinarily limited. She could either walk, run or sprint back to the forest. Then she would hunt down the naughty elf who had pulled her into the book and convince him to put her back where he had found her. For now, until she could get back to the forest, all she had to do was stay out of her host's way and out of his pit.

Of course, that plan assumed the forest contained some magical element that would take her back to her time. The very thought made her want to weep. What if she were truly stuck in medieval Scotland? She would live out her life and die without ever seeing her parents again, her brothers, her nephews and nieces . . .

The rumble of voices sent a thrill of fear through her body. She closed her eyes tightly, praying she would be left alone. The bedroom door opened and shut with a soft click.

"But, Jamie, you can't just send her out on her own."

"Angus, I've no use for a woman. Complain, that's all they do."

"I've yet to hear Elizabeth say aught, and look what you've done to her. And the hall could use a woman's touch."

"She's a lady, you old fool. She likely knows nothing of servant's work."

"Let her stay another night. 'Tis the least you can do for her."

Jamie's sigh could probably have been heard down in the village.

"Go prod Hugh about supper. I'm starving."

"But you'll see to the lass—"

"Go!"

Elizabeth winced in spite of herself at the sound of Jamie's bellow. The door closed, and she let out her breath slowly.

"I know you're awake."

She opened her eyes and watched Jamie light a candle in the fire and come to stand by the side of the bed. There was no getting around how big he was or how fiercely he scowled.

"You've slept enough. There are clothes on the chair. Dress and come downstairs."

She nodded and waited until he left before she rose from the bed. What else could she do but comply with his wishes? There was much to be said for humoring the volatile lord of the keep.

She dressed in a long cotton shirt, then looked at the blanket and belt on the chair. So this was what a plaid looked like. She fingered the coarse wool, marveling not only at the texture but the colors.

The door opened, and she whirled around in surprise. Jamie stood there, the frown still plastered to his face. Perhaps he didn't have any other expressions in his repertoire.

"I was certain you would not know how 'tis worn," he began gruffly. "The plaid," he added, his eyes dipping lower.

Elizabeth vainly tried to pull the shirt down further over her thighs. The look Jamie had given her legs sent heat flooding to her cheeks. Why didn't they make those shifts a few feet longer?

Jamie picked up the plaid and pulled it around her neck. He tossed one end of it over her shoulder and then belted the rest of it around her waist. He stood back and looked at her critically.

"You'll do," he said. "Come downstairs."

"I don't have any shoes."

Jamie leaned over the chair and reached for something. He dropped a pair of shoes at her feet, then folded his arms over his chest and waited.

Elizabeth tried on the leather slippers. They were, predictably, too small but she forced her feet into them anyway. Until she found where her sneakers were hiding, these would have to do.

"Come."

She followed Jamie from the room, not exactly eager to leave the relative safety of it. Once she walked out into the passageway, she was hit square in the nose by an odor that rivaled her dirtiest dishes.

"Dinner," Jamie threw over his shoulder as he eagerly thumped down the stone steps.

Elizabeth followed him more slowly, putting her hand out against the wall to steady herself. Her palms were sweaty, her head was spinning, and she knew she was on the verge of being ill. Was this stage fright? The mere thought of facing who knew what downstairs made her want to hike up her long skirt and run back up to Jamie's room.

"Elizabeth, now!"

She stumbled down the rest of the steps—too quickly because she caught the edge of her plaid under her toes and went sprawling headfirst into the great hall. Jamie's arms broke her fall. He set her back on her feet, frowned at her, then walked over to the long wooden table set up near the fire. Twenty men sat there already with another twenty or so sitting around another table on the opposite side of the hall. There was another table at the back of the room, set on a raised dais, but Jamie did not go there. Elizabeth wondered about that, then caught sight of the forty odd pairs of eyes that turned to look at her.

She concentrated on putting one foot in front of the other. She ignored the thick scum covering the floor and the way it squished under her feet as she walked. Jamie shoved one of his men off the bench and gestured for Elizabeth to sit. She obeyed, doing her best to ignore the man who sat next to her, drooling like a sailor who hadn't seen a woman in a decade.

Dinner was something smelly in a bowl. Well, at least it wasn't moving. Elizabeth managed to down some coarse, brown bread and a liberal amount of wine. The men, however, seemed to find nothing wrong with their meal, what they noticed of it. They spent most of their time gaping at her and blindly shoveling food into their mouths.

After dinner there was a good deal of ale flowing and a great deal of talk. Most of it revolved around politics and clan wars. Elizabeth sat at the table and listened, again congratulating herself for having a maternal grandfather who had thought it necessary for his wee granddaughter to learn Gaelic. At least she recognized most of the words they were using. Now, if she just hadn't understood references to the Bruce. There wasn't a more medieval king of Scotland than Robert Bruce.

Elizabeth thought she was holding up very well. It wasn't every day a girl discovered she was breaking bread with men who had lived 700 years before she was born. She hadn't begun to hyperventilate, nor had she run screaming out the door. She was very proud of herself. Jamie had only looked at her strangely a time or two, when she spoke up to ask for clarification on some tidbit or other. Maybe he couldn't believe she was so up on current events. Maybe her accent wasn't all that far off, though she hoped she wouldn't be around long enough to acquire a charming medieval lilt.

Shortly after sunset, the men rose from the tables. Elizabeth jumped up as the bench was pulled out from underneath her. The tables were cleared, then stacked against the walls. The dogs settled down by the hearth, and men began to vie for choice places in the hall to bed down for the night. Jamie headed toward the stairs without giving Elizabeth a backward glance. She fought the sudden surge of panic. He didn't plan on leaving her alone, did he?

Well, she had a different idea. There had to be a guestroom of some sort in the place, and she would find it. She walked to the stairs as if she knew where she was going. Jamie was coming down them without looking, and they collided. Elizabeth caught the arm he threw out to steady her, then gave him a weak smile.

He shoved a blanket into her arms. "Here."

She smiled uncertainly. "Do you have another room . . ."

"I've no time to see to you further today. You have a blanket. Use it."

With that, he turned on his heel and climbed the steps without looking back.

Elizabeth stood at the bottom of the steps and clutched the blanket to her chest. She wanted to sit down in the scum and bawl like a baby. James MacLeod had no heart. She watched as he disappeared upstairs, taking with him her only hope of protection. She looked over her shoulder hesitantly, wondering if everyone would be standing in line to have a turn at her.

There was an empty chair by the fire. She looked at it, then looked at the front door. What was the lesser of two evils? Maybe Angus was handy. If things went poorly, he would rescue her again, wouldn't he?

Then again, maybe not. Angus wasn't in the group of men around the fire. Nolan, however, was. He was standing in front of the fire with his hands behind his back, watching her. His expression was not pleasant. She had little doubt about what she would face at his hands if he caught her alone. With any luck he would get tired of watching her and go away.

An hour later, she stood in the same place. Nolan had sat in the chair she had eyeballed. He was leaning lazily against the back, watching her with narrowed eyes. Elizabeth couldn't stand to watch him watch her anymore. She sidled toward the door, allowing herself only to concentrate on what she would do once she was outside. The landscape was unfamiliar, but she knew the forest was to her right once she exited the hall door. She put her hand on the wood and pulled on the heavy latch. She heard footsteps behind her. With a mighty jerk, she opened the door and fled down the steps.

Jamie paced the length of his bedchamber. He'd been pacing thusly off and on all day. Damn the wench. Why could he not rid her image from his mind? Not even casting her from his chamber had aided him. He walked over to the trunk under the window and opened it, then he pulled out her cloak and put his hand in the pocket. It was an action he had performed a dozen times over, ever since he had found the tokens the night before while washing her garments. The slick pieces of parchment were like nothing he had ever seen.

He walked over to the hearth and squatted down, holding up the objects to the fire where he could see them clearly.

"American Express," he read aloud, stumbling a bit over the last word. She had not lied about *american,* whatever that meant. He put the little green speckled object on the floor and took up the other. Driver's License.

There, before his eyes, was Elizabeth. Just her face, but 'twas her. He ran his finger over the surface of her face and found it to be flat. Just as flat as it had been all evening. What sort of witchcraft was this? The image was far too clear for any artisan to have fashioned it.

Jamie knew how to read and had no trouble reading the word *birthdate* and understanding what it meant. It was the numbers underneath the word that shook him to the core. 9/10/1970. The 1970 was clear enough. It was a year.

Elizabeth had said her america had won its freedom from England two hundred years ago. Two hundred years ago, England was Normandy trying to overtake Saxony in the Year of Our Lord 1111.

He closed his eyes, and a shiver went through him. There was no place called america that he had ever heard of. And there was no place in Scotland where parchments such as these were fashioned.

Elizabeth wasn't a witch.

She was from the future.

A scream tore through the stillness of the night, and Jamie jumped to his feet. He tossed Elizabeth's tokens into the trunk and bolted from his room. He took the steps four at a time and skidded across the great hall. He pulled up short outside the hall door, momentarily stymied by the silence. Then he heard the sound of struggles coming from the darkness to his left.

Jamie ran toward the stables. He came to a halt just inside the door. "Cease!" he thundered.

Elizabeth was being held down in the hay by four men. Nolan had her skirt tossed over her face, and his own plaid lifted purposefully. Jamie flung himself at his kinsman and took him to the ground.

"Release her," he barked curtly to Elizabeth's captors, and they instantly obeyed him. He reached over and yanked Elizabeth's skirt down, shooting his men a murderous look of displeasure.

He turned back to his errant kinsman only to find himself shoved aside. Elizabeth threw herself at Nolan, her claws unsheathed. Blood exploded down Nolan's face as her fist connected with his nose. Jamie was so surprised that he could only kneel in the dirt, astonished. Until Nolan's fist glanced off Elizabeth's cheek. Jamie felt a rage such as he'd never felt before crash over him. He jerked Nolan to his feet and shoved him toward the stable door.

"Out," he said. "Out of my stables and off my land."

Nolan stared at him open-mouthed. "She's just a wench, Jamie. Lord knows we've shared them before."

"Out," Jamie commanded. "Never set foot on my land again. If you do, I'll kill you. And if you ever touch this girl again, I'll do worse than that." He was so furious, he was shaking. How dare Nolan lay a hand on her!

Nolan's face turned a fierce shade of red, and the veins stood out on his neck. "Then you chose a wench over me."

"Go!"

With a foul oath, Nolan turned and stormed from the stables. Jamie hauled Elizabeth to her feet and pulled her behind him. He swept the remaining men with a glare.

"The next man who touches her will not receive such mercy."

"I can take care of myself," Elizabeth protested.

Jamie tightened his grip on her hand so quickly that she squeaked.

"If anyone is to touch her, 'twill be me," Jamie snapped. He met each man's eyes and stared them down until he was satisfied they would obey. Without another word, he turned and dragged Elizabeth behind him back to the hall. Angus plowed into him in his haste.

"Jamie, lad, I'll watch over her."

"As you did this night? I think not."

"I was in the village and didn't hear her. Come now, and let me have her. I'll take good care of her and treat her kindly."

Jamie ignored him. The very idea of Angus looking after Elizabeth was ridiculous. He would have no idea how to care for a woman from the future. Aye, the mere mention of her birthdate would likely leave Angus wheezing far into the next decade.

Jamie slowed as he realized where his thoughts were leading him. As if he himself would be the one to watch over her!

Nay, he couldn't. He nodded to himself hastily. He had no use for a woman, especially a woman as fetching as Elizabeth. The very *last* thing he needed was another night such as this, with his heart racing when he'd heard the scream and the blood pounding in his ears as he had seen Elizabeth almost harmed.

And keeping her would ruin his men. He'd marked the way they'd gaped at her over supper. Nay, the lads were rough and ill-mannered, perfectly trained warriors whose greatest pleasure came from meting out well-deserved revenge. Jamie forbade them to rape, but he hardly wanted to make soft-bellied, faint-hearted women out of them. And that is just what would happen if by some malevolent quirk of fate he found himself saddled with a wench. By St. Michael's toes, he couldn't bear the thought of coddling a weak, whimpering female!

He flinched at the crack of a palm against his face. His eyes focused, and he realized he was standing in front of his bedchamber door facing Elizabeth, who was wearing what was obviously her most intimidating frown. He might have been convinced if it hadn't been for the remains of fear lingering in her eyes. He rubbed his cheek and looked at her crossly.

"What?"

"I said, let go of me, you barbarian! I want to go home!"

"Barbarian?" he echoed. "Damn me, girl, I just rescued you!"

"To rape me yourself," she accused.

"I've no mind to rape you!"

"Oh." She looked at his chin, as if she couldn't quite bring herself to meet his eyes. "I see."

"So you do," he said with a scowl. He started to pull her inside his bedchamber, but she put her hand on the wood and held on. Jamie rolled his eyes and looked at her again. "What now?"

"I need to use the bathroom."

"The what?" By the saints, these americans spoke strangely. She searched for the word. "Garderobe," she said finally, coloring a bit.

He grunted and led her down the passageway. He waited while she went in. And then he waited some more. Finally his impatience got the better of him, and he banged on the door. "Be quick about it!"

He could hear her sniffling, but she opened the door soon enough, keeping her head lowered. He put his hand under her chin and lifted her face to the light. Her cheeks were tear-stained. A feeling came over him, something he didn't recognize. It started in the pit of his stomach, groped at his heart on its way up and finished with a stinging sensation behind his eyes. He had the most ridiculous urge to gather the lass into his arms. To do what, he surely didn't know. Before he could understand what he was feeling, much less express it, Elizabeth jerked her face away.

Och, but that was offensive. Jamie scowled at the sting to his pride and took Elizabeth none too gently by the arm to drag her back down the passageway and into his chamber. He bolted the door behind them and then reached for a blanket from his bed. He flung it at her.

"Sleep on the floor." He stripped and crawled into bed, ignoring the fact that Elizabeth stood in the middle of his chamber, looking like a child who had lost its mother. He turned away with a curse and buried his face in his pillow.

"I want to go home."

"Tomorrow," Jamie said, his voice muffled. " 'Tis far too late tonight."

He heard her settle in and then slowly lifted his head to see where she was sleeping. He swore again. She'd never sleep a wink sitting bolt upright in a chair. He crawled from the bed and stomped over to stand in front of her. Her eyes were on level with his naked groin, and bright color flooded to her cheeks. He pursed his lips as he squatted down in front of her. Then he noticed the discolored flesh of her cheek. His eyes narrowed, and he suddenly regretted having allowed Nolan to leave so easily. He lifted his hand slowly.

"Don't touch me," she warned, sticking her chin out in what he was fast coming to learn was a show of stubbornness.

"Don't be foolish," he said, attempting to sound gruff. That same warmth was spreading rapidly through him. It was doubtless from supper. Hugh's skills were definitely not improving with time.

Elizabeth's foot square in the middle of his chest caught him completely unawares. He landed on his backside in a very undignified sprawl. By St. Michael's nose, the woman was going to make him daft!

"If I don't kill you myself before this night is through, 'twill be a miracle!" he thundered, swinging his legs back to the floor and glaring at her. He rose and gave her a wide berth as he made a valiant attempt to swagger back to bed, which wasn't an easy task as a girl half his size had just given him the humbling of his life.

He lay back with his hands behind his head, trying to scowl. The wench was cheeky, disrespectful, and she had absolutely no idea of her place or how to humor a man. No doubt that was how women comported themselves in Elizabeth's day. Perhaps she had a lord there who had grown weary of her sharp tongue and had sent her packing. Jamie had little choice but to agree with the man, whoever he was. Elizabeth had certainly been more malleable when she'd lived only in Jamie's dreams.

On the other hand, she was certainly a fierce warrior. Jamie stared up at the ceiling, turning that over in his mind. There was much to be said for a woman with spine. And those eyes! Surely the most fetching shade of blue-green he had ever seen. Aye, and her face was something an angel would envy.

He frowned. Perhaps a few more days of keeping her near wouldn't hurt.

Just to have answers, he reminded himself quickly. No other reason. He would question her about the future at his earliest opportunity. He'd been more than generous with his hospitality. A few tales in return was the least she could do for him.

That settled, he rolled over and closed his eyes. He would see to her tomorrow, when he had the time.

Chapter 4

ELIZABETH PULLED HER head out from under the bed and sneezed. A person would have needed a big game permit to hunt the dust bunnies under Jamie's bed. Unfortunately dust was all she had found. There was no sign of her clothes. She rose and crossed the room to the trunk she couldn't open, then gave it a kick. She had no doubts her comfortable sneakers and warm sweater were hiding right in front of her.

More than her clothes, she wanted her driver's license back. About the time Jamie saw it, he would have a fit. She could just imagine the bellow he would bellow at the sight of her birthdate. Assuming he could read, of course. Even if he couldn't, her picture would convince him beyond doubt that she was a witch, and she would find herself slow roasting on a spit.

Perhaps she would just give up on her things, find Jamie, thank him for his hospitality and leave. Though his manners hadn't left her too impressed so far. Sleeping in the chair while he snored contentedly in his bed hadn't exactly endeared him to her.

She walked over to Jamie's door and opened it, gathering her courage along the way. Jamie had seemed clear enough when he'd told his men to leave her alone the night before, but how long would that last? She would just have to be on guard. After all, she'd grown up with five brothers. She wasn't helpless, and she certainly didn't intimidate easily. She hadn't been thinking clearly last night when she had run, or Nolan never would have gotten the better of her. No, she would be more in control of herself in the future. She left Jamie's room and walked down the stairs, trying to achieve a balance between caution and confidence.

She turned the corner at the bottom of the stairs and ran smack into a solid chest. She jumped back with a gasp, then put her hand over her heart and forced herself to breathe deeply. No reason to panic just because the man in front of her was enormous. He was taller than Jamie and easily as broad.

Elizabeth lifted her chin and tried to look haughty. "Excuse me," she said, stepping past him.

He dropped to his knees before her, blocking her way. "My lady," he began miserably. "I've come to beg pardon."

Elizabeth looked down into his face and felt the tension ease out of her a bit. To call him boyishly charming just didn't do him justice. He was cute, and cute was directly at odds with his size. Long blond hair hung in tangles to his shoulders, and his bright blue eyes shifted when she met them.

Then she realized that they had already met. He was one of the four who had held her down the night before while Nolan groped.

"Get out of my way," she said coldly.

A tear glistened as it dropped to the floor. "My lady," the giant croaked, bowing his head, "I never meant to hurt you, and I swear I didn't look at you when Nolan had your skirts up. The lads tease me about being soft, and I had to prove I wasn't. I'm sorry you suffered for it."

"They tease you?" she asked, skeptically.

"My face, my lady. They think I'm still a boy."

More teardrops fell on the stone floor at her feet. The sight of such an enormous man weeping with remorse was her undoing. Elizabeth couldn't remember the last time she'd made a man cry. She reached out and put her hand on his shoulder.

"It's okay," she said, patting him. "Really."

The giant shook his head. "Nay, my lady. I should be flogged for it."

"Well, let's not go overboard," Elizabeth said, patting him

some more. "Just promise me you won't do anything like it again, and we'll call it even. All right?"

"Truly?"

"Truly," she said.

The young man jumped to his feet and took her hand, crushing it in both his own. He reminded her of a very large, very enthusiastic sheepdog. She earnestly hoped he would not lick her face.

"Thank you, my lady," he said, nodding furiously. "Malcolm is my name. I'd be pleased to be your guardsman, if you'll have me. I've already asked the laird, and he gave me leave. Do you say aye?"

"If that's what you want," she said, wondering just what she was getting into. Then she looked up into those bright blue eyes and felt the last of her reservations disappear. This one wouldn't hurt her. "So that makes you kind of a bodyguard type, right?"

"Bodyguard?" he echoed.

"You know, you'll look after me."

"To my dying breath," he said, pounding his chest dramatically.

Elizabeth would have laughed, but it looked as though Malcolm was completely serious. She certainly wasn't going to pass up his help for the time she would be there. He was big and intimidating, and now he was there to protect her from the others who might not accept her so readily. She nodded regally to Malcolm and walked past him.

"My lady," he said, jumping to catch up with her, "where go you?"

"I have to find Jamie."

"But you need something to break your fast. Hugh has prepared a tasty repast for your pleasure."

After last night, Elizabeth couldn't believe Hugh could prepare anything edible, much less tasty.

"Later. I've got to talk to Jamie now."

"But he is training the men," Malcolm said. "You mustn't disturb him. He willna like it."

"Tough," she muttered under her breath as the kink in her

neck she had earned sleeping in the chair acted up and shot pain down her back and arms. "I have to see him immediately."

Malcolm began to wring his enormous hands as he walked along beside her.

"He willna like it," he repeated, punctuating his words with little sounds of distress. "The laird is powerful fierce when he's angered. He willna like it one bit."

"Too bad." Elizabeth slipped and slid over the last few feet of floor near the door, then opened the door and stepped outside. It was cold, and she wished she'd had a jacket. Unfortunately, her brother's jacket had gone the way of her nice, correctly sized sneakers. "Where is he?"

"My lady . . ."

"I command you to tell me," Elizabeth said, hoping intimidation would work. It was hard to intimidate a man who was almost a foot taller than she, but Malcolm seemed susceptible enough to threats.

"To your left, my lady."

He crossed himself, then followed her.

Elizabeth strode ahead confidently, following the sounds of battle. So Jamie was putting the troops through their paces. It would be good for research purposes to see it. She rounded the corner and walked into the fray before she realized what she was doing.

She had expected chaos. Jamie's hall and his bedroom gave every indication of a man who couldn't organize himself to save his life. But his lists were another story. Several men practiced swordplay in pairs. Others wrestled. Still others practiced with bows. They were all in various states of undress. Only a few of them were wearing armor. That surprised her at first until she remembered where she was. These were the Highlands, and money was tight. Armor was expensive, and it probably got in the way when they stripped down to their altogethers and shimmied up trees to drop on unsuspecting enemies.

Elizabeth spotted Jamie immediately. He was training in his boots and kilt. He wore no shirt, even though it was anything but balmy outside. Elizabeth stared in fascination as he wielded his great broadsword. The muscles in his arms, shoulders and

back worked powerfully as he swung the blade. His leg mus
cles flexed in mighty definition as he lunged and retreated. His
dark hair hung over his shoulders, flowing as he moved. All
things considered, he was easily the most handsome man she
had ever laid eyes on. It was no wonder he was laird. He even
made Malcolm look a bit on the wimpy side.

She stood there for several minutes, watching. Actually, she
was indulging in a healthy bit of lust. This was the kind of man
she'd always dreamed about, one who was manly enough to
protect her if the need had arisen. If she and Stanley had been
mugged on the street, Stanley would have handed her over with
the same alacrity he would have a five-dollar bill, then run the
other way. She had the feeling such a thing wouldn't cross
Jamie's mind.

She sighed. Along with all that strength certainly came a
forceful personality, and she had her doubts she would change
any of his thinking. From all appearances, he was a dyed-in-
the-wool chauvinist, and there wasn't much she could do about
that.

Good grief, not that she'd want to. She shook her head,
laughing at herself. As if she'd be around long enough to try.
Jamie was great as a dream hero, but his medieval manners,
coupled with his medieval surroundings, were just too much to
take.

And she really had no business hanging around in the past.
The sooner she got home, the better. But she would write one
incredible book from all this. Talk about firsthand research!

She strode out onto the field, ignoring Malcolm's cries of
panic and trying to avoid the men who seemed not to notice
that she was trying to cut through them. It was a bit different
than negotiating a path through a dance floor. She walked up
behind Jamie and tapped him on the shoulder.

"Excuse me," she said, clearing her throat.

Only her reflexes made her duck in time to miss being lev-
eled by his arm as he spun around. She straightened and smiled.
"Hi."

He closed his eyes briefly, and she wondered if he were mentally counting to ten. Then he looked down at her. Oh, yes,
that's what he'd been doing, all right.

"Go back to the hall," he said, through gritted teeth.

"I know you're busy, but I really need to get home. Now, if you wouldn't mind just pointing me in the right direction—"

"Woman, go back to the hall!" Jamie bellowed. The veins popped out at his temples and on his neck. "Malcolm!"

"Aye, my laird," Malcolm said, bowing and scraping.

Jamie picked Malcolm up by the front of his saffron shirt and held him off the ground. Jamie's muscles bulged with the effort, but he seemed to have no trouble hefting Malcolm, nor keeping him hefted. Elizabeth watched, open-mouthed, as Jamie shook her keeper.

"She could have been slain," Jamie roared. "I could have cleaved her in twain without realizing it, you fool! Take her back inside and see that she stays there, else you will answer to me!"

"But, Jamie, she's a headstrong wench—"

"She's half your size! If she disobeys, sit on her! By St. Michael's thumbs, Malcolm, use the few wits God gave you and keep this disobedient wench in check!"

He dropped Malcolm to his feet, then turned his glare on Elizabeth.

"Go back to the hall. I will see to you when I've the time for it. And never, *never* come out to the lists again. Do you hear me?"

He was shouting so loud, the king of England could have heard him. That, added to the suspicious looks Jamie's men were giving her, was enough to make Elizabeth realize she'd just made a big mistake. She nodded and spun on her heel, towing Malcolm back to the hall with her. She shut the door, leaned back against it and let out a long, slow breath. Then she looked up at Malcolm.

"You were right."

Malcolm's teeth were chattering. "I'd have to s-sit on you if you m-misbehaved, Lady E-Elizabeth, so you'd b-best be comporting yourself w-well."

"You take things far too literally, Malcolm," Elizabeth noted. She pushed away from the door and sighed in resignation. She would have no help from Jamie that morning. It had probably been a bad idea to interrupt him outside anyway. He would be much more amenable to suggestion after lunch. Thinking about lunch reminded her that she hadn't eaten much for dinner the night before.

She followed her nose to the kitchen, no great task as it smelled worse, if possible, than the rest of the hall. She came face-to-face with Hugh, who looked as if he couldn't tell one end of a spoon from the other. He had bright red hair, a faceful of freckles and a nose that had seen better days. It was either red from being tweaked for his poor cooking, or he had a perpetual cold. When he blew his nose on the floor, she strongly suspected the latter.

"A fine meat pie for you, my lady," Hugh said, grasping the pie with his nose-blowing fingers and handing it to her.

"How about an apple?" she suggested, fighting the urge to gag. "Or something a little less filling? We'll save the pie for Jamie."

Once she had her apple in hand and had cleaned it as inconspicuously as possible on her plaid, she looked around Hugh's kitchen. His staff was in worse shape than he was. It was no wonder supper was so bad. She didn't want to think about the extra little goodies that were surely finding their way into the stew pots every day.

An hour later, lunchtime arrived and brought with it a hall full of hungry Highlanders. Elizabeth sat at Jamie's right hand again, only this time Malcolm sat on her right, protecting her from the lusty-sailor types. Elizabeth kept her eyes on her meal after the first time she caught one of the men staring at her as if he looked for horns. Maintaining a low profile was obviously a very good idea.

She waited until Jamie had devoured his meal and most of the men had gone before she voiced her desire again.

"Jamie," she began quietly, "I have to say your hospitality has been really great, but I need to be getting home. I realize you don't have any men to spare as escorts, but if you'll just—"

"Nay," Jamie said. "Not today."

Elizabeth stared at him in silent irritation until he finally cursed under his breath and met her gaze.

"What?" he asked crossly.

"How hard can it be to draw me a map of your land?" she asked.

"I haven't the time." He rose. "Malcolm, do not allow her outside the hall. And see that she doesn't stir up any mischief inside either."

"Wait," Elizabeth began, but Jamie was already on his way out the door.

She sat until the table was empty, then put her head down and sighed deeply. It was obvious Jamie wasn't going to be of any help. She lifted her head and looked next to her.

"Malcolm?"

"Aye, my lady."

"Will you help me get to the forest?"

He looked horrified. "Whatever for? There are beasties in the forest, lady. Powerful, hungry ones who'll eat a man alive as soon as look at him."

Elizabeth didn't believe that. She'd spent an entire morning in the forest and the only beastie she'd encountered had been Nolan. She sighed and rose.

"Well, thanks anyway. I'll be seeing you."

"My lady, where go you?"

"To the forest, Malcolm. I've got to get home. I think I left my curling iron on."

"Lady, nay—"

She ignored him and started toward the door.

And the next thing she knew, she was facedown on the table, and Malcolm was crushing all the bones in her pelvis and lower back.

"Malcolm, get off me," she gasped. "You're breaking me in two!"

The weight eased. She found herself pinned only by Malcolm's sturdy legs, one over the small of her back and one over the backs of her thighs.

"Malcolm, Jamie wasn't serious about this!"

"I don't mean to hurt you, Lady Elizabeth, but Laird Jamie's powerful fierce when he's been disobeyed, and I fear his wrath much more than I fear yours."

"What if I promise not to leave?"

"Forgive me, lady, but I don't believe you."

Elizabeth rested her cheek against the wood of the table and contemplated her situation. Moving Malcolm was out of the question. Logic wasn't going to work either, if their recent conversation was any indication. It looked as if the only way to be free was to have Jamie come countermand his order.

She took a deep breath and shouted Jamie's name at the top of her lungs. Malcolm didn't seem to have the courage to clap his hand over her mouth, so she continued to yell.

She yelled until she saw a body come stand at the end of the table. It wasn't Jamie, though it was dressed similarly, without a shirt and sporting only a short kilt. Elizabeth lifted her head and then she blinked. The boy couldn't have looked any more like Jamie if he'd been a clone.

"Who are you?" she asked.

"Jesse MacLeod," the boy said, making her a low bow. "At your service, lady. My father sent me to see to your comfort."

"Jamie is your father?" Elizabeth asked, in a strangled voice. Jamie was *married?* "What about your mother?"

"She died birthing me, my lady." Jesse knelt so he was on eye level with her. "Not that my sire would have wed her. She was a mere village wench."

Well, at least Jamie wasn't happily wed. The term "mere village wench" raised Elizabeth's hackles, but she would give Jesse a lesson in women's emancipation later, once Malcolm allowed her to breathe again. She took the deepest breath possible, ready to give Jesse an earful to relay to his father.

"Now," Jesse interrupted her, frowning a frown Jamie probably would have been proud of, "what sort of distress are you in, lady?"

Elizabeth gritted her teeth and summoned all her reserves of patience.

"Malcolm is sitting on me."

Jesse stroked his chin thoughtfully. "I daresay he wouldn't be sitting on you without good reason. Malcolm never does anything without good reason."

Elizabeth started to laugh. She felt a bit like Alice in Wonderland, having fallen down a rabbit hole into a world where nothing made sense. She put her head down on the table and laughed until she was crying. This wasn't happening. She hadn't been dumped in medieval Scotland into the hall of a man who didn't seem to care for the female species in general. She wasn't being pinned to a hard wooden table by her bodyguard who took everything literally. And she wasn't being helped to see reason by a bastard son who seemed to find none of this out of the ordinary.

"Malcolm, you've made her weep," Jesse said disapprovingly. "Let her up. If we both watch over her, perhaps she will stir up no mischief."

Malcolm swung his legs off Elizabeth and hopped off the table. He helped her sit up, then reached out to dry the tears from her cheeks. Jesse elbowed him aside and did the honors himself. Elizabeth judged him to be about sixteen or so, which either made Jamie well over thirty or a very young father.

"Your father must be very old," she said, trying to be subtle.

"A score and ten, I think," Jesse said, drying the last bit of moisture from her cheeks. "Very old indeed." He sat down on the table next to her and looked at her closely. "You came from the forest, didn't you?" he asked.

She nodded slowly, still stunned to learn Jamie had sired this child when he was no more than a child himself. She was also very unsure where Jesse's line of questioning was going.

"Malcolm, fetch us wine," Jesse ordered. "I'll watch over Elizabeth." He waited until Malcolm had shuffled over to the kitchen before he looked at her again. "My uncle lost himself in the forest," he said carefully. "Came home only once, babbling of the things he'd seen. Things from the future."

"Oh, really," Elizabeth said, her heart pounding against her ribs. She could get home. She didn't realize how deeply worried she'd truly been until now. She closed her eyes briefly in thanks.

"His name is Patrick. He looks like my sire, only he laughs more."

"How nice," Elizabeth said. What else could she say? *Gee, Jesse, I'm new to this time traveling, and I haven't run into your uncle yet. Give me a few more years.*

"You came from the forest," Jesse said, his gaze never leaving hers.

"Jesse, that doesn't mean . . ."

"But it could. Couldn't it?"

The last wasn't exactly a question. Elizabeth realized she had misjudged Jamie's son. Jesse reminded her of her brother Alex, who could have witnesses squirming on the stand with only a pointed question or two and a piercing look. And she had to admit she was a rotten liar.

"Jesse, it would probably be better to leave this alone." She attempted a smile. "There are some things it's just better not to know."

"He said he was journeying home to 1996."

Elizabeth flinched before she could stop herself. Jesse smiled.

"My uncle said it was the future. I can't imagine counting that high, but Patrick wouldn't lie."

Elizabeth could only stare at him, unable to speak. If Patrick had managed it . . .

"Is it possible you might have met him?" Jesse asked.

Why fight it? Elizabeth had no idea what sorts of shocks she would send through time by admitting anything, but Jesse deserved to know. She shook her head. "I'm sorry, Jesse. I don't know him."

"A pity," Jesse said softly. "My father misses him deeply." He looked around him to make sure they were alone, then leaned closer. "Is it true the future has wagons that move without horses? And that men fly like birds through the skies?"

Elizabeth swallowed convulsively. Oh, the things Jesse would never see! She put her arm around him and smiled gently.

"Maybe it's better if we don't talk about it. I don't think your father would take kindly to this conversation; nor would the rest of your clan. They all think I'm a witch as it is."

"But it's true, isn't it?" he whispered. "About the wagons?"

She paused. Then she nodded.

"It must be a world of marvels."

"It is." She sighed, then looked at him. "Would you help me get back to the forest?" she asked hopefully.

He shook his head slowly. "Nay, Elizabeth. The forest beasts are very fierce, and my sire is the only one who could stand against them. You should wait for him to take you."

Well, there didn't look to be any alternative. Maybe she could get Jamie alone after dinner.

Malcolm returned, and soon he and Jesse were talking her ears off. She tried to listen but had a very hard time concentrating.

There was a doorway in the forest.

And if Patrick MacLeod could get to 1996, so could she.

Elizabeth had counted on dinner sweetening Jamie's mood, but it wasn't to be so. The food wasn't any better than it had been the night before. Elizabeth winced at the hearty curses that were thrown Hugh's way. He really did need a few cooking lessons.

After the meal, Jamie got to his feet. Elizabeth didn't have to ask to talk to him. He took her by the wrist and pulled her along after him up the stairs and to his bedroom.

Once there, he tossed her a blanket, stripped, then crawled into bed, as if he had nothing better to do than go to sleep. Elizabeth stood in the middle of the room, much as she had the night before.

"I need to talk to you," she managed, clutching her blanket and looking at him.

He put his hands behind his head and frowned at her. "Talk."

"I want to go home."

"Nay."

"Why not?" Elizabeth asked, very carefully. It was an enormous effort to keep control over her temper.

"You're still tired. When you're better rested."

Elizabeth gritted her teeth. She was going to chip something if she didn't lower the stress level in her life. The very first thing she was going to do once she got home was tear up her Forbidden Sweets list. A quart of Chocolate Decadence was sounding better by the moment.

She glared at Jamie. "I'm not going to get any rest sleeping in that chair, Mr. Hospitality."

"I haven't the time to see to you," he countered, his own expression darkening. "When I've the time, then you'll go home.

Until then, be you silent and let me sleep. And if you let me sleep *now*," he said pointedly, "I will see to you tomorrow. Let that be enough. I've several things to discuss with you."

"Then let's get them over with—"

"Tomorrow," he interrupted. And with that, he rolled over and began to snore.

Elizabeth sat down with a choice swear word or two to keep her company. She would go tomorrow, even if it took her all day just to elude Malcolm. She had to leave soon. Any more exposure to Jamie's lack of manners and she wouldn't be able to use him for hero material.

She settled the blanket over herself and closed her eyes. Yes, she'd get back to New York tomorrow, then maybe fly home to Seattle for a month or two to recover. Living in New York just wasn't what it was cracked up to be. She could move back home and write in the spare room above her parents' garage for free.

One thing was for sure: she was never opening another book on Scottish history again.

Chapter 5

JAMIE DRESSED SILENTLY in the darkness, then built up the fire. He wanted to leave his chamber without looking at Elizabeth, but his body had a different idea. He knelt down before the chair and looked at her, noting the bruise on the side of her head where she had hit the table. It was fading slowly.

He reached for her wrist and laid it on her leg. She stirred and opened her eyes.

"Hush," he said, gruffly. "Does this pain you?"

She nodded sleepily.

He felt it gently, then wrapped it in the stiff cloths he'd prepared the day before. Hopefully the wrist was merely bruised, not broken, and would heal with time. Jamie rose to his feet, then scooped Elizabeth up in his arms. He was past fathoming his own actions, so he gave them no more thought. He laid his woman from the future very carefully on his bed, then covered her with a blanket.

"You're weary," he announced. He used the tone he customarily used with errant young lads in training. "You'll rest here until I come to fetch you. Is that clear?"

She smiled. It hit him right behind the knees and almost knocked him flat. Merciful St. Michael, she was a beauty! He turned and strode from the room while he could still walk. A wench. Why did the Fates despise him enough to saddle him with a wench? Particularly a fetching one with a sharp tongue and a vast amount of courage? He could have borne it much more easily if she'd wept at every turn. Instead, she bellowed, just as he would have done. Malcolm was completely under her spell, and Jesse was fast falling that way. The lad spent all the moments he could snatch away from his training with Elizabeth, talking her to death.

Unfortunately, Jesse hadn't managed to wrest much information from her. Jamie had no intentions of failing at that. He wanted to talk to her openly. Was it possible she knew his younger brother? How were things in her day? Surely it was a time of great miracles. How else could a man capture a part of another's soul and fix it to a piece of parchment that it never faded or grew dim? Aye, those were questions he would have answers to. Her reluctance to talk wouldn't last long against him.

He trained for an hour before he decided she'd slept long enough. He marched up the stairs to his chamber, his purpose fixed. He threw open the door. Elizabeth was poking a dirk into the lock on his trunk. She jerked around in surprise, then quickly hid the blade behind her back. Jamie frowned at her.

"Thieves are hanged, you know," he said, with a pointed look at his trunk.

How she had the gall to look affronted, he surely didn't know, but she managed it.

"I was looking for my clothes. Where are they?"

Jamie had planned to give them back to her. Aye, he surely had. Now, though, he found himself hesitating. If he gave her her clothes, she would be on her way before he had aught to say about it. So, being that he *was* laird, he chose the wisest course: he would keep them and keep her. Until she had answered his questions, that is.

"There are several things I would discuss with you," he said, in his most lairdly tone.

She lifted one eyebrow. "Such as where my clothes have gone?"

"Such as where you came from," he countered. "Or, more to the point, *when*."

She went absolutely still. "I see you've been talking to Jesse."

Jamie frowned. "Aye, but he told me nothing I hadn't already divined on my own." He wasn't about to tell her how. "And now I have questions I wish to have answered."

She quietly moved to the mantel and put his dirk back on it.

"I think there are some things you really would prefer not to know," she said. "If you would just help me back to the forest, I'll leave you in peace." She turned around and looked at him. "Please."

The *please* was almost his undoing. But, with an effort, he put his shoulders back and recaptured his stern look.

"I've need of tidings of my brother, Patrick. I have cause to believe you might know him."

She shook her head, slowly.

"You came from the forest," he pressed on. "Your clothing was like nothing I've seen before, and your accent is one I've never heard. If that hadn't convinced me, talking to Jesse would have. My son says you have seen these things of the future. I'm sure that if you know of these things, then somehow"—he took a deep breath—"beyond reason, you are from then. The future."

Now that he'd put it in words, he realized how daft he sounded. From the future? Saints, he was babbling just as much nonsense as Patrick had! Her driver's license was something an artisan had fashioned. Perhaps she was from the Continent. Her accent was strange enough for that to be true.

"1996," she whispered.

Jamie swallowed—hard. "1996?" he repeated. The numbers felt strange on his tongue. "Aye," he said, "1996."

She nodded. "That's the year I came from."

"Patrick said he was going back to then. That time," he amended. He tried to smile confidently, but he feared it came out as a grimace. "I thought he was daft."

"I don't think he was."

He fought to take a normal breath. It wasn't all that strange. If he could believe Patrick, he could surely believe Elizabeth.

"Perhaps that was where my brother went," he went on. "Your 1996. Surely you saw him there."

"He looks like you, only he smiles more," Elizabeth said. "Right?"

Jamie's eyes widened in surprise. "Then you know him?"

She shook her head. "Jesse told me. Jamie, the city where I come from, the land where I come from, is so full of people, I could go days and not see the same person twice. You can't imagine it."

Jamie knew friend and foe alike for miles around. What a terrible place that future must be, where you knew no one, saw no friendly face on your journeys.

"I wish I could help you," she said, softly. "I really do. I'm sorry."

So was he.

"Ah," he said, grasping for something to say, "it is nothing. I suspected as much. There are, however, other questions I would put to you."

She sat down on his trunk and looked up at him. "Jamie, knowing what's coming isn't how life works. Your future is my past. It's already happened the way it should. If I tell you things about your future, you might make different decisions and that would change what to me has already happened. I've probably already said more than I should." She looked at him and smiled gravely. "Do you see?"

See what? Trying to picture his future as her past gave him pains in his head. She already knew what would happen to him, his clan, his enemies, and yet he had no inkling of any of it? Saints, it was more than he could face before a meal.

"Be that as it may," he said, frowning for her benefit and praying he didn't look as bewildered as he felt, "I will still have my questions answered. Later. When I've the time for it."

He left the chamber while he still had hold of the last shreds of his wits. Saints, what he needed wasn't answers, it was a keg of ale! Aye, a cup or two to fortify himself wasn't such a poor idea.

By the third cup, his frown had become deep. Perhaps she was right, and he was better off not knowing what would befall him. And, since she could provide him with no tidings of his brother, he knew it was past time he sent her home. The last thing he needed was to fall prey to her as his son and Malcolm had done.

His good intentions lasted until the midday meal. He sat at the head of his table with Elizabeth on his right and found his eyes continually drawn to her.

But it was only because she didn't eat what was put in front of her. There was surely no other reason for him to look at her. There was also no reason for him to linger after, except that Elizabeth looked to be plotting something. Already he recognized the disobedient gleam in her eyes.

He caught her in the act of corrupting Angus.

"Just help me get past Malcolm," she was whispering.

Jamie stood directly behind her and folded his arms over his chest. Angus met his gaze and gave him a wry smile.

"She's persuasive."

Elizabeth whirled around and gulped. "Jamie."

"Jamie, lad, she wants to go home," Angus said softly. "Perhaps—"

"She isn't going anywhere," Jamie said stubbornly. Damn her anyway, why was she in such a bloody hurry to rush off? Anyone with sense could see she was still spent from her journey into the past. He wouldn't be accused of being remiss in his hospitality. He looked down at her and felt a deep scowl settle over his features. "Where have you hidden your keeper?"

At that moment, the door to the hall burst open, and Malcolm tumbled in.

"There she is!" Malcolm exclaimed, running full tilt toward them.

Jamie snatched Elizabeth out of the way the moment before Malcolm would have plowed her over.

"Carefully," Jamie exclaimed. He retrieved Elizabeth out from behind him and handed her back to Malcolm. "I don't want you more than a pace away from her, is that understood? Whatever excuses she gives you, ignore them."

"Jamie," Angus said, clearing his throat pointedly, "Elizabeth isn't your prisoner. Why won't you let her go?"

Jamie suppressed the urge to wring Angus' neck.

"She's still weary," Jamie said gruffly.

"I am not," Elizabeth retorted.

"Aye, you are." He shot another displeased stare at Malcolm. "Watch over her well, or you'll answer to me."

Malcolm bobbed his head obediently. Jamie left the hall, cursing under his breath. He should have let her go. It would have been far easier on his peace of mind.

He hadn't been training a quarter of an hour before he heard Jesse shouting his name. Jamie resheathed his sword and stomped off toward the hall, his anger near the boiling point. Then he saw the lack of color in his son's face, and his chest tightened painfully.

"Elizabeth?"

Jesse shook his head. "Kenneth. He wandered off into the forest—"

Jamie brushed past his son and ran to the keep. There was already a cluster of men in the hall near the fire. Jamie parted them and knelt down by his clansman. He was not faint-hearted by nature, but the sight of his mauled and bloodied kinsman made his stomach turn. He wanted to take Kenneth's hand, but there was nothing left to take. So he met Kenneth's remaining eye.

"Quite the tussle," he said gruffly.

Kenneth smiled, then grimaced in pain. "I followed . . . a stag. Met a few boars. Something . . . else. Could have been a dragon." He coughed and arched his back suddenly. "See to my . . . son, Jamie."

"I will," Jamie said, but Kenneth wasn't alive to hear that promise. Jamie brushed his hand over Kenneth's eye and closed it. Then he heard the hastily muffled gasp and looked up in time to see the flash of Elizabeth's skirt as she fled.

"It was the witch who cursed him," a man muttered.

Jamie rose and glared down at the man. "She's no witch."

"She looked at him and he died," the older man repeated, stubbornly.

"He died of his wounds!" Jamie exploded. He stood up, disgusted. "Saints above, she's naught but a girl, and a frightened one at that." He looked about the circle until he found Ian. "Take word to his family. I'll go pay my respects tonight."

Ian nodded. "I'll do it and have Kenneth seen to."

Jamie left the hall and climbed the steps to his chamber. He closed the door behind him and leaned back against it.

Elizabeth stood at the open window, sucking in great gulps of fresh air. He understood completely. Not only had she likely never seen a man so torn before; she had doubtless realized that going into the forest alone was a foolish thing to do.

He crossed the room and stood behind her, not daring to touch her.

"Is he dead?" she whispered.

"Aye, lass."

She said nothing more, but her shoulders shook.

Jamie had no idea what he was to do now. Should he draw her into his arms? To do what? He couldn't have borne it if she'd begun to weep. His own emotions were far too close to the surface for that.

He also knew some of Elizabeth's fear was for herself. She wanted to go home. He could understand that. Had he been in her place, wouldn't he have longed for the Highlands? Would not the pain of losing his family have driven him to do anything to see them again? He bent his head and dragged his hand through his hair. He didn't want her to go, but he couldn't think of a good reason to make her stay. He sighed deeply.

"I'll take you."

She turned and looked up at him. Her eyes were moist.

"Thank you."

Jamie cleared his throat roughly. "Aye, you should."

She put her hand on his arm. "I'm sorry, Jamie. About your friend."

"He was foolish to go alone."

"But that doesn't make it any easier, does it?" she asked gently.

Jamie pulled away, her touch having burned him. "Rest while you can. We'll leave at first light tomorrow."

He left the chamber before he broke down and sobbed.

And he wasn't sure what he would have wept over—that he'd lost a fine clansman or that Elizabeth was leaving.

Saints, what a tangle she had made of him!

Chapter 6

JAMIE WOKE WITH scum covering him from head to toe. That hardly improved his humor. He'd been fool enough to give Elizabeth his bedchamber the night before. Yet it had been either leave it all to her or join her in it, and he'd known he couldn't force himself on her. So he had bid Malcolm guard her and had retired to sleep in the great hall with his men.

He took the time to wash some of the filth from him, then went up to fetch his guest. Just a few more hours and he would be rid of her. Now that the decision was made, time couldn't pass swiftly enough for him.

He entered his chamber to find her standing at the window, in the same place he'd left her. She turned once she heard him enter.

"Do you have my clothes?"

He tried to look puzzled. "Clothes? Nay. I had them burned."

"Oh."

He hoped God wouldn't smite him for lying. Elizabeth would find more clothes in the future. He wasn't about to give the ones in his trunk back to her. Or her tokens. On nights to come, when he'd slipped powerfully far into his cups, he would pull out her driver's license and look at her. A legion of demons couldn't have convinced him to give up that small comfort.

He pulled his extra cloak down off the peg near the door and draped it around her shoulders.

"You'll chill else," he said, looking above her head. He settled the cloak, then suddenly pulled his hands away when he realized he'd been about the task far too long. "Come," he said, spinning on his heel and striding from the chamber.

He waited for her on the steps to the hall. Half the household was gathered there. He looked over the lads, noting the ones who had lusted after Elizabeth and the ones who were suspicious of her yet. He swept them all with a look that made them, to a man, back up and lower their eyes.

"Elizabeth's lord is coming for her, and I'm taking her to meet him," he lied. "I need no escort save Jesse and Malcolm."

"Nay, I'll come too," Angus said. He was already mounted.

"As will I," Ian added. He stood next to his gelding. "You might need my common sense, Jamie lad."

Jamie couldn't manage even a decent retort for that slur. Ian was the only one Jamie could count on to hear his deepest secrets and never repeat them to anyone. Romantic fool though Ian might have been, he was at least good company. Jamie knew he would be grateful for that companionship on the way back to the hall.

Without Elizabeth.

He heard the collective intake of breath and knew Elizabeth had come out. Untrusting or not, his men were moved by her beauty. Jamie's expression darkened. Perhaps it was best she leave, before his entire clan lost their wits. He turned around and took her by the arm.

"You'll ride with me."

"Ride?" she echoed, looking around his arm at the powerful stallion saddled and ready.

"He's spirited, but I control him well enough."

"That horse?" Elizabeth said, stalling.

A terrible suspicion began to bloom in Jamie's mind. "Do you mean to tell me," he rumbled, "that you cannot ride?"

Her pale eyes were huge in her face. That was all the answer Jamie needed. He clapped his hand to his forehead and groaned. The day was off to an unenviable start.

"Trust me," he said with a deep sigh. He boosted Elizabeth

up into the saddle, then held his mount steady as she fought with her loose skirts to get herself settled astride his horse. Jamie yanked her dress down over her calves, looked over his shoulder and glared at the men he had correctly assumed were gaping at her legs, then vaulted up behind her.

Astronaut was a beautiful horse, the most powerful and intelligent Jamie had ever owned. Jamie reached around and took the reins, then patted Astronaut's neck. "Rest easy, Elizabeth. You'll frighten my stallion else."

"Him?" she asked tightly. "What about me?"

Jamie put his arm around her waist. It immediately became latched onto by two cold hands.

"I'll not let you fall, Elizabeth. Don't squeeze Astronaut so tightly with your legs. He will think you wish him to gallop." Jamie clucked his tongue and urged his mount forward.

"Astronaut?"

Jamie waited until they were well past the village before he answered.

"Aye. A future word my brother taught me."

She was silent for several moments before she spoke.

"It's the word for a man who travels to the stars."

Jamie cleared his throat. "Aye," he managed. "So it is."

He closed his eyes and memorized how she felt in his arms. He burned into his mind the way her hair felt against his cheek as the wind lifted it, how her lithe body felt pressed back against his chest. Saints above, she disturbed him! She was like no other woman he'd ever known. Foolish though it might have been, he wanted her sweetness, her gentleness, her courage in his life. Those were all the things he'd never had and, until that moment, had never known he wanted. Never in all his days had he encountered a woman who haunted him so.

And now he was on the verge of sending her away.

"Know you where we should go?" he asked, opening his eyes and seeing the forest loom up before him.

"I think it's south of here. I'm not sure. I'll know the spot when I see it."

Jamie didn't say anything. He merely guided Astronaut into the forest and turned south. The sounds of their passage filled his ears, sounds he knew he would never forget. The leather of his saddle creaked, Astronaut snorted and tongued his bit as they rode, birds chirped in the trees above them. The bracken snapped under his mount's hooves. Jamie listened to the men behind him speak in hushed voices, as if they were in some holy place. Elizabeth's hands rested over his and, despite himself, he wished they would remain there forever.

"I think that's it up ahead," Elizabeth said, suddenly.

Jamie held up his hand, and the men behind him stopped. In truth, it wouldn't have mattered had the four continued on. Jesse, Ian and Angus knew of Patrick's disappearance and return from the future. Malcolm was too dimwitted to make anything of what he would see. But Jamie wanted privacy when he watched Elizabeth go, so he continued on alone and reined in Astronaut just before an open glade. He swung down from his mount and held up his arms for his lady. He set her on her feet and straightened her cloak.

"Go on," he said gruffly. "I know you're anxious to be gone."

She hesitated, but he refused to look at her. He heard her sigh and turn away. Once her footsteps had receded, he flipped Astronaut's reins over a tree limb and approached the edge of the glade.

The sunlight fell down through the trees like heavy threads of pale yellow silk. Jamie watched Elizabeth hungrily as she walked into the midst of the glade and then turned to look at him. The sunlight fired the strands of red scattered through her dark hair and turned her eyes to a pale aqua, more beautiful than the finest beryl he'd ever seen. She looked like something out of an enchantment, with her long hair streaming about her shoulders and her fair skin pale in the morning light. Jamie's heart lodged in his throat along with a lump of emotion he couldn't swallow past. Merciful saints, he was going to lose her. He'd never truly understood until that moment how much he'd wanted her, and now he could never have her. He clenched his fists at his sides.

"Take her," he whispered to the Fates. "Take her, damn you!"

Elizabeth couldn't have heard him, yet a single tear spilled over and ran down her cheek. She took two steps toward him. Jamie didn't think; he merely crossed the remaining distance and yanked her into his arms. He buried his face in her hair and breathed, fighting that excruciating stinging behind his eyes. He had no reason to care for this troublesome wench, none at all.

But, saints above, he couldn't release her.

It was Elizabeth who pulled away, finally. Jamie released her and hardened his expression until not a trace of emotion could have been revealed there. Elizabeth reached up and touched his cheek.

"I'll miss you. I was almost beginning to like your grumbles."

Jamie grunted. She hadn't paid him much of a compliment, but perhaps he didn't deserve more. She was likely still annoyed with him for having put her in his pit.

"If I ever do see Patrick," she said, "I'll tell him hello."

"You do that."

Elizabeth leaned up on her toes and brushed his cheek with her lips. "Thank you, Jamie."

He pushed her away and cleared his throat, as if his life depended on being able to swallow easily. He stepped back a pace.

"Go on, you troublesome baggage," he said gruffly. "And keep the clothing. It suits you very well."

She smiled. It was like a dirk in his heart. He turned around and walked away while his legs were still steady beneath him. He put his hand on Astronaut's neck and kept his back to the glade. He couldn't bear to watch her disappear. Would she fade to nothing, like a spirit? Or would she vanish in a bolt of lightning?

He wasn't sure how long he waited, but he'd counted as high as he could count more than once. He almost mounted without looking in the glade, but he couldn't help himself. With a deep sigh, he turned.

Elizabeth was standing in the same place.

"Elizabeth?"

Her face was ashen. "Nothing is happening."

Jamie walked to the edge of the glade. "Perhaps you are doing something amiss. What were you doing when you came here?"

"Lying down."

"Then do so." That was simple enough.

She lay down and closed her eyes. Jamie watched her, waiting silently.

Nothing happened.

"Maybe you have to go away," she said hoarsely.

"Aye." He walked away, as far as he dared. Any number of beasts could have come crashing out of the trees, and he wouldn't have been able to save her. So he stayed close enough and kept his dirk in his hand just in case something came along to harm her.

He waited. And he waited. And he thought he heard the sound of weeping.

"Father! A boar!" Jesse's shout broke the stillness.

Jamie didn't think; he reacted. He leaped up into the saddle and spurred Astronaut toward the glade.

"Elizabeth, up!" he bellowed.

She had only crawled to her feet when he raced by, caught her by the arm and hauled her up in front of him. As an afterthought, he hoped he hadn't pulled her limb free of her shoulder.

He sent Astronaut wheeling around and they rode east, toward the edge of the forest. Jamie heard the squeal of the boar behind him, then heard answering hoofbeats as his company gave chase. He clutched Elizabeth to him with one arm and held his drawn sword in his free hand, guiding his mount with his knees. They reached the meadow, and Jamie heard the distinct dying scream of a future night's supper. He reined in his stallion and waited for his men to come to him. Angus arrived first, and his expression was grave.

"Elizabeth?"

"Leave her be," Jamie growled, sheathing his sword and tucking Elizabeth more closely against him.

"Nothing happened?" Jesse panted as he came to a stop alongside them.

"What was supposed to happen?" Malcolm asked, completely bewildered. "Didn't her lord come for her? Why would we want him to? I say we keep her."

"Be silent, dolt," Ian said, cuffing Malcolm smartly.

Jamie ignored them all and nudged Astronaut into a walk. He pulled back slightly, trying to catch sight of Elizabeth's face. He'd expected to see rivers of tears flowing down her face.

Her cheeks were dry.

"Elizabeth?"

She didn't respond.

"You'll stay with me, of course," Jamie continued, as if she'd answered him. Of course he would keep her. He was the only one with any inkling of how to care for a woman from the future. "That agrees with you, doesn't it?"

She reminded him of how she had looked when he'd descended the pit to retrieve her. Her eyes were open, but unseeing. In truth, he couldn't blame her. What if she could never return? What if she were consigned to live out her days in the Highlands, never to see her family, never to leave his hall, never to leave his side?

He was torn between elation that he would be allowed to keep her and terror that he would be forced to keep her. Saints, he had no idea what to do with a finely bred wench!

He forced away thoughts of what would come. He would allow her to stay in his hall. That in itself was much for her to be grateful for. He certainly hadn't honored any other woman thusly. Aye, he would give her a home, warm clothes and food. She couldn't ask for anything else.

By the time they reached the keep, she was trembling violently. Jamie slipped off his horse with her in his arms. His household was still gathered before the hall doors.

"Her lord changed his mind," Jamie barked, anticipating dozens of questions he had no intention of answering. He carried her up the stairs to his chamber, set her down in his chair and built up the fire in his hearth. He poured wine and held the cup to her lips. "Drink."

She didn't move.

"Damn you, Elizabeth, drink!"

Her eyes focused on him, and she obeyed him. He forced a cup of wine down her, then pulled blankets off his bed and covered her with them. And then his inspiration ceased. He had done for her what he would have done for himself, and now he had no idea how to proceed. He was terrified she would break down and sob. Comforting an hysterical woman was not in his list of daily tasks. So he pulled up a stool in front of her and sat, prepared to give her something akin to the words he might have given to the young ones in his clan whom he prepared for battle.

"You've no time for tears," he began briskly. "There is much to be done, and you're just the lass to do it. We might have failed today, but there will be other days, and we will be victorious then." He waited for her to agree with him. She didn't move, so he plunged ahead. "Perhaps we chose a day when the Fates were feeling fickle. We will try again in a few days. Until then, there is plenty to keep you busy here around the hall. I'll see that you have warm clothes and hearty food to eat. In truth, there isn't much more a body could ask for than that, is there?"

Elizabeth didn't exactly overwhelm him with her enthusiasm. Indeed, she didn't make any move to acknowledge she'd even heard him. Jamie frowned.

"Perhaps you're chilled and cannot appreciate my words." He tucked the blankets around her more securely, then rose. "I'll be back to fetch you for supper. Rest until then."

He left his chamber, feeling as if he'd failed in his efforts to reassure her. In truth, he wasn't sure how he could have succeeded. If he'd been in Elizabeth's shoes, hundreds of years out of his time, then found he couldn't return, what would he have done?

Likely sat down and bawled like a bairn.

He descended the stairs and found a cluster of Elizabeth's staunchest admirers there. Hugh's eyes were as red as his nose. Malcolm was almost beside himself with worry. Angus looked grim, and Jesse hadn't even taken the time to change his blood-soaked clothes. Ian looked at Jamie so piercingly, Jamie wanted to squirm. He ignored his cousin and turned his attention to the others.

"She is fine," he announced.

"But she couldn't go forward—" Jesse began.

Jamie held up his hand. "No one is to know what happened this morn, is that clear? Whatever you know, keep it inside yourselves. I remember very clearly the last witch I saw burned, and I won't sentence the girl above to that same fate.

She is an innocent, and only our silence will keep her that way. Understood?"

All but Malcolm nodded solemnly. Malcolm looked confused. Jamie reached out and clapped the blond giant on the shoulder.

"Just watch over her carefully, Malcolm, and don't open your mouth to anyone about her."

"Aye, Jamie," Malcolm said, nodding firmly. "I'll do that."

The group broke apart and went their separate ways. Ian remained behind, looking at Jamie closely. Jamie shot him an annoyed look.

"Don't you have anything pressing to do?"

"Other than speculating about your motives?" Ian asked, a smile tugging at his mouth. "Nay, that sport will be entertaining enough."

"She needs a home," Jamie growled.

"And is that all you intend to offer her, my laird?"

"Fool," Jamie said, disgruntled. "You would do better to use your sword arm more and your brain less."

Ian only laughed. "Och, but you're pitifully easy to read, Jamie. She is fetching, is she not?"

"I couldn't care less how she looks," Jamie said, growing increasingly uncomfortable. "She's just a wench. She means nothing to me."

"Of course."

"She doesn't!"

Ian only smirked as he made Jamie a low bow and then walked away, whistling a cheerful melody.

Supper was a very quiet meal. Jamie watched Elizabeth sit and stare into the fire, obviously seeing nothing. The men didn't talk, didn't jest. Indeed, they hardly made any noise at all as they ate. Even the ones who had been against Elizabeth looked subdued. Jamie knew there would be no more talk of Elizabeth being a witch. It was obvious to any fool there that she had suffered a tragedy of immense proportions. Everyone knew witches didn't have tender hearts to break. Elizabeth's broken heart was there for all to see.

After supper, Jesse supplanted Malcolm's place next to Elizabeth and tried to tease her into speaking to him. She ignored him. Ian flattered her from the opposite side of the table, lavishing compliments on her that would have had any other maid blushing furiously. Elizabeth's expression didn't change.

Jamie took her upstairs long before the hall had settled down for the night. She didn't say a word as he bolted the chamber door, then led her over to the fire. He left her standing there as he built up the blaze. That seen to, he sat down in his chair and looked up at her. She stood before him as still and emotionless as a statue. It frightened him. He reached out and pulled her, unresisting, down onto his lap. She made no move to stop him. Saints, had the shock been so great that it had damaged her permanently?

"Elizabeth," he said quietly, situating her more comfortably. "Elizabeth?" He put his arm around her and shook her.

Oh, merciful saints, she was going to weep. Jamie watched the tears gather in her eyes and knew he was done for. He groaned silently as he pulled her close and patted her back as gently as he knew how.

"Not so hard," she said, coughing.

He winced and stopped patting. Saints, he was inept! He took his hand and very carefully rubbed her back, hoping it would soothe her.

It didn't have the desired effect. She broke down and sobbed. It was the most heart-wrenching weeping Jamie had ever been privy to. She made little sound, but her body shook with violent tremors, and her tears burned his neck where they fell. Jamie felt more helpless than he ever had in his life. At that moment he very much regretted the lack of a mother in his life. Perhaps he might have been more skilled at comforting Elizabeth had things been different in his youth.

As it was, he could only hold his woman from the future. He tried to make soothing noises, but they sounded foolish, so he stopped. And still she wept.

After a time, which seemed very long indeed to him, she simply rested in his arms, breathing harshly.

"Elizabeth, we can try again."

It was the wrong thing to say. Where she dredged up more

tears, he certainly did not know, but she had an entirely new batch to drench him with. She cried until she was choking.

"It might work," he offered.

She cried out as if he had struck her. "It will never work!"

Jamie had to agree with her, but he did so silently. He rocked her gently, giving his soothing noises another try. Perhaps he was improving his skill with them, for Elizabeth's tears subsided. Soon she was only clutching him, as if he were the only thing that saved her from sliding into the pit of hell. Jamie used the hem of his sleeve to dry her cheeks.

"There, there, lass," he said gently. "Let me fetch you something to drink. You're likely thirsty from weeping all those tears."

He was thirsty from just listening to her weep all those tears. He put her off his lap and procured a cup of wine. He made her drink a few sips, then drained the rest of the cup himself.

He sat back down and held open his arms for her. She came to him willingly, and he had the most ridiculous feeling of pleasure come over him. It wasn't the pleasure he felt when contemplating bedding a particularly delightsome wench. It was a warmth in an altogether different part of his body, in the vicinity of his heart. He tightened his arms around her and settled her head more comfortably on his shoulder.

"You may weep more if you wish it," he announced, feeling exceedingly generous.

"I think I'm finished for the moment," she whispered, her voice hoarse from her tears. "But thank you just the same."

Jamie felt a hint of a smile cross his face, and his worry receded. If Elizabeth could attempt even a weak jest, then she would survive. It had somehow become very important to him that she did.

He froze.

When, by St. Michael's sweet soul, had this woman become so necessary to him? Mayhap she *was* a witch, and she had enspelled him well enough that he'd lost all his wits.

Her hand rested so trustingly on his chest, burning him even through the cloth. He sat, panicked, as he felt her relax and fall asleep. He was a fool! He'd wanted nothing more that morning than to keep her near him, not truly thinking what it would mean. Now he had her, and what was he to do with her? Already she had begun to ruin his reason. Her pain had become his pain. Who knew what sorts of tortures lay in wait further along the disastrous path he'd just put his foot to?

The memory of the agony he'd felt at losing Patrick was too sharp for him to forget and become lax. He couldn't risk caring that deeply about anyone again. For a reason he couldn't fathom, he knew losing Elizabeth would be much more painful. Merciful saints above, he couldn't bear even the thought of it!

Distance. He latched onto that thought with all his strength. He would leave for a few days and see to his affairs. Aye, it was past time he did that. Already Elizabeth had been a distraction, just as he'd known she would be. Distance was his only hope. His reason would return, and his heart would reconstruct those defenses it had somehow lost. He would allow her to stay in his house, but he would keep her far from him. And the sooner he began, the better. Before sunrise, he would be gone.

Elizabeth stirred, then pressed her face against his neck and drifted back into slumber.

Jamie closed his eyes and groaned silently. The girl was acting as if she trusted him. That only made matters worse.

If she hadn't suffered such a tragedy, Jamie told himself, he would have risen right then and fled for safer ground. But Elizabeth needed him at present. Truly, there was no sense in disturbing the lass before he had to.

Sunrise was soon enough.

Chapter 7

Elizabeth STARED OUT Jamie's window, too weary and heartsick to move. She'd slept the night before only when she couldn't stay awake any longer and cry. Each time she'd woken, Jamie's arms had tightened around her. He had comforted her, just as sweetly as she ever could have hoped for. Then he had laid her on his bed at dawn and disappeared.

She turned away from the window and looked over Jamie's room. So this was how she would live the rest of her life. She would never again see a car or a plane or a movie. The phone would never ring and wake her up, taxis wouldn't honk their horns outside her window, and she wouldn't have to worry about that Forbidden Sweets list. She'd never get close enough to another chocolate chip to have it affect her saliva glands, much less her blood sugar level.

She let out a ragged breath. Her parents would be frantic. Her brothers would turn the United States upside down looking for her. In a few years, they might give up hope and let her memory die a peaceful death. She would be stuck back in time, and her family would never be the wiser.

Well, moping wouldn't do her any good. She would just have to get over it. Her family would have expected her to go on and be brave. Her father would have told her, "Look for the good in every situation." Eldest brother Jared would have said, "Nothing happens without a reason." Alex would have told her to call if things got really bad, and he would send her a plane ticket. She smiled at the thought. Alex could always be counted on for a good rescue.

Well, since United wasn't flying the friendly skies yet, she would stick with the other two pieces of advice. After all, what choice did she have? She'd tried the forest and found it unresponsive to her pleas. Jamie had offered to try again, but she knew there was no point. There had been no hint of magic in the air, nothing that felt as it had that blustery fall day in the park. Perhaps it had something to do with Jamie. When it had come right down to it, she hadn't really wanted to leave him, especially after his good-bye hug.

Now it looked as if she was going to get that wish. All she could do was make the best of it and think of it as medieval research. She might eventually figure out the forest. She could keep her eyes and ears open and maybe try again in a few months. Though, for all she knew, she had gone back in time seven hundred years for a purpose.

Though she certainly couldn't bring one to mind at present.

She opened the door to find Malcolm leaning against the far wall. He straightened the moment he saw her and gave her a cheerful smile. Then his smile faltered. He crossed the passageway and lifted the hem of his sleeve to dry her cheeks.

"Your eyes were leaking, Elizabeth," he noted. "Come, let us see what Hugh has prepared for you. That will cheer you."

Elizabeth couldn't exactly agree, but she was touched by Malcolm's concern, so she tried to smile for his benefit. She took his proffered arm and walked with him down to the great hall.

Hugh and his lads were walking on eggs around her, just as Malcolm was. Elizabeth knew she couldn't stand a lifetime of living with people who pussyfooted around her. It was best to bring things back to normal as quickly as possible. And if there was anything that made her feel normal, it was getting organized. She didn't have pen and paper to make a list, but then again, in Jamie's hall, the priorities were blindingly obvious. She couldn't live in Jamie's home the way it was, so she'd just clean it.

"Come on, Malcolm," she said, tossing the remains of her breakfast apple into a bucket of pig slop. "We've got a lot to do today. Let's go find Jamie."

She left the kitchen, Malcolm trailing behind her dutifully. Angus was standing near the hearth, so she crossed the slippery floor to him. He turned when he heard her coming and smiled gravely.

"How do you fare today, little Beth?" he asked, giving her his grandfather's smile.

"Well enough," she said. "Where's Jamie?"

"Ah, well," Angus said, shifting his weight to his other leg, "he's out."

"Out?" she echoed.

"Out," Angus said, with a nod. "I believe he's off visiting an ally or two with Ian."

"Is he?" Malcolm asked, sounding puzzled. "But he planned to break those new mounts from Andrew MacAllister today. He was powerful anxious to see it done."

"Ah, well," Angus said again, "he had a change of heart."

"But," Malcolm said, scratching his head, "I thought he was just out for a ride to get his distance from the disturbance in the hall. What did he mean by that, Angus? Things have been quiet enough of late."

Angus colored. "He meant nothing by it." He looked at Elizabeth apologetically. "Truly."

"I see," she said.

And, quite suddenly, she did.

"Elizabeth, lass, Jamie isn't used to having a woman about. And for all I know, his plans might have changed. He's been needing to visit a few of his allies—"

Elizabeth ignored Angus' attempts at pacifying her. She'd known Jamie didn't want her there at first. He'd made that plain enough. But after how sweet he'd been the night before!

She put her shoulders back and frowned. She certainly didn't have anywhere else to go at the moment. Jamie would just have to get used to her. And he would also get used to sleeping with the men because she was sick of sleeping in the chair. Only one of them was going to use his bed, and it sure as hell wasn't

going to be him. She worked herself into a fine, affronted temper within moments and felt one hundred percent better.

Anger was certainly preferable to tears.

"I'm going to clean this place," she announced, giving
Angus a look that said he'd be smart not to argue.

"Of course," he said, clasping his hands behind his back.

"Jamie willna like it," Malcolm muttered under his breath.

Elizabeth favored him with a glare, and he ducked his head.

"I've said my piece," he muttered again.

"I've heard your piece, and I'm ignoring it," Elizabeth said
briskly. "Angus, I'll need help moving the furniture. Do you
think you can find me a few strong bodies to do so?"

Angus went off immediately to see to her wishes. Elizabeth
recited a list of supplies to Malcolm and sent him off to the
kitchen for them. Then she turned and looked down into the
fire, forcing a frown to her face. Jamie's disdain was the final
blow. It wasn't enough that she had lost her entire life in a single stroke. She'd lost any hope of gentleness from her laird just
hours later.

Damn, it hurt.

Angus returned with clansmen in tow. Some of the men still
seemed wary, but they weren't carrying kindling, which she
took as a sign she wasn't going to be barbecued any time soon.
She picked a few stocky ones and a few who looked as though
they needed to be taken down a peg or two. There was nothing
like cleaning to bring a man to heel. She led her crew upstairs
and set to work with them, hoping the exercise would keep her
from thinking.

Jamie's bedroom wasn't as frightening as the great hall, but
it came close. She closed her eyes as she scrubbed the floor and
scraped layers of dirt off the walls and windows. By the time
the room was clean, she was cross and bedraggled.

But at least her bedroom was livable. She was half tempted
to toss all Jamie's clothes out into the hallway, but she thought
better of it. He would be bellowing loudly enough when he
learned his sleeping quarters had been shanghaied.

Her anger disappeared with the setting sun, to be replaced by
a dull numbness that seeped through her. She'd known from the
very start that Jamie didn't have any use for women. Maybe she

should have been relieved he had let her stay as long as he had. He could have just as easily turned her out and not lost a wink of sleep over it.

But not only had he kept her, he had comforted her. Each time she'd woken during the night before, it had been to find him awake with his arms around her. He'd held her close, tried to stroke her back gently. Last night, she'd seen her knight in shining armor and found him lacking not a single romantic requirement.

And then the cold light of dawn had intruded and dealt romance a bitter blow indeed. She sighed as she leaned on the windowsill and looked out at the mountains.

Life was so much easier in books.

Supper was disgusting, as always, and Elizabeth knew that revamping Hugh's staff would have to be bumped up on her priority list. She let her eyes roam around the table and winced at the way the men wolfed down their food and threw the bones over their shoulders to be caught by the numerous dogs in attendance. That was something that would have to stop if she ever hoped to have the hall clean.

She had just choked down the last of a very inedible meal when she felt eyes on her. She looked across the table at the very dirty teenager sitting next to Jesse. She gave him a smile and received a scowl in return. Jesse rose and dragged the lad over. He held him there by the scruff of his neck.

"Megan, give a greeting to Elizabeth."

"Megan?" Elizabeth looked up at Jamie's son. "This is a girl?"

Megan hurled a foul curse at Elizabeth and fled from the hall.

Elizabeth looked at Jesse. "Where is that child's mother?"

"Died of consumption a pair of years after Meg's birth. I found Megan starving to death and brought her here. Father wouldn't let her into the hall as a girl, so I dressed her up as a lad." Jesse smiled ruefully. "He pretends not to notice."

"I see," Elizabeth said, not having any difficulty at all believing James MacLeod to be that heartless. Poor Megan. The girl was probably hopelessly confused about what sex she really was, and it was all Jamie's fault. And then another thought occurred to her. She looked up at Jesse.

"She's what, twelve?"

"Thirteen."

Elizabeth felt her first true smile of the day come out. "And what, pray tell, did you plan to do with him once *he* became a *she*?"

Jesse looked supremely uncomfortable. "Ah, well," he stalled, "I was hoping to avoid that day as long as possible. I've managed well enough so far . . ." He smiled hopefully. "I don't suppose you'd care to take over, would you?"

"I wouldn't think to usurp your place."

Jesse dropped to his knees. "I beseech you. I know nothing of these womanly matters. Already she is too old to run with us." He took Elizabeth's hands and clasped them between his. "Please?"

She couldn't tell him no, especially since she was just itching to get her hands on Megan and give her a bath.

"I doubt she'll like being watched over by a dreaded girl, but I'll see what I can do."

"Thank you," Jesse said, kissing Elizabeth's hands fervently. "I vow she'll accustom herself to you in time."

Elizabeth ruffed Jesse's hair affectionately. "Go rescue your lad one last time. The next time I catch her, she'll have a cleaning just like the rest of the hall."

Jesse rose and bounded over to the door. Elizabeth stood with a sigh, and Malcolm jumped up right along with her.

"I'm just going to bed. I'll be fine."

"I'll sleep outside your door," Malcolm said, casting a dark look at the rest of the men. "Just in case."

Someone threw a huge chunk of soggy bread at him.

"As if we'd harm her," the man said, disgruntled.

"Aye," another piped up. "Have you gone daft, lad? She's a kinswoman now. I'll kill the first man who thinks to touch her!"

Malcolm grunted. "See that you all remember that. I'm her bodyguard, you know."

Elizabeth winced as she realized she would definitely have to watch what she said, or there would be words inserted into Highlander vocabulary centuries too early.

Malcolm saw her to her door, then made her a low bow. "I'll sleep right here, my lady."

Elizabeth nodded and closed the door. She bolted it, too, then banked the fire and undressed by candlelight, as if she'd been doing it all her life. She slipped into bed and immediately noticed how big and empty it felt.

She flopped over onto her stomach and buried her face in Jamie's pillow with a curse. It was never going to feel anything but big because she was never going to share it with anyone.

Especially a pigheaded, cowardly laird named James.

Chapter 8

JAMIE LED ASTRONAUT into the stables and rubbed him down, taking the time to gather his thoughts. A se'nnight had passed, easily enough time for him to have regained control over himself. He'd bolted from his hall like a frightened whelp, but it wouldn't happen again.

After all, he was laird.

He experimented with a few fierce frowns before he left the stall and strode back to the hall. He would speak to Elizabeth and inform her he had decided she could remain in his house but that she wouldn't disturb him in the lists or while he was lecturing his men on their duties. And she most certainly wouldn't torment him in his bedchamber again. One night of catching a chill from her tears had been more than enough. She would have to find another place to sleep. He would keep her at a distance, and his heart would be protected.

He opened the door to his hall as the sun was setting, and was hit square in the nose by a smell that almost brought him to his knees.

Supper.

He walked to the kitchens, dazed. Hugh squeaked when he caught sight of Jamie, but Jamie ignored him. He walked straight over to the pot and scooped up a ladle of something that smelled fit for the king's supper table. He tasted hesitantly, on the chance that his nose was deceiving him.

Nay, it was nothing short of delicious.

"Lady Elizabeth's doing," Hugh said, pulling forth a cloth and blowing his nose vigorously into it.

Jamie slurped up another scalding mouthful before he looked over his kitchen help, wondering how in the world Elizabeth had taught them to cook. The lads were fresh-scrubbed and standing at attention. Jamie reconsidered. Perhaps having Elizabeth in his hall wasn't a bad thing after all. As long as she confined herself to the kitchens, of course.

"Let me go, you bastard whoreson!" A young voice echoed behind Jamie in the hall.

Jamie tossed the spoon at Hugh and strode out into the hall. He was greeted by the sight of Megan struggling to free herself from Malcolm's long powerful arms.

"You miserable cur!" Megan cried. "Bloody, diseased, loose-boweled woman!"

"Keep hold of her," Elizabeth called out, hurrying across the rushes.

Megan sank her teeth into Malcolm's arm, and he released her with a yelp. She bolted across the rushes toward the door, cursing for all she was worth. Elizabeth started after her, then slid on the muck. Jamie leaped forward and caught her; only his movement tipped them both over, and he went down flat on his back with a thump, Elizabeth landing heavily on his chest.

She kneed him in the groin getting to her feet, and Jamie gasped out a curse. He rolled to his feet, then hunched over with his hands on his thighs, panting until he'd regained his breath. He limped across the hall, out the front door, and around the corner of his hall. Then he pulled up short. He leaned back into the shadows, reaching out to snag Malcolm, who had come lumbering out of the hall behind him.

"Hush," he said, putting his finger to his lips. Malcolm nodded wisely and tucked himself into the shadows behind Jamie. Jamie looked around the corner, wondering which one of his women was weeping.

It was Megan. Elizabeth sat on the ground with Megan

curled up in her lap. Megan had flung her arms around Elizabeth's neck and was bawling with all her might.

"I hate you," she cried.

"Now, Megan," Elizabeth said gently, rocking her, "of course you don't. You're just angry because I wanted you to take a bath."

"You're bloody right I am!"

Elizabeth laughed softly. "Megan, my sweet, if you knew how good being clean feels, you'd want a soak. I would guess you hadn't taken a bath in a few months, isn't that so?"

"Years," Megan said, choking on her tears.

"You see?" Elizabeth said. "You've just forgotten how nice it really is. Tomorrow we'll have Hugh's lads heat you some water, and you'll scrub off some of this dirt. I'll cut your hair a little better, and then we'll find clean clothes for you. Lad's clothes, if you'd rather, though I think you'd be very pretty in a dress."

Megan in a dress? Jamie shook his head at the thought.

"Think you?"

Jamie pursed his lips at Megan's suddenly interested tone. Then he scowled some more at the purely maternal way Elizabeth went about smoothing Megan's shorn hair back from her face and mopping up her remaining tears. He hadn't even given Elizabeth his instructions, and already she was meddling.

"I think you would be a beautiful girl," Elizabeth said.

"This means I can't play with the lads anymore?"

"They'll have to learn they can't treat you as roughly as they do now. And perhaps your interests will change. I used to run around with my brothers, but then I found there were other things I wanted to do, like write."

"Write?" Megan echoed, aghast. "As the monks do? Lady Elizabeth, women aren't supposed to write."

"Honey, women can do whatever they want to do."

Jamie snorted silently to himself. Elizabeth filled the child's head with foolish notions. Women couldn't write. They weren't capable of it.

"But," Megan said slowly, "Jesse won't like me if I'm a girl."

Well put, Jamie noted.

"And Laird Jamie won't let me stay," she said, her chin beginning to tremble. "You know, he doesn't care for girls at all."

"Well, we'll just have to change his mind about that, won't we?" Elizabeth put Megan off her lap and rose. "Let's go have supper, Megan. It smells much better than usual, doesn't it?"

Jamie watched as they came around the corner. Elizabeth didn't even spare him a glance as she walked past him, leading Megan by the hand.

Jamie gasped. How dare the wench saunter by him without even giving him a look. By the saints, he was *the* MacLeod! Had the woman no idea just how feared he was among his enemies and his allies alike? He shoved Malcolm out of his way and stomped back to the hall, intent on giving Elizabeth a dressing-down she wouldn't soon forget.

She wasn't visible when he entered the hall, so he strode straight to his place and sat down, his expression dark. He leaned back in his chair and drummed his fingers against the top of the table, waiting to be served. The rest of his men were gathered about the tables in their normal loud and mannerless fashion. Gone was the reticence they'd used the night Elizabeth had come home and everyone had believed her lord did not want her.

The memory of that night brought a deeper frown to Jamie's face, a frown he used to cover the sudden twinge of regret he felt. Ah, the poor lass. She had nowhere to go, and here he prepared to make her feel even less welcome? He leaned his head back against the chair and drew his hand over his face. He was going daft. That was the only reason he found himself with so many feelings he couldn't fathom. One moment he wanted to haul her into his arms, and the next he wanted to cast her far from him.

He opened his eyes just in time to see her take her place. By the saints, she was a beauty. It was all he could do to pay heed to his supper, delicious though it was. It wasn't that she was simply beautiful, which she was. There was a light that radiated from her, a goodness that drew him to her as surely as a light draws a moth. He could scarce take his eyes from her.

Looking around the table, he found his men suffered the

same plight. Every last one of the fools panted for the gift of a smile from her lips.

Jamie started to frown. He could fall as much under her spell as he wished. He was in complete control of himself. His men, however, were a different tale entirely. Having them besotted was dangerous. They had to be sharp, as sharp as the edge of a blade, not gentled by a woman's smiles. He stood up suddenly, and all eyes snapped to him. That at least was somewhat satisfying.

"I want every one of you up before dawn," he said. "We'll train until we drop. It angers me mightily to see you men sitting here smiling as if you were a-wooing at court. I'll not stand for it. Elizabeth," he said, "go upstairs. You're a distraction my men do not need." With that, he walked around the end of the table and made for the door.

He slammed out of the hall before he could hear her reply. He walked around the keep a dozen times, hardening his heart against her. And then he walked about the keep a dozen more times, testing his feelings and assuring himself they would withstand the sight of her. He recalled the words he had planned to say to her, the warnings about not disturbing him and remembering her place. Aye, she deserved them even more than she had when he'd first returned.

Once he felt completely prepared, he reentered his hall. His men were all diligently doing something proper. Some sharpened their swords; others worked on selected bits of their battle gear. Every last one of them wore a grim expression befitting a seasoned warrior. Jamie grunted his approval on his way up the stairs. And then he saw Malcolm standing before his door. He frowned at his kinsman.

"She'll have no further need of you tonight, lad."

Malcolm shifted uncomfortably. "I don't think she wants you to come in, Jamie."

Jamie tried the door and found it bolted.

"Elizabeth, open this door!"

"Go away, you jerk!"

"Jerk?" Jamie echoed. "What is *jerk*?"

"My laird," Malcolm interjected, "I daresay you don't want to know. She called the Fergusson that when she learned the man was our enemy." Malcolm lowered his voice. " 'Tisn't a compliment."

Jamie gritted his teeth. "Elizabeth," he began tightly, "open this door before I break it down."

"Forget it, buster," she called. "This is my room now. I've cleaned it, and I'm going to sleep in it. Go sleep in your pigsty."

"My laird," Malcolm said, cutting Jamie off before he could gasp in outrage, "I believe she means your thinking chamber. She doesn't mean that you should sleep with the swine."

Jamie forced himself to unclench his hands. "Elizabeth," he said, dredging up what little patience he had left, "I'll give you to the count of five before I break down this door. If you're wise, you'll open it."

"Go to hell!"

Jamie came close to throwing himself at the wood. Then he reconsidered. It wouldn't serve him to break down his own door when he had every intention of sleeping in his chamber that night. So he shrugged.

"Very well, then. I will."

He walked past Malcolm, then flattened himself against the wall. He wasn't the most powerful laird in the Highlands for nothing. He knew Elizabeth would open the door soon enough just to see that he'd gone and when she did, he would slip inside the chamber and toss her out all in one motion.

He didn't have to wait long. He clapped his hand over Malcolm's mouth as the bolt slid back, then pushed his cousin out of the way when the door opened. He stepped inside his chamber, then slammed the door behind him, discarding the idea of throwing Elizabeth out. The thought of keeping her captive while he shouted at her was much more appealing. He slid the bolt home, then crossed his arms over his chest and looked down at her, suppressing the urge to throttle her.

"You forget who is laird," he growled.

She folded her arms and frowned right back at him. "I'm not sharing this bedroom. You can leave."

"This is *my* chamber, not yours."

"There isn't anywhere else for me to sleep."

"Sleep downstairs, wench, with the dogs."

She looked as if he'd just slapped her, and he instantly regretted his words, in spite of himself.

"Move, and I will," she said, her voice hollow.

Jamie struggled to regain his composure. Damnation, she was just as much trouble as he suspected she'd be!

"I'm not finished speaking with you," he said sternly. "Go sit you down by the fire and prepare to listen to me. I've several things to say to you."

"If you'll just get out my way, I'll leave and save you the trouble."

"You'll go nowhere. Sit down."

He saw that his tone was irritating her. Some of the fire began to come back to her eyes. Jamie gestured arrogantly, hoping to provoke her further. He wasn't disappointed. She cursed him under her breath as she sat down in his chair. He walked over to pour himself wine from the pitcher on the table near the hearth and caught her movement. He banged the cup down and leaped across the chamber. He lunged for the door, slamming it before she could open it more than a thumb's width. Then he spun her around and backed her up against the door, pinning her hands over her head. He jerked the bolt home with his free hand and glared down at her.

"Don't," he warned as he reached down and caught her knee just before it made contact with his privates.

"Let me go!"

"Just where is it you'll go, Elizabeth?"

"Home," she said, trying to pull her arms down.

Jamie held her wrists against the door easily with one of his hands. He looked down and met her pale eyes.

"You can't go home, lass," he said quietly. Saints, the words pained him as much as they surely pained her.

"You don't want me here," she said, her voice hoarse. "Just let me go."

He put his hand under her chin and lifted her face back up. He met her eyes and winced at her haunted look. He considered all the things he'd planned to say to her, all the admonitions, all the warnings to leave him in peace. They were logical enough. He'd never wanted a woman in his hall. He'd lived his entire life in peace and quiet without one.

And then he considered the feelings he'd had while he'd carried Elizabeth to the forest, believing that he was sending her from him and he would never see her again. He thought of her tokens in his trunk, the tokens that he had kept for himself that he might retain something of her once she was gone.

But she wasn't gone. She wasn't able to go. He held naught but trouble in his hands, yet he couldn't find it in himself to keep her far from him. Saints above, he was losing his wits. He released her hands and slipped his arms around her back.

"Jamie—"

"Hush," he said roughly. That stinging sensation was back behind his eyes, and he had the terrible feeling it was the beginning of tears. He bent his head and pressed his face hesitantly against her hair. "God help me, I canna let you go," he whispered.

"You don't want me here," she said, her voice catching on the words.

O merciful saints, she was going to weep. Jamie gathered her closer and slowly began to rock from side to side, as he'd seen her do with Megan. She trembled as he held her, and he cursed himself for being a hard-hearted bastard. The girl had just lost her family, everything that had ever meant anything to her, and all he could think of was how she might complicate his life?

As if the latter were actually something he could stop. Elizabeth had already complicated things. He'd felt more emotions in a fortnight than he'd felt in his entire life. Just looking at her was as painful as a dirk in his belly, twisting and turning. Her beauty hurt him. Her sweetness humbled him. Thinking of how terribly lonely she must be made him want to break down and sob.

Nay, he couldn't chastise her for her actions or her words. In time he could teach her that it was dangerous for her to wander the lists, that it made him look weak when she questioned him before his men, that he truly did know what was best for her. But for now, he hadn't the heart to teach her anything, except perhaps that she could trust him. The feelings he'd had the night he'd held her while she wept returned, but this time they didn't frighten him. At least not as badly. He was strong enough to show her a smidgen of gentleness, wasn't he?

Now if he could just divine how one went about doing the like.

He pulled away from Elizabeth, then put his arm around her shoulders and led her over to the fire, snatching up a blanket on his way. He sat down, then reached out and pulled Elizabeth to him. It took him several moments to arrange her to his liking on his lap, and then he spread the blanket over her. He leaned his head back against the chair and looked at her solemnly.

"Would you care to weep?"

"Would it bother you?" she whispered.

He couldn't bear the tremor in her voice. Nay, he would do nothing again to put it there. He was much more comfortable when Elizabeth was shouting at him than when she was looking at him as if she didn't trust him. He lifted his hand and awkwardly drew her hair out from beneath the blanket.

"Nay, Elizabeth," he said, purposely putting a bit of gruffness in his voice so she wouldn't think him weak, "it wouldn't trouble me." He met her eyes again. "Can you start on your own, or do you require aid?"

He thought she was going to smile, but then her eyes grew moist and she leaned against him, pressing her face into his neck. Jamie wrapped his arms around her, prepared to suffer as great a drenching as he had the other night she'd wept. But Elizabeth shed no tears. She mostly trembled, as if she were cold. So he gathered her even closer. And then he rocked her again, just a little. She seemed to like it well enough, for soon even her trembles ceased. Then she lifted her head and looked at him.

"I should be going now."

"Going? Where are you going?"

She shrugged. "I know you want me to leave."

He put his palm to the side of her head and forced it back to his shoulder.

"I've changed my mind."

"You don't want any women in your hall."

He cleared his throat. "I daresay I was enjoying my peace and quiet far more than was good for me. A wench or two trying my patience won't bother me too greatly."

"You want me to go sleep with the dogs."

He pursed his lips. "Are you going to remind me of everything I said this night?"

"I'm doing my best."

He twisted so he could look at her face.

"I was angry when I said those things. I daresay I didn't mean them. And I don't want you to sleep with the dogs."

She considered. "Well, if I sleep here, where will you sleep?"

He shrugged. "In here with you."

"I really hadn't planned to let you in."

"You would become lost and chilled in that great bed without me."

Elizabeth shook her head. "Forget the bed, buster."

Buster? He didn't know the word, but he had the feeling it wasn't any more complimentary than *jerk* had been. Did she actually think he would just bed her as if she were a common whore?

"I will not bed you, Elizabeth."

"I am *not* sleeping with you."

"You cannot sleep any longer in this chair."

"Exactly."

"I have no intentions—"

"—of sleeping anywhere but on the floor," she finished for him. "Since you're planning on sleeping in this room anyway."

Her words surprised him so, he could only gape at her.

"You're a very chivalrous soul, James MacLeod, to give up your bed for me."

"I never agreed—"

Then he looked into her clear aqua eyes. Och, but that was a mistake. No woman had ever looked at him with such gratitude before. He paused and considered. Then he looked again at the angel who was looking at him as if he were indeed something very chivalrous.

Hell. If she wanted the bed so badly, she could bloody well have it.

He sighed deeply, waving a fond farewell as all his reason fled. He leaned his head back against the chair and closed his eyes, surrendering. Elizabeth rose, and he didn't stop her. The battle was won, at least for the night, and he had no more head for strategy.

He opened his eyes when he felt her tuck a blanket around him as he sat bolt upright in his chair.

"By all the bloody saints," he spluttered.

Elizabeth smiled. Jamie groaned silently. If she would just cease with those smiles, he might stand a chance against her.

"You're very sweet," she said.

"Off with you, you troublesome wench," he muttered. "I hope you find naught but lumps in that bed."

"Now, Jamie," she chided.

He cast her a baleful glance. "Perhaps a flea or two, also."

"I cleaned in here. There are no fleas."

He grunted. But he couldn't bring himself to move from the chair. After all, she had arranged the blanket nicely enough.

He listened to her make herself at home in his bed and indulged in a bit of regret that he wasn't there with her. The things he was driven to do already!

"Jamie?"

"Aye?"

"Chivalry is a good thing."

"'Tis bloody uncomfortable."

He made a few complaining noises, and he grumbled a good long while under his breath so she knew at what cost his chivalry was had, but he didn't untuck her handiwork.

Life was certainly simpler without a woman in the house.

But, he admitted grudgingly to himself, not nearly as pleasant.

Chapter 9

ELIZABETH MADE HER way down to the great hall. It was empty except for Hugh cursing in the kitchen and Megan sitting alone by the fireplace. Breakfast was an appealing thought, but it could wait. Megan looked too forlorn to be left alone. Elizabeth walked across the rushes, grimacing for the hundredth time at the feel of them under her shoes, and sat down on the bench next to Megan.

"Good morning, Sir Megan," she said.

Megan smiled up at her wanly. "And to you, Lady Elizabeth."

"What's wrong, honey?"

"Jesse's out training."

"Doesn't he do that often?"

"Aye," she said glumly. "But Laird Jamie won't let me out with the men anymore. He says it's no place for a girl."

Elizabeth mulled that one over for a bit. It was encouraging to find that Jamie had begun to soften where Megan was concerned.

"Isn't there somewhere we could watch them and they wouldn't know it?"

Megan's eyes lit up. "We could stand on the battlements. But Jesse won't let me go up there without him. He's afraid I'll fall." She scowled. "He worries like an old woman."

Elizabeth smiled. "He just loves you, sweetheart, and he doesn't want you to get hurt. If I go up with you, I'm sure he won't mind."

"Laird Jamie said you were not to go either. He thinks you might be afeared of how far above the ground it is."

Elizabeth wished desperately that she could take Laird Jamie to the top of the Empire State Building. That would teach him a thing or two about heights. She took Megan's hand in hers.

"I'm not afraid of heights, honey. Let's find a snack, and we'll have a picnic on the roof while we watch the men work."

"Honey? Snack? Picnic?" Megan looked completely confused.

Elizabeth bit her tongue. She would have the entire keep talking like Americans if she weren't careful. She gave Megan's hand a squeeze.

"What I meant was we'll fetch an apple or two and break our fast on the battlements. How does that sound?"

"Strange," Megan said slowly, "but I think I'll find it to my liking."

Elizabeth almost regretted her brave words when she and Megan opened the door to the roof and walked out into the morning sunshine. It was a long way down. Megan held onto her hand tightly.

"Look at your feet, my lady, and I'll lead you to the wall over the field. Then you can hold onto the stone and look down safely."

Elizabeth managed a weak smile as she nodded and allowed Megan to take the lead. The girl was surefooted and obviously used to wandering around on walkways no more than three feet in width. They reached their destination quickly, and Elizabeth let out a ragged breath. Then she lifted her eyes and gasped.

The view was breathtaking. She was looking due north, to the mountains. The tops of their peaks were already dusted with a light covering of snow. What she had originally thought to be a meadow was actually the top of a flat mountain. There were certainly mountains taller than the one Jamie's keep rested on, and there were also deep-plunging valleys, just hinted at by the way the mountains dipped down in the distance. The rugged beauty of the scene before her rendered her speechless. It was harsh and rough and completely untamed. Very much like the laird who invaded her thoughts so frequently. It was no wonder Jamie had little time for gentleness. How could he, when this was the environment he faced each day?

But surely the beauty of his home moved him. Why would he work so hard to protect it otherwise? She wished she had been an artist. Capturing the magnificence of the scene before her would have been worthy of any amount of time.

"Elizabeth!"

The thunder of Jamie's bellow almost made her lose her balance in surprise.

"Don't you dare move from that spot!" he shouted.

Elizabeth looked over the wall in time to see Jamie toss his sword to Jesse and sprint back to the house. Elizabeth looked at Megan and winced.

"I think we're in trouble."

Megan paled. "Think you?" She began to tremble. "Laird Jamie's so fierce when he shouts."

"Don't worry," Elizabeth said reassuringly. "I'll calm him down."

She bit her lip as she turned to wait for Jamie to burst through the battlement door. Calming him down was the least of her worries. Keeping him from strangling her was her first priority.

Jamie didn't burst, he *eased* through the door. He put his finger to his lips and walked to them slowly, as though he were afraid they'd bolt at the slightest provocation. Elizabeth looked behind her, wondering if there were someone sneaking up behind them.

"Don't move," Jamie commanded in a loud whisper.

His urgent tone made her nervous. "Why?" she whispered back. "Is the roof going to fall down?"

He put out his hand to her. "Just don't look down, Elizabeth. Watch my hand. I'll be there to fetch you before you know it."

Elizabeth looked at Megan with her mouth open. Megan put her hand over her mouth to hide her grin.

"He thinks we're afraid," she whispered into Elizabeth's ear.

"We'd better not tell him otherwise. It might embarrass him."

Megan nodded, her eyes twinkling. Elizabeth turned back in time to find Jamie almost to them. He approached carefully, his eyes locked with hers. Three more steps and she was crushed against his chest. So was Megan.

"I'm going to beat you for this," he growled into her ear. "Damn you, Elizabeth, you frightened me witless!"

"If you plan to beat me, I'll just stay up here, thank you just the same."

Jamie groaned and settled Megan on his hip. "Put your arms around my neck and hold on tightly, Megan," he said quietly. "There's a good girl. Elizabeth, hold on to my hand and don't look down. Understood?"

"Yes, Jamie," she said dutifully, exchanging a solemn look with Megan. She followed him all the way down the stairs and to the great hall. He sat her and Megan down on a bench and paced a time or two before them. Finally he stopped and glared down at them.

"You two will drive me to madness!" he bellowed. "What in heaven's name were you doing crawling about on the roof?"

"Watching you and Jesse," Elizabeth said meekly.

"You could have fallen and killed yourselves!" he shouted. "I'm so furious, I cannot decide which of you to turn over my knee first!"

"Stop bellowing so loudly. You're frightening Megan."

"Better her frightened than dead!" he thundered. "And that goes for you too, Elizabeth. You are forbidden to go up on the roof, is that understood? Both of you!"

"But the view is so lovely," Elizabeth protested.

Jamie threw up his hands in disgust. "Your life means so little to you that you would risk it for a look at mountains you can easily see from the ground?"

"We wouldn't have fallen—"

His roar cut her off in mid-sentence. He clenched his fists at his sides and looked as though he were truly trying to stop himself from beating her senseless. He finally turned a fierce frown on them both.

"You will not set foot on that roof without me. Is that understood, Megan?"

"Aye, my laird," she squeaked.

"Elizabeth?"

"Yes, Jamie."

He grunted. "Obedience at last. Perhaps now you two can stay out of trouble long enough for me to train for a bit?"

"Of course, Jamie," Elizabeth said.

"Megan?"

Megan jumped like she had been stuck with a pin. "Aye, my laird."

Jamie mumbled something unintelligible and stomped out of the hall. Once he was gone, Elizabeth let out a sigh of relief and relaxed.

"That was close."

"He was furious," Megan said in a small voice.

Elizabeth put a hand under her chin and lifted her face up. "Do you know why?"

"Because he doesn't like us?"

"Because he likes us very much. If he didn't care, he wouldn't be so upset that something bad could have happened to us."

"Truly?" she asked, wide-eyed. "Is that why Jesse yelled at me the other day when I tried to break the new stallion?"

Elizabeth gasped. "You did *what*?"

"One of the lads dared me to. I was making a fine showing until Jesse pulled me down." Her eyes widened again. "He swatted my backside, Lady Elizabeth, right there in the stables. Then he hugged me, then he yelled at me."

"It's exactly the same idea, love."

Elizabeth smiled to herself. Maybe Jamie's bellows were a good thing after all, if that's what they were disguising.

The bath was a great success, as far as Elizabeth was concerned. Underneath all the layers of dirt, Megan was a very beautiful young girl. Elizabeth did her best to even out Megan's hair with Hugh's sharpest kitchen knife. It was a poor substitute for scissors, but she made do.

A dress was also easily procured. Hugh had a daughter Megan's age and sent his son down for a dress as soon as it was requested. Elizabeth could hardly wait to see Jesse's face when he saw his little lad turned into such an enchanting young lady. Megan was still far too young to be wooed by him, but it was never too soon to start him thinking about marriage. Nothing would have pleased Elizabeth more than to have seen the two of them together.

After waiting until the men were seated and bellowing for supper, she and Megan made their grand entrance. Elizabeth hung back and allowed Megan to walk ahead of her. Jamie looked, rubbed his eyes and then looked again. But it was Jesse's reaction Elizabeth was waiting for.

He was sitting facing the kitchen, talking to Ian. He looked up at Megan and smiled, then continued his conversation. Then all of a sudden he stood up, slapped his palms on the table and gaped.

"By Our Lady, who in the world is this?" he thundered, in a well-done imitation of his father. "Since when did this poor keep acquire two angels of such loveliness?"

Megan's hands were clasped tightly behind her back, and she turned quickly to look at Elizabeth with wide eyes.

"Go on," Elizabeth said.

Jesse leaped over the table. He came immediately to Megan and made her a low bow.

"My Lady Megan, if you would do me the honor of being my companion this evening?"

"Do I have to serve you?"

"Would this vulgar knave ask a lady of your breeding to serve him? I think not." He offered her his arm. She looked up at him blankly, and Elizabeth smiled at his long-suffering sigh. "Megan, you're to put your hand on my arm, and I'll lead you to the table. That's how it's done."

"Oh," Megan said, blushing. She shyly put her hand on Jesse's arm and cringed all the way to the table.

Jamie didn't bother offering Elizabeth his arm. He pulled out her chair and beckoned to her with a kingly gesture. She sighed and tromped across the floor, vowing to teach Jamie a few things about good manners.

"This is what was under all that dirt and horse manure?" he asked, when she'd taken her place.

She nodded. "Amazing, isn't it?"

"I'd best have a talk with Jesse. 'Tis too soon for that little lass to bear him a son."

"I beg your pardon?"

Jamie gave her an amused smile. "He's a man, Elizabeth, and has had more than his share of village wenches."

Elizabeth reached for her goblet of wine and drained it, unwilling to know more.

She turned back to her meal. It was haggis. She just couldn't do it. Jamie finally took her bowl away and finished it himself.

When he made to rise, she put her hand on his arm. She could at least make one attempt to save Megan's innocence.

"Jamie, where does Megan sleep?"

He leaned against the back of his chair. "With Jesse, of course."

"We've got to find her a bed. She's too old to be—"

"Woman," Jamie rumbled dangerously, "you sound disconcertingly like a wife with your nagging. I will not tolerate being told what to do in my own home."

"But . . ."

"Go up to bed, Elizabeth."

"Jamie," she began miserably.

"Now!" he exclaimed.

She rose without another word and climbed the stairs to his chamber. Megan wasn't going to sleep with those men, no matter what Jamie said. Elizabeth would sleep with her before she allowed that to happen.

She paced the length of Jamie's chamber, waiting for him to arrive. As she paced, she fumed. Damn him for being so stubborn. She snatched his knife off the mantel and faced the door. So this wasn't exactly her street-mugging class, and it wasn't exactly pepper spray she held in her hand. She could make do. The important thing was to teach Jamie a few things about how one went about raising a teenage girl.

She fingered the knife purposefully and waited.

Chapter 10

JAMIE LEFT THE table and walked up the stairs. He had best settle this before it went much further. Future women had the oddest ideas about how to treat their lords. It was past time he instructed Elizabeth in the finer points of the art.

He walked into his bedchamber and stopped still. Elizabeth held his dirk in one of her hands. The sight was so absurd, he almost laughed. As it was, he couldn't stop his smile.

"Saints, Elizabeth, what are you doing?"

"I'm going to protect Megan," she said shortly.

"With what? Harsh words?"

She held the dirk up in front of him. "You think I don't know how to use this?"

Jamie almost said her nay, but he had seen the damage she had done to Nolan's nose.

"I think," Jamie said, slowly, "that you might know how to use your fists. But a dirk? Nay, I think not."

"I'll learn, no thanks to you." She gave him a look that was so cold, he flinched. "You're unfeeling, James MacLeod, to force a child to sleep with a hall full of men. I'm well acquainted with what your men are capable of."

Jamie frowned. Hadn't he rescued her that night? And, saints, he'd just seen Megan settled . . .

"Never mind. I'll just go see to her myself. I can see you're going to be of no help."

He folded his arms over his chest, his pride mightily stung. He watched her walk to the door, jerk it open, then pull it to behind her with a bang. He was half tempted to follow her and see what her expression was when she realized her mistake. But nay, he would likely enjoy it more if he only waited for her to return and apologize.

He stood in the same place, waiting. It didn't take long. Only a handful of moments passed before the door opened quietly. Elizabeth stepped in, her expression grave.

"I'm sorry," she said softly, closing the door behind her.

He nodded. "You should be. I am not the ogre you think I am."

"I know."

He waited. And when she said no more, he frowned. "That is all? You've need of lessons in the fine art of begging for forgiveness, Elizabeth."

She crossed the room to him. "Building her her own room is much more than even I could have asked for. And it was quite a sacrifice to give up even part of your private thinking room so she'll be comfortable now. You've a very generous heart, James MacLeod."

Jamie had to agree with her. And somehow, he just couldn't make any more of it. He wasn't over fond of apologizing, and no doubt Elizabeth wasn't either. He looked up at her for a moment or two with pursed lips. Finally he nodded.

"Forgiven. I also spoke with my son, in case you were wondering."

"And?"

"I told him to leave her be. He'll not trouble her in that way, at least for another year or two."

"Thank you, Jamie."

He sighed in resignation. "It's the very last whim of yours I plan to see to, Elizabeth. I've more important things to do." His voice hardened along with his expression. "And do not begin to work your magic on my son. What you do with Megan is your affair, but I'll not have you fussing over Jesse. The boy is mine to raise, and I want no interference from you. You can keep your opinions and womanly ways to yourself."

She turned away from him, but not before he saw the look of hurt on her face. Saints above, what had he said now?

"Elizabeth . . ."

"Just leave me alone," she said curtly.

Jamie felt an overwhelming urge to throw up his hands and leave his chamber. By all the saints above, what had he been thinking to let a woman into his life? They were nothing but trouble, and he had known that from the first. They certainly required more apologies than he had suspected. The saints only knew what else would be required at his hands before the tale was finished.

He walked to the hearth and sat on his stool, where he could get a good look at Elizabeth. Of course, it was a look at her back, for the very moment he could see her face, she turned it from him. He rubbed his jaw thoughtfully. At least Elizabeth hadn't turned tail and fled.

She was ignoring him. It was also clear he had said something to hurt her feelings. There was no sense in that. He was fast finding he did not care for that look in her eye. Better that she be shouting at him than weeping.

" 'Tis obvious I said something amiss," he ventured.

She remained silent. Jamie rubbed his chin another time or two, then took to rubbing the back of his neck. That always provided him with better answers.

"Would you care to tell me what that was?" he asked.

Her back was ramrod straight. Jamie shook his head in silent admiration of her stubbornness. Aye, he had met his match in this one.

"Elizabeth?"

She turned around. "Do you really want to know?" she asked.

Judging by the look in her eye, Jamie was half tempted to say her nay. But cowardly he wasn't, so he nodded. Hesitantly.

"First," she said, holding up her hand as if she intended to tick off her list on her fingers, "you skedaddle out of here the other day like you can't wait to get away from me. Just how do you think that made me feel?"

Skedaddle? Jamie opened his mouth to ask for the meaning of that, then shut it at the look of ire on her face.

"I thought I had uncovered a veritable mother lode of sweetness under all those grumbles after we came back from the forest. You were so wonderful! And then—"

She swallowed suddenly, hard, then put her shoulders back.

"You dealt romance a killing blow," she said, stiffly. "If that weren't bad enough, now you tell me you don't want me messing with your son. Oh, and let's not forget the part about me being seen and not heard. Next you're going to have me in a Donna Reed outfit, chained to the stove. Good grief, Jamie, it's the most unattractive display of Neanderthalism I've ever witnessed!"

Jamie could only stare at her, openmouthed. He hadn't understood half of what she had said. She spoke his tongue rather well, as a rule, and generally he could puzzle out the strange words she slipped in occasionally. But now she was obviously tossing in more than the occasional future word into her Gaelic. He had no idea what he had displayed, but it was certain it had been displayed unattractively. He checked his plaid as unobtrusively as possible. Nay, everything seemed to be covered well enough.

"And furthermore, Mr. Chauvinist, if you had enough romance in your soul to understand the concept, you would realize that what I really want is to be held. I want to be told you can't live without me. I do *not* want to be told you've no time to see to my whims. I don't even have any whims! I am a very reasonable woman!"

With that, she shot him another displeased glare and turned her back on him again.

Jamie paused and considered the last. Indeed, she was not an unreasonable woman. He likely should have taken more time for her, but, saints above, he hadn't dared! He'd done his damndest to keep her far from him so he didn't fall further under her spell.

He sighed. It was too late for that. The more days that passed, the more fond he grew of her. She was like no other woman he'd ever known. He'd wondered at first if it was because she was from the future. Now he began to suspect it was just because she was Elizabeth.

Perhaps it would be wise to appease her a bit. He cleared his throat.

"I filled the pit today," he announced.

She was silent for a goodly time. Thén she turned around and faced him.

"You did?" she asked softly. "Why?"

He shrugged. "I shouldn't have put you there." He looked at her and shrugged again. "I did it to make amends, I suppose."

She smiled. It was like sunshine after a fierce storm. Jamie congratulated himself silently. An apology was a small price to pay for this.

"But what will you do with your prisoners?" she asked.

"Have you guard them with your dirk, I suppose."

She laughed softly. "Oh, Jamie. You have a wonderful sense of humor."

"Humor? What have my humors to do with this? I am never ill."

She crossed the room and knelt in front of him. "I meant that you jest very well."

"Ah," he said, wisely. "Indeed I do."

"Thank you for the amends. I think you have more chivalry than I give you credit for." She leaned up and kissed him on the cheek.

He blinked, startled. But he wasn't so startled that he didn't mark a pleasant thing when he saw one.

"Do that again," he commanded.

"What? Say 'Thank you'?"

She jested with him. He recognized the twinkle in her eye and resolved to put it there more often.

"Indeed, but not with words." He gestured to his cheek. "The other."

She leaned forward and kissed him again, a soft kiss that he barely felt.

"Again."

He met her lips this time. Then he pulled back slowly and looked at her, trying to judge her reaction. Chivalrous he might have been, and he secretly thought Elizabeth very wise for noting that fine characteristic in him, but he was hardly adept at kissing. He wondered if Elizabeth would notice his lack of skill, and the thought of that embarrassed him.

"Don't," Elizabeth said. "Don't frown at me any more today, Jamie."

He hadn't realized he'd been scowling. So he tried a smile. It wasn't his best effort, so he leaned forward and kissed Elizabeth, hard, then sat back before his pride could suffer any more blows.

"Again."

He met her eyes. "Again?"

She smiled. The gentleness of it almost hurt him. "Again."

He scooped her up in his arms and set her on his lap. She looked startled enough, but Jamie ignored it. No sense in not being comfortable while he was at his work.

He leaned forward and kissed Elizabeth again, very firmly. He saw her wince. Embarrassment flooded him, for he knew suddenly that he'd hurt her. The room became stifling. When had it become so hot? Saints above, he wished he hadn't kissed her in the first place.

"That was nice," she said softly, putting her arm around his neck. "Wasn't it?"

He'd already bruised her mouth. Merciful St. Michael, he was beyond all aid! He ventured a look in her eyes and saw nothing but trust there. He could hardly believe it, but there was no denying what he saw.

So, he took his courage in hand and leaned forward again. Only this time, he barely touched her lips with his. Indeed, his kiss was softer than a breath against her lips. A shiver went through her. Jamie was on the verge of tossing her off his lap to save his pride, when she opened her eyes and smiled at him.

"Oh, Jamie."

The tone of her voice said it all. If he could have swaggered while sitting in a chair, he would have done it. He leaned forward and kissed her again, exactly the same way. Her eyes closed, and her other arm came up around his neck. Jamie hardly dared breathe, fearing he would break whatever spell he was weaving. He shivered when he felt her finger a lock of his hair. Och, but the lass could do terrible things to him with just a touch.

And then a most distressing thought occurred to him. What if she had learned such skills with another man? Perhaps a husband? He pulled back and looked at her, feeling a dread chill settle in his heart.

"Elizabeth?"

She opened her eyes and smiled at him. "Yes, Jamie."

"Are you betrothed?" Even voicing the question pained him.

Her smile changed. It could have been rueful. Or it could have been wistful. He didn't dare speculate.

"Sort of."

"Sort of?"

"Stanley Berkowitz."

"Stanley Berkowitz?" he repeated. "What by the blessed name of St. Michael is a Stanley Berkowitz?"

She smiled. "You sound like my father. Oh, Jamie," she said, with a sigh, "he would have liked you so much."

Jamie watched her as she turned her face away and stared into the fire.

"You miss this Berkowitz so much?" he asked grimly, dreading her answer.

She shook her head, a faint smile on her lips. "I just miss my family."

A wave of relief washed over him. Maybe he'd just throw the ring into the forest, and somehow it would find its way back to Lord Berkowitz and that would be an end to the tale.

The missing of her family was something he could understand. His father had died on the end of a Fergusson sword when Jamie had been but sixteen. Though he and his father had never been particularly close, it had been a blow to lose his sire. An even deeper pain had been the loss of Patrick. Jamie had never wept, but he knew he should have. His grief had been deep, and still weighed heavily on him at times. But how to ease Elizabeth's pain? Perhaps the only way was to send her home. He wanted to turn away from the thought, but he couldn't. Who was he to add to her pain when he could possibly be the one to take it away?

"Elizabeth," he said slowly, "I could try to take you back to the forest again if you wish it."

"Then you want me to go back." It wasn't a question.

Jamie pulled her to him again and closed his eyes. At least she sounded as if she wanted to stay. "Of course not," he said, mustering up as much gruffness as he could. "There are several reasons you must remain."

And he wanted to voice none of them. Telling Elizabeth he wanted to keep her because he found he was growing accustomed to her was just something he couldn't admit quite yet.

"Megan needs a bath, and I daresay no one else could convince her to take one."

"Of course."

"And you need me to teach you how to kiss. This Berkowitz was obviously terribly unskilled. I certainly hope he never took you to his bed."

He could have sworn he felt heat in her cheeks. He peered down at her out of one eye and saw that she indeed blushed.

"He didn't bed you, did he?"

"He didn't even kiss me."

"Did anyone else? Do anything else?"

"Jamie," she exclaimed. "That's none of your business!"

"Ah, I see." Perhaps she was a virgin. "How old are you, Elizabeth?"

"Twenty-four." She lifted her head and glared at him through her blush. "I'm saving myself for marriage, so don't get any big ideas, buster."

There was that word again. Slur or not, Jamie didn't care. He was simply happy to see the fire back in her eyes. He leaned forward and kissed her just as gently as he had before. Elizabeth would stay. Somehow, the thought wasn't unappealing at all. He gave her a smile, just to let her know where his thoughts had taken him.

She reached up and touched his cheek. "You have a very nice dimple," she said.

He frowned immediately. "I have no marks."

"It's not a mark, Jamie; it's a dimple. It's cute."

"Cute?" he echoed doubtfully.

"Charming," she clarified. "Endearing. Sexy."

"Sexy? What is *sexy*?" Now *this* sounded like a future word he definitely should know.

"Enough of this conversation," she said quickly, pushing out of his arms. "It's past time for bed."

"I think I would rather stay and have you look at my sexy dimple again," he said, reaching for her.

"And I think you would really rather go to sleep. Go away."

Jamie toyed with the idea of arguing, then decided against it. There would be time enough to learn all Elizabeth's future words and encourage her to give him more compliments such as she had that eve.

Jamie rose and went to fetch a blanket off his bed. He turned away as Elizabeth undressed and crawled under his blankets. He stretched out on the floor and resigned himself to an uncomfortable night's sleep.

"Good-night, Jamie."

He grunted, trying to find a comfortable way to lie. He forced himself not to remember all the solemn vowing he'd made about not letting her complicate his life.

It was far too late for that now.

"A pity this Berkowitz of yours was fool enough to let you go," he said.

"And why is that?"

Jamie grunted. "Think you I would give you back to him now? After you've caused me at least a fortnight of grief? You've completely disrupted my life. I'll not let you leave so easily."

"Oh, Jamie."

He cursed himself for being on the floor instead of next to her on the bed, because he had the distinct feeling he would have had another kiss for that flowery sentiment.

He sighed and rolled to the fire. Aye, she would stay. She would stay, and he would try his best not to bed her, despite himself, as wedding her was out of the question. He had an heir, and he certainly didn't want a wife.

But he would take a woman from the future and somehow learn to live with her.

It was a far sight more appealing than learning to live without her.

Chapter 11

ELIZABETH WOKE TO intense pain. She put her arm over her stomach and groaned, knowing immediately what it was from. Why hadn't she thought to stuff an extra tampon box into her pocket before coming to the Middle Ages? As near as she could tell, she'd been in Scotland for three weeks. Amazing how time flew when you were century hopping.

She didn't dare move, not knowing how far the damage had already spread. She looked over to find Jamie sleeping soundly in front of the hearth.

"Jamie," she called softly. "Jamie, wake up."

He sat bolt upright, his sword already in his hands. "What?" he asked, looking around with startled eyes. "Fergussons?"

"Jamie, we're not under siege. I need you to get me a basin of water and some cloths. And then you can stand out in the hall for a few minutes while I take care of some things."

He looked at her blankly. "What things? Why do you need water? It's the middle of the night!"

"Jamie," she said patiently, "it's my time of the month."

The blank look did not leave his face.

"For what?"

She groaned. "For not being able to have a baby, that's for what."

"Why would you worry about being with child?"

"Don't be so dense! I'm bleeding, Jamie."

"You're bleeding!" He leaped up. "Who did this to you?" he demanded. "Who touched you while I slept?"

The sound of running feet echoed down the corridor. A banging soon commenced on the door.

"Father, open up!" Jesse called frantically.

"Jamie, command me!" Malcolm shouted, just as frantically.

Elizabeth dropped her face into her hands and moaned with embarrassment.

"Jamie, it's just something women go through every month. Didn't you know?"

Obviously not.

"Jesse, be silent!" Jamie thundered. He knelt on the bed and laid his hand on her shoulder. "What is this mystery?"

She sighed. "Get me water and cloths, and then leave. Once I've taken care of things, I'll tell you all about it."

He immediately did as she asked. He came back in with her requested items, his face as white as a sheet. Elizabeth shooed him from the room and hurriedly did the best she could with what was available.

Jamie was through the door the moment she said he could come back in. He propped his sword up against the table and sat on the edge of her bed.

"Is the bleeding staunched?"

He looked as bad as she felt. She nodded, trying to put on a decent smile.

"It's okay. Happens every month."

"God help me."

Her sentiments exactly. Jamie's concern was almost enough to make her feel better. She laid her head back on the pillow and made herself comfortable.

"I'm sorry I woke you like that."

He brushed aside her apology. "Tell me of this womanly mystery. It seems a powerful bother."

"It is. And I'm not giving you any details."

"I know of horses and men. I know nothing of women, and I would learn more. Now."

Well, he might say he wanted to know more, but Elizabeth

could guarantee him he wouldn't want all the details, no matter how emancipated he sounded at the moment.

"It's just something my body does every month I don't have a baby."

"Every month?" He looked at her incredulously.

"Yep."

He rubbed his hand over his face. "Saints above, you women are strange creatures. I am powerfully glad to be a man. Now, how long will this torture of yours last?"

"Three or four days. Just long enough to make me incredibly cranky."

"Cranky?"

"Irritable. Short-tempered."

"Wonderful," he grunted. He looked at her closely. "It pains you still?"

"A bit."

"You're lying."

"I'm being brave."

"Aye, you would never be anything but, would you?" He reached for her hand and brought it to his lips. He kissed her knuckles. "Take your rest, brave one. I'll see to you well enough."

"Thank you, Jamie."

"You should. Saints, Elizabeth, but you have turned me into a witless fool."

Elizabeth smiled. Somehow cramps didn't seem so bad when she had Jamie's medieval grumbling to distract her.

Jamie waited until Elizabeth had drifted back off to sleep before he moved. The candle on the little table next to his bed gave off a faint light, light enough for him to see the darkness beneath her eyes. How could she survive such affliction each month?

He leaned back against the footpost of the bed and watched her. It was odd the things he never learned, not having a woman in the keep. He had been turned away by a village wench once because she said the time was not right. He had assumed it was some sort of superstition she believed in. Perhaps she had been suffering this monthly torture also.

He rose before dawn and walked around his keep, trying to understand what he felt. The thought of anyone having hurt Elizabeth had sent him into a rage, the force of which he had never felt before. The thought of her upstairs suffering twisted his gut.

Damnation, but it was frightening to think he could actually care for the girl.

He entered the bedchamber to find Jesse and his mates hovering over her anxiously.

"What is the meaning of this?" he bellowed.

Jesse jumped to his feet, and the rest of the lads scattered like leaves before a strong wind.

"We were cheering her," Jesse said.

"Jamie, leave him alone," Elizabeth said, frowning.

"Out," Jamie commanded, pointing toward the door. "She needs to rest."

The lads scampered immediately. Jesse left more slowly. Jamie caught his son around the neck and shook him.

"Go train, whelp."

"Aye, Father."

Jamie released his son, then moved to stand next to the bed. Elizabeth didn't look much better than she had the night before. He poured her a cup of wine, then squatted down by the bed while she drank it.

"I'm pleased to see you bearing this pain bravely," he noted.

"Thanks a whole hell of a lot, buster."

He lifted one eyebrow. "Ah, I see," he said. "This then is the crankiness you spoke of, aye?"

"It sure is," she said, glaring at him. "You got a problem with that?"

"Judging by the look in your eye, my lady, I think I would be wise to say you nay."

Elizabeth looked at him for a moment in silence, then laughed.

"Oh, Jamie, you are just priceless." She paused, then sniffed. "I just don't know what I would do without you."

Merciful saints above, now it looked as if she might weep. The woman wasn't cranky, she was daft. How could she snap at him one moment, laugh the next, then weep? Jamie rose quickly, before she did anything else he wouldn't understand.

"Do not rise until I give you leave," he ordered, then fled from his chamber.

He could have sworn he heard the sound of a goblet hitting the door.

The next time he returned, late in the afternoon, it was to hear Elizabeth spinning tales for Megan. Megan had turned out to be a beautiful girl. 'Twas no wonder Jesse had kept her covered with dirt and manure all those years. Jamie had laughed the day before at the wounds his son had inflicted on his mates for gaping at her.

Elizabeth had already given Jamie a lecture on Megan's care and feeding that morning. Then he'd been instructed to hasten the building of Megan's chamber. That had been during another bout of crankiness when Jamie had half feared Elizabeth would rise from her bed and take a blade to him if he disagreed. He'd crossed his heart as she told him to do, then escaped again before she could fling anything else, commands or goblets, at him.

Presently the bed-curtains were closed at the foot of the bed, and Jamie knew Elizabeth and Megan couldn't know he was listening.

Elizabeth's stories were enchanting but hopelessly impractical. Since when did a man risk all for the woman he loved? What man would be fool enough to find himself so besotted of a woman that he would go to any lengths to make her his? It was complete nonsense.

But Elizabeth could indeed spin a fine tale. She had told him that she was a weaver of tales in her own day; only she wrote them down on parchment for others to read. He couldn't imagine how many monks it would take, scribbling into the wee hours, to copy enough books to give to everyone in the future. Elizabeth said that, instead of men, they had machines that did it. Jamie couldn't imagine that either, so he let it pass.

But she did have a way with words, and that he could understand. He especially liked the tales with the mythical creatures she seemed to invent on the spur of the moment. Each story possessed a maiden in some sort of distress and a handsome, brave knight to rescue her. Invariably the maiden's name was Megan, and Jamie smiled dryly at Megan's delight over that discovery.

The powerful knights, however, seemed a bit familiar, though he couldn't quite lay his finger on why. The lads always seemed to have dark hair and green eyes and be extremely fond of showing off their strength at every turn. He puzzled over it for quite some time, then gave up. Perhaps he'd question Elizabeth about it when he had the chance.

And, much as he grumbled at her, she simply would not stop mothering Jesse and his mates. Jamie watched them critically as they trained and could not see that they were much worse for the wear, but her gentleness still didn't sit well with him. The lads didn't have time for a mother. They heartily disagreed.

As did Megan. As far as she was concerned, Elizabeth was a gift from above. Once her bed had been set up in his thinking room, she found it impossible to go to sleep without a kiss and a story from Elizabeth. Elizabeth found it delightful; Jamie found it senseless. What did a child need with such foolishness scampering about in her head each night before she slept? It would trouble her dreams.

Yet he found himself hovering at the doorway each night, listening to Elizabeth tell her stories and gently put Megan to bed with a kiss. One night the sight even brought tears to his eyes. It was a beautiful picture: the beloved mother hovering over a beautiful child. Megan soaked up every ounce of gentleness Elizabeth gave her and blossomed before Jamie's very eyes. At times he had to smother his smile as he watched the girl follow Elizabeth everywhere, imitating her every move. It was sweetness he never thought he'd ever see in his own home.

The last week of October Jamie woke to a pounding on his door. He leapt up from the floor, already pulling on his clothes.

Angus stood in the corridor, his face ashen. " 'Tis young Innis and his bride. And several others after them. Lord, Jamie, you don't want to see what's been done to them."

"Rouse the keep," Jamie barked. "Leave Jesse and the lads here, as well as half the men to guard Elizabeth."

Angus nodded and turned before Jamie could bang the door shut.

"Jamie?"

He lit a candle in the fireplace and strode across the room. Elizabeth was sitting up, her hair tumbling over her shoulders, looking more beautiful and desirable than he thought possible. He jerked her to him with one arm and crushed her against his chest.

"Some of my people have been killed," he said hoarsely. "I'll leave men to guard you. You'll be perfectly safe."

"Jamie," she gasped, "I worry for you! Take your men to protect you."

"I'll leave who I care to leave, and there'll be no discussion about it," he growled. He kissed her forcefully, trying to leave a mark on her which would never be erased. He released her abruptly. "Stay inside the keep, Elizabeth. Do not go anywhere without Malcolm or Jesse."

"Be careful," she pleaded, her eyes wide.

He nodded curtly and banged from the room.

Thoughts of her haunted him as he rode to the outskirts of his land. He'd only brought a score of men, leaving at least that many behind to guard Elizabeth. Had he left enough? Saints, what would he do if he returned to find her harmed? Well, it was sure enough that Malcolm and Ian would protect her, or die trying. Somehow, though, it wasn't enough to ease his mind.

It was late in the morning when he finally saw the smoke in the distance. There was no telling what mischief the Fergussons had wrought.

He pulled up at what was left of the first hut. He dismounted slowly, the scene before him almost making him ill. His young crofter Innis MacLeod and his wife lay on the ground, their naked bodies horribly mutilated.

Jamie threw back his head and gave vent to a hoarse battle cry that echoed in the stillness of the morning. He swung up into the saddle and sent his company thundering east with a motion of his hand.

His agony wrenched at his insides until he thought he would never be free of the pain. Over and over again, he saw Elizabeth's face in the place of Heather MacLeod's. It was Elizabeth's body he saw mutilated, Elizabeth's hair pulled out in clumps, Elizabeth's beautiful eyes staring up lifelessly at the sky.

His breath came in gasps. He couldn't go on like this. How in the world had he ever let her come so close to his heart? Why had he been such a fool as to think he could remain unaffected by her?

It wasn't too late. He could send her to a convent. Or find a husband for her. One of his allies, Robert McShane, had just lost his bride. He had a wee bairn in need of a mother. He wasn't much to look at, but he had a good heart. At least he'd never beaten his wife as far as Jamie knew.

Whatever he did, he would have to do it when he returned. He would send her away, and then his life would return to normal. His men would once again sharpen their swords at night to the accompaniment of bawdy jests. They wouldn't mill about the kitchen late in the afternoon, hoping for a taste of Elizabeth's latest creation. Jesse would no longer put on his best manners when eating with Elizabeth at the table. Jesse's mates would start throwing food again. That was always good for a few chuckles.

But most of all, he would never feel terror again. He would never wake at night and wonder if she still breathed. He would never spend hours on his knees while she suffered her monthly time, praying she would recover. He would never look at another dead woman and imagine it to be the woman he loved.

He hardened his heart and his expression as he pushed his stallion even harder.

Elizabeth would just have to go.

Chapter 12

ELIZABETH ROSE AND dressed quickly, but not quickly enough, because by the time she had descended to the great hall, Jamie was gone. She looked at the men still sitting at the table before the fire. They were some of Jamie's fiercer guardsmen and she paled, wondering whom he had taken with him and if they'd be able to protect him.

"My lady, come sit," Malcolm said, rising and lumbering across the floor to escort her to the table. "You will be quite safe here with us."

"It's not me I'm worried about, it's Jamie!"

The men looked up at her as one, every last one of them astonished.

"But why?"

That question came from a dark-haired man Elizabeth recognized as Jamie's friend Ian. Maybe he was Jamie's cousin. It was hard to tell just how the family tree went. Why had Jamie left Ian behind? He was very skilled with a sword.

"My lady," Ian continued, "Jamie will not come to harm. No one would dare touch him."

Elizabeth sank down onto the chair. "How long do you think he'll be gone?"

"Three or four days, unless it turns into a full-scale war. Then we will be summoned to help."

"Ian!" Malcolm exclaimed. "It willna turn into a war."

"I may as well know the truth," Elizabeth said weakly. "Tell me the worst, Ian, and don't spare the details."

"Lady Elizabeth, Jamie will be just fine," Malcolm said, throwing Ian a warning look. "He always comes out unscathed in these encounters. He does but check on those crofters who've been having a bit of trouble near the border. Once he rights things to his satisfaction, he'll come straight home."

Elizabeth accepted a cup of ale. Beer for breakfast wasn't exactly what her mother had provided all those years, but the men of her house hadn't been riding off to war either. Stronger circumstances called for stronger drink.

"What happened to the crofters?"

Ian sighed and rubbed the back of his neck. "Several Fergussons attacked them. The scouts who returned said the Fergussons had burned the huts and raped the women. The worst of it is they slew every living thing, including the cattle. The deaths of his people infuriate Jamie, but what angers him the most is the slaying of the beasts."

"Pardon me?"

He looked at her seriously. "It's not as coldhearted as it sounds. Raids are a part of life. What Jamie can't understand is why their laird Fergusson doesn't kill the crofters and then steal the cattle. That kind of man he could fathom. A man who slays everything for the sake of destruction is a man none of us understands."

"What will Jamie do?" she asked, dreading to hear the answer.

"If he can find the men who did the deed, he'll kill them. Then he'll lift as much Fergusson cattle as possible." He smiled grimly. "Starvation is a powerful weapon here in the Highlands. Our resources are few, and we guard them jealously. Jamie's not about to kill the Fergusson's beasts just to spite him. If Jamie is going to make off with spoils, he's going to see those spoils feed his people over the winter."

The talk then turned to preparations for the upcoming winter, to which Elizabeth listened with only half an ear. It was astonishing to hear firsthand what had only been written about in history books. How she could have rewritten the chapter on the Clan MacLeod.

She sat up with a start. She searched back through her memory, trying to recall the chapter she had read on Jamie's clan, the chapter that had contained the pen and ink plate of the forest. She remembered vividly the drawing, and she could even remember the title and author of the book. But she could not, for the life of her, remember what she had read about the MacLeods.

"Lady Elizabeth?"

She shook herself and focused on Ian's face. "Yes?"

"My lady, you look pale. Perhaps you should go lie down."

She smiled weakly. "I'm fine, Ian, thank you just the same."

"My lady, please do not fret. Jamie will return safely. I'm sure of it."

Elizabeth wished she could have been. She had read pages and pages about Jamie's wars and enemies. Why couldn't she remember what she had read when it might have meant the difference between Jamie's living and dying?

As far as rewriting history went, it made sense. She could have really fouled things up if she'd known what was going to happen to Jamie and his kinsmen before it happened. But that was all academic. This was the man she was coming to love, out in the wilds of the Highlands, possibly going to war. If she could have at least remembered the date of his passing, she could have locked him inside his room until the day was over and so kept him safe.

How she wished she'd used that book as a pillow that day in the park!

With Jamie away, Elizabeth knew she either had to do something or drive herself crazy by pacing. Fortunately, cleaning always had been her favorite way to assume some sense of control over her life. The great hall certainly was high on her cleaning list. After a good deal of deliberation, she decided on a plan that was sure to drive the twenty-odd Highlanders left in the hall right over the edge.

There was a new addition to the tables during lunch in the form of tablecloths. The men sat down hesitantly and looked at each other as though they wondered if they had stumbled into the wrong place.

Elizabeth stood, and all eyes snapped to her. She suppressed a smile. No wonder Jamie liked to stand up at meals. It was a powerful feeling.

"I suppose you are wondering what these cloths are."

"And where are the dogs?" one of the men asked.

"Out," she said. "In pens."

"But who'll eat the scraps we throw on the floor?" another asked, scratching his head.

Elizabeth beamed her approval at him. "How clever of you to bring up the very subject I want to talk about. Aren't any of you a bit tired of the smell of the rushes?"

The volume of response wasn't exactly what she had hoped for, but it was a start.

"If you were having a go at one of your mates, wouldn't you prefer to wrestle on a clean floor?"

That sparked a bit more interest. The mention of reduced slipping due to absence of dog droppings and animal fat was met with an even more enthusiastic response. Elizabeth smiled her most winsome smile.

"That's what the tablecloths are for. If you have something that's not quite edible, just put it aside. Not over your shoulder onto the floor. Hugh and his lads will clean off the tablecloths into the dog pens. That way the hounds still get fed, and we have a clean floor."

"Was this Jamie's idea?" Ian piped up.

"Of course," she lied firmly. "You don't think I could have come up with this on my own, do you? Jamie's concerned that you men be in top form at all times. That means good food and a clean place to sleep. A man can't train as well if he doesn't sleep at night. Isn't that so?"

A vigorous chorus of assenting ayes answered that question for her.

"Good. We'll practice now, and again this evening, and then I'll clean the floors tomorrow."

The meal proceeded in a very civilized fashion, with each man carefully placing his unwanted items near his cup. Elizabeth was enormously pleased with them. After lunch, Ian cornered her.

"You're a brave one." He grinned.

"You don't think Jamie will approve?"

"Will he have a choice? Once he finds out this was all his idea, he'll have to. You'll hear about it in private, though."

"The hall is a pigsty, Ian. Jamie's always grumbling about it. I'm sure he'll like it when he returns."

Or so she hoped. With the way Ian was laughing as he walked off, she wondered if she'd made a very large mistake.

The changing of the rushes began the very next morning after breakfast. Elizabeth had fully intended to do it herself but found that there were others with a different idea entirely. She turned away several of Jamie's more burly kinsmen, sure that she would be strung up for having put them to such menial labor.

She was trying to move one of the tables when another man came to her.

"Lady, allow me to help."

She looked at him out of the corner of her eye. No, he was too sturdy too. She gave him a fleeting smile.

"Thanks, but I'll manage. I'm sure you have other things to be doing."

"But I don't, my lady. They've no use for me outside. I'd be pleased to help you in here."

Elizabeth turned to look at him fully and gulped. He was missing his right arm and one of his eyes.

"I'm so sorry," she said instantly. "That was thoughtless of me."

"No need to apologize, my lady. I gave up what I did in defense of my kin and my laird. There's no shame in that."

"Of course there isn't," she agreed, moved by not only his courage but his healthy sense of self-esteem. "And to be honest, this isn't really woman's work. The tables are very heavy, and scraping the rushes off this floor may take more strength than I have. I'd be pleased to have a strong man or two at my disposal. You're hired."

He looked faintly puzzled and then smiled. "You mean, you'll have me?"

"Gladly. I'm Elizabeth."

"I know. I'm Everett. What will you have me do first?"

"Find us some help?" she suggested.

"Perhaps a few lads who might not be missed?"

"If you value my life, that might not be a bad idea."

He chuckled as he made her a low bow. "I will return immediately with several lads who are itching to be about some sort of mischief."

By the end of that day, a quarter of the room was done. It had been a full day's work even for the ragtag crew Everett had rounded up. Elizabeth went to bed feeling the day had not turned out half badly after all.

Jamie rode wearily up the way to his hall. It had been an exhausting se'nnight. He hadn't caught the culprits, but he had lifted enough cattle to make the Fergusson regret his actions. He had no doubts there would be retaliation, but that was simply a fact of life.

Things hadn't changed while he'd been gone. The blacksmith still filled the morning air with the sound of his pounding; the grunts and curses of his men could still be heard from the training field; smoke still wafted lazily up into the sky, assuring him that at least someone was cooking inside.

No doubt *she* was still inside. Heaven wouldn't have taken pity on him and sent her home while he was gone. Nay, she'd still be there, interfering in every facet of his life, stirring up trouble and confusion wherever she went. He could just imagine what a woman she had made out of his son while he was away.

He opened the hall door and pulled up short.

"What in hell's name is going on here?" he thundered.

There were men in his hall, on their hands and knees, scrubbing his floor. Elizabeth was there with them, scrubbing just as diligently. She looked up in surprise at the sound of his voice. Then she jumped to her feet, looking as guilty as sin itself.

"Jamie, you're home."

"And not a moment too soon," he said angrily. He stomped

across the floor, noticing the lack of rushes. "Just what do you think you're doing?"

"Why, cleaning the hall," she said simply, looking at him as though he had gone daft.

"I can see that!" he shouted. "Who gave you permission to drag my men away from their work?"

"But—"

"Out!" he yelled.

"Jamie!"

"Out!" he repeated, just as loudly, pointing to the door. "I need no woman in my hall tearing it to pieces. Go! Begone! And take your womanly ways with you!"

He expected her to burst into tears. Instead she gave him a look that felt like a slap, then walked swiftly past him. She slammed the hall door behind her with a resounding bang. Jamie swept his men with a glare.

"Don't you have anything better to do than woman's work?" he demanded.

His bluster evaporated abruptly as Everett stood and faced him.

"Of course, my laird," he said softly. He beckoned to the rest of his crew, and they one by one filed past Jamie, all giving him respectful nods.

Jamie walked wearily to his chair by the hearth and sank down into it. He thought to reprimand himself, then sat up with a curse. So the men scrubbing his floors couldn't wield swords. They shouldn't have sunk to doing a wench's job. It was Elizabeth's fault for humiliating them so. Jamie'd had nothing to do with it.

So why did he feel as low as the scum which now covered only a portion of his floor?

Dinner was a very uncomfortable affair. Megan sat next to Jesse, weeping, until Jamie finally bellowed for her to be silent. She fled upstairs, sobbing with little-girl tears that tore at his soul.

His men would not look at him. Worse than that, the first time he threw a bone over his shoulder, he could have sworn he heard several of them gasp. The sissies were putting their leavings next to their plates. *Sissies* was a future word he had learned from Elizabeth, and it suited his womanly warriors quite well, to his mind.

He finally stood up. At least their eyes still snapped to him. Somehow, it wasn't as satisfying as it usually was.

"Would someone care to explain to me why the tone in this keep is so poor?"

Not a man moved a muscle.

"Jesse?"

" 'Tis but a quiet night, Father. Nothing more."

Jamie banged his fist on the table. "I am still laird here! Your laird is a man, you fools, not a woman!"

"Of course," Ian said quickly. "We were waiting for tidings. What will you tell us?"

Jamie sat down, not appeased in the least. He told the tale in as few words as possible, letting his men know by his tone alone that he was anything but pleased with them.

He retired early and went directly to his chamber. He gritted his teeth. Damn her, there was a mug full of wildflowers on the mantel! He took them and tossed them out the window. That didn't make him feel any better. He flung himself down in the chair before the hearth and glowered into the fire.

He could still hear Megan weeping. The child was hopelessly overindulged. She'd never been such trouble when she was a boy. He listened to her for a goodly while before irritation overcame him. He stomped down the passageway to his thinking chamber and stopped at the half-open door. Jesse was speaking softly. Jamie pulled back, then stopped himself. Eavesdropping was a father's right. He leaned in closer.

"Megan, hush," Jesse said gently. "You'll make yourself ill weeping like this."

"But she's gone!" Megan wailed.

"You know that isn't true. I saw her to Friar Augustine's myself. She'll be just fine there, what with Malcolm standing guard over her. Tomorrow morning you and I'll go visit, and I'll leave you there all day."

"Leave me there for always," she wept bitterly. "Your father hates Elizabeth, and he hates me too. He doesn't want me in his house."

"Meg, you know that isn't true. And what will I do if you're not here? I'll miss you very much."

Jamie peeked around the door in time to see Megan throw her arms around Jesse's neck and cling to him.

"I love her so much, Jesse. She's the only mother I've ever had."

"We'll have her back, you'll see. Now, lie down and go to sleep. I'll be right here."

"You promise to stay?"

"Aye, love. I'll not move from this spot."

"Will you take me to Elizabeth first thing?"

"The very first thing."

Jamie stood in the shadow of the half-open door and watched his son soothe Megan until she fell asleep. He sighed and turned back to his own chamber. When had Jesse become such a gentle young man? A few weeks ago he would have sooner slapped Megan than held her tenderly.

Or would he have? Jamie began to wonder if he had been blind. Jesse was a fine warrior, but he had never possessed the cruelty Jamie had seen the other lads exhibit from time to time. Perhaps gentleness wasn't such a bad thing. Jesse didn't seem to suffer in his swordplay from it.

So Elizabeth had run to the priest. Fitting. At least she would be safe there. Several of Malcolm's more sturdy mates hadn't been at supper. No doubt they were keeping watch also.

As he should have been doing. But couldn't. Once he set foot inside Friar Augustine's gate, it would be as well as admitting he loved Elizabeth. He just couldn't do that. Especially since he fully intended to send her away.

Aye, *then* he would finally have some peace in his hall. Elizabeth had disturbed him for far too long.

He was up before dawn, pacing. The thought of Elizabeth likely weeping herself ill at the friar's had kept him awake most of the night. Damnation, but she had him so twisted about he scarce recognized himself!

And if that wasn't enough to foul his sunny disposition, she had also left him feeling a remorse he'd never felt before. He had come home fully intending to pack her off to seek other lodgings, and now all he could do was brood about what grief he had caused her. Aye, the churnings in his belly were all her fault. He should surely seek her out and instruct her in the art of never causing her lord grief. He would, once he'd fortified himself with a few cups of ale.

He made his way down to the hall only to find it almost empty. Ian alone sat at the table. Jamie sat down across from him, and a mug of ale appeared instantly, along with a hearty meal.

"Where is everyone?" Jamie asked, with his mouth full.

"Out training, my laird," Ian said respectfully.

"Since when do you call me 'my laird?' "

"It seemed fitting. Or perhaps I should call you 'my laird horse's arse.' "

Jamie's eyes narrowed, and he fingered his eating knife purposefully. "I see. So, you take her side in this."

"In what? This war over clean floors? Jamie, don't be a fool."

Jamie sat back and looked at his kinsman coolly. "Since you seem to be so wise, you tell me how I should be acting, if not like a fool."

"You should be grateful."

"I never asked her to do this."

"That was obvious, even though she said you did, to credit you with being so bloody concerned about your men's welfare."

Jamie blinked in surprise. "She did?"

"Aye, she did. It amazes me that she would care to save your pride even while you're not here. You certainly haven't made the same effort for her."

"She can do what she likes as long as she doesn't interfere with my men," he growled. "I won't tolerate that."

"Did you by chance mark any of the men who were so diligently helping her yesterday?"

Jamie sighed heavily. "I saw."

"Did you also stop to think that yesterday was the first time in years Everett has actually done something besides watch the rest of us with longing as we trained outside? Or that it was the

first time in years Dougan has felt like he had a purpose, besides being fed and helped to the closet three times a day?"

Dougan had only one arm left, and it was minus a hand.
Jamie scowled at Ian. "And what, pray tell, did she find for him
to do?"

"Dougan has a brother who is a friar, a friar who does astonishing things with herbs. A knowledge, I might add, which he
gave to Dougan in great detail. This sweet scent which rises to
greet you this morn from your floor is one of his concoctions."

"That still doesn't excuse her from putting men to women's
work. How are they to find satisfaction in that?"

"Keeping a hall clean is backbreaking work. If you had seen
what they went through to scrape the filth off your floor, you
would realize that. That's the way Elizabeth put it to them, and
that's the way they considered it. And," he said, cutting Jamie
off, "she had quite the chat with the more vocal of the other
lads. When she described to them what they would be eating at
your table for the rest of their days if they mocked her workers,
they were more than willing to keep their mouths shut. She
needn't have even threatened them. When they saw how much
it meant to her, they clapped hands over their mouths of their
own accord."

Jamie sighed. "Any more arguments?"

"Give me time. When are you going to fetch her?"

"Who says I'm going to fetch her?" he grumbled.

"You will," Ian said briskly. "And more's the pity."

"I hate you, Ian."

"I hate you too, Jamie, you heartless bastard."

Jamie threw his ale in Ian's face. Ian leaped across the table
and took Jamie to the ground. It wasn't a fair fight, and Jamie
had the distinct feeling Ian was landing most of his blows
merely to avenge Elizabeth.

A quarter of an hour later, they were both lying on their
backs, panting.

"Ian, she frightens me."

"Falling in love frightens you," Ian corrected.

Jamie turned his head to look at him. "Doesn't it you?"

"Normally it would. But not with Elizabeth."

"I've no intention of keeping her."

"Then you're doubly a fool to let her go."

"Bloody romantic," Jamie grumbled.

"Lackwit whoreson."

Jamie rose and hauled Ian to his feet. "Swords this time, my friend. I think I'd like to carve you to bits. Perhaps it will sweeten my humor."

Jamie scowled to himself as he walked outside with Ian. Unfortunately the only thing that would sweeten his humor was most likely bawling like a bairn in Friar Augustine's cell.

Chapter 13

ELIZABETH STOOD AT the doorway of the little house off the chapel and watched Megan drag Jesse along by the hand. Once Megan was within running distance, she broke away and threw herself into Elizabeth's arms. Elizabeth laughed as she hugged the girl tightly.

"I missed you, honey. Yesterday was a very long time ago."

Jesse pushed Megan out of the way and kissed Elizabeth on the cheek.

"You look as bad as my father does."

Elizabeth stepped away and took Megan's hand. "I could not care less about your father, Jesse MacLeod."

Jesse started back down the path. "You're a terrible liar, Elizabeth," he called over his shoulder.

Megan tugged impatiently on Elizabeth's hand before Elizabeth could hurl a rejoinder at Jesse's retreating back.

"I want to work some more on the tale," Megan said. "I know how I want the dragon to look."

"Then let's get busy." Elizabeth smiled, putting all thoughts of James MacLeod aside, where they certainly belonged after his treatment of her. She walked with Megan into the house, trailed by her constant shadow, Malcolm. Malcolm took up his post outside her chamber door, frowning fiercely as if he expected to be assaulted at any moment. Elizabeth closed the door behind her, grateful for the protection. Not that she expected any assaults any time soon. Especially from the keep.

Friar Augustine had been gracious enough to offer her hospitality when she came banging on his door a week ago. The old monk had been delighted to have company, and he had immediately set Elizabeth up with her own chamber. He had been overjoyed to find she could read and write and had soon brought her several of his own compositions. His script was so ornate as to be almost illegible, but he mistook her inability to read his hand for slowness with her letters and had patiently taught her what characters were what.

Only a few hours after arriving, Elizabeth found herself seated at a desk with a generous amount of parchment before her and a full inkwell. She had written far into the night, detailing everything that had happened to her from the moment she'd woken from the dream she had had of Jamie. It felt good to be putting things on paper again.

The good father had begged to read her little story, and she had obliged only after several hours of pleading. She was afraid the old man would have heart failure when he read it. He merely lifted his snowy eyebrows a time or two and nodded at certain places in her narrative. He had set the pages down once he read of Angus' bringing her to the keep.

"Lass, Scotland is a magical place. Celtic enchantment runs thickly in these hills. And forests," he had added pointedly.

She had twisted the folds of her plaid with her fingers. "Do you think I'll ever go home again?"

"Do you want to?"

Now, that was the question that had plagued her ever since she had been summarily ejected from Jamie's hall. Though Jamie was completely impossible, she found herself taken with him just the same. He was gruff and grumbly, but when he was sweet . . .

Father Augustine had continued to read and laughed uproariously over her descriptions of Jamie's malleable personality. He had finally dried the tears from his eyes and handed her back her scribblings.

"Lass," he had said, "perhaps you should read your own tale

once more. To me, it says you miss your family desperately, but you've found another one here that suits you fine."

"Beth, you're ignoring me!"

Elizabeth pulled herself back from her reverie. "I'm sorry, Megan. Let's see what you've done."

"This is Montague," Megan said proudly, indicating the fierce-looking dragon looming over a hapless knight.

Elizabeth's appreciation of the illustration was genuine. Megan had a gift for bringing creatures to life on paper. The dragon stood over a knight and wore what could only have been termed an expression of smugness.

"Isn't this the knight who thrashes Montague to rescue the princess?" Megan asked.

"Yes, sweetheart, it is. What did we decide to call him?"

"Let's call him James."

"After anyone we know?" Elizabeth asked dryly.

Megan giggled. "You wanted to name the knight that Montague ate 'James.' I think Laird Jamie wouldn't see the jest in it."

"Probably not. Very well, love. This brave lad is now dubbed Sir James, subduer of fierce dragons and rescuer of beautiful ladies in distress."

They had started the book two days earlier, once Elizabeth had discovered it was getting too cold to work out in the garden. Elizabeth had been mending one of Friar Augustine's frocks when she caught sight of Megan doodling on a piece of paper at the desk. Megan had been mortified to find Elizabeth had learned of her sinful activity, but Elizabeth had been enchanted. It was then she suggested that they do a story together. Elizabeth would provide the tale, and Megan would draw the characters.

Only the friar knew about their project, and he had been sworn to secrecy. He often hovered at the doorway, trying to steal a glance at the work in progress. When he had been treated to a rare glimpse of the book, he had gushed with such enthusiasm that Elizabeth had promptly promoted him to proofreader.

It would have been a wonderful time in her life except for the fact that she had seen neither hide nor hair of Jamie in over a week. Megan said he did nothing but mope, and when he wasn't moping, he was yelling for no reason at all. It comforted Elizabeth to know he was out of sorts, but she would have much rather had an apology and a request to come home.

She knew she probably should have prepared a scathing tongue-lashing for Jamie, should he have dared to show his face, but somehow she couldn't find it in her to expend the effort. He had changed so much from the time she had first met him. It was no doubt taking him a while to become adjusted to the thought of a woman in his house.

Two women, she corrected herself with a smile. Megan had reported that Jamie had even tucked her in the night before. Gruffly, of course, but it had been a tucking-in nonetheless.

"Elizabeth," Megan said patiently. "You wear the same look Laird Jamie does when he's ignoring me."

Elizabeth laughed ruefully and kissed Megan on the cheek. "That's the very last time you'll see it today, I promise. Now, where were we?"

"Sir Jamie just had his eyebrows singed off."

Elizabeth grinned. "Well, we'll put his helmet on him and send him back into the fray."

"Father, I'm going for a walk. Care to come?"

Jamie looked up from the column of figures he had spent the last hour trying to total.

"Walking anywhere in particular, son?"

"Down to the friar's to fetch Megan."

Jamie grunted. "The little imp has you completely besotted, Jess."

"I'm not suffering too much from it. Even you'll admit that."

"You've become intolerably cheeky."

"That's hardly Megan's fault."

Jamie rose with a sigh. "I suppose a bit of fresh air wouldn't hurt me either."

He pointedly ignored his son's smug smile.

The walk to the chapel seemed shorter than usual, perhaps because Jamie wanted to delay it as long as possible.

Friar Augustine opened the door. He bowed to Jamie then put a finger to his lips.

"Come along, Jamie lad," he said with a smile, "and tell me if this isn't the most beautiful sight on God's green earth."

Jamie followed the friar with Jesse trailing in his wake. Then he stopped at the doorway to a chamber, leaned against the wall for support and drank in the vision before him.

Elizabeth sat in a chair before the fire with Megan curled in her lap, both of them sound asleep. Jamie had never seen anything so peaceful in all his life. A feeling of tranquillity dodged past the barriers he hastily tried to erect and settled itself comfortably in his heart. Much as Elizabeth had done when she settled herself in his home.

So this was why men married; this was why men went out and fought. Simply to protect the ones they left behind, the sweet souls of their homes and hearths. Aye, this was something worth fighting for.

And it was something too valuable to lose. The McShane could find someone else to mother his wee bairn. Convents acquired wenches enough without adding anyone of his acquaintance to their number.

Saints, how could he have ever thought to send her away?

Jesse put his hand on his shoulder, startling him.

"Have you ever seen two more beautiful creatures?" he asked softly. "We should be on our knees day and night thanking the good Lord for giving them to us."

Jamie looked quickly at his son, surprised at the depth of feeling in the lad's voice. Jesse's smile was one Jamie had never seen before. He blinked. The boy was actually in love!

"I'm going to take my lady back to the house. If I were you, I'd do the same."

Jamie was too astonished by his realization to even reprimand Jesse for his cheek. He watched as his son gently disentangled Megan from Elizabeth's arms. Megan opened her eyes and smiled as she put her arms around Jesse's neck.

"You came for me."

"Didn't I say I would?"

Jamie watched the exchange with complete amazement. Those two had lived in his house all their lives, and he had never noticed what was going on? He looked back at Elizabeth, his eyes still full of wonder.

She was staring up at him, a soft smile curving her lips. She didn't move, didn't leap up to curse him; she simply sat in her chair and watched him. She didn't bother to beckon to him either, which made him nervous. He put back his shoulders and shook himself mentally. After all, he was still laird. She would do well to remember that.

" 'Tis high time you came home," he said gruffly.

"You want me to come home?"

"Would I have said the words if I didn't mean them?" he retorted, frowning.

"I suppose not." She smiled, but she did not rise. He sighed heavily.

"I suppose now I am to carry *you* back to the hall?"

Her face fell. "Of course not," she said, rising and walking away from him. She went to the table and shuffled papers into a pile. Then she put them in a small trunk and locked it. She stood there for several moments, fiddling with the long key, as though she waited for something.

He dragged his hand through his hair. So she wanted an apology. Well, he supposed she deserved one. He crossed the room and put his hands on her shoulders.

"I'm sorry I shouted at you," he grumbled. "I did not mean to shame you."

She turned around. "After the way you threw me out of your hall the other day, I should think—"

He put his hand over her mouth and cut off the rest of her words. The vision of Innis' wife was still bright in his eyes. He had long since resigned himself to the fact that the reason he had yelled at Elizabeth was because he was afraid of losing her. Tossing her out of his hall had been a convenient way to rid himself of possible pain. It would have worked too, if he'd been able to do anything besides think of her every moment of the past se'nnight. He cleared his throat.

"I had my reasons, but they are not the reasons you think."

She pulled his hand away from her mouth. "Were you angry I didn't ask your permission first?"

Her subtle dig wasn't lost on him, but his heart was too constricted to allow him a suitable retort.

"That was not my reason. How could it be when you told

every last one of my men that 'twas my idea? They thought me daft for casting you out."

"Then what was it?"

Jamie sighed. Had he ever thought his woman's stubbornness to be a good thing?

"There were crofters killed, brutally. Women and children." He cleared his throat roughly. "It pained me to think something like that might happen to, ah . . ." He paused and groped for a name. "To Megan," he finished with a triumphant smile.

"I see," she said.

And if her searching glance told the tale, indeed she did. Jamie could only stare at her, helplessly. What was he to say, that he had thrown *her* out of his hall because he had been so terrified of losing her and having his poor heart broken that it had seemed the only thing to do? Was he to tell her that he loved her? That he couldn't live without her?

Before he could completely gather his thoughts, much less express them in a manner that wouldn't humiliate him, Elizabeth had given him a small smile, as if she had understood everything he hadn't said.

"Oh, Jamie," she said, still wearing that faintly amused smile. "What am I going to do with you?"

Then she leaned up and pressed her lips against his.

"You are forgiven, my lord," she whispered against his mouth.

Well, whatever else she chose to do with him, she could certainly give him more of her sweet kisses. He put his arms around her before she escaped.

"Forgive me again," he said.

She laughed softly before she kissed him again. He closed his eyes and savored the feeling of her lips against his.

"You could forgive me with more enthusiasm," he murmured.

"I would if you'd apologize properly for not appreciating the cleanness of your hall."

He lifted his head to look down at her. "And the little tablecloths my men use with nothing less than religious fervor? Have you any idea the looks I received the first time I threw a bone over my shoulder?"

"I can only imagine."

"I do appreciate what you've done. I never thought to walk across my floor and actually keep my footing without struggling."

"So you like your hall clean?"

"I like my hall clean and you forgiving," he whispered. "I've missed you, Elizabeth."

"Oh, Jamie."

There was that tone again. Jamie's knees almost buckled, but he forced himself to stand firm. Saints above, he wanted to ravage her mouth until she couldn't breathe, until he had made her so much his that she could never leave him. He shoved aside his sudden nervousness. He could kiss her properly, gently and carefully, and she would find it very much to her liking. Hadn't she already been kissed by him several times and thought it pleasant indeed?

But those kisses had been chaste. He hadn't dared enter her mouth, for fear he would be too rough and frighten her. It was fortunate that today he was feeling terribly in control of his passions. Aye, he could kiss her deeply and see if she cared for it.

Which she would, of course. After all, he *was* laird.

He slipped his hand up her back and buried it in her hair. Too roughly, if her wince told any truth. He flinched as if he'd been the one pained and tried to cover his mistake with a hasty cough.

"It's okay," Elizabeth whispered, putting her arms up around his neck. "I didn't comb my hair very well today."

That was a lie. There were no tangles in that beautiful mane that he could feel. So he carefully cupped the back of her head in his hand, then bent his head and kissed her softly. When she didn't stiffen in his arms, he closed his eyes and kissed her again, more firmly this time. He continued to kiss her, tasting her lips as if he nibbled at an especially tasty dish. Elizabeth relaxed in his arms, allowing her body to lean against his. Jamie felt his poor form respond immediately to her nearness, but he took his desires by the throat and kept them captive. The very last thing he wanted to do was frighten the woman in his arms.

But being the slightest bit bold with his kiss was another thing entirely. He opened his mouth a bit and touched Elizabeth's lips with his tongue. She trembled as she clutched at his shoulders. Jamie didn't think to ask her if she liked it. That she was holding him and not pushing him away told him all he needed to know.

He parted her lips with his, urging them open, then slipped his tongue inside her mouth. Saints, the heat that raced through his veins at such a simple touch! He wrapped his other arm more tightly around her and pulled closer, wanting nothing more than to feel her body pressed against his. He forgot about breathing, about his men who were likely waiting for him to train with them, about the cattle he had stolen from the Fergusson. All he could think about was Elizabeth, her mouth open beneath his, her slender body pressed against his.

He kissed her more forcefully, groaning even as he did so. He wanted to be invading another part of her. Aye, he ached to do so. Perhaps just feeling her under him while he kissed her might be enough to satisfy him for the moment. He opened his eyes and espied the bed, then eased Elizabeth back toward it.

"Ahem," a voice said clearly from the doorway. "Jamie, you were about to take Elizabeth up for supper?"

Jamie cursed silently, then lifted his head. He looked down at Elizabeth and met her wide-eyed gaze. She was flushed. He felt flushed.

"Jamie, lad?"

Elizabeth escaped Jamie's arms before he could make a grab for her. He sighed and rubbed his forehead, then turned and looked at his priest.

"Supper? Aye, Father. We were just about to take our leave of you."

The friar hustled them out the door and clapped Jamie heartily on the back. "Bring her right back after supper, lad. A bonny lass like Elizabeth shouldn't be deprived of her rest."

Jamie frowned as he found himself shoved out the front door. "I do not plan to bring her back. Her place is with me."

Friar Augustine looked down his nose skeptically, a feat indeed, as Jamie was a head taller than he. "Am I to understand that you plan to keep this maiden in your hall this eve?"

"Aye, you do," Jamie said curtly.

"In her own bedchamber, of course."

"She'll sleep in my chamber."

The friar's eyebrows went up so far they almost disappeared into his hair.

"I will not touch her," Jamie growled. "I give you my word. I will not touch her tonight."

"And tomorrow?"

"Tomorrow will take care of itself."

The friar didn't look convinced. "Well, then, I'll rely on your honor to keep her virtue intact," he said in a purely paternal tone. "See that you don't disappoint me, lad."

"I won't," Jamie grumbled. "A good night to you, Friar."

"And to you, lad. And to you, Elizabeth."

"Thank you, Father."

Jamie took Elizabeth's hand and strode back to the hall with her.

"You're in a hurry," she remarked.

He scowled. "He ever makes me feel like I'm a bairn, off to do something I shouldn't."

She only laughed.

Jamie ushered her into the hall, watching her face closely. Her mouth hung open, and she looked around as if she had never laid eyes on the place before.

Everett and his crew had been busy. They had scoured the place from top to bottom, repaired crumbling stone, broken tables and benches and hung new torches. All in all, it was a place to be proud of. Jamie stood back and folded his arms over his chest, pleased not only with his hall but with the look on Elizabeth's face.

She gave him another in her series of heart-stopping smiles and then threw her arms around his neck and hugged him.

"You are a wonderful man, James MacLeod. It's beautiful."

For a moment he buried his face in her hair and breathed deeply, relishing in the feel of her arms around him. Then he put her away and frowned, hoping none of his men had seen his moment of weakness.

"The floors are clean at least," he said gruffly. "Well, go on. I've no doubt you want to gush over Everett."

She didn't eat dinner. She was too busy flitting from place to place, having a personal chat with each and every one of his men. Everett was back to his old self, cocky and swaggering, after she finished heaping compliments on his head. Jamie was impressed.

He had never been quite sure how to approach Everett after his wounding. He was grateful to Elizabeth for her miracle, for Everett had been a very proud and arrogant warrior, constantly boasting of his considerable skill. Perhaps he would never fight again, but at least now he felt he had a purpose. He had come to Jamie just that morning full of plans for running the hall more efficiently. Jamie had promptly dubbed him steward, relieving Angus of a job he detested. And it was all because of Elizabeth.

By the time he was ready to go up, Elizabeth was almost asleep at the table. He lifted her in his arms, ignoring what he was sure were numerous stares from his men. Elizabeth couldn't have cared less; that much was obvious by the way she wrapped her arms around his neck.

He carried her to his chamber and set her on her feet inside the door.

"I should go check on Megan," she said sleepily.

"I'll do it. I doubt you could stay awake long enough to finish the task."

He crossed the passageway to his thinking room. The moment he opened the door, Megan sat bolt upright in bed.

"Jesse?"

"Nay, girl, 'tis Jamie."

"Is Elizabeth home?"

Jamie crossed the room and perched carefully on the side of her bed. "Aye, lass, she's home. Safe and sound." He laid her back down gently and smoothed her hair from her face. "And 'tis past time you were asleep."

"I worried Beth wouldn't be safe."

"And how is this, with me to protect her?"

"And you'll protect me, too?" Megan asked hopefully, reaching for his hand.

Jamie felt tenderness for the imp before him well up in his heart. He raised her hand to his lips. "You too, Megan. Now," he said sternly, "your task is to fall asleep as quickly as possible. Understood?"

"Aye, Jamie," she said, snuggling down into her blankets.

Jamie rose and tucked her in carefully before he straightened and crossed the room.

"Jamie?"

"Aye?"

"I love you."

Jamie wouldn't have been more surprised if she had sprouted horns and cursed him from head to toe.

"Hrumph," he managed, completely at a loss for words. "I'm sure you do, lass. Now, good-night."

He shut the door hastily and walked back across the corridor to his own bedchamber. Megan was half asleep. That had to be it. The girl was overcome by weariness and babbled things she couldn't possibly understand, much less intend. That problem solved neatly, he banked the fire in his hearth, stripped and lay down on the floor.

"You were very sweet with Megan," Elizabeth said.

He grunted, not quite trusting his voice. Megan's words had left a suspicious lump in his throat.

"She loves you very much."

"That's enough of that kind of talk," Jamie said gruffly, wincing at the crack in his voice.

"You know, I think I just might love you too."

With that, she rolled over and promptly proceeded to sleep the sleep of the just.

Jamie could not find words in his vocabulary to express his complete astonishment, not that Elizabeth would have been awake to hear them had he succeeded.

It was the most bewildering day he had ever passed.

He had the feeling, as sleep finally claimed him near dawn, that those kind of days would soon be his lot in life.

Merciful heavens, 'twas a frightening thought.

Chapter 14

ELIZABETH SAT IN her bath and rested her chin atop her bent knees. The wooden tub was the largest in the house, having obviously been fashioned for Jamie. Elizabeth closed her eyes and enjoyed the warmth from the water and from the fire in the hearth. She never had been much on baths, having preferred showers, but when in Rome . . .

The door opened behind her, and she looked around to see who had invaded her privacy, cursing herself as an afterthought for not having bolted the door.

Jamie stood there. He blinked.

"Oh," he said, as if he hadn't a clue that he really should turn around and go back the way he had come.

"Jamie, get out of here," Elizabeth exclaimed.

He swallowed. It looked to have been a very unsuccessful attempt.

"Do you require aid?" he managed.

"I require that you beat it," she said, trying to sound tart.

"The buckets of rinse water are heavy."

"They'll seem especially heavy when I bonk you over the head with one. Get lost!"

Jamie dithered. He started toward her and Elizabeth shrieked. Then he spun on his heel and left the room. Elizabeth let out her breath slowly. Oh, she recognized the look in his eye all right. And she had no intentions of indulging him.

Unless he wanted to marry her, of course.

She finished her bath, then dried her hair in front of the fire. It took her most of the morning to gather up the courage to leave the bedroom. Jamie needed time to cool off, and she fully intended to give it to him. She went downstairs eventually and hoped Jamie would just forget whatever bare flesh he had seen and continue to be his semicharming, gruff self.

But by the time evening arrived, she had the sneaking suspicion he hadn't forgotten anything. Something was definitely up. Jamie hadn't left her side since the moment her foot hit the great hall floor. He had sharpened his sword while she sewed. He had lounged on the kitchen table while she cut up vegetables for dinner. He would have followed her into the garderobe if she hadn't shut the door in his face. All day long he gave her looks, as if he couldn't quite believe she was there.

And then there were the other looks, the ones which sent the blood thudding in her ears and tingles down her spine. She felt like a lone chocolate chip cookie sitting exposed on a plate, waiting to be devoured.

By the time they retired, she was on pins and needles. Jamie held her hand as they climbed the steps and didn't release it once they had entered his chamber. There was a bottle of wine and two goblets resting on the table near the hearth. She looked up at him in surprise.

"What is this?"

He shrugged dismissively. "Nothing. You seemed a bit on edge. I thought wine might soothe you." He bolted the door behind him and walked across the room to sit in the chair. He poured wine into the goblets and held one out to her. "Come and sit, Elizabeth."

She looked around for another chair. There was only a small stool near the fire. She took the wine and sat down, frowning a bit. He could have offered her the chair. She looked at him to find him smiling faintly.

"Drink," he said.

"Why?" she asked suspiciously. "Is it poisoned?"

He only shook his head. She drained the glass in one, slow

pull. Then she put her hand to her head as the room began to spin. When her eyes focused again, she saw Jamie holding out his hand.

"What?"

"This is the chair you were to sit in."

"You're sitting in it now." The man was dropping IQ points by the moment.

"Aye, I am."

It dawned on her what he was saying. "Oh."

Before she knew it, she was cradled in his lap.

"I see."

"So you do," he said, taking her cup away. "Do not fear me, Elizabeth."

Now this was a James MacLeod she had never seen before. He was slicker than an L.A. lawyer, and if she'd been thinking clearly, she would have hightailed it out of there.

Then again, maybe not. She felt her resistance begin to melt away. Jamie took her hands and slipped them up around his neck, his eyes never leaving hers.

"Hold me," he demanded softly.

A soft whimper escaped her lips. Or it might have been an anguished moan of resignation. Whatever it was, she knew she was in for something overwhelming.

He slipped his hand under her hair and pulled her head relentlessly toward his. He kissed her and she knew she was lost. His skin was smooth as a babe's next to hers, and she realized he had shaved. She knew then that he had been planning this entire event for several hours. What could she do besides smile? Here was a man who never wanted a woman in his home, and now he was planning evenings to please her?

She felt a tug at the belt of her plaid and she pulled away.

"Jamie, no—"

"I won't," he said, pulling her back to him. "I won't do anything you don't want as badly as I do. Just let me kiss you."

She nodded and closed her eyes, surrendering to him again. He was a passionate man, but she was sure he was as good as his word. Several minutes later he pushed her plaid off her shoulders. Her eyes flew open.

"Sshh," he said, putting his finger to her lips. "Elizabeth, 'tis but warm in here."

"But Jamie," she began, blushing.

"You are still clothed. Unfortunately, so am I."

His matter-of-fact tone caught her completely off guard. She laughed at his disgruntled look.

"Are you too warm?"

"Aye," he nodded, looking very hopeful.

She laughed as she rose unsteadily to her feet, pulling her plaid back around her. "I suppose your plaid is a bit hot."

It was gone instantly. His tunic still covered the vital parts, so she couldn't argue with that. He spread his plaid out on the floor before the fire and stretched out, holding up his hand.

"Join me."

"On the floor?"

"On my plaid," he said. "There's a very great difference."

The man had a way with words. She blushed as she sat down next to him, clutching her own skirts nervously.

"Relax," he said. "I'm no bear this eve, Elizabeth. And if I am, I'm very tamed. You should be delirious with joy."

If she had a reply to that teasing, she lost it the moment his lips touched hers.

Her plaid somehow made its way across the room. Her tunic and shift were thin, but with Jamie's strong arms around her, she just didn't mind. He had removed his shirt almost immediately, and the heat from his bare chest made her own temperature rise considerably.

She realized with a start that his hand was pulling her shift up her bare leg.

"Jamie," she squeaked, "what are you doing?"

"Elizabeth, I truly thought I could leave you be, but . . ." He paused and looked at her. "Then I saw you today."

"You saw my back, buster."

"It was enough." He reached up and trailed his finger over her cheek. Gently. That he was obviously being so careful was her undoing. "Beth, let me," he said hoarsely. "I vow I'll pleasure you well."

"But—"

Jamie didn't wait for an answer. Or perhaps he saw his answer in her eyes. He leaned over her and kissed her again. Elizabeth held her breath as he did so. He was so incredibly gentle, as if he expected to break her. His fingers traveled lightly over her face and slid into her hair.

Elizabeth groaned as his lips left hers. He kissed his way down her throat, across her shoulder. Maybe he was more practiced than she gave him credit for, or maybe she was just head over heels in love with him; all she knew was she was feeling things she'd never felt before in her life.

She'd never made love before. She'd come close a couple of times, but it had never felt right. It was hard enough breaking up with someone when you'd just scratched the surface of intimacy. But after making love? It was just a side of herself she hadn't been ready to share. She'd decided during college that waiting for marriage was a very good idea.

That had been before Jamie. Maybe she'd never felt this desire before because she'd never been in love before. She knew at that moment that she really did love Jamie, grumbles and all. Things would work out in the end. If he wanted to make love to her, then she wasn't going to tell him no.

Because, she realized suddenly, she wanted it as much as he did.

"Jamie," she said, escaping his lips to catch her breath, "when are we going to the bed?"

He stiffened for only a split second. "The plaid will suit us better."

"But the bed would be softer."

"The bed is too symbolic of marriage," he murmured, burying his hand in her hair and urging her head back. He bent his head and pressed his lips against her throat.

"Oh," she whispered.

Then she froze. "What did you say?"

"Hush, love."

She put her hand firmly in the middle of his chest. "The bed is too symbolic of marriage?" she repeated. "In the sense that I'm just a *bit of sport* for you until you find a wife?"

"Now, Elizabeth . . ."

Elizabeth rolled away from him and crawled to her feet. She snatched up her plaid and threw it around her shoulders.

"Don't you dare now-Elizabeth me, you jerk," she said hotly.

"But . . ."

Elizabeth shot him a displeased glare before she opened the door and stomped out into the corridor.

"I was going to share my plaid!" he exclaimed from behind her. "Have you no idea what an honor that is?"

Elizabeth pulled up short at the top of the steps and turned slowly to look at him.

"Let me get this straight," she said. "I'm good enough for you to take on the floor, but I'm not good enough for your bed, is that it?"

"I do not wish for a wife—"

"I'm not a slut, James MacLeod, and you're sure as hell not going to treat me like one."

"And just what is that to mean? I have never shared my plaid with anyone before!"

"And you're not going to start with me."

She turned on her heel and descended the steps, then stomped across the great hall.

Malcolm and a half dozen other men immediately jumped up and followed her. She strode straight to Friar Augustine's house. A torch spilled its light out onto the path as the friar opened the door. She stopped at the threshold and threw up her hands in despair.

"He's driving me crazy!" she exclaimed.

"Come inside, lass," the friar said, with an amused smile, "and I'll fix you some soothing tea."

She knew tea wasn't going to fix what had gone wrong that night. She had a great deal of thinking to do, and most of it concerned what she truly wanted from life. There were some things worth holding out for, and she had to decide what those things were.

She sincerely hoped Jamie had a miserable night's sleep and found the *bed* entirely too comfortable for his black soul.

The morning brought Elizabeth a decision but little relief from her heartache. Once the temperature had warmed up to above freezing, she took to pacing in the friar's garden, mulling over his advice from the night before. He seemed to feel sure Jamie was just having cold feet and had encouraged her to wait for marriage. Elizabeth couldn't dismiss Jamie's actions so easily.

She stared out over the far wall of the garden. The view was almost breathtaking enough to distract her. The level of snow seemed to drop farther down the mountains with each week that passed. She wasn't looking forward to a winter spent in Friar Augustine's little house. It was well kept but drafty. Perhaps she'd enlist Everett's aid in putting it to rights before the year waned any further.

She walked until she couldn't walk any more, and she had traversed the garden paths a hundred times. Maybe writing another chapter in her diary would take her mind off things. Even if all she had to write about was Jamie being a jerk, getting it out on paper might help her get a better perspective on things.

She ran smack into an immovable shape before she realized there was someone standing in front of her. She stepped back a pace and looked up into troubled, deep-green eyes.

She stepped back another pace and clasped her hands in front of her.

"Jamie," she said flatly.

"Come home," he said. "Please."

A "please" from his lips a week ago would have had her in tears of joy. It was amazing how much more one wanted after giving it some thought.

"No."

"I'll ask nothing more of you than that, Elizabeth. Just come home."

"Why? So that you might favor me with a night or two on your plaid as the mood strikes?"

He flinched. "Nay."

"What then?"

He looked at her helplessly. "I don't know, Elizabeth. All I know is I can't live without you. I thought I'd slit my own throat before I said those words to a woman, but there they are."

She paused, wrestling with herself. If she'd had half a grain of sense, she probably would have taken the offer and run with it. But to what end? To be his mistress? What would happen if he suddenly decided to take a wife? Would she find herself packed off into some isolated convent?

"No, I want more than that, Jamie."

That obviously wasn't the reply he had been expecting. He began to frown. "Such as?"

"I want you to court me. If I were ever to see my father again, I want to be able to look him in the eye and not be ashamed of what I've done."

"Court you?" he echoed, obviously not having heard anything past that. "You want me to *court* you?"

"I do."

"To what end?" he growled.

"Marriage."

"Marriage?" he gasped, his voice rising. "Marriage?" he shouted.

"Yes!" she shouted back. "I want you to court me and then marry me. Like you actually loved me. And when you do take me to bed, it will be as your wife, or you won't take me there at all!"

He threw up his hands in frustration, then turned and stomped off, banging his way out of Friar Augustine's garden.

"Elizabeth, 'tis time for a bit of tea," Friar Augustine called merrily from his door. "Come out of the cold, lass."

Elizabeth obeyed him out of habit. He seemed to be in a fine humor and chattered on about this and that while Elizabeth consumed three cups of soothing tea. It was beyond her to comprehend what he was saying.

She had blown it. Jamie would never in a million years come back.

Chapter 15

JAMIE PACED THE length of the great hall, muttering under his breath. So she wanted to be wooed. Women were all the same. They wanted trinkets, trinkets and more trinkets. Courting trinkets were the most costly of them all. The last time he had been at court, he had marked the gold laid out by men to woo their ladies. The amount was staggering! How in heaven's name did Elizabeth expect him to part with that quantity of gold, merely to see to her whims?

They didn't live in the Lowlands. Their fields were not overflowing with more crops than they could harvest. His kin didn't own more cattle than they could care for. It was a harsh life, a meager one. Every smidgen of food Jamie put on the table, he sweated for. He had no gold to squander on numerous bolts of cloth, foolish ornaments for her hair and useless trinkets to clutter her chamber with.

An hour later, he found himself pacing in his thinking room. He could never afford what she would wish to have. But how could he shame himself by admitting that?

He walked back over to his desk and looked again at the last column of his ledger. It had been a very fruitful summer. The larder was full, and he possessed double the head of cattle he had the year before. It would see his people through the winter easily.

And there was gold to spare. He had promised a goodly amount of it to Everett for use in repairs, but there was yet some he could take for his own.

"Damnation," he swore as he unlocked the chest behind the desk. He pulled forth a pouch and emptied the gold into his hand. What he held in his hand would purchase a dozen bolts of fine cloth and perhaps a trinket or two for her chamber. *His* chamber, he corrected himself with a scowl.

It would have also purchased several of Andrew MacAllister's finest stallions and enough ore to produce two dozen new blades.

He closed his eyes and prayed. He didn't want it to come down to a choice between Elizabeth and his kin. He sighed and opened his eyes, once again looking at the gold in his hand. Perhaps there was no choice. Elizabeth was good for his people, and she was good for him.

He put the gold back into the pouch and stood, straightening his clothing. If marriage was what she wanted, he'd give it to her. Maybe wedding her would ease the ache she caused in him. He gave that further thought as he walked down the stairs to the great hall. That was probably the last thing marriage would do for him.

Minutes later he stood at the door of Friar Augustine's house and knocked. The good friar himself opened the door and beamed at Jamie.

"I see you've come to your senses, Jamie lad."

"Aye," Jamie grumbled. "Though I'm sure it will be bloody expensive."

The friar only chuckled and clapped Jamie on the back, welcoming him into the house. "She's in her chamber, laddie. Scribbling, as usual."

"She truly can write?"

"Very well. You should read it sometime. You'd find it very entertaining."

Jamie didn't doubt that, but he had no desire to pursue it. He opened the door without knocking, sure that Elizabeth would never let him enter if he asked permission. She looked up in surprise from where she sat at the table.

He strode over to her and dropped the bag of coins on the table near her hand.

"There."

She looked down and then back up at him, confusion plain on her face.

"There what?"

He frowned. "I've had no time to purchase you all the courting gifts you're sure to demand. The gold's a pledge against the time I'll go to market to buy them."

"Jamie, I don't understand what you're talking about."

"I have no trinkets on hand with which to sweeten your mood," he said, his voice raising with each word. He knew he was shouting but couldn't stop himself. "Damnation, woman, this will have to do!"

"Trinkets?"

Jamie swore in frustration. There were times Elizabeth's inability to grasp the simplest concept threatened to make him daft.

"I'm wooing you. Isn't that what you demanded? Wooing requires trinkets of all kinds—usually purchased at great cost!"

Elizabeth only smiled.

"The gold is not enough?" he asked stiffly, the very question costing him much.

"You *want* to marry me?"

"Isn't that why I am here?" he snapped. "Damn you, Elizabeth, you are trying my patience sorely this day."

She rose and took the gold in her hand. He allowed her to lead him over to the chair before the hearth. He sat down heavily, still frowning at her. Damn her if she still wasn't wearing that amused smile.

She pulled up a stool and sat down before him, then took his hand and put the gold back into it.

"Jamie, you don't have to buy me anything."

He frowned. "What are you babbling about, woman?"

"I do not require trinkets to be wooed."

"Then what, pray tell, will you require?" he demanded. "My hall? A keep of your own?"

She grinned. Jamie almost rose and left.

"Damnation, Elizabeth, stop laughing at me."

"Jamie, I wasn't laughing at you. Your sweetness just tickled me."

He grunted, somewhat appeased. "That is another tale entirely. Now, if you do not require trinkets, and you do not require a keep of your own, what is it you do require?"

"A walk in the garden."

His mouth fell open.

"A ride in the meadow. An afternoon on the roof. You know, romantic things."

"Romantic?" he echoed weakly. The woman *was* daft.

"Romantic," she nodded with a dreamy look. "Love letters, picnics by the lake, long evenings spent snuggling in front of the fire. Can you write poetry?"

"I've no time for such foolishness," he managed, stalling for the time to regain his wits. He could hardly believe his ears. The women of the future had the oddest ideas about wooing.

"Oh," she said in a small voice. "I suppose you don't."

He stole a look at her downcast face. Then he began to understand. This was why she loved the little tales she made up for Megan, the ones about the brave knight who wooed his lady with sweet words and gentle kisses. Och, but the lass had a tender heart.

"Well, perhaps we should discuss what this wooing of yours entails," he said, trying to sound as if it were really his idea. "You want me to walk with you in the garden?"

"Yes," she said softly.

"Write you love letters?"

"If you have time."

"Rescue you from dragons?"

She looked up at him in surprise. "You were listening."

"I admit it, and I was as charmed as young Megan by your tales. As there are no dragons in present-day Scotland, is there anything else you would like vanquished?"

"No," she said, with a smile.

"And what is this snuggling you spoke of?"

"It means holding."

"Ah," he said wisely. "So, I would take you to my chamber,

sit in my great chair and hold you in my arms before the fire, stealing the occasional kiss?"

"You do understand what romance is."

"It costs far less than I had thought originally," he said dryly.

She laughed. "Jamie, you are very sweet."

"Nay, love, 'tis you who are sweet."

He wondered why in the world he had fought his feelings so long. It was so much easier to just admit he loved her. In a few short weeks, she had become like air to him. How could he have ever thought he would survive without her?

"Don't you have things to do?" she asked.

He reached out and tucked a lock of hair behind her ear. "If I do, I don't remember what they are. I'm quite sure the lads will survive without me for a few hours. What say you we stay here and snuggle for a time?"

She nodded and came willingly into his arms. He rested his cheek against the top of her head. If something as simple as holding her earned him such brilliant smiles, he would spend the rest of his life doing just that.

It was very late in the afternoon when Jamie knew his arm would likely fall off if he didn't move it. It was with a sense of regret that he shifted, for he had truly enjoyed this snuggling business.

"Howdy, handsome," Elizabeth whispered, stirring.

"*Handsome* I believe I understand, and I compliment you on your keen eye. *Howdy* I do not understand."

"It's just a greeting."

"Then howdy to you too." He smiled at her and then bent his head and softly brushed her lips with his. "Is this wooing pleasing you so far?"

"Very much. Are you bored yet?"

"Not quite yet. I'll give a yell when that day comes, some two or three hundred years from now."

Her look of shock almost made him laugh.

"Are you drunk?" she asked.

He shook his head with a wry smile. "Resigned is a better word."

"To what?"

"To the fact that I cannot live without you, and there is no use in pretending I can."

"Oh, Jamie," she breathed.

The plain truth was, he couldn't hear that tone from her enough. So he closed his eyes and let her kiss him, finding that future wooing was a very fine thing indeed. And what a sweet lass the future had provided him with. When she pulled away, he trailed his fingers over her cheek as gently as he knew how. She was good and kind, and he vowed to do all in his power to keep her safe always.

He sobered at the thought. Elizabeth knew so little of the harshness of war. Or the harshness of his world, for that matter. What would she do the first time she saw a man killed? What if she were the one to do the killing? She was more innocent than Megan. How could he keep her gentle spirit sheltered from the realities of life?

"What are you frowning about, my lord?"

He focused on her face to find she was smiling. He wondered if he would ever become accustomed to that knee-buckling smile. How was it no man had caught her before? They had all been fools.

He took her hand and pressed it to his lips. "I feared you would think I was ill if I did not frown every now and again."

She laughed. "Jamie, you have a wonderful sense of humor."

He would have stood on his head a dozen times a day to hear more compliments such as that. He kissed her hand again and racked his brain for something clever to say just so he could hear her laugh. Coming up with nothing, he settled for the first thing that came to his mind, wanting nothing more than the sound of her voice washing over him.

"Elizabeth, what is it with the men in your day that one of them did not spirit you away to his hall long ago?"

"They were afraid of my brothers."

Jamie knew she had five, but he'd been afeared to speak too much of them, lest it grieve her. She didn't seem overly sad at present. Perhaps he might venture a question or two.

"How fierce are these lads?"

"Very fierce," she said with a wistful smile, "though not strong enough to subdue you, certainly."

Ah, more compliments. He looked quickly to see if she was teasing him. When he saw she wasn't, he puffed out his chest slightly.

"I never doubted that," he said smugly. "And I suppose I should thank them for keeping you safe for me. Not that I would have cared if you had been betrothed to another man, however. He simply would have taken one look at my blade and turned tail and fled. Nay, if I had the chance, I would certainly thank those lads of yours for their aid. Think you they would have challenged me? Just to see if I could stand one against five?"

Her sniffle drew his attention. "Oh, Jamie," she said quietly, "I wish they could have met you. And I wish they could be here to see us married."

Jamie could plainly see how much the thought grieved her. The saints knew he couldn't bear the thought of losing her, but perhaps he was wrong in keeping her. He took a deep breath.

"Elizabeth," he said slowly, "I do not want to, but if you have changed your mind, I can try again . . ."

He couldn't finish his thought.

She was silent for several moments, during which time Jamie prayed with more fervor than he ever had in his entire life. If she left him . . . nay, the thought didn't even bear entertaining. It terrified him to think he loved her so desperately, but he was helpless to do anything about it. She was lodged in his heart as surely as a spiny burr in a plaid.

She lifted her eyes and looked at him unflinchingly. At that moment, she could have asked for all the silk and jewels on the Continent, and he would have cheerfully gone to procure them. The love in her eyes stunned him.

"I miss my family," she said softly, "but I'd miss you so much more. This is my home, Jamie. I'll stay."

He forced himself to kiss her gently, when what he wanted to do was kiss her until she couldn't breathe. He tried not to squeeze her as tightly as he wanted to, but even so he heard a faint popping sound. He hoped he hadn't broken her back.

"I take it the news pleases you, my lord?" she managed, once he released her lips.

"I knew it all along," he assured her.

"Of course you did."

"Do you still grieve? You may weep if you wish it."

She hugged him so tightly, *he* couldn't breathe. He almost wished her brothers were on hand so he could have given them a piece of his mind. They had trained her entirely too well.

"Jamie, you're so sweet. I don't know what I'd do without you."

"You'd have no one to choke."

She pulled back and smiled. "I love you."

The gentleness in her glance and in her voice brought that annoying stinging sensation back to his eyes. She loved him? Nay, 'twas impossible. She said things she didn't mean. He blinked rapidly.

"Tell me of your family," he said, wanting to distract her. "Unless it would grieve you."

"Not at all. Who do you want to hear about first?"

"Start with your father and work down. What is your sire's name?"

"Robert. He's a pediatrician."

"A what?"

"Healer. He works just with children." She smiled wistfully as she spoke of the gentle man who had raised her and taught her respect for life and its mysteries.

Secretly Jamie couldn't help but feel a bit sorry for the man. Was he so unskilled that he was only allowed to ply his craft on children? Obviously Elizabeth didn't realize what an insult the men of her day had paid her father, and Jamie wasn't about to point that out to her.

"And your mother?" he asked, wishing he could speak to the woman in person and tell her what a wonderful daughter she had given life to.

"Her name is Mary," Elizabeth answered. "She's kind and giving. She would have loved you immediately."

"And what of your brothers?"

"Jared, Stephen, Alexander, Sam and Zachary."

"Merciful heavens," he said weakly. "And what do these ruffians do? Besides chase women and stir up mischief?"

"All but Alex and Zach are happily married. Jared and Stephen are doctors. Sam has his own band, but he hasn't quit his day job yet. Alex is a lawyer, and Zachary just graduated from college."

It was a bewildering list, to be sure. Jamie was almost tempted to write it all down to get it straight in his head. The most pressing question was about the surgeons. He hoped her answer would be a good one.

"And these healers, Jared and Stephen? Do they cure grown men or only children?"

"Grown men," Elizabeth assured him.

Jamie sighed in relief. At least her sire would have some reason to be proud.

"It pains me to admit it," he said, "but I did not understand a thing you said after the two oldest ones."

"It's a lot to digest all at once. Suffice it to say, none of them has as difficult a task as you have, nor could any of them do the things you do each day. They are good men, but you are a better one. My father would be delirious with joy to have you as a son-in-law."

"Think you?"

"I do."

He was pleased by her words. He would wed Elizabeth and treat her well. Robert Smith would never have a reason to be displeased with his daughter's choice.

He started to tell her just how well he would treat her when a banging on the door interrupted him. He toyed with the idea of rising and beating the intruder senseless. Nay, it was too much trouble to stir.

"Go away," he called.

"Father, supper is ready. May I enter?"

"He's a wonderful son," Elizabeth whispered.

"He's a pest," Jamie grumbled, secretly pleased by her praise. He looked at her, trying to keep a neutral expression on his face. "You find him tolerable?"

"I know just how proud of him you are, Sir Jamie, and you have every reason to be. And yes, I find him very tolerable."

Jamie grunted in answer. "Come in, Jess," he called.

Jesse poked his head in the door, then grinned.

"I see you're occupied."

"Very."

"Are you coming back to the hall . . . ?"

Jamie sighed. "Presently. Now that you've satisfied your curiosity, you may go."

Jesse grinned again and slipped out the door. Jamie raised Elizabeth up to her feet, then held her close for a moment or two, relishing the feeling of her arms around him. Even if he couldn't find the words to tell her how he cared for her, he felt it deep in his heart. At first he thought that burning sensation had been Hugh's cooking, but he knew better now.

It was love.

Elizabeth had the feeling the peace and tranquility of the afternoon wasn't destined to last. And she was prepared to have the other shoe drop with a very loud thump.

It did.

When darkness fell and the keep settled down for the night, she walked with Jamie to his chamber. She stopped him at the door.

"I'll sleep with Megan," she said softly.

Jamie's jaw hung slack. "What?"

"Surely you don't want to give up your room . . ."

"Aye, I do not." He put his hand on the door to open it, but she stopped him.

"Jamie, I won't sleep with you until we're married."

He opened his mouth to express what surely would have been a bellow, and Elizabeth quickly put her finger to his lips.

"You'll wake the entire household," she whispered. "And you agreed, Jamie."

"I agreed to no such thing!" he exclaimed.

She folded her arms across her chest. "After, Jamie. Not before."

"I'm not going to bed you. That much I promised. But this," he gestured helplessly, "this staying out of my own chamber I did not agree to!" He folded his arms across his chest and looked down at her stubbornly. "Absolutely not, Elizabeth. I forbid it."

Ten minutes later, Jamie was glaring at her from Megan's bed as she pulled the covers up to his chin and planted a chaste kiss on his forehead.

"Sweet dreams," she said with a gentle smile.

"I cannot believe the foolish things I am driven to do because of you."

She smoothed the hair back from his face. "Do you want me to tell you a story?"

"Aye," he growled, "about a lackwit laird who let himself be led about by a ring through his nose to the everlasting delight of his lady and the never-ending laughter of his clan. And entitle it 'Elizabeth and the Dolt.' "

She would have laughed, but she didn't think Jamie would join her. Instead she decided on flattery.

"Jamie, you are a most chivalrous knight. It's very romantic of you to give up your chamber for me while you're wooing me."

He grunted, only slightly mollified. "Off with you, then," he said, nodding toward the door with a frown. "If you're to have my chamber to yourself, you'd best make use of it while you can."

"Good-night, Jamie," she said as she rose and walked to the door.

"Bolt your door," was his only response.

She turned at the door and looked back at him. He looked terribly uncomfortable in that short little bed, and she almost relented. Then she shook her head. She wanted her wedding night to be special. It wouldn't kill Jamie to sleep in the fetal position for a few nights.

"Go if you're going," Jamie rumbled.

She smiled at him. "I love you."

His frown darkened. "Aye. Now, go to bed."

Elizabeth smiled to herself as she pulled the door closed. He would unbend enough one of these days to say the words. And she would turn that day into a clan holiday.

She went to bed, thinking about the celebration.

Chapter 16

JAMIE WAS ALREADY grumbling before he rolled out of bed just after dawn. He had been up a dozen times during the night to check on Elizabeth. Putting his ear to the wood revealed nothing but silence. At least she had bolted the door as he had commanded her to do. It was pacifying to know she had obeyed him in that.

But it hardly eased his irritation. He was laird of the most powerful clan in Scotland, and he was banned from his own bedchamber by a slip of a girl who demanded as part of her wooing his absence from his own bed? It was nothing short of humiliating. Wooing. What fool had ever invented the bloody custom?

Jamie stomped down the steps, his mind already searching for someone he could vent his frustrations on. He gave the rushes a hearty kick as he stomped across the floor. Then he identified a choice victim and strode over to him purposefully.

Ian held up his hands and sat back in his chair. "Don't start with me this morning, Jamie."

"Hugh!" Jamie bellowed. "Bring me ale!"

Poor Hugh scurried across the rushes as fast as his spindly legs would carry him, sloshing ale all over his person and the floor. He earned more than his share of hearty curses for being such an oaf by the other men who had become accustomed to a clean place on which to wrestle.

Jamie ignored his men and turned his attention back to Ian. "Enjoy your meal," he said darkly, "for 'twill be your last."

Ian raised his mug in salute and drained it in a long pull. He grinned over the lip of his mug as he watched Jamie toss back the contents of his own cup with angry abandon.

"Sleep poorly, my lord?"

Jamie slammed his cup down. "I'm going to thoroughly enjoy slicing you to ribbons."

Ian chuckled. "I've no doubt of that. But you've done the right thing, you know."

"Meaning?"

"Giving up your chamber for Elizabeth."

"How did you know?"

"Jamie, you were bellowing loud enough last night for the Fergusson to hear you. The gossips in the village were sure you had bedded Elizabeth. Now they're equally as sure you didn't. Whether you intended it or not, your little sacrifice last eve saved your love's good name. That alone should be worth the score of times you rose to check on her."

" 'Twas only a dozen," Jamie said gruffly.

"Well, you do count better than I. I'll take your word on the affair."

Jamie grunted. He'd never stopped to consider what others would think of his taking Elizabeth to his bed. To be honest, he never cared what others thought. But she would. It would have hurt her deeply to know others looked down on her. Well, perhaps his suffering was worth something after all.

But even so, he had a kink in his back from sleeping with his knees curled to his chin, and someone would have to pay for that. He looked at Ian and decided he would do quite well. He rose.

"Come with me outside, Ian, lad. I still owe you for a slur or two."

After all, chivalry had its limits.

Windows were certainly at a premium in Jamie's hall, and Elizabeth desperately wished there were a way to enlarge the ones on the main floor. She knew they were small bordering on nonexistent simply as a safeguard, but that didn't stop her from wishing.

She was picking at the decaying mortar of one ground-level window when she heard deep voices approaching. Eavesdropping wasn't a habit of hers, but once she identified the speakers, she couldn't tear herself away.

"Damnation, Ian, but I'm in sore need of wooing ideas."

"I still say you should hie yourself over to the McKinnon's fair and part with some of your precious gold. All women love trinkets."

"Not my Elizabeth. She's a dreamy lass, not one given to accumulating masses of baubles."

"*All* women love trinkets," Ian repeated firmly.

"And I say they don't," Jamie repeated, just as firmly. "Think of something else."

"Jamie, you're asking the wrong man. I've never had to woo a woman. One look at my fine form, and I'm fighting them off. I toss them a coin on my way out, and the tale is finished."

"Damnation, Ian, this is my future wife, not a village whore!" Jamie exclaimed. "I'm not about to *toss her a coin on my way out*, as you so tenderly put it." He paced back and forth, the gravel crunching under his boots. "What think you of love letters?" he said, stopping suddenly. "Verse perhaps?"

"Hire a minstrel, Jamie."

"Flowers?"

"Jewels instead."

"Long walks in the garden?"

"Whatever for?" Ian asked in astonishment. "Jamie, you've gone daft."

"And you've no romance in your soul," Jamie growled. "I'll just have to think for myself, as usual."

"Don't harm yourself by the effort," Ian laughed.

The conversation ended abruptly, and a great amount of dirt flew into the window, making Elizabeth jump back hastily. She coughed and waved her hand in front of her face, congratulating herself on receiving her just desserts for listening.

So she was *his* Elizabeth. The remembrance of his possessive tone made her positively beam with pleasure. Her laird was a romantic and didn't even know it.

Jamie didn't come in for lunch, and she began to worry about what sort of shape he'd be in when he finally arrived for dinner. The man could eat all five of her brothers under the table and still look around for dessert. If he wasn't fed on a regular basis, he wasn't fit to live with.

She wrapped her cloak around her and left the hall, wondering where Jamie would be keeping himself. The blacksmith's hut was silent, and only an occasional whicker came from the stables. She thought about strolling over to the friar's house, then dismissed the idea. Jamie wouldn't go to him for wooing ideas.

The lists were empty, so she walked around the keep and headed toward the garden. She peeked over the wall, then put her hand over her mouth to stifle her gasp. Jamie and Jesse were there, crawling on their knees in the foliage. Jamie was cursing a blue streak.

"Damnation, Jesse, those are weeds!"

"Father, they're wildflowers. All the other flowers Malcolm planted last spring are gone."

No wonder Malcolm got teased. Elizabeth could hardly imagine that giant tenderly caring for rosebushes.

Jamie sat back on his haunches. "And you'd give these to Megan?"

"Saints, nay. They would make her sneeze."

Jamie threw up his hands in despair. "As I said before, they're *weeds*!"

"I don't understand why you're doing this in the first place. Megan would much rather have a dirk or a new mount as a gift."

"All women love flowers," Jamie said, as if he quoted from a book of great wisdom. "That's what they love, and that's what I mean to have."

Jesse sighed and rose. "Then you'll have to find them yourself. I've no idea what to look for."

"You've two eyes and a nose," Jamie bellowed. "Come back down here and help me search! And keep a lookout over your shoulder. About the time anyone sees me doing this, I'll be laughed out of my own keep."

Elizabeth beat a hasty retreat and vowed to gush over whatever Jamie brought back to the house.

She was standing near the hearth when he came into the great hall. When he saw the hall was still half full of his men, he hastily shoved something under the length of plaid tossed over his shoulder. Before he could take even a step toward her, he was cornered by Angus. Angus' audience was very short-lived.

Jamie stalked over to her, a disgruntled expression on his face. Without a word, he took her by the arm and dragged her up the steps to his chamber. He ushered her inside, banged the door closed behind him and dug inside his plaid. He thrust a fistful of very wilted, completely crumpled vegetation at her. She didn't dare call them flowers. If they had been originally, their trip up the stairs inside Jamie's plaid had rid them of all petals.

She couldn't have cared less about their condition. She accepted them with the same reverence and astonishment she would have the Hope diamond. Then she threw her arms around her love's neck and hugged him tightly.

"Thank you," she whispered into his ear. "They're beautiful."

He mumbled something completely unintelligible. When she pulled back to catch it, he yanked her against him again, denying her the opportunity of looking at his face. Or his blush. She grinned into his hair.

"You're very sweet, Jamie."

He grunted and let her slip back down to the floor. He bent and kissed her hard on the mouth before he turned and walked to the door.

"Got things to do," he threw over his shoulder as he banged out of the room.

Elizabeth looked at the flowers in her hand and smiled. On closer inspection, a few blooms had survived the trip in Jamie's great paws. She arranged them in a cup and set them on the mantel. The beauty was Jamie's love, which was reflected in every broken stem, missing petal and crushed blade of grass.

They were sweeter than any corsage she'd had in high school and infinitely more precious than the dozen roses with baby's breath Stanley had sent her every Friday afternoon.

She much preferred weeds from her love.

Jamie sat in his chair at the high table and looked longingly at his customary seat near the fire at one of the lower tables. Ian had assured him sitting in the laird's chair would impress Elizabeth, and Jamie hadn't been able to argue with that. Impress her he might, but he was certain he would catch his death from the draft before he would see the fruits of his labors.

He cast a dubious look at Ian's second suggestion for the evening. The minstrel was a tall, gangly youth with more stars in his eyes than sense in his head. Jamie snorted. Now, *there* was a romantic. Jamie wasn't convinced this was the way to woo his lady, but Ian had been adamant. Ian never lacked for women to warm his bed, so perhaps there was some merit in the idea, though Jamie was reserving judgment until after the evening was over.

He watched the callow lad's eyes fair pop from his head and his jaw hang to the floor and knew that Elizabeth had come downstairs for supper. Jamie rose and intercepted her halfway across the hall. He tucked her hand under his arm possessively and led her to the chair next to his, giving the minstrel a look that should have sent the young man scurrying for the first convenient hiding place.

Instead the witless lad approached the high table in a daze and made Elizabeth a deep bow.

"Fairest lady," he said, "surely my life 'til now has been naught but darkness. The radiance of your loveliness has brought a light to my life which will never be dimmed, even should I find myself cast from this hall and consigned to a hell without your beauty."

Jamie stole a sideways glance at Elizabeth to find her looking at the minstrel in shock.

"Your lips are the deep red of sparkling rubies, your eyes the pale blue of the beryl, your skin an alabaster fairness that puts the fairest of pearls to shame. Would that I were an artist and could capture the exquisiteness of your being on even a small slip of parchment to ever carry with me, to gaze upon in the darkness of my wretched soul and remind myself that an angel has indeed come to earth and now deigns to grace my worthless being with the goodness of her perfect soul."

Elizabeth leaned up and whispered in Jamie's ear.

"He's kidding, right?"

Kidding was completely out of Jamie's vocabulary, and he surely did not want to mistake her meaning.

"How was that?" he whispered back.

"He jests," she repeated. "He doesn't mean all those silly things, does he?"

The lad had babbled nothing but the exact sentiments in Jamie's heart, and Jamie cursed himself for not being eloquent enough to have said them first. He sighed and raised her hand to his lips.

"I fear he is very much in earnest."

"Well, tell him to stop it. He's embarrassing me."

Jamie took heart and waved away the young man, who looked momentarily crushed until he was informed he would be allowed to sing. He dragged up a stool in front of Elizabeth and began to put his flowery sentiments to music.

"Jamie," Elizabeth whispered irritably, "tell him to move down. He's driving me crazy."

A flick of Jamie's wrist sent the lad scurrying, though no doubt not far enough to suit Elizabeth. Jamie puzzled over her reaction during supper. Surely she knew she was beautiful. Or didn't she?

"Is he unable to sing about anything but me?" Elizabeth said with a frown, pushing away the remains of her meal. "I'm going to boot him right from this hall if he doesn't shut up."

Jamie laughed. His lady was starting to sound as foul-tempered as he was. He turned to the minstrel.

"My lady will hear something else, lad, or you will be out on your ear. Mind you, she's very fierce."

The young man hastily complied and began to sing about anything but Elizabeth's beauty. He even made up a song about the fine stew he had smelled but was not allowed to eat yet. Jamie gasped with laughter over the lad's cleverness and cheek.

He looked down at Elizabeth and found her grinning at his mirth.

"The lad pleases you?" Jamie asked.

"He's very good."

"Shall we keep him?"

"I thought minstrels just traveled, never staying in one place more than a night or two."

"The lucky ones find a lord who is pleased with their skill and keep them on. Of course, there are men who will not stay bound to a place more than one night. But judging from the mournful look in the lad's eye, being cast out into a hell without your beauty to gaze upon would be a sorry fate for him indeed."

"Jamie, he wasn't serious."

"But everything he said was true," he admitted. "Life without you would indeed be hell."

"Oh, Jamie," she breathed, her eyes glowing. Before he knew what she planned, she leaned up and kissed him square on the mouth.

The silence in the hall was deafening. Jamie realized that only after she pulled back and the blood stopped pounding in his ears.

The men in the room choked on their laughter and then began to applaud.

"Minstrel," Jamie bellowed, riding high on the knowledge that his own compliments pleased Elizabeth far more than the flattery of a mere boy. "My lady will speak to you now."

The minstrel skidded to a halt in front of them. "Aye, fairest angel?"

Jamie pressed a kiss against Elizabeth's forehead, ignoring Ian's heckling. "Elizabeth, question the lad to your satisfaction. If he suits you, you may keep him." He sat back in his chair and watched, supremely interested in the outcome of the conversation.

"Will you just stop looking at me like that?" Elizabeth said to the young man.

"I'm helpless against the chaste love I feel for you, my lady."

Elizabeth sighed. "How old are you?"

"A score and four, my lady."

"Where is your family?"

"Perished, my lady. My uncles and father ever fought among themselves until most were dead. The king took away our lands, which was nothing more than my kinsmen deserved, believe you me. I snatched up my lute and fled before the king could mistake me for one of my wicked cousins. That was fourteen years ago. Since that time, I've been roaming, singing for my keep."

"You must miss your family deeply."

"It would ease my pain greatly if I were allowed to serve you," he said, his eyes pleading. "Not only can I sing, but I know a few of my letters. I can count quite high if I have my shoes off and can use my toes. And I know recipes which would tempt the palate of the Bruce himself. I'm even handy with a blade if need be."

His chatter abruptly stopped, and the blood drained from his face as Jamie rose to his full height. Jamie rescued the lute from the young man's trembling fingers and laid it on the table.

"Well?" he asked Elizabeth. "The lad has no Gaelic, and 'tis true I should likely slay him for it, but he sings well enough. If he suits you, he may stay."

"Jamie, you can't just keep him as if he were a stray cat."

Jamie shrugged. "He'll have food and a roof over his head. What more could a lad want than that?"

"Aye, my lord," the young man agreed. "'Tis a fair bargain you offer me."

"Your name?"

"Joshua of Sedgwick."

"Saints, yet another Englishman in my keep," Jamie said, sighing in resignation. "Well, consider yourself a Scot now, man. Find your supper in the kitchen, then ask Angus for a blanket and some warmer clothing."

He immediately dismissed Joshua of Sedgwick from his mind and reached for Elizabeth's hand. She was looking up at him with a mixture of pride and gratitude.

"Let us go snuggle for a time," he whispered, "then you will tell me what that look means."

"But Megan is sleeping with me in your chamber . . ."

"We'll use my thinking room. You may check on Megan first, if you like."

"You're very gracious to allow it."

"I am forced to order you about several times a day that you do not forget that I, not you, am laird here."

He opened the door to his chamber and stood near the bed, waiting for an appropriate opportunity to hasten Elizabeth's bedtime story along. When he saw his chance, he dove in.

"And then," he said, interrupting Elizabeth, "the brave knight bowed to Lady Megan and beseeched her to be a good lass and take her rest, as he had many plans for the sweet Lady Elizabeth before evening shadows lengthened too far. And the Lady Megan replied, 'Of course, Sir Jamie. I will gladly do your bidding and fall asleep instantly that Lady Elizabeth might go with you and allow you to woo her, for I know you have a great amount of snuggling in mind for the eve.' Sir Jamie praised Lady Megan for her goodness, gave her a kiss goodnight—" he leaned over and gave her a gentle peck on the forehead—"and bade her sleep quickly. Go to sleep, Megan. Come along, Elizabeth." He took Elizabeth's hand and pulled her toward the door before she could protest.

"Jamie?"

"Aye, Megan."

"I love you."

How was it a child of no more than thirteen summers could leave a grown man wanting to weep? He put his shoulders back, walked around the bed and leaned down to kiss her gently.

"I do too, imp," he said, cursing the crack in his voice. "Now, go to sleep before I must needs beat you."

Megan only giggled and pulled the covers up to her chin.

Jamie groaned as he walked around the bed to collect Elizabeth. He caught sight of his flowery offering sitting in a cup on the mantel and groaned again. Women. All it had taken was two of them to turn him into a soft, tear-prone fool.

The saints be praised he'd had the good sense to keep them both.

Chapter 17

JAMIE WAS UP the next morning well before sunrise, having not slept most of the night. And it wasn't the smallness of the bed that had disturbed his sleep so thoroughly. A feeling of dread weighed heavily on him, a feeling he was not unaccustomed to. He'd had it often enough in the past, and it had proven to be a fairly accurate indicator of approaching danger. Hadn't just such a forewarning saved his life the year before?

He'd been out hunting with Jesse when he'd had a vision of an arrow coming toward his back. Not an hour later, he'd heard the sound of a bowstring being released. Leaping off his horse and diving to the ground had been instinctive. The arrow had come to rest in the trunk of a tree, and his assassin's head had soon come to rest beside his lifeless body. Jamie had neither the time nor the mercy to spare on Fergusson's roaming scouts, especially when they roamed on MacLeod soil.

He walked heavily down the steps to the great hall, praying it was just his imagination coupled with a bit of stale brew. He fully intended to take Elizabeth to the McKinnon's fair and woo her properly, even though taking her from the keep made him nervous. Indeed, he'd almost changed his mind about going until he heard Megan telling Elizabeth what she would see. How could he deny his love the sight of her first fair? Especially since Ian considered it a most important wooing ritual.

Elizabeth was ready well ahead of the required hour and did his bidding without question. Until she saw the horses waiting in the courtyard.

"We're riding? Again?"

"Astronaut will not hurt you," he said, boosting her up into the saddle before she could protest. He held his mount steady while Elizabeth arranged herself astride in the saddle, then he swung up behind her. He took the reins and turned his horse toward the gates. "Hold onto my hands. I will teach you as we ride. You will have your own mount on the way home."

She nodded without making a sound. He knew she was petrified and so did Astronaut, but the beast was too wise to buck them both off.

"Relax," he said soothingly. "Elizabeth, you're frightening my horse. If you want us to both keep our seats, you will concentrate on loosening the death grip your legs have on Astronaut's sides."

"I'll fall," she said tightly.

"And how is that, with my arms safely around you?"

"We'll both fall then."

"If we do, I'll fall under you, and you'll have nothing but the cushion of my hard body to land on." He smiled in spite of himself. "Does that ease your mind any?"

"Not one stinking bit," she said.

He puzzled for most of the morning about her usual method of transportation. Had she walked everywhere? She had beautifully fashioned legs that could have come from that sort of exercise, but walking was a slow process. Perhaps she always rode in those wagons that moved by themselves. Aye, that would explain her not knowing anything about horses.

He called a halt at midday for a meal and to allow Elizabeth time to rest. He swung down to the ground and then held up his arms for her. He took his time setting her on her feet.

"Can you stand?" he asked.

"I think so."

"Fetch enough food for us both and sit down," he said, pushing away from her suddenly. "I'll be along shortly."

He turned and walked away without waiting for a response. He had to leave, force himself to think of anything else besides

Elizabeth. He knew he had to have her, and he fully intended to wed her, but he honestly didn't know how he would survive either. She made him lose control. He was nearing the border of his land and should have had his mind on his surroundings. All he could think about was the sweet scent of her hair filling his nostrils and her delicate hands clutching his so trustingly. He shuddered to think of how preoccupied he would have been had he already lain with her.

That wasn't the worst. Never in his life had his emotions been so close to the surface. Not even when Jesse had almost been trampled by an unbroken stallion at the tender age of five had Jamie been so overcome by emotion. Lately he was ever on the verge of something: joy, tears, desire.

Perhaps it was love. He wanted to pick Elizabeth up in his arms, carry her to his bed and lose himself in her, over and over again until they were both too weary to move. He wanted to take her fiercely and unleash her passion. He wanted to take her slowly, with infinite care and touch her soul. He wanted to feel her soft hands on his body, on his face, in his hair. He wanted to hear his name torn from her lips as he brought her pleasure.

That was the one reason he never let himself kiss her with too much fervor. Once he ravaged her mouth as fully and as thoroughly as he wanted to, her body would follow. Once he had made her his, he would never be able to hold back his soul from her. Then his weakness would ever be just below the surface, instead of buried deep where it should have been.

It was a losing battle and he knew it. She had gone from a witch in his pit to a thorn in his side to an ache in his heart.

He strode back purposefully to camp and ate lunch without speaking to Elizabeth at all. She was more relaxed as they rode in the afternoon but still ill at ease in the saddle. By the time they made camp and sent a messenger to the McKinnon keep, she was almost asleep. He could have easily found shelter under Guilbert's roof, but he wasn't about to let the McKinnon put Elizabeth in a chamber of her own. The man had too much the reputation for womanizing.

After seeing to his men and the securing of the camp, Jamie sought Elizabeth. She was near the fire, asleep. He slid under the blankets behind her and pulled her back against his chest.

"Jamie, what are you doing?" she murmured.

"Protecting you. Do not argue with me on this."

She didn't. She merely snuggled back against him.

"You aren't angry with me anymore?" she asked, lacing her fingers with his.

How could he blame her for his troubles? She couldn't help being sweet, loving, gentle—everything he wasn't. And she wasn't responsible for the nagging worry in his mind.

"Nay, love," he said, "I'm not angry with you. I never was."

"I just don't understand you sometimes."

"I don't understand myself either," he said with a sigh.

He closed his eyes and buried his face in her hair. The morrow would bring what it would, and his fears would either be confirmed or eased. Premonition was a terrible thing. It had saved his life more than once, but that was small comfort as reward for the hours of unease he passed while looking over his shoulder, waiting for the blade to appear from out of nowhere.

Elizabeth woke the next morning and burrowed closer to the warmth. A large hand cupped her chin and lifted her face for a kiss. Once he released her, she sighed.

"I suppose it's time to get up."

Jamie pulled her closer. "We've little reason to today. We'll wait until well after sunrise and then show ourselves to the McKinnon before we attend the fair."

She pressed her face against his warm neck. "Who's the McKinnon?"

"Guilbert McKinnon is a womanizing bastard of the worst sort. He's ruthless, conniving, dishonest and possibly one of the best allies I have."

"I don't see much there that recommends him."

"There's nothing to recommend him but that he has a large clan, and he hates the Fergussons as much as I do. He's a man to be trusted only with your wars, not your gold or your lover. I certainly do not intend to leave you alone while he's about."

Two hours later, Elizabeth clutched Jamie's hand as they made their way up to the keep. She was intensely reluctant to meet Jamie's ally. She had passed muster among his own people, but how would she explain her presence to someone else?

"Jamie," she whispered quickly, "perhaps I shouldn't go. How will I explain . . ."

"I have thought of it all, Elizabeth. Leave Guilbert to me."

"Why did we come?" she asked miserably.

"I thought the fair might amuse you."

Elizabeth nodded and fell silent.

The McKinnon was everything she had always pictured a Highlander to be. He was straight from the movies with his bright red hair, his short, compact frame and his piercing blue eyes. A harsh scar ran down his cheek, making him appear terribly dangerous. She almost fell to her knees in gratitude that she had wound up in Jamie's keep and not Guilbert McKinnon's. The look Jamie gave her told her he was thinking the exact same thing.

After Guilbert's first lustful look, Jamie's arm went immediately around her shoulders. He pulled her so tightly against him, she could hardly breathe. He made up some story about them having been betrothed from birth. Evidently Jamie had a distant cousin of some fame in the Lowlands, and that cousin had just been elected to be her father.

Elizabeth tried not to shudder as she and Jamie were ushered into Guilbert's hall. There were serving girls aplenty, but they were seriously lacking in domestic skills. The hall was a sty and smelled like a sewer. She accepted ale and prayed she wouldn't die from it.

Jamie had her chair so close to his and her so far out of it toward him, she might as well have been sitting in his lap. She wasn't about to argue. What Guilbert lacked in lustful looks, his men more than made up for. She felt like a slab of meat being dangled in front of a dozen hungry pit bulls.

The pleasantries were exchanged with all haste, and Jamie finally led her from the hall. She had never in her life been so glad to escape a place before.

"MacLeod, a word in private," the McKinnon said as they left the hall.

Jamie locked eyes with Ian, who immediately took his place at Elizabeth's side. Malcolm flanked her on her left, and a dozen of Jamie's other linebackers surrounded her, effectively cutting off her view of anything but the sky above her. She held on to Ian's hand tightly.

"Och, Elizabeth," he complained, "you're about to snap my poor fingers in two. Have pity on your humble servant."

"Ian, I don't like it here."

Ian squeezed her hand gently. "We'll keep you safe, even if Jamie's away. We're your kinsmen now."

It was an eternity before the front line parted and Jamie came to stand before her. His expression was chiseled straight out of granite. She shrank back from him, then stopped. Here was the one person she should have been able to count on, and he was turning on her? Not if she could help it. She took a step forward and looked him square in the eye.

"What?" she demanded.

"Hold out your hand."

She did, hesitating only slightly.

Jamie dropped a pouch onto her palm. She looked down at it and then back up at him.

"What's this?"

"Gold," he said flatly. "Go buy yourself whatever you need."

"Jamie, you know I don't need anything."

The slabs of stone softened only slightly. "Elizabeth, you need things. I'm sure of it." His face softened a bit more. "Go on," he said with a poor imitation of a smile. "Buy yourself something beautiful."

She put the gold back into his hand and folded his fingers over it. "You keep it. If I see something I can't live without, I'll let you know." She slipped her hand through his arm. "Jamie, please smile."

His smile didn't reach his eyes, but it was an improvement. He led her over to where the cluster of carts and booths were already set up. Throngs of people milled over the grounds. Elizabeth clutched at Jamie's hand and prayed she wouldn't get separated from him.

She soon lost her fear in the delight of what she saw. There were carts containing every type of ware imaginable. There were bolts of fabric, mostly rough-spun woolens, but things which would have been deliciously warm. She pored over a cart containing various odds and ends. She finally stumbled upon a silver-handled comb. She looked up at Jamie.

"Can we make something like this at home?"

Jamie's face had again taken on that hard edge. "If you desire it, purchase it."

"It isn't for me," she said impatiently. "It's for Megan. Do we have a silversmith in the area?"

Jamie's eyebrow lifted in surprise. "Aye. He could fashion something like that."

Elizabeth handed the comb back with a smile and moved on to the next place that caught her eye. It was another fabric merchant, but this one had ribbons and lace and all manner of delicate embroidery. She asked the price of a length of ribbon and had no idea what the amount was. A questioning look at Jamie earned her only a frown and a coin in her hand. She paid the man and happily curled up the ribbon and tucked it into the pouch at her belt.

"Perhaps by Christmas her hair will be long enough," she said as they strolled through the crowd.

"Pardon me?"

"Megan," Elizabeth smiled. "She'll love the color, don't you think? I'd like to find something for Jesse now. Is there anything special he likes?"

Jamie stopped still. "You bought that for Megan?"

"Of course," she smiled. "What do I need with hair ribbons when you hate my hair braided?"

Jamie sighed and put his arm around her shoulders. "Jesse needs nothing. Find something for yourself. Do not these trinkets please you?"

A flash of blue caught her eye, and she made a beeline for it. There, in a secluded corner of the fair, surrounded by burly men, was a jewelry maker. Or a gem owner. She hardly knew what to call the man. All she knew was he had the aquamarine in his hand that she wanted to put in Jamie's wedding ring. It was enormous, and she was sure it would cost a fortune. Fortunately she had brought Stanley's engagement ring with her for just such an occasion as this. She shoved it into Ian's hands while Jamie's back was turned.

"Get me that blue stone," she whispered urgently. "Trade this for it. Whatever this doesn't cover, I'll find a way to pay you for. Don't let Jamie see you."

Ian closed his hand over the ring and nodded. Elizabeth tugged on Jamie's hand and smiled brightly up at him.

"I've changed my mind. I think I want to buy everything. Where shall we start?"

She kept browsing until she knew Jamie's patience was at an end. Finally she bought herself enough lace to make a slip of a collar, should she ever come into possession of material for a dress. Jamie tossed a coin at the merchant and pulled her away. She looked frantically for Ian, who saluted her behind Jamie's back.

Angus appeared at that moment, and Elizabeth blessed him for his good timing. She and Ian walked on ahead.

"Did he trade you?" she asked.

Ian plunked a pouch down into her hand. "Your big blue stone and several other gems, two or three of which just might match Jamie's eyes. I think you were robbed, but you have your treasures."

Elizabeth thought to look in the bag, then she saw Jamie bearing down on them. She hurriedly put the pouch behind her back and smiled up at him. Her smile died at the look on his face. He thrust out his hand. She looked up at him in surprise and put his money pouch into his hand. His expression only darkened.

"The other. I want to see what it is you've spent all my gold on."

"It wasn't your gold."

"It certainly wasn't yours," he bit out. "Guilbert dared me to allow you to purchase anything you wanted, saying you would empty my coffer in one day. I boasted that you cared not for gold and jewels to adorn yourself with. You've made a fool and a liar out of me. Now, let me see the evidence of your guilt."

Elizabeth blinked, finding the change in Jamie very hard to understand. But she didn't have any trouble understanding the accusation in his eyes. She slowly opened the pouch and poured the gems into his hand.

"These, my lord," she said, looking up at him coolly, "are what *Stanley's* ring purchased. The large stone is to be bound into your wedding ring. I hadn't decided quite whom to give the other gems to. I had thought perhaps they would serve well in a sword for your son or a ring for Megan."

With that, she turned and walked away. She was guilty and sentenced before the jury even went out. She was well aware of the precariousness of Jamie's situation and had never thought to ask for luxuries. She didn't need them. She had a warm bed, decent food and a family to love. There was nothing material she needed that she didn't already have.

An ear-piercing scream rent the morning air. Elizabeth pulled up short at the sight that greeted her.

A woman was tied to a pole and surrounded by piles of dry wood. The first torch had already been set to the dry tinder, and the smoke wafted toward the heavens.

They were burning a witch.

Chapter 18

THE SCREAM TORE through Jamie's consciousness. He dragged his eyes away from the small fortune of gems in his palm and searched the surrounding field. His eyes fell first on the witch at the stake and second on Elizabeth, who stood nearby, motionless. He shoved the jewels and his gold at Ian and sprinted the distance that separated him from his love.

He whirled her around and wrapped his cloak around her. "Put your fingers in your ears," he commanded hoarsely.

She didn't move. If he had not felt the tremors that shook her so violently, he would have thought her stone dead on her feet. He turned her head and pressed her ear against his chest. He covered the other side of her head with his palm, praying he would cut off the shrieks coming from the woman writhing in the midst of the flames.

The girl was no witch. Jamie knew her for one of Guilbert's servants who had been in high favor with him during the spring. Either she had been found gotten with child, or she had taken a fancy to someone besides the laird. Either way, her fate had been sealed long before she knew what was coming. Guilbert McKinnon put more witches to death than the rest of Scotland united.

The smell of burning wood and charring flesh almost made Jamie retch. How did Guilbert live with himself?

"Fine sport, isn't it, MacLeod?" Guilbert drawled from beside him.

Jamie didn't bother to look at him. "I can think of finer."

"Why do you hide your betrothed? She should see what we do to witches here."

Jamie didn't miss the thinly veiled accusation. He favored Guilbert with a frosty look. "She has been sheltered the whole of her life. I see no reason to upset her by your sport."

The McKinnon's eyes narrowed. "I find it odd you never spoke of a betrothed before, MacLeod. You have an heir; what need you with a woman to tie you down? I spoke with your cousin Nolan a few days back. He says the wench came from the forest, and we all know what the forest spews out. Indeed, you carry yourself like a man enchanted."

Jamie allowed his mouth to curve into a very unpleasant smile. "You don't want me as an enemy, McKinnon."

Guilbert backed down. It obviously galled him to do it, but he knew he had gone too far. He stepped back a pace, then turned and strode away.

The woman's screams had long since faded, but the melting of her flesh was no less gruesome. Jamie swept Elizabeth up into his arms and carried her back to their camp. His men were mounted and waiting.

Ian held Elizabeth while Jamie mounted, then handed her up to him. She was still, not even trembling anymore. He tilted her face up and looked into her vacant eyes. She was so far away, he knew he wouldn't be able to reach her until she calmed.

He pulled his cloak close around her and spurred Astronaut on. He never should have brought her. He had originally intended to make the required visit to Guilbert and then shower Elizabeth with gifts from the market. Her response to his flowers had delighted him so; he couldn't resist the thought of giving her a bit of material and a foolish trinket or two. He knew she didn't require them, but he had been sure she would have accepted them with gladness just the same.

Guilbert's taunt had stung him into anger, and he had been fool enough to take that anger out on Elizabeth. And what had she purchased with the gold he forced on her? Something for Megan and a scrap of lace no wider than his thumb for herself.

His expression tightened into a frown. She deserved yards of lace with which to adorn her dresses, chests full of ribbons for her hair and bags of jewelry for her fingers and clothes.

He had given her the key to his trunk, but he had never thought she would take her ring and use it for something so foolish as a stone for him. He deepened his frown until it blocked any emotion that might have shown on his face. She had bargained away the only thing of value she possessed for a stone the color of his eyes. For his wedding ring. He continued to frown until the urge to weep receded.

He didn't even try to rationalize away his guilt. He had been a bastard and deserved every wave of remorse that washed over him. Elizabeth loved him. She loved his kin. She was not one of the grasping, selfish women he had met at other keeps, women who lusted after his body and his ruthless reputation. Those women came to his bed only to boast of having been there. They cared nothing for him.

Not like the sweet girl in his arms who had grown weepy at the sight of a fistful of crushed weeds. He groaned. He had been three times a fool. He pulled Elizabeth closer to him. Never again. Never again would he misjudge her. And he would do everything in his power to shield her from the harsh realities of his world. He only prayed her morning's viewing hadn't left her permanently scarred.

"Elizabeth, we're home."

Elizabeth struggled to rise to the surface of her misery and found it impossible. All she could hear were the screams. And Guilbert McKinnon's words. He'd called her a witch. She'd been coherent enough to understand that.

Jamie carried her up the stairs to his chamber. She couldn't find her tongue to greet either Megan or Jesse. Megan immediately began to weep, and Jamie reassured her all was well. Jesse took Megan away.

Jamie put her to bed. She didn't protest. Food was brought, but she couldn't bring herself to eat. Jamie pleaded, cajoled, commanded and then bellowed, but she ignored him. Eating was completely beyond her.

She slept for hours at a time, not caring enough to stay

awake. Each time she opened her eyes, Jamie was there by her bedside, sitting in his chair, watching her with grave eyes. He looked worse every time she woke up.

Finally she was resigned. It might have taken only a couple of days, it could have taken a week—she wasn't sure. All she knew was what she had to do.

She rose early one morning and wrapped her plaid around her. She opened the shutters and looked up at the mountains that stood so proudly behind Jamie's home. The beauty of the scene took her breath away. It was just one more reason she had to go. Jamie would never again enjoy the sight if it were the backdrop to her being burned at the stake.

"Beth?"

She hadn't heard him enter the room. But now he was there, she might as well tell him what she had to.

"I can't marry you," she said clearly, not able to look him in the face as she voiced her decision.

She heard him cross the room to stand behind her. His strong arms went around her waist.

"Beth, you're weak and sorrowful. Listen to my begging for forgiveness, and then forget what you've seen. I never should have taken you from the keep."

She turned around and backed up against the window, hoping to put distance between them.

"Jamie, I'm serious. I can't marry you. It would never work. How could I do that to you? Or to our children?"

"Damn you, Elizabeth, you are no more a witch than I am!"

"But they do not know that."

"No one would dare accuse—"

"I don't love you."

He looked as surprised as if she'd just slapped him across the face.

"I don't," she pressed on mercilessly. "I never have. It's all been a game to cheat you from your gold. You're a rich man, Jamie—"

"You're lying!"

"I'm not. I can't marry you, Jamie, and those are my reasons."

Silence fell in the room like a soft blanket of snow. It trickled down from the ceiling, stifling every sound until she couldn't even hear her own heartbeat. All she could see was the agony in Jamie's eyes.

He turned and left the room, closing the door quietly behind him.

Elizabeth slid to her knees. Tears wouldn't even come to her eyes. Her breath was always just a gasp away, but she never could quite catch it. He'd forgive her in time. He'd realize she had done it because she loved him so desperately. Her ruined life didn't matter. She'd go back to the forest and take her chances again with the wild beasts. At least she'd never cause Jamie deeper hurt.

Through a thick cocoon of misery, she heard the door slam with a force that should have knocked it off its hinges. Before she could blink away the burning tears which had finally come to her eyes, she felt fingers bite into her arms.

Jamie shook her until she thought her neck would snap.

"Damn you, you're lying," he said harshly. "You love me." His voice cracked. "Elizabeth, you love me. I demand you say the words!"

She couldn't speak, couldn't breathe, couldn't do anything but stare at him in silent agony.

"I refuse to accept this!"

She could only shake her head, mute.

He hauled her into his arms. After only a moment's hesitation, she threw her arms around his neck and clung to him. Tears coursed down her cheeks.

"You love me," he repeated. "And I will not let you go until you say the words."

Elizabeth choked on her tears. "Oh, Jamie," she cried softly, "I love you more than life."

"Then why did you do this?" he asked plaintively.

"I just didn't want to hurt you."

"I do not understand your logic!" he exclaimed, pushing her back and glaring at her. "Damn you, Elizabeth, your words were like a dirk in my heart!"

"You love me then?" she asked, dragging the plaid across her eyes.

"Of course, you empty-headed female!" he shouted. "Why do you think I want to beat you senseless?"

He looked almost shocked at his own words. A half laugh escaped her before she shuddered and wound her arms around him again.

"Jamie, I'm so frightened," she said, her teeth beginning to chatter. "What if—"

"Hush," he said harshly. "Hush and listen. Not even the Bruce would dare make such an accusation. To you I may be a simple man full of naught but sweet words and kisses. To both my allies and my enemies I am a man devoid of the smallest smidgen of mercy or compassion. When a man injures what is mine, I kill swiftly and without hesitation. The scars you see on my body are far fewer than the ones you would see on Ian's or Angus', for I do not wait to hear pleadings for forbearance. My world is a harsh one, and it has tempered me to its harshness. There isn't a man in this realm who does not know of me. Those who are wise fear me. Those who do not usually die by my hand before they realize their mistake."

He pulled back, and his eyes were as chilly as the frigid air blowing in from the window. "Guilbert McKinnon is not so great a fool as to anger me, for he knows my revenge would not be quick and painless. He would suffer until he thought he could bear no more, then suffer again. Not even my king would dare accuse my wife of witchcraft. He has my loyalty but not at the expense of your life. You have nothing to fear."

"But what if you're gone?" she asked softly. "What if someone comes while you're away?"

"There is not a soul in this keep who would not lay down his life instantly for yours," he said simply. "The men who guarded you most closely while we were traveling have, to a man, come to me and vowed again to protect you with their lives. Before we left, I had to command the rest of my kin to stay home. They feared you would not have enough men of my house to surround you to keep you from harm."

Elizabeth's eyes burned again with tears at Jamie's words. It was the same feeling of being protected she'd had with her brothers, only this time it was even sweeter. She reached for Jamie's hand and held it in both her own.

"Then I do not shame you?"

"Nay, you do not," he said gravely. "Having you bear my name would bring nothing but honor to me. Now, do you take back your words? You hurt me deeply."

"I'm sorry, Jamie," she whispered. "I only wanted to spare you greater hurt."

"And life without you would do that? Woman, your logic is terribly flawed." He reached out and drew her into his lap. "Now 'tis my turn to beg forgiveness. I'm truly sorry I treated you so poorly at the fair. Guilbert angered me, and I punished you in his stead. I would ask you to forgive me. I will behave from now on."

"Jamie, our tempers are both too close to the surface for that."

"I never said I wouldn't shout at you. I just said I wouldn't shout at you without good reason."

She found it in herself to smile. "I fully intend to shout back."

"I'd be disappointed if you didn't."

"You spoiled my surprise," she chided. "Do you still have the aquamarine?"

"The beryl? Aye, 'tis in your trunk. Along with your other treasures. But I have forgotten completely what it looked like. Is it large enough, do you think?"

She smiled. "Was it a stupid thing to do?"

"Nay, Elizabeth. When we travel to court and I sit in the company of great lords, they will gaze with envy on the king's ransom my wife placed on my hand."

"That bad?"

He smiled. "Nay, 'twas a most generous gift."

"And you felt like a slug when you realized what I'd done."

"Aye, lower even," he agreed. "The fair will come here in another few days. This time I will pamper you as you deserve."

"You won't because I need nothing."

"You need new gowns and ribbons for your hair and then you will need—"

"Supper," she finished, crawling to her feet. "I'm starving, Jamie. Let's go eat."

Jamie stopped her at the door. "Tell me again that you love me," he commanded, lifting her face to his.

"You're very demanding."

"Wrong words."

She laughed and leaned up on her toes to kiss him softly. "I love you."

"Now you will agree to wed me," he announced.

"I'm thinking about it. Let me eat first, and then I'll see if I'm equal to the task of enduring you for the rest of my life."

"You'll agree."

"Do I have a choice?"

He paused and looked at her thoughtfully. "You dreamed of me before you came to my time, didn't you?"

She nodded.

"I also dreamed of you. I think I knew then you were mine," he said quietly. "Perhaps we chose long ago, but time somehow erred. Now it has wrought the impossible to bring us together. What think you?"

Elizabeth's mouth fell open. It was the most romantic thing she had ever heard anyone say, and she could hardly believe it had come from the lips of the battle-seasoned warrior standing before her. "I think I'll marry you before time changes its mind," she breathed.

He took her face in his hands, then kissed her.

"Time will never take you from me again."

Chapter 19

THE WEEK MARCHED by much too quickly for Elizabeth. Jamie was determined to wed her on Saturday, and that was that. He completely ignored her excuse that she had nothing to wear. He found the idea of her redoing the hall in preparation for their guests laughable. From the moment she learned they would even be having guests, she was in a panic. Jamie assured her Angus and Everett would take care of all the arrangements, but that hardly eased her mind.

He tried to distract her by wooing her. Elizabeth was completely helpless against his efforts. He kidnapped her for a picnic one afternoon, arrogantly pleased that he had thought of everything.

Except separating the food items in his saddlebag.

Extremely soft-boiled eggs had ruptured and polluted an open jug of wine which had in turn tipped over as they rode, dousing a meat pie that had become a gooey layer of slime covering the soft leather interior of the pouch. Jamie hurled the entire mess into the lake, accompanied by several foul oaths. Elizabeth praised him for his planning, which had left them with nothing to do but kiss for the afternoon. Taking his cue, he swaggered back from the edge of the water and proceeded to leave her wondering why anyone ever took food on picnics. It was too much of a distraction.

*   *   *

Elizabeth was up at dawn on Saturday, not having spent much
of the previous night asleep. It wasn't so much the getting married that had kept her tossing and turning, it was the after part.
Jamie was such a big man, all over. She almost felt as though
she was going in for surgery—just a bit of agony and then it'd
be done with. She wondered if all women felt that way about
losing their virginity.

Once she had bathed and dressed, Elizabeth looked around
the room, smiling at the subtle changes. It was cleaner, certainly. She looked at the wildflowers sitting in the mug on the
mantel. Jamie had given her some the day before, and the current batch had actually survived the trip under his plaid. He was
still adamant that no one know of his weakness.

She walked to the window and gazed out at the mountains,
taking pleasure from their rugged beauty. It was hard to believe
that beauty was hers to gaze at for the rest of her days. Her only
regret was that her family wasn't there. Her father would have
loved Jamie so.

Angus called for her as the sun was peeking over the mountains. She walked to the chapel on his arm, telling him once
again how grateful she was he'd found her that day. Friar Augustine was waiting for them, simply beaming. She lifted her
eyes to meet Jamie's and promptly lost her breath.

He looked magnificent. She had managed to drum up a
newly fashioned plaid for him, and it was tossed over his shoulder and wrapped around him with casual grace. His long legs
were bare from knee to calf, the muscles standing out in crisp
definition. His boots had been cleaned for the occasion and
came close to gleaming. His long, bright sword hung at his
side.

But his face was what held her attention. His long dark hair
was pushed back off his shoulders and out of his eyes. His features were schooled into a grave mask, but his eyes simply
glowed with love. She knew, as she walked to meet him, that
the love in his eyes was for her alone. She had a hard time not
just throwing her arms around him and hugging him right there.

Jamie was having a hard time controlling the same urge.
Elizabeth was a vision. She wore the dress he'd had made for

her, a dress to go with the color of her eyes. He had imagined how it might look and what it might do to her eyes, but his poor imagination had in no way prepared him for the reality. Then again, perhaps it wasn't just the dress that made her so beautiful. It was the joy in her face. He was stunned by the love he saw in her eyes. He came close to looking behind him to see whom she was staring at.

He spoke his vows clearly and strongly, wanting there to be no doubt in Elizabeth's mind that he meant what he said. She repeated her vows in that husky, melodious voice that ever left him breathless. He slid her ring onto her finger and grinned at her surprise. The emerald had put a hefty hole in his personal cache of gold, but it was worth every bit of it to see her astonished look.

She slid his king's ransom onto his fourth finger, and he closed his eyes briefly, praying no one would kill him for it before he could bolt himself into his bedchamber with his wife. He gave her a wry smile and knew she had read his thoughts.

Then she was his. He took her into his arms and kissed her with all the gentleness in his soul. She was a slight thing, ethereal not only in body but in soul. He swore then that he would spend the rest of his life protecting that innocence of spirit.

The afternoon was spent in merrymaking, though the ale did not flow as freely as it might have otherwise. Guilbert McKinnon was in attendance, and Jamie didn't trust him further than he could throw him. What he wanted to do was throw Guilbert all the way to France.

Elizabeth danced and laughed and found herself even kissed a time or two until the overzealous revelers caught Jamie's watchful eye. His look of displeasure saved her from any more unwanted advances. Andrew MacAllister, who informed her personally that he was Jamie's favorite ally, ignored Jamie and danced with her until her feet were ready to fall off. He would only leave her be when Jamie removed him bodily to the side of the hall.

When evening shadows fell, she felt Jamie's hand under her elbow.

"Let us be away," he whispered. "Before some fool decides that standing us up would be fine sport."

"Pardon me?"

"The bedding ceremony. They strip the poor couple and then stand them up facing each other. 'Tis done in the event that taking a look at each other makes them believe marrying wasn't such a wise idea after all."

"You're kidding," she whispered in disbelief. "They don't really do that, do they?"

"Jamie," Andrew boomed, coming to clap a hand on Jamie's shoulder. "Time to go up, don't you think?"

"Cease before 'tis too late," Jamie rumbled, giving Andrew a dark look. "You'll regret it."

Andrew laughed. "You did the honors for me, my friend. I'm only returning the favor."

Elizabeth found herself swept up into Jamie's arms and carried up the stairs before she could protest, or before anyone could stop him. Only Ian tried and received a black eye as reward.

Jamie entered their room and set her on her feet. Elizabeth watched as he made a production of closing and bolting the door. Then he took an inordinate amount of time building up the fire, then checking the shutters. Finally he ran out of things to do and simply leaned against the mantel, frowning at her.

"You hardly ate anything today."

"I wasn't really hungry, Jamie."

He wiped his hands on his plaid and then clasped them behind his back. "I see."

She could hardly believe it, but he looked nervous as hell. She walked over to him slowly, afraid he just might run if she weren't careful.

"I'm not about to bolt," he grumbled.

She laughed and crossed the distance between them. Jamie gathered her close and sighed.

"I'm in my own bedchamber, *finally*, and I'm as uncomfortable as a horse with burrs under his saddle."

"That bad?" She smiled, pulling back to look at him.

"Aye, I feel as giddy as young Joshua sounds. And 'tis all

your doing. Never did I doubt my skill betwixt the sheets until I wed you. Now I haven't the faintest idea what I'm to do."

"Liar." She grinned.

"I am in earnest. Damnation, Elizabeth, I'm afraid I'll hurt you!"

"I'm sure you will," she said, "but I know you won't mean it."

"I cannot believe what a shambles my poor mind is in," he muttered darkly, staring into the fire. "A waif of a girl sneaks into my hall, then into my chamber, then into my heart. I can barely tell east from west anymore, and my men are no less confused." He glared at her. "You tell me what I'm to do with the mess that is now my life."

"I think, my lord," she smiled, "that you should deal with the shambles tomorrow. Your men are in fine shape. I worry even less about you, as you are just as grumbly and impossible as you were the first day we met. I'm quite sure that means you have survived my arrival into your life. Marriage will not worsen your humor."

"Ah, Elizabeth," he said, with a deep sigh, "you know my grumbles are nothing but show. I bless the day I came into my hall and saw you sitting in my chair. Though it galls me to steal words from Joshua's mouth, I cannot do anything but admit that before you came to me, my life was bleak and gloomy. Should I lose you now, my life would be hell."

"Oh, Jamie," she said, "you do have a way with words."

"Perhaps you should add minstrelsy to that long list of my finer qualities," he said.

"I'll do that."

He held her in silence for a very long time. Elizabeth shifted in his arms.

"Do you want to sit?"

"Nay."

She waited some more. Finally, she cleared her throat. "Anything else, then?" What she couldn't have done with a six-pack of Pepsi and a batch of chocolate chip cookie dough about then. It would have calmed her jitters.

Jamie pulled back and looked at her grimly. He cast a look

heavenward before he frowned again and reached for the belt
of her plaid.

He turned the bow into an impossible tangle. Soon he was
down on his knees, cursing as he struggled to get it undone.

Finally, he gritted his teeth and reached for his dirk.

Jamie stood at the foot of the bed and looked longingly at the
beautiful woman sleeping there. He still had trouble taking in
the fact that Elizabeth was his. And she loved him. It was such
an astonishing notion. Certainly his father had been fond of
him, but he doubted it had gone as far as love. Even if it had,
Douglas MacLeod had never been one to reveal his feelings too
openly.

But Elizabeth did. It continually brought Jamie up short
when he would catch her watching him with that gentle smile
playing around her mouth. And that was not the only way he
knew how deeply she cared for him. She laughed at his grumbles. She saved his pride when it needed saving. She even
thought his dimple a sexy thing indeed.

And she accepted him in her bed willingly even though he
knew he had hurt her. When he'd woken in the night to find
himself aching for her, she'd opened to him willingly, smiling
all the while. The only sign of her distress had been the tears
she hadn't known were trickling down her temples.

He walked over to the hearth and built up the fire, then
hunched down in front of it. What knew he of loving a wife?
All he knew was bedding the occasional whore. It was a completely impersonal act, easing himself when his needs became
too great. He knew nothing of soft touches. Even his journeys
to other keeps had taught him nothing. Women begged for a
night in his bed, but the couplings had always been fast and furious, with little or no talking before or after, much less any
touching. How was he to learn from that?

He sighed as he rose. Ian would know. Women flocked to
him like flies to manure. There had to be a reason for it. He
walked back over to the bed and looked down at the sleeping
form of his wife. Aye, pleasing her was worth the humiliation
of admitting his ignorance to his cousin.

Elizabeth stirred and opened her eyes. "Howdy, handsome," she smiled, holding up her arms.

He knelt down and drew her into his arms.

"Howdy to you too, beautiful one," he murmured into her hair.

"Jamie, where are you going? It's still dark."

He pressed a kiss against her hair and then laid her back. "I've a thing or two to inquire into, love, and then I'll return."

"Hurry back," she said. "I'll miss you."

"I'll miss you, too," he said gruffly. "I'll be so quick you'll never know I was away."

He practically fled from the room.

Angus was standing at the bottom of the steps, keeping watch. He smiled when he saw Jamie.

"You're up and about early, Jamie. All is well here. Go back to your bride."

"The lass is due a bit of rest since she got not a wink of sleep during the night," Jamie said with blustering arrogance. "Where's Ian?"

"Down in the village. He's been there all night celebrating your wedding."

"Hell," Jamie muttered under his breath as he threaded his way through the great hall, avoiding stepping on servants and guests who were sleeping off their merrymaking. He waved off several of his guardsmen who immediately rose and followed him. This sort of thing called for privacy.

It took him only minutes to find the cottage where Ian was currently making his bed. Jamie was aided greatly by the thunderous shouts of passion, from both Ian and his evening's entertainment. He rolled his eyes and leaned against the wall, determined to wait. After all, how long could Ian last? Shouting like that, surely he would be finished with his pleasure soon.

Jamie was sure an hour had passed before Ian fell silent. "Finally," he said, and began to pound on the door.

Ian himself opened the door, naked, holding his sword and a candle. His eyes widened in surprise. "Jamie, what is it?"

"I must speak with you immediately about a matter of the utmost importance," Jamie said gruffly. "In private."

Ian turned back to his companion and motioned toward the
door with his head. "Go bed down with your sister, Natalie."

The girl left only after trailing her hand suggestively down
Ian's chest.

"I'll be waitin'," she purred.

"No doubt," Ian said, giving her a gentle swat with the flat
of his sword. Once she was gone, he ushered Jamie in and
pulled up two chairs in front of the hearth. He tossed his plaid
around his shoulders and then went to fetch something to drink.

Jamie took his seat heavily and accepted a cup of ale. He
waited until Ian was seated and then waited some more. When
he'd gathered as much courage as he possessed, he looked at
Ian bleakly.

"I need help."

"Anything," Ian said, without hesitation.

"These words do not go further than this room," Jamie
growled. "I'm not opposed to cutting out your tongue to assure
myself of that."

"And lose all those glorious insults I plan to pay you over the
next few years? Don't be a fool."

Jamie relaxed a bit, knowing Ian would not betray his confidence. He downed the ale in one long pull and then tortured the
empty mug in his hands.

"Ian, I've bedded my share of whores and such, but . . ." he
sighed, "I fear that . . ." He sighed again and swore as he felt
himself coloring.

"Bedding a virgin is a tricky thing, my friend," Ian said gently.

"I hurt her badly, Ian," Jamie said, with a groan. "God knows
I didn't mean to and she didn't complain, but her tears were
proof enough of it. I know nothing of soft touches and things."

"But of course you do," Ian said matter-of-factly. "Jamie,
I've seen you soothe your horse after a fright, speaking to him
in whispers and patting him gently."

"My wife is not a horse!"

"Jamie, lad, I only sought to point out to you that you're not
beyond hope. Now, let me tell you of the last virgin I bedded.
Just in case you were wondering," he added, with a grin, "it was
the Fergusson's eldest daughter. 'Twas a fine night indeed."

"Tales of revenge will not help me, Ian."

"When I took her to my bed, she became a woman to be wooed with gentleness and care," Ian replied seriously. "I planned to ruin her virginity for revenge's sake, but once I had her alone, I loved her as sweetly and as tenderly as I knew how. Now, be you silent and listen."

Jamie walked back to the keep with an embarrassed grin on his face. Ian had no shame and divulged the most intimate of details as calmly and bluntly as if he discussed fodder for the horses. Jamie knew he'd done nothing but blush furiously for the past hour or two, but 'twas well worth it. Perhaps he would still be a bit awkward at first, but his patience was sure to be rewarded. Elizabeth's pleasure was not something he would give up on easily.

He strolled into the kitchen and lifted a loaf of fresh-baked bread right from under Hugh's nose and then snatched a slab of cheese and a handful of small apples.

"Wine," he barked, and Hugh fled to the larder. Jamie smiled pleasantly at his cook as he took the bottle from him. "The bread smells wonderful," he said, giving Hugh the first compliment the man had ever had from his lips. "See that the guests are fed well today, Hugh. I've other things to attend to. And send up water for a bath as quick as may be."

"Aye, Jamie," Hugh squeaked.

Jamie whistled as he picked his way over his guests. Andrew shot him a glare from one open eye.

"Do you have to be so bloody cheerful?" he growled.

" 'Tis the morn after my wedding. I should be complaining already? See to the keep for a day or two, will you, Andy? There's a good lad."

He smiled pleasantly at Andrew's hearty curses and continued blithely on his way, thinking of no one but the lovely woman in his bed who was about to be loved until she fainted.

Chapter 20

ELIZABETH WOKE TO the sound of the door closing softly. Jamie came in, carrying what looked to be goods for a picnic. She sat up, holding the sheet to her chin, and smiled at him.

"Breakfast?"

"Aye. I don't know about you, but I'm starving. Come and sit with me by the warm fire."

She didn't have to hear that twice. Sleeping with Jamie's warmth had made her forget how she usually had to turn up the electric blanket to high. She looked around, fully intending to then find the warmest of Jamie's plaids and wrap it around her.

Jamie beat her to it. He stripped off his plaid and draped it around her shoulders. He busied himself with the fire until it was crackling. Elizabeth had barely gotten her toes warm when a knock sounded on the door. Jamie opened it and ushered in a handful of his men bearing a tub and buckets. The tub was filled with steaming water and the buckets left near the hearth. Jamie shut the door, bolted it and then came to stand before her.

"Your bath, my lady."

"This is very nice of you." A bath was just the thing to soothe her jumpy nerves.

He held out his hand, waiting.

Elizabeth looked at him. "What?"

"Your bath grows cold."

She frowned. "Then leave so I can take it."

He only smiled. "I think not."

"You think not?" she echoed. "Jamie, you're not going to watch me take a bath."

He looked at her for a moment or two in silence, then sighed and turned his back to her. "Very well, then. But make haste, Elizabeth."

Elizabeth gave in. She had her doubts Jamie would leave, but at least he had turned around. She dropped his plaid and stepped into the tub. The water was deliciously warm, and she sank down into it with a heartfelt groan. Jamie knelt beside the tub and rolled up his sleeves.

"What are you doing?" she squeaked.

"I am preparing to bathe you."

"You're what?" she exclaimed, realizing she was very close to shouting. Heaven help her, she was powerless to do anything else. Making love was one thing; having her husband give her a bath in broad daylight was another thing entirely.

"I'm going to bathe you. 'Tis easily done."

She crossed her arms over her chest. "Forget it. I can take my own bath. Do something else. Go sharpen your sword. And wipe that infuriating grin off your face."

Jamie, of course, ignored her. He took her hand and pressed her palm against his mouth. "I promise 'twill be enjoyable. Relax and let me do this thing." He opened his mouth and touched the palm of her hand with his tongue.

"What in the world are you doing?" she breathed, feeling a tingle run up her arm and then down her spine.

"Nothing," he said innocently. "Close your eyes and relax."

His tongue made slow, lazy circles on her skin while his thumb caressed the inside of her wrist. Elizabeth wanted to fight him. She nodded to herself over that one. Having him bathe her was just plain out of the question. But somehow she just couldn't manage to pull her hand away. Or keep her eyes open. She leaned her head back against the tub and surrendered.

"You know, I have never served anyone before," he murmured.

Elizabeth forced herself to hang on to rational thought, and it was an effort. Just what had turned Jamie into such a seducer? Their wedding night hadn't been much to shout about. She had contented herself with thinking that as time went on she would learn to relax, and Jamie would learn to slow down.

It looked like the latter was going to happen sooner than she had thought.

Jamie was positively lingering over her skin. And then, far too soon, his mouth left her hand. She opened her eyes to protest this turn of events only to find him smiling arrogantly.

"You have another hand yet to be seen to, wife."

She blushed.

"You know," he said conversationally, "I intended to bathe you simply for your pleasure, but now I find it pleases me as well." He slid his fingers slowly up her arm. "Your skin is very soft."

He traced her collarbone slowly, then cupped her chin in his hand and turned her face to his. Elizabeth closed her eyes as he leaned closer and covered her mouth with his. Heat rushed through her. He kissed her until she thought she just might pass out.

Then he was gone.

She managed to force her eyelids open to look at him. He was wearing a self-satisfied smirk.

"Lean up for a minute, Elizabeth," he said, cheerfully, "and I'll wash your back."

Elizabeth wanted to smack him. She gave him a weak glare and was rewarded with another grin before he moved behind the tub.

She leaned forward and rested her chin on her bent knees, contemplating how best to get hold of his mouth again without seeming too obvious. Goodness, but bathing seemed to bring out the best in her husband.

A tingle went down her spine at the feel of Jamie's fingers sliding under her hair and lifting it forward over her shoulder. She sighed in pleasure as he ran the soap over her back and then groaned as he began to gently massage her muscles.

"Too hard?" he asked, stopping instantly.

"Perfect," she groaned. "Jamie, you're a master."

He was. He seemed to be able to search out each little bit of tension and convince it to disappear. By the time he cupped the water in his hands and used it to rinse off the soap, she was half asleep. She allowed him to pull her back against the tub and then she closed her eyes, certain that no woman had ever felt such bliss even after an afternoon in a fancy New York salon.

"Your leg, my lady," he said, putting his hand on her knee.

"You forgot my other arm," she murmured. "And my hand."

"I will get there in my own good time," he assured her.

"How did you learn how to do this?" she asked, opening one eye and looking at him.

"Bathe you? I do it myself often."

"But not like this."

He gave her a half smile that was part smugness and part mystery. "There are things a man knows from the cradle, and one of them is how to please the woman he loves. Well, at least a little about it," he added hastily. He held out his hand. "Other leg."

Elizabeth leaned back, closed her eyes and enjoyed the feeling of his hands on her legs. His touch was perfect. And then he tucked her leg back into the tub. A tingle went down her spine as he held out his hand.

"Your other hand, wife," he said in a silky voice.

She gave it to him, already anticipating what he would do. She wasn't disappointed in the least. There was hardly an inch of her hand that he didn't either tease with his tongue or nip at softly with his teeth. She shivered as his lips trailed up the inside of her arm and to the crook of her elbow.

By the time his mouth had traveled over her shoulder and up her neck, it was all Elizabeth could do not to beg him to kiss her. He seemed to read her mind, for his mouth closed over hers just as she started to speak. He slid one hand under her hair and held her head up while he plundered her mouth.

He slid his hand down over her ribs, making her muscles jump of their own accord. He trailed his fingers over her hipbone and frowned. "You're too frail. 'Tis high time we put meat on your bones."

Now, that was a compliment she couldn't let go unnoticed. She pulled his head to hers and kissed him passionately, trying to show him how much his tender bathing had pleased her and how grateful she was he didn't think she was pudgy. Every twentieth-century woman should have had a fourteenth-century husband who thought ten pounds overweight to be a bit "too frail" for his taste.

"Put your arms around me," he whispered hoarsely, slipping his arm underneath her back and pulling her half out of the tub against him.

She clung to him, meeting his searching mouth with a passion of her own. The longer he kissed her, the more she thought she'd die if he stopped. Jamie held her tightly against him, the strength of his embrace robbing her of breath.

Just when she thought she couldn't bear the heat he stirred in her any longer, he released her. Elizabeth collapsed back against the side of the wooden tub. She smiled up at Jamie weakly.

"Wow," she breathed.

She wasn't sure, but she thought he might be blushing. She angled her head to get a better look, but he ducked his head.

"Sit still," he mumbled. "Your water grows cold, and I've still to wash your hair."

"Is the water cold? I hadn't noticed."

Yes, that was definitely a blush. A fiery one, from what she could tell. She smiled to herself and let him have at her hair. By the time he had finished, she barely had the strength to stand up and let him dry her off. And when he tucked her into the chair next to the fire so he could take his own bath, she closed her eyes and shivered. Jamie had somehow acquired patience that morning.

And what breathtaking patience it was.

Jamie munched contentedly on a piece of soft bread as he watched Elizabeth sit facing him on the plaid with her hair thrown over her head. The soft light of the fire played over the dark strands of her hair, bringing out deep red scattered here and there. He reached out and fingered a drying lock, marveling at its softness.

Elizabeth peeked at him from under her masses of hair. "Something wrong?"

He smiled. "Just making sure it was real."

She laughed, a sound that never ceased to charm him. She winked at him before she hid again and continued to separate the strands with her fingers to encourage them to hasten their drying.

Jamie stopped his hand on its way to his mouth, realizing that he had just about consumed the whole of their meal. But how could he apologize? It took strength to love a woman, and he had no intentions of feeling faint when the moment of truth arrived. He would wait until Elizabeth asked for him, but he felt sure she would soon enough. She had reacted very well to his kissing before. And what pleasure he would give to her when he loved her fully!

Ah, blushes, he noted as she flipped her hair back over her head and looked anywhere but in his eyes.

"Come sit closer," he said smoothly, bending his head to catch her downcast eyes. "You are too far away from the fire, love."

The small distance she moved was not measurable by any of his methods. He pushed aside the food and pulled her onto his lap.

"Did I please you?" He gestured toward where the tub had been an hour before.

She wrapped her arms around his neck and pressed her face into his hair, denying him the opportunity to look at her expression.

"Oh, Jamie," she said, in that tone of voice that ever left him weak in the knees.

Och, the smugness that spread itself over his face. He wondered if he'd ever be able to wipe the expression off. Aye, she'd been pleased. His sweet, dreamy wife had found his kisses beautiful. Already he had been repaid for his embarrassing talk with Ian.

He nuzzled her neck, smiling at the giggles that escaped her lips. She didn't know him well enough to know that he was even more ticklish than she. He had the feeling he'd regret it if she ever learned of his weakness.

"You must be hungry," he whispered. "Eat your supper and then perhaps we'll have a nap here in front of the fire."

He put her off his lap and then watched her as she ate. Her fingers were long and slender. The longer he watched her, the more he began to long for the feel of those slender hands on his body. How would it feel to be touched by a woman? How would it feel to be lingered over and caressed? The thought of it sent fire rushing to his cheeks.

He tugged on his tunic, billowing it out to hide just how badly he wanted her. Aye, 'twas the thought of her loving him that set him so aflame. Perhaps once he had learned to love her well, she would wish to touch him also. He could imagine worse ways to spend the night than at the mercy of his beautiful wife. Would she run her fingers lightly over his chest, or would she rub his muscles with strength? Would his body frighten her? He knew the scars caused her distress, but he had come to believe that it was because she feared for his skin. Would she find the rest of his body pleasing to her eye and hand?

He surreptitiously took a sniff near his underarm. Nay, there was no odor there to offend. He'd bathed after her, and the scent of her rose soap still lingered on his skin. He rubbed his hand over his chest, pretending to scratch. Aye, the muscles were firm. His belly was flat. There was no fat to spare on his work-hardened frame. But would it please her? Had the men of her day been soft and white? Unmarked, unscarred? Perhaps she only found pleasing a man she could sink into like a soft pillow.

"Jamie, what's wrong?"

Her soft voice broke through his reverie. "Nothing," he said curtly, still smarting from the sting of his thoughts.

Her look of surprise annoyed him. She obviously had no idea what she'd done to irritate him, and that irritated him further. Had she no concept of how a man's mind worked?

"Tell me of Stanley's form," he demanded.

"Excuse me?" she said, looking a bit dazed. "Where in the world did that come from?"

"His form," Jamie growled. "Was he fair to look upon? Tall? Strong?"

She laughed. "Jamie, he was a wimp."

He softened his frown only enough to raise one eyebrow.

"Wimp? What is *wimp*?" He wasn't sure if her grin was because she was laughing at him or with him.

"A wimp is a person who is sort of a weak, cowardly type. I told you before that Stanley meant nothing to me. But if you insist on a description, I'll give it to you. He was only a bit taller than I am, with watery blue eyes and not much hair left on top of his head."

Jamie dragged his hand through his hair before he could stop himself. Aye, a thick thatch still grew there. It would be a cold day in hell when the top of his head glinted in the sun like a polished shield.

"And," she continued, "he was soft and pampered. In fact, his hands were softer than mine." She turned his palm over and traced the calluses there. "He didn't have strong hands like yours." She smiled up at him. "You have beautiful hands, Jamie."

He cleared his throat. "They're mightily scarred."

"They're hands of a man who is not afraid to fight to protect what is his. And your hands can be very gentle, despite their strength. I've seen the way you tuck Megan in at night. And the way you touch me," she added, color leaping to her cheeks.

He couldn't hear that kind of confession enough to suit him.

"Then Stanley's softness did not catch your eye? Not entirely?"

She laughed, then lunged at him and tipped him back onto his plaid. Had he seen the movement coming, he might have been able to protect his dignity. As it was, he was pinned to the floor with his laughing wife sprawled on top of him before he could expel a breath to curse her. Then, before the frown even reached his brow, he realized he was just exactly where he wanted to be. But he frowned anyway as he put his hands behind his head. There was no use in letting her think she had the upper hand.

"You, my lord, are fishing."

"Fishing?"

"For compliments," she grinned.

"I am not," he retorted hotly.

She propped herself up on her elbows and continued to grin

at him. "Don't I tell you often enough what a handsome man you are?"

"Not often enough to suit me," he muttered darkly. She was already laughing at him. What use was there in salvaging the rest of his pride?

"Oh, Jamie, you've such a gentle heart."

"Remove yourself," he said gruffly. "Now."

She smiled. "Much as I think the floor would be softer than your rock-hard chest, I prefer it where I am. You make a most comfortable resting place."

It was quite by accident that her hands grazed his sides, but when she felt him jump, she took full advantage of the fact that his hands were behind his head. His bellow of miserable laughter drew forth giggles from his lady. When he finally managed to dislodge her fingers from his armpits, he whipped her over onto her back so fast, she lost her breath. He straddled her hips and took both her hands in one of his. With a slow, deliberate motion, he pinned her hands over her head.

"Jamie, please," she laughed.

"Fishing, Lady MacLeod?" he said menacingly, beginning to count her ribs. "You think me so daft as to fish for compliments?"

"I compliment you all the time!" she shouted, trying to catch her breath, laugh and squirm away from him all at the same time.

Her laughter was contagious, and he found himself laughing just because she was. And then he laughed at the curses she managed to hurl at him when she could catch her breath. When she looked to be fair ready to faint, he took pity on her and simply grinned down at her. Who would have thought he would be spending the morn after his wedding tickling his wife on his plaid and actually enjoying it? He thought to comment on that, but the feel of her body underneath his distracted him. He slowly stretched out on top of her, putting his legs on either side of hers and taking as much weight as he could on his knees and elbows.

"Am I crushing you?"

"No," she said, her voice suddenly gone hoarse.

"Frightening you?"

"No, my laird."

He lowered his head and brushed her lips with his. Ah, how sweetly she opened her mouth to him, already anticipating his desire to taste her.

But he had no intentions of moving so quickly. He forced himself to kiss her slowly, leisurely, as if he had all the time in the world. She was impatient, though, and tried to kiss him more passionately. Jamie hurriedly bent his head to kiss her neck, only intending to hide his smile. He was doing something right. Ian had told him Elizabeth's responses would guide him.

"Jamie . . ."

He returned to her mouth and surrendered to her, kissing her deeply. He groaned at the flash of desire that surged through him. It burned through his body like bad whiskey burns the throat. He suppressed the urge to move against her the way he wanted to.

The heat of her bare skin caught his attention and, without moving, he noted that the plaid she had wrapped around her like a blanket had parted quite nicely, leaving a good portion of her uncovered. He moved off her to take his weight on his side. His tunic had ridden up over his hip, but he wouldn't have noticed had his wife not been tugging at the material. He looked at her in surprise.

"Take this off," she said softly. "I mean, if you want . . ."

He yanked the garment over his head, then pulled Elizabeth back into his arms. He groaned as she slid her hands up into his hair and dragged her fingers through his long locks. Pleasure was indeed a two-edged sword. He could not give without having it back in like measure.

It seemed he had only begun to kiss her again in earnest, when she put her arms around his neck.

"Take me to bed, Jamie," she whispered. "Take me to bed because I think I just might faint the next time you touch me."

He didn't have to hear that twice. He hauled her up into his arms and stalked across the chamber to his bed. He laid her down gently and then followed her. He knew he was crushing her beneath him, but she seemed not to care and, to be honest, he just couldn't bring himself to do anything about it. She had welcomed his kiss, and now she would welcome the rest of him. He knew because she was opening to him, beckoning to him to take her.

And so he did. His only regret was that it did not last a lifetime. It was like nothing he'd ever experienced before. He almost drowned in the pleasure that washed over him again and again.

He came to himself to find he was crushing her in an embrace that most likely had broken half her ribs. She was smoothing his hair back from his face. He closed his eyes and felt like he'd died and gone to heaven.

"Oh, Beth," he said softly, pressing his face against her neck. "My sweet, bonny Beth."

Jamie couldn't find the words to express what he'd felt or the joy he now knew in having loved his wife well. And something more had happened that morning, but he wasn't sure what it was. Something inside him had changed somehow, leaving him softer perhaps. Or more arrogant, he thought with a grin. Whatever it was, 'twas Elizabeth's doing, and he fully intended to blame her for whatever change she'd wrought.

"Elizabeth," he murmured into her hair.

"Yes, Jamie."

He cleared his throat. "I . . . I love you."

She tightened her arms around him. "I love you too," she whispered.

He remained motionless for some time, savoring not only the deed but the words that had followed. Finally, he pulled away from her. She put her hand to her ear.

"What?" he asked.

"I'm deaf," she grumbled.

He looked at her in puzzlement. "And how is that?"

"Your shouts of passion, you bellowing bear," she said, with a sudden grin.

He blushed. Damn her, she could still make him blush. He rolled from the bed and pulled up the blanket to cover her. She was grinning madly, and he contemplated the merits of either wringing her neck or merely covering her face with a pillow. Instead, he knelt down at the bedside and leaned over to kiss her softly.

"You are very pleased with me," he stated.

"Very," she agreed, reaching up to push his hair out of his eyes. She looked him full in the face. "Jamie," she began, shaking her head in wonder, "I just don't know what to say. Maybe something along the lines of 'I don't think there will be enough nights in my lifetime for you to love me as often as I'd like.'" She stopped suddenly and blushed. "Put bluntly, that is."

His chest puffed out of its own accord. The woman was going to make him absolutely impossible to live with if she kept up her sweet compliments. He grinned arrogantly.

"Then we'll just have to make good use of the daytime, my love."

He rose and ambled over to the fire, grinning until his face ached. It was exceedingly hard to not let fly a shout just to rid himself of the excess of pride that gathered in his body.

Aye, 'twas a fine morn indeed on MacLeod soil.

Chapter 21

ELIZABETH SAT IN the large chair in front of the hearth in Jamie's thinking room and listened with only half an ear to Megan, who was relating the events of the past few days. They were events Elizabeth had missed out on as she had been held captive in her husband's chamber, slave to his every whim. She smiled at the memory of his expression when she'd accused him of it. Then she blushed at the memory of what he'd done after that.

She leaned her head back and smiled into the fire. It had been four days of pure bliss. They'd left their room only to use the closet or sneak up to walk on the battlements. She'd had Jamie completely to herself. And how he'd loved her! It made her knees weak just thinking about it. And oh, was he ever arrogant about it all. It never ceased to tickle her when he would boast of his skill. She was left with no choice but to heartily agree with him.

"Beth, you aren't listening," Megan chided.

Elizabeth smiled down at the girl sitting on the stool in front of her. "Sorry, honey. You were talking about our book?"

Megan sighed the sigh of a teenager who was struggling to be patient with her less-than-intelligent elders. "We finished talking about that a long time ago. I was asking you if I could call you 'Mother.' "

For the first time Elizabeth noticed the bright blush staining Megan's cheeks. She was so touched by the question that tears sprang to her eyes. She gathered Megan close and pressed a gentle kiss to her forehead.

"Of course you can, sweetheart. I'd love to have you as a daughter."

Megan burst into tears and clung to her. "I was so afraid you'd say me nay."

"My sweet Megan, why would I say no?"

Jamie entered the chamber just as Megan's tears had subsided to mere sniffles. He cocked one eyebrow up in question and Elizabeth smiled. He walked across the room, hauled Megan to her feet, then bent and gently brushed away her tears with his thumb.

"What's this?" he asked gruffly. "Why these tears, imp? Don't you know the tale of the girl who cried so much that her tears filled her chamber and floated away all her furniture?"

Megan put her arms around Jamie's waist. "Elizabeth said I could call her Mother. I'm just happy."

"Hrumph," Jamie said, frowning thoughtfully. "I see." He stroked his chin with his free hand and looked off into space. "And if you chose her for your mother, it means that you must needs also name a sire. Is that not so?"

Elizabeth watched the girl watch Jamie miserably, too afraid to voice her fragile hope. Elizabeth prayed Jamie would choose his words well. When she saw him looking around for a chair, she stood up and motioned for him to sit.

Jamie sat in the chair and snuggled Megan close in his arms. "Let us speak awhile of this sire you must choose. He should be strong, aye?"

Megan nodded.

"Perhaps laird of a powerful clan," Jamie added. "Of course he must be well respected so as to have his pick of husbands for you. Although he could no doubt find you a man of his own house to wed. A lad who perhaps resembles him just a bit."

"Think you?" Megan asked shyly.

Jamie grunted. "We'll see what the lad makes of himself. I daresay this sire of yours will be choosy about whom he allows to have you. Have you any other preferences about your father?

He perhaps should be gruff and grumbly, and certainly he should beat you regularly to keep you obedient. And of course, he will expect you to call him Papa and fetch him ale when he bellows for it." He drummed his fingers on the arm of the chair. "I daresay he would expect you to continue learning your letters and snatching the occasional hour to draw, or however it is you call that infernal scratching I hear in your chamber at all hours." He looked at her arrogantly. "All in all, I would say I am your best choice. You agree, of course."

Jamie squeaked involuntarily as Megan threw her other arm around him and hugged him with all her might. Elizabeth smiled. Jamie was such a marshmallow.

"I love you, Jamie," Megan said, her voice quavering.

"Papa," Jamie corrected.

"Papa," Megan said reverently, laying her head against his shoulder. She smiled at Elizabeth. "Isn't this great?"

Elizabeth laughed and reached out to tug on Megan's dress. "Yes, sweetheart, it is."

"Might we show him the book now?" Megan asked eagerly.

Elizabeth nodded and smiled at Jamie as Megan scrambled off his lap. "I love you," she mouthed to him.

He tried to look stern but failed miserably. Elizabeth knew Megan's request had touched him more than he cared to admit. Jamie oohed and aahed over the book, and it was easy to see his admiration was genuine. Then he made Megan lock it up in the trunk and showed her where the key was hidden. After one last great hug, he issued his first command as her father and bade her leave him in peace. Megan departed joyfully after several hugs and kisses from each newly acquired parent.

Once she was gone, Jamie pulled Elizabeth onto his lap.

"Howdy, wife," he smiled. "I've missed you this morning. Did my kiss good-bye leave anything to be desired?"

His kiss good-bye was more aptly described as a passionate joining that left her breathless for a good hour after he'd donned his clothes and strutted from the room.

"Yes, it did," she said solemnly.

He was instantly offended. "What?"

"Just more of the same," she murmured as she pressed her lips against his ear.

His arrogant grunt left her grinning. Good heavens, what an ego her laird had.

"I actually came to fetch you for a purpose other than ravaging your sweet body."

She pulled back and looked at him. "And that was?"

"I have decided you must learn to defend yourself." His expression sobered. "I have wrestled with this decision long, and much as it grieves me to force this loss of innocence on you, I think it necessary. I have planned that you shall never be without men around you, but ofttimes plans go awry, and I will not leave you defenseless."

"Jamie, I'm not helpless," she said gently. "I grew up with five brothers, remember?"

"Did they ever come at you with a dirk? Or a sword?"

She sighed. "You know they didn't."

"Then perhaps your world is a less violent one than mine. But, as these are the times you must endure for my sake, ours are the dangers you must also learn to face. I will not have you at the mercy of someone you could escape if you but had the knowledge. We will take what you learned from your brothers and improve on it." He smiled sadly. "You've no idea how this grieves me, Elizabeth. If there were any other way . . ."

Elizabeth knew she would have been a fool to disagree. Jamie's world was indeed far different from hers.

"All right," she sighed. "What do you want me to do?"

"Dress in the warm woolen leggings and tunic you'll find on our bed. And wear your boots. I will await you below."

A half hour later she found herself facing Ian in the garden, holding a knife in her hand and looking at the dagger in his. What she wanted to do was walk away. The expression of determination on Jamie's face kept her where she was.

After what seemed to her hours of learning to avoid Ian's thrusts, she'd had enough. She could defend herself well enough, but she couldn't for the life of her get that blade out of Ian's hand. Finally, his mocking smile made her so mad that she came at him with every trick she'd learned in the mugging class she'd taken. It wasn't pretty fighting, it was street fighting, and Ian had no idea how to respond. Before he knew it, he was flat on his back with her knee jammed uncomfortably in his groin and her fingers pressing against the inside corners of his eyes.

"You honorless wench!" Ian gasped. "Did no one teach you there are lines which are not crossed?"

She rolled off him and sat cross-legged on the ground, looking up at Jamie wearily. "I can't take anymore today. Please, Jamie."

Jamie's face was expressionless. "Not a bad showing. We'll work again tomorrow."

"Not a bad showing?" Ian echoed, thoroughly offended. "I never receive such flowery praise." He sat up and glared at Elizabeth. "I let him abuse my fine form each day just for sport, and I don't even have so much as a thank-you from him."

Elizabeth smiled wearily. "I think he loves me, Ian."

"And I think you've bewitched him," a caustic voice said from behind Jamie.

Elizabeth looked up and met Guilbert McKinnon's hard eyes. There was more in them than hatred; there was lust. Her skin crawled. It was too bad all the wedding guests hadn't gone home already. Seeing Guilbert McKinnon again was something Elizabeth could have done without.

Ian jumped to his feet and hauled Elizabeth up behind him, shielding her. She peeked around his beefy arm and prayed she wouldn't see swords drawn. She clutched at Ian's plaid to hold herself upright when she saw the look on Jamie's face.

"I assume that was a poor jest," Jamie said calmly, his tone soft and pleasant.

"It's the plain truth," Guilbert snarled. "She's a witch, MacLeod, and I intend to see her burned."

Jamie's change of expression was frightening in its swiftness. He spat at the McKinnon's feet.

"No man will speak of me and mine thusly and escape unscathed."

Elizabeth noticed that Guilbert's brother, Richard, was standing a pace or two behind him, along with a dozen McKinnon clansmen. She saw something out of the corner of her eye and realized that the rest of the garden had suddenly become full of MacLeod kinsmen, who all wore the same looks of fury their laird did.

The sharp sound of metal on metal snapped her eyes forward.

"No," she breathed, but Ian pushed her back before she could take even half a step forward.

"Be still," he hissed. "You will hinder him if he must fret over you. Instead, watch the finest warrior in the Highlands best the man who accused you and therefore the rest of your clan unjustly. Stand proudly, Elizabeth, and remember whose wife you are."

It was just so primitive. But she stiffened her spine and forced herself to maintain her composure. What else could she do? She had no hope of stopping whatever was about to happen. All she could do was pray, and she did that fervently.

She didn't want to watch, but she couldn't help herself. Ian wouldn't allow her to stand next to him, so she looked around him as best she could. She tried not to wince every time Jamie's and Guilbert's swords would meet with such a loud clang.

Never had she seen such a look of fury on Jamie's face. It was no wonder there wasn't a man within miles who didn't fear him. She would have been blubbering at just his expression.

Either the McKinnon was braver or more stupid than she because he didn't back down at all. He was just as angry as Jamie, but his anger made him sloppy. Jamie's strokes were clean and controlled; Guilbert's were wild and random.

Guilbert's sword went flying suddenly. She gasped as she saw that several of Guilbert's fingers followed it. Guilbert clutched his hand to his middle and came at Jamie with a knife in his left hand. With a casual gesture, Jamie tossed his sword to Ian, who caught it just as casually. The McKinnon was soon relieved of his knife, and Jamie tossed it hilt first to Guilbert's brother, giving Richard a look that made him pale. It was unfortunate that the sensible one of the family was not in charge.

Guilbert's bellow of rage made her jump and she watched, still horrified, as he charged her husband. Jamie sidestepped him easily, and Guilbert went sprawling. He rose as Jamie stood there with his arms folded across his chest. Jamie waited patiently until Guilbert charged him again before he lashed out viciously with his fist and caught Guilbert full in the face.

Elizabeth stopped keeping track of the blows exchanged

after that. All she knew was Guilbert was taking probably the worst beating of his life, and she didn't feel sorry for him in the least. Jamie beat him until his own hands were raw and bloody. When Guilbert was nothing more than a barely breathing heap at his feet, Jamie turned to Richard.

"Take him off my land. We are allies no longer."

Richard stood his ground. "I do not share my brother's opinions, Jamie. You know that."

"While he lives, you certainly do," Jamie shot back. "And while he lives, any McKinnon who sets foot on MacLeod soil will be sent back to your hall in pieces. Your brother is the one in league with the Devil, not me or mine. We'll speak of an end to this feud your laird's begun when the day comes that he's dead and buried."

Richard could say nothing else. His men gathered up Guilbert's sword, Guilbert's severed fingers and his bruised body. Jamie watched dispassionately as they left the garden. MacLeod men immediately followed to see them to the border.

The spell was broken. Elizabeth shoved Ian aside and threw herself at her bloody warrior.

He was still and unyielding for only a small moment. Then he wrapped his arms around her and held her tightly.

"Do you now see why a man is a fool to speak against me?"

She nodded, her head jerking spasmodically. "I do." She struggled to keep her teeth from chattering. "I'm sorry I forced you to do that."

He pushed her away. "I defend what is mine."

She'd never seen him in such a harsh mood before and hardly knew how to handle him. Well, praise couldn't go wrong. And she was awed by the fact that he had taken his life in his hands to defend her. Stanley would have handed her over to Guilbert without a second thought.

She took a courageous step forward and put her hands on his chest, looking up into his fury-hardened face unflinchingly.

"Forgive my words," she said quietly. "I said something I didn't mean because I was overcome. You risked your life to defend me, Jamie, and that is something no one has ever done for me. You were magnificent. The McKinnon was a fool to think to raise his sword against you."

Jamie grunted and put his bloody arms back around her. "Now you begin to speak as a laird's wife should." He patted her back in the unconsciously bone-crushing way he had. "Go call me a bath. There are well-deserved compliments I would hear from your lips before evening falls."

She nodded and pulled away, more than willing to think up a hundred compliments to shower on him before the afternoon was gone. Malcolm and another of his mates fell in on either side of her as she walked back to the house.

"He's very skilled," Malcolm said in a hushed voice.

Elizabeth looked up at him haughtily. "He's the MacLeod, Malcolm," she said, feeling every inch the proud Highlander wife. "You actually think he would be anything less than invincible?"

"Nay, my lady. There's none to equal him, to be sure."

Elizabeth smiled to herself. She was beginning to sound just like Jamie, and somehow that thought made her only stand up straighter and frown a bit, just to make sure Malcolm took her seriously.

There was only one thing that nagged at the edges of her mind, and that was what Guilbert McKinnon would do when he recovered from what Jamie had done to him. There would be retaliation, of that she was certain. She had a hunch the retaliation would be directed solely at Jamie. Jamie was impossibly skilled with a sword, but he didn't have eyes in the back of his head. Maybe learning to use a sword and a knife would be worth the effort after all. If nothing else, she could defend his back until he could turn and do it himself.

She shook aside her thoughts and strode purposefully back to the house. Her laird wanted a bath, and damn Hugh if he didn't provide one on the double. Her frown was intimidating and her bearing regal. Her father would have been proud.

A month after throwing a very quiet Guilbert McKinnon off his land, Jamie sat in his thinking chamber, thinking. Megan's quarters had been completed the week before, and he found he missed her popping in and out of the chamber for this item or that. The little imp had instigated herself in his heart just as firmly as Elizabeth had. He was powerless against the combined force of their sweetness.

Not that he even pretended to fight it anymore. He grumbled at Megan just to hear her laugh. She was an angelic girl, needing little reprimanding to keep her obedient. A quiet word spoken was all it took to make her gravely regret whatever action had displeased him, but he spoke those quiet words infrequently.

As for Elizabeth, he only grumbled at her to remind her who was laird. That, and to watch her grin behind his back. She was surely convinced she had him tamed. Perhaps he was. He found himself still doing ridiculous things to please her. But he complained loudly about each fistful of flowers he fetched her, each bolt of cloth he just happened to have come across, each purposeless walk and ride he took her on just to have her close. She ignored his complaints and accepted each of his gestures with the same surprised, delighted, awed expression she had worn the first time he had shoved a fistful of weeds at her.

Of course, it was not all peace and tranquility. Just the night before, she had thrown his pillow into the corridor, then his blanket, finishing her tirade by ordering him out of his own bedchamber. Not even attempted kisses had sweetened her humor. Had he not felt so guilty about shouting at her for almost no reason, he wouldn't have gone. But he went. And he sat outside the door and sang almost tuneless melodies far into the night. Joshua had soon taken pity on him and joined him on the top step, playing his lute just loudly enough to keep Jamie on key.

Sometime during the second watch, Elizabeth had given in. She'd opened the door and listened to his apology, then graciously allowed him back to his own bed. He'd loved her sweetly, just to show he held nothing against her. She accepted his loving just as graciously.

Not to say she was never in the wrong. Though he might have had a ready temper, hers was just as ready and just as hot. Perhaps it wasn't such a bad thing. Apologies from either side usually led to their chamber and, once there, the bed was only a step or two away. He smiled. It was a fitting way to restore the peace between them, and he hoped it would always be so.

He folded his hands under his chin and stared at the wall, letting his thoughts flow freely through his mind. Immediately an image of the McKinnon assailed him, but he pushed it aside. What was done was done. When Guilbert was able to crawl from his bed, there would be retaliation, but Jamie seriously doubted that Guilbert would find many of his kinsmen willing to forfeit their lives for their laird's foolish accusations. Nevertheless, the man bore watching.

What caught and held Jamie's attention was the things he had read in Elizabeth's daybook, or whatever it was she named it. It told of her strange journey and of the time spent in his house. Her descriptions of him had been at once flattering and humiliating. Did he strut about so arrogantly? He suspected he did, but by now it was a habit hopelessly ingrained in him.

Her descriptions of her time intrigued him greatly. She knew much of the happenings of the past, and he had quizzed her thoroughly on her knowledge of Scotland. A pity she had somehow lost the memory of the words she had read about his clan and the other Highlanders of his day. He knew she wasn't lying. She was just as puzzled by it as he.

Perhaps it was just as well. Had he possessed knowledge of the future, it no doubt would have led to grief somehow or another. But it would have been a fine thing to have wind beforehand of the wars to befall his kin. Or a disaster to befall his love.

But how could that be? How could men of the future have written about Elizabeth when she was from their own time? The very effort of trying to reweave the strands of time gave him a sharp pain in the head and made the room begin to spin. Aye, perhaps there were mysteries better left alone.

A pity, though. Knowing the future would have been a fine thing indeed.

Chapter 22

ELIZABETH WOKE TO a pounding on the door. She recognized that sort of frantic, thugs-are-at-the-gate type of pounding, and she groaned. The peace of the past two months had been far too enjoyable, and she'd known it couldn't last.

Jamie was out of bed and dressed before she even managed to unstick her eyelids from each other. She yanked a shift down over her head and crawled out of bed, pulling a blanket around her as a robe. Angus was at the door, sweating.

"They killed the lookouts," he panted, "but they're drawing back at our show of force."

"Who?" Jamie demanded harshly, tucking various weapons into his boots and belt.

"Fergussons. I could have sworn I marked several of the McKinnon's men in the company, but I've been wrong before."

"Not since I've known you," Jamie retorted. "See to rousing the men. We'll kill every last Fergusson we find on our land. I want the McKinnons taken alive."

Elizabeth swallowed, a completely futile effort, as her mouth was dry as cotton. Man, there was just no getting used to this. No matter how often it happened, she knew she would never accustom herself to the brain-numbing fear she felt at the thought of Jamie going into battle.

He put his hands on her shoulders. "Bolt the door." He

looked pointedly at the sword he had made her, which leaned against the trunk under the window. "Use that if need be. I will see it does not come to that, but should it, kill first and regret later."

She nodded, her movements jerky.

He released her and left the room. Elizabeth dressed while Jesse brought Megan in. Jesse gave Elizabeth a quick hug before he disappeared into the passageway. Megan was completely composed, a feat Elizabeth wished she could have accomplished. It was all she could do not to scream from the tension. Would an arrow find its way into Jamie's back? Would someone throw a knife at him and he not be the wiser until he felt it nick his heart?

She began to pace. Torturing herself with gory possibilities was not helping. Jamie would survive. He'd survived thirty years without her worrying about him. With any luck, he'd survive another fifty or sixty.

The day ended, though she wouldn't have believed it if she hadn't seen the shadows lengthening outside. She heard Jamie's voice calling her name from below. She unbolted the door and stepped out into the hallway, her heart in her throat.

Jamie stood near the top of the circular stairway and smiled at her grimly. " 'Tis over."

Tears sprang to her eyes and blinded her. That was surely the only reason she imagined she saw a shadow in the stairwell behind her husband. But then Jamie started up the remaining steps, and Elizabeth saw the dull gleam of a blade descend with sickening speed toward his back.

"Behind you!" she screamed.

Jamie whirled around and fell backward up the steps, holding onto his attacker's arm. His attacker's good arm. The other was minus several fingers.

"I'll see you in hell," Guilbert McKinnon spat, forcing the knife closer to Jamie's chest.

"I think not," Jamie said coldly. He slipped a knife from his belt and plunged it upward into Guilbert's belly. Guilbert gasped, stiffened, then slumped over him.

Jamie shoved the corpse off him and turned to lurch up the

remaining steps. He was covered from head to toe with blood, but Elizabeth didn't care. She threw herself at him and clung to him.

"All's well, Elizabeth," he said, soothingly.

Elizabeth closed her eyes and shook.

"All is well," he repeated, softly.

The rest of the evening passed like a nightmare. Elizabeth sewed up wounds and gave what comfort she could. Time and time again, she replayed in her head the scenario of what would have happened had Jamie died. Not only would she have lost her love, she would have met her end only after rape, she was sure of that.

Once the men were seen to, Jamie took a seat in his chair by the fire and beckoned to Angus.

"Bring him in," Jamie rumbled, his eyes glittering in the firelight. "If he's foolish enough to show himself, then I'll at least have a good look at him before I send him along to hell with his brother."

Richard McKinnon was ushered roughly into the hall. He submitted without complaint to the insults and taunts hurled his way. He was brought to stand before Jamie and looked at him unflinchingly.

"I am not my brother," Richard said quietly. "He is now dead, and I am free of his opinions. The men who followed him and shared his views are dead. The kinsmen remaining me are loyal to me and therefore to you. Our clans have been allies in the past. I would have it be so again."

"And what guarantee do I have you will not stab me once my back is turned?"

"Again, I am not my brother. Guilbert was obsessed with the thought of having your wife. He knew the only way he would find success would be to slay you." Richard smiled grimly. "Though your lady is indeed beautiful, I am not fool enough to try to steal her away from you, Jamie. If you are willing, I think you'll find me to be quite a different man from my brother."

Jamie looked at Richard so long in silence that even Elizabeth began to squirm, wondering if her husband would just as soon strike the man down as to answer him. Finally Jamie nodded.

"I've known you many years, Richard, and know you for the just and true man you are. There will be peace between our clans. I will offer you hospitality."

"Perhaps another time," Richard said, inclining his head slightly. "I've many dead to carry home, and I would be about it before another sun sets."

After a few words in private with Jamie, Richard left. Elizabeth let out the breath she realized she'd been holding. Another disaster successfully avoided.

Then, without warning, memories flooded back. She had to sit down, faint from their assault. Before her mind's eye was the book she had read on Clan MacLeod. She saw the history of the family through the earliest records kept, through the attempted conquests by the Romans, then the Normans, then the English. She saw the words detailing the lairds down through the years as clearly as if the book were open in front of her. She scanned the lines, looking for something useful.

Douglas MacLeod, born 1264, died 1297. Slain by a member of the clan Fergusson. His son, James, began to rule at age sixteen. Renown for his prowess in battle, James led the MacLeods against the clan Fergusson to avenge his father's death. After slaying Kincaid Fergusson in 1311, James himself met his end in 1312 at the hands of one of his allies, Guilbert McKinnon. James's son, Jesse, began to rule at age seventeen. He was wedded to Megan MacLeod that same year.

"Elizabeth?"

She came back to herself slowly, looking at Jamie in horror.

"Elizabeth!" he exclaimed.

Elizabeth swallowed convulsively.

"Elizabeth, damn you, speak!"

"Jamie," she whispered, "I remembered what I read." She swallowed again. "According to the history books, Guilbert should have succeeded." She paused. "You should be dead."

And Jamie, that proud, peerless laird, feared by all in the

Highlands for his ruthlessness in battle, his fierceness in protecting his kin, his sharp intelligence that left no man capable of outwitting him; aye, he did what any sensible man hearing that kind of news would have done.

He fainted.

Jamie woke with a groan, his head fair splitting with the pain. Too much ale. Aye, that was it. Perhaps he would do well to avoid such an abundance of drink in the future. He sighed as he felt a cool cloth pressed against his forehead.

"Elizabeth?" he asked, not bothering to open his eyes.

"Yes, husband."

"How much ale did I drink yestereve? 'Twas surely Richard's gratitude that drove me to it."

"You didn't drink anything."

The hesitancy in her voice was enough to make him open his eyes. He frowned at her.

"But of course I did," he said sternly, wondering why his wife had suddenly gone daft. "Why else would my head feel like John had been using it as an anvil for his hammer all night? I spoke with Richard, then watched you look as if you'd seen a ghost, then I listened to you babble something . . ." He stopped short and looked at her with wide eyes. "Something about me being dead?" He pinched himself strongly. "Am I dead?" He certainly didn't feel dead.

"Jamie, you're very much alive, thank heavens."

He sat up and rubbed the back of his head, wincing as his fingers encountered a bump. "Who hit me over the head?" he demanded.

"You fainted."

His head shot up, sending the chamber spinning wildly. "I what?" he thundered.

Her grin gave him the distinct urge to throttle her. He threw off the covers and swung his legs to the floor, hoping the sudden rush of air would cool his temper. He glared at his wife.

"I fail to see the humor in your little jest. The MacLeod never faints."

She laughed and threw herself at him, tumbling him back onto the bed.

"I don't mean to laugh," she said with a grin, "but you really did faint. The reason you have such a fine goose egg on the back of your head is because we were all too shocked to catch you."

The wear and tear of the last few days was beginning to tell on his wife. That was surely the only reason she was babbling such idiotic tales. He never fainted. There was not a day in his life that he was not in complete control of his body and the events around him. Aye, his fine form wouldn't dare desert him so thoroughly.

He was so busy forcefully stating those reassurances to himself that he failed to catch the beginning of what his wife was saying.

"Of course, we all took a solemn vow never to mention it. You would have been impressed with Ian. I think he wanted to giggle, but he suppressed the urge completely."

The caress of her light fingers against his cheek was extremely distracting, as was the length of her lithe frame against him, but he forced himself to concentrate on her words.

"To tell the truth, we were more worried about you than anything. It took Ian, Angus, Malcolm and four others to carry you up the stairs. They were most impressed with the sheer weight of your body. And, of course, the men are completely convinced Guilbert bewitched you temporarily. You know, he was rumored to be a warlock."

Jamie felt the blush begin in his toes and travel relentlessly upward. He looked at his wife in disbelieving horror.

"I fainted?" he squeaked, then cleared his throat hastily. "Loss of blood," he said gruffly, deepening his voice an extra bit. "And the strain of fretting over you. Any man would have been prone to a bit of weakness under such circumstances. I blame the event on you. Aye, 'tis all your doing."

"I knew it would be," she said, and he didn't miss her dry tone, though he chose to ignore it. "Of course, I beg your pardon for causing you such disturbance."

"Hrumph," he grunted. "Then I forgive you." He truly did not wish to hear any more about his moment of weakness than necessary. He put his hands behind his head, careful to avoid the bump, and frowned up at her. "Now, tell me why it is I should be dead?"

She related the words from the book she had read about his clan. He would have thought to discount them, but she told him details about his father he was certain he'd never revealed to her. When she spoke again of the death of Douglas's son James by the hand of Guilbert McKinnon, Jamie felt the hair on the back of his neck stand up. He rolled her off him and sat up slowly.

"Then I *should* be dead," he said, his voice full of quiet astonishment. "Saints, Elizabeth, Guilbert *should* have killed me. How was it that things finished from there?"

"Jesse killed Guilbert and then went on to become laird. He married Megan, and they had a son named James. Then there was Stephen who ruled after that, then Ian, then Angus. And by the way, that great-great-great-grandson of yours, Angus, was a terrible womanizer. The total number of his bastards was so high, no one ever got an accurate count."

Jamie put his hand to his head, trying to stop the chamber from spinning. He felt perilously close to fainting again. He was so close to it that he didn't even protest as Elizabeth laid him back on the bed and leaned over him, smoothing the hair back from his face.

"It's a bit of a shock, isn't it?"

"Aye," he said thickly. "More than a shock. I feel as though I've gone through a great, turbulent storm and come out to find nothing the same as it was before." He looked at her helplessly. "I should be dead. If not for you, I would be."

"I know," she said softly.

"What are we to do?" he asked, pained. "I cannot continue to walk about my land when I should not be there. If Jesse is to be chieftain of our clan, how can it be if I am still here?"

"I don't know, Jamie," she whispered. "We're changing history even as we speak. Every minute we remain is another minute of history that has been altered." She looked at him helplessly. "Maybe that's why it's only now that I remembered. Because we're both in a place in time where we shouldn't be, and it doesn't matter what either of us knows. Or maybe we're supposed to know what's to happen so we can let events proceed as they should have."

Thinking of the consequences of all that made his head throb painfully. "Och, I am too tired to puzzle this out today," he said. "Let us think on it. Perhaps in a few days we will come to a decision about what we should do."

Even as the words left his lips, he knew what he would have to do. He would have to leave and allow events to progress as they would have originally. He looked up at his wife and managed a wan smile.

"You know, I've always wanted to see a man travel to the stars and come back to tell the tale."

She put her finger to his lips. "Let's talk about it later. All of a sudden, I'm hungry for a certain handsome laird I know."

Jamie closed his eyes as Elizabeth's mouth came down on his softly. He would think about their future later. If he was to leave his time and travel to hers, there would be preparations to be seen to, plans to be made. Aye, there was much to be done.

But later. His wife was demanding his full attention. Who was he not to give it to her?

His decision was made just before dawn. It had been made long before that, but the sun was just rising as he resigned himself to it. How was he to do anything else? He would have left Jesse if he had died; there was little difference in what he was about to do. His only consolation was that he would be going with Elizabeth.

Or so he prayed. Aye, they would enter the forest together, and he would bind her wrist to his. Time had given her to him; time would not take her away without a struggle. Without her, he might as well have died by Guilbert McKinnon's hand.

Elizabeth stirred in his arms and then snuggled closer to him. "You're awake early," she murmured sleepily.

If there was one thing his woman had never learned, it was to rise before the sun. He doubted that would ever change. He rested his cheek against the top of her head and tightened his arm around her, being careful not to crush any of her ribs.

"Elizabeth, I feel odd walking about my keep when I should be dead. I do not think I can bear many more days of this."

"And your solution?"

"The forest," he said firmly. "Though it failed you the time you tried it, perhaps it will not fail us together."

She lifted her head and looked at him bleakly. "But what about Jesse and Megan?"

He smoothed the hair back from her face. "They'll learn to do without us. We'll keep them ever alive in our hearts, but nothing more. Elizabeth," he said earnestly, "I've given it much thought. We must go. Much as it grieves me to leave my son behind, I would have left him just the same had I been slain. I will not rob him of the life and duty that should now be his. He is a man full grown and ready to lead our kin. Megan is old enough to wed him and give him bairns. That is their fate. We must leave them to it."

Tears leaked from her eyes. Jamie drew her close, understanding well the emotions that raged within her. Hadn't he felt the same pain thinking about leaving Jesse? And young Megan, who had become so very dear to his heart?

That did not begin to cover the rest of his kin. Angus had been a father to him for so many years. It would be grievous indeed to bid him farewell. Jamie couldn't bring himself to think about Ian. They weren't cousins, they were brothers. Aye, bidding Ian farewell would surely drive him to weep.

But he had no choice. He saw his course as surely as if fate had drawn a path for him in the dirt. He would take Elizabeth back to her kin and somehow find a way to survive in her world. He could do nothing but.

"When will we go?" she sniffed.

"In a few days."

"And we can see Megan and Jesse wed?"

Jamie smiled. "And this from the woman who ever scolded them for kissing? Now you want them safely wed and bedded?"

"Of course not," Elizabeth exclaimed, her head shooting up. "He can marry her, but he certainly isn't going to sleep with her. That can wait for a few years."

Jamie was so surprised, he laughed. "Surely you jest."

"Jamie, he's not about to have his way with that *child*!"

"She's no longer a child, love. She's more than capable of giving him a bairn."

"That hardly makes her a woman," Elizabeth countered. "Jamie, she's barely fourteen!"

He grinned and pulled her back down to lay in his arms.

"You tell me this, wise one," he whispered in a conspiratorial tone of voice. "If you had been fourteen and I seventeen summers and we had been wed, would you have barred your bedchamber door to me had I come knocking?"

"You know I wouldn't have. But," she said, rising in spite of his efforts to keep her tucked under his arm, "you and I are not the players—"

He put his hand over her mouth. "She'll be fine, Elizabeth. I'll speak with Jesse about the ways to love a woman gently. He won't hurt her. Now come you here and be silent. I've a mind to make sure my theories still hold true."

Chapter 23

JAMIE TUCKED THE blankets up around his slumbering wife and kissed her forehead softly. She moaned.

"My head is killing me," she mumbled.

"Too much ale, my sweet," Jamie chuckled softly. "Sleep will cure the pain. You should be able to sleep in peace, as I'm sure the rest of the keep shares your desire for a bit of quiet."

He didn't say as much, but her pain was surely what she deserved for having tried to drink herself into a stupor the day before. And on the day of Jesse and Megan's nuptials, no less.

"Go if you're going, would you?" Elizabeth grumbled crossly, opening one eye to glare at him.

"As my lady wishes," he grinned, making her a small bow. A pillow hit him square on the backside as he turned and walked to the door, but he didn't bother to retaliate. He'd take his revenge later when his wife was coherent enough to enjoy it.

He descended the stone steps to his great hall, wondering how many more times he would do it before he gave up his home forever. It was a sobering thought. He had taken so many things for granted over the course of his life. And now to lose them! He vowed then to take what days remained him and etch into his memory the sights, sounds, smells and feel of his world, that he might remember them in the future.

Aye, the future called to him. He was torn between agony at leaving his land and his kin and intense excitement at seeing the wonders of Elizabeth's world. It was truly a sorry state of affairs inside his being. Talking it out was perhaps the only way to ease his pain, and Ian was his first choice. He needed to speak with Ian just the same. It was wrong not to let his closest friend know his plans.

Ian was sitting on a stool by the hearth, looking bleary-eyed. Jamie suppressed a grin as he reached his cousin and gave him a hearty slap on the back.

"A fine morn," Jamie boomed.

Ian glared up at him. "I could have sworn you ingested more ale than I last eve, yet here you are, looking virginally pure and healthy."

Jamie laughed and hauled Ian to his feet. "A walk down the meadow and back will clear away the thick cobwebs in your brain, cousin. I promise it."

"Will you also promise to whisper at me, not shout?" Ian asked crossly. "Jamie, my skull is fair splitting with this pain!"

"Very well, old woman," Jamie whispered loudly. "I will humor you."

Ian followed Jamie from the hall, grumbling the entire way.

They walked in silence for some time, Ian wincing at every step that jarred his head and Jamie losing himself in the smell of the heather and the feel of the rising sun on his face. Aye, leaving would be difficult indeed.

"What devilry are you about?" Ian asked bluntly.

Jamie looked at Ian and sighed. "Elizabeth and I have to leave."

"A journey to court? Aye, a fine idea. Elizabeth should see the Bruce. I'll keep an eye on Jesse while you're away."

"Nay, Ian, much further than that." He waited for that to sink in. "Much further," he repeated softly.

What reaction he had expected was surely not the one he received. One moment he was standing, the next he was flat on his back, wincing from the aftereffects of Ian's fist in his face. Then he was gasping for breath, breath which he was not able to draw thanks to Ian's hands at his throat.

"Enough," Jamie protested weakly.

"Damn you," Ian snarled, "when did you plan to tell me? After all we've shared, did you simply intend to wander off into the forest and leave a note behind bidding me a fond farewell?"

"Air . . ." Jamie pleaded earnestly, "Ian . . ."

Ian released him with a foul oath and got to his feet. He stood with his arms folded over his chest, glaring down at Jamie.

"Well?" he demanded.

Jamie sat up slowly, rubbing his offended neck and then loosening the saffron shirt to give himself more room to breathe. He rose slowly.

"I couldn't bring myself to tell you," he said gruffly, trying to tramp down the disconcerting emotions that threatened to bring tears to his eyes. " 'Tis obvious we do not wish to leave."

"Then stay," Ian said, looking at Jamie as if he'd lost all sense. "We need you here."

Jamie sighed and looked up at the sky, searching for a way to explain to Ian what had taken him days to understand himself. He sighed again. "Walk with me, brother. I'll explain as best as I can."

He gave Ian the barest details about Elizabeth's house of books and what she had read about their clan. Then he related in as few words as possible what she had read about the succession of lairds. Ian shook his head as he listened to Jamie speak of his own death.

"Impossible."

"Is it?" Jamie mused. "Think on it, Ian. Had Elizabeth not been there, I never would have known Guilbert was behind me."

"Had Elizabeth not been here, you never would have gone back into the house," Ian countered.

Jamie shook his head. "I didn't go back in to fetch her. I went back in to see that the hall was secure."

"Guilbert never would have tried to kill you if he hadn't wanted Elizabeth," Ian said.

"Richard told me yesterday that Guilbert had wanted my death for years. She was nothing but a convenient excuse."

Ian sighed. "I see you have given this much thought."

"Aye, I have. Now you see why I must go."

"Nay, I do not. You have been given a new life. Use it!"

"It is now Jesse's life," Jamie said, stopping and looking at Ian seriously. "If events had progressed as destiny had wanted them to, Jesse would now be laird. I cannot rob my son of that duty."

Ian frowned. "How came you by this notion?"

"If I were dead, as I should be, Jesse would be named chieftain." He struggled for something to show Ian what he meant. Finally, he pulled up the edge of his plaid. "See you here how the strands of wool begin at the bottom and are fashioned in a pattern?" He pointed to an intersection of plaid. "One strand ends, then begins again here. One strand, Ian, not two. Were there two strands from this point on, the pattern would be flawed, and the flaw would only become more apparent the further it went through the cloth. That kind of disorder is what I would make of the future if I stayed. Don't you see?" he asked, looking at Ian earnestly. "Every year I spent in a time where I was supposed to be dead would be another flaw in the fabric of life." He stopped suddenly and smiled proudly at his own words. Perhaps he would be a philosopher in Elizabeth's day. Surely the men of her time could benefit from a bit of Scottish wisdom.

Ian put his hand to his head. "Och, the pain it gives me just trying to make sense of your words."

Jamie clapped a hand on Ian's shoulder. "I understand, believe me. 'Twill take a goodly bit of time before it comes clear in your head, but it will."

"I'm coming with you," Ian announced suddenly.

"You cannot," Jamie said sharply. "Ian, have you heard nothing I've said? You are destined to be in this time. If you leave, you remove a thread from the fabric. It may be that you will damage the cloth irreparably if you do not stay and fulfill your lot here."

Ian turned abruptly and began to walk back to the hall. Jamie caught up with him and walked alongside him, wishing he could say something to ease his dearest friend's pain, but knowing there was nothing to be said.

By the time they reached the keep, Ian's walk had slowed and his shoulders had slumped. They paused on the steps leading up to the great hall.

"You won't sneak out some night like a thief and leave me cursing you for eternity, will you?"

Jamie managed a wan smile. "You know I won't."

"I'll follow you one of these days," Ian vowed. "See if I don't."

Jamie found it in himself to grin at Ian's vehemence. "I wouldn't expect any less of you. And I'll have a handsome wench or two waiting for your pleasure."

"Has Elizabeth a sister?"

"I fear not. I'll see what else is available and choose wisely."

Two days later Jamie sat in his great chair before the hearth in the great hall and grinned at Megan's squeals as she fled from Jesse up the stairs. Jesse's throaty laughter echoed back down to them, and then there was meaningful silence. Jamie looked next to' him to find his wife smiling wistfully. He reached for her hand and brought it to his lips.

"Are you remembering all the times I chased you in like manner?" he teased.

"Jesse's just following your poor example. I seem to remember running up those steps just last night."

He smiled arrogantly. "You allowed me to catch you, just to have more of my fine loving. You cannot help but admit the truth of that."

"Of course," she agreed.

He rose and swept her up into his arms before she could open her mouth to protest. Ignoring her blushes and the grins of his men, he stalked across the rushes and climbed the stairs purposefully. Her anguished groan stopped him halfway up to his bedchamber.

"You wished to chase me instead?" he asked politely.

She smiled. "Not tonight. I'd rather be at your mercy just now."

Jamie obliged her, reveling in his power to make his wife weak and trembling in his arms. Having her fierce and demanding didn't displease him either, though he found the scratches on his back to be a bit distressing at times. When they were both exhausted from too much play, he gathered her close in his arms and relished the feel of her soft body pressed close to his.

And then he knew. It brought tears to his eyes, but he knew he could delay the inevitable no longer. He felt hot tears scald his chest and knew his wife had come to the same conclusion.

"We won't pack until tomorrow morning," he said softly.

"Oh, Jamie," she wept, "this is so hard."

"I know, love," he whispered, holding her tighter, "but there's nothing else to be done." He lifted her face and kissed her gently. "Sleep for a bit, wife, then I'll love you again before the sun rises. We'll leave this bed many fond memories of us for it to cherish."

"Jamie, do you think we'll stay together?"

"Of course," he said firmly. "I'll allow nothing else."

"And you think the forest will work?"

Jamie's next words were determined.

"I won't give it any choice."

They were up and gathering their belongings together well before dawn. Elizabeth chose only a few things to take with her. It came down to her wedding dress, an emerald green dress Jamie had given her to go with his eyes and a plaid with a fine saffron shirt. The clothes she had come to his time in were long since gone, having been buried deep in a place by the pond. If she ever saw Alex again, she hoped he would forgive her the loss of his jacket.

The only other things she packed were her journal and a few of Megan's drawings. The story they had worked on together, Elizabeth left behind. Megan would need bedtime books for her own children, and that would be a good start.

Jamie's belongings were not many more. He took his weapons, the fine clothes Elizabeth had made him for their wedding, a bag of gold and a bag of precious gems.

They broke their fast with their kin. Megan wept openly and clung to Elizabeth as they sat together after the meal was cleared away. Elizabeth tried to comfort her as best she could, but what could she say? They would certainly see each other again when they both passed beyond the veil that separates this life from the next, but it would be many years until then.

Elizabeth held onto Megan's cold hand as she bid farewell, one by one, to Jamie's kinsmen. *Her* kinsmen. Everett leaned down and gave her a hug that knocked the wind from her. Malcolm wept openly, kneeling at her feet and hugging her. Joshua threatened to break his lute if they did not relent and bring him along. Hugh did nothing but blubber, holding onto his kitchen spoon as if it were a life raft. Angus kept his arm around her as he spoke softly into her ear, telling her how much like a daughter she'd been to him and promising to look after Jesse and Megan and keep them safe.

She watched Jamie fight his tears as he bid farewell to each of his kinsmen. He'd told them nothing more than that he and his lady were going far away, and they feared they would not be back. Elizabeth had the feeling more of the men knew what Jamie was up to than they let on.

Jamie walked to the door of his hall, and Elizabeth followed him. Ian bid farewell to her first.

"You know I'll come to you before I die," he whispered into her ear. "Have a few lusty wenches on hand for me, my lady."

Elizabeth put her arms around his neck and hugged him tightly. "If you promise to leave the kegs in the cellar alone until that day, I just might."

He grinned. " 'Tis a harsh thing you require. Let us say only that I will be an infrequent visitor. Will that satisfy you?"

She nodded, suddenly finding a large lump in her throat preventing her from answering.

Ian released her after giving her a hearty kiss on the mouth and then turned to Jamie. Elizabeth watched the scene with wistfulness.

"I hate you for this, Jamie," Ian said hoarsely.

"I know," Jamie replied, the same hoarseness in his own voice. "It wouldn't bother me too much to find you knocking on my hall door in a few years."

"Should I escape certain death, I will be there. Wouldn't want to mar the cloth of the future."

Jamie hugged Ian fiercely, blinking back tears. After a few more hearty slaps on the back, Jamie bade Elizabeth say her final good-byes to Megan and then boosted her up into the saddle. He swung up onto his own mount, and they set off toward the gates with only Jesse as an escort. Elizabeth only looked back once. The scene was something she knew she'd never forget.

The household was gathered on the steps to see them off. She took one last look at the faces who had come to be family for her: Angus, Hugh, Malcolm, Friar Augustine, Ian and sweet Megan. Then she turned her face forward and tried to ignore both her tears over leaving and her apprehension over the future. How in the world could they predict where they would wind up? Perhaps all the tears and good-byes were for naught. They might just wander through the forest for a pleasant day or two and then return to the keep.

But even as the thought took shape in her mind, she knew it wouldn't be that way. Their time in the fourteenth century was over. Even if their destination was still up in the air, that other fact was undeniable.

They stopped at the edge of the forest. Jesse dismounted and held up his arms for her. She put her hands on his shoulders and let him help her from her horse. She smiled at him, remembering the first time she'd seen him and what a little copy of his father he'd been. She reached out and smoothed his bangs from his eyes.

"Take care of yourself, Jesse. And of Megan. She'll need you close for a while."

He nodded obediently. "I will."

"You'll make a fine laird."

He hugged her to him and pressed his face down against her shoulder. "I'll miss you," he said, his voice hoarse with tears. "We'll never forget you."

"Nor we you," she whispered, patting his back.

"You'll name your first son after me?" he said, pulling back and smiling crookedly at her.

"What would we need with another son named Jesse?"

"Well spoken," Jamie said from behind Jesse. He turned his son around and pulled him into a bone-crushing hug.

Jesse wept openly, drawing tears from his father also. Elizabeth cried just watching them together. In some ways she felt so responsible for Jamie's grief. If she'd never come, he would never be leaving.

Then again, if she'd never come, he would be dead. How many times had he said those very words? Still, that didn't make it any easier to watch the two men struggle to regain their composure.

"I'll miss you," Jamie said gruffly, giving his son a shake. "You be sure to mind the borders well. I daresay your troubles with the Fergussons aren't over. And see that the cattle aren't lost. Your kin will starve without them. Raid the McKinnon a bit, just for me. Richard will understand."

Jesse managed a weak smile. "Aye, Father. I'll do it."

"Don't forget all the grandchildren you promised me. I'll read about it in some book, you know. And you take care of that wife of yours. She's young yet. There's still time to teach her obedience."

Jesse smiled. "I will."

"Hold fast, Jesse, to the land. Lead the clan well."

"I will not fail you."

"Why do you think I'm leaving you my hall? Of course you will not fail me." He kissed Jesse and then pushed him back. "You will do that favor I asked of you?"

Jesse produced a length of leather from his belt. Jamie held out his hand, and Jesse wrapped the length around his father's left wrist. Elizabeth watched the entire operation with wide eyes. Then Jamie beckoned to her, and Jesse fixed the other end of the strap around her right wrist.

"That I do not lose you," Jamie explained.

Jesse held onto them both for another long, heart-wrenching moment. Finally he pulled away and put his shoulders back.

"You'll never be dead to me," he said, his eyes still brimming with tears. "And I'll make you proud. Don't forget me."

"We won't," Jamie and Elizabeth said in unison.

It was finally Jamie who gathered the reins to their horses in his hands and bade Jesse one last farewell. Then he turned and led his wife into the forest.

They walked silently through the trees, hand in hand, not speaking. Emotions were still too close to the surface for that. They walked at a leisurely pace, for there was no reason to hurry. Why hurry when the future wasn't hastening off without them?

* * *

Jamie stopped before nightfall. He wouldn't even untie Elizabeth as he gathered wood for the fire. After making a meal on a bit of bread and cheese, they curled up near the fire in blankets. Jamie lay behind Elizabeth, holding her against his chest.

"Elizabeth?"

"Yes, husband."

"Think you we'll go to this America of yours?" he asked in a hushed voice.

"Jamie, I have no idea. I thought you had this all figured out."

"Finally my woman allows me to take the lead, and 'tis the one time I have no inkling of the destination. Why I'm surprised at this, I don't know."

"As long as we're together, I'm not really worried about the destination."

Jamie nodded, though in truth he had a very specific destination in mind. He would see Elizabeth's America eventually. What he wanted to see was Scotland in her time. He wanted to see his descendants and what they had done with the knowledge they'd gained over the centuries.

And he wanted to see his hall. With any luck at all, it would have survived the centuries and remained intact.

He felt Elizabeth drift off after a short while, then struggled to keep his eyes open. A strange weariness took hold of his limbs and rendered him as weak as a babe. After one last, heartfelt petition, he succumbed to weariness. Within moments, he too was asleep.

Chapter 24

THE CHILL FINALLY forced Elizabeth to wakefulness. She groaned sleepily and pulled the blanket up around her ear. Damn Jamie and his early mornings anyway. Didn't he know a husband's first and foremost duty was to keep his wife warm? That was surely the only reason men generated heat like four fireplaces combined.

Suddenly, and almost on top of one another, two realizations came to her: she was lying on the ground, and she was alone. She sat up, gasping to draw air into her burning lungs. Her chest felt like some powerful giant had it in his fist and was squeezing ruthlessly. The leather thong was still around her wrist, but there was nothing else attached to it. She clenched her hands in her lap and threw back her head to cry out mournfully into the morning calm.

"Jamie!"

If there had by some miracle been an answer, she wouldn't have heard it for the thunder of blood in her ears. It wasn't fair! How could she have slept all through the night without noticing his being taken away from her? All she had to live for had been ruthlessly ripped away. She was alone, bereft, abandoned, cursed . . .

"Elizabeth!" Jamie exclaimed, pulling her into his arms.

"Woman, you're bellowing loud enough to bring all the clans of Scotland down on us!"

She opened her eyes long enough to see that it was Jamie's own beloved face so close to hers, then she threw her arms around him.

"Oh, Jamie, I thought I'd lost you! I woke up and you weren't there."

"Hush, love," he said soothingly, rocking her gently. "I was just beyond the trees gathering wood for the fire. I told you I wouldn't leave you. We'll be together many long, happy years. Let me build up this fire, and then we'll snuggle together for a time until you warm up. Your hands are freezing."

Elizabeth waited, then stretched out with him after he had finished his task. They lay under the blanket, not speaking. Elizabeth's mind was working too furiously for speech. Now that she knew Jamie was safe, other things began to clamor for her attention. They were still in the forest. What did that mean? She wasn't sure what she had expected, but it hadn't been to wake up where she'd gone to sleep.

"Elizabeth," Jamie rumbled.

"Yes, Jamie."

"Maybe we haven't left my time," he said. "The forest seems no different to me."

It didn't. Elizabeth looked around her and saw that much. Trees were trees, and Elizabeth hadn't really paid that much attention the night before, but she had to agree with him.

"I think you're right."

Jamie sighed and sat up. "Then all we can do is keep traveling and hope we come across something that allows us to know in what century we find ourselves. I daresay I shouldn't have come without men to guard us both. Though I could defend us against many, I must admit I would be hard pressed to defend us against the entire Fergusson clan."

Elizabeth rose and started to fold the blankets, trying not to think about the truth of Jamie's words. What if they did run into a band of unfriendly Highlanders? Worse yet, what if they were still in the fourteenth century? Where would they go? They couldn't go back to their hall. It was Jesse's right and privilege to lead the clan, and she knew Jamie wouldn't take it from him.

Jamie's hand under her chin startled her. She looked up and met his eyes.

"I'll care for you well, Elizabeth," he said quietly.

She put her arms around him and hugged him. "I know, Jamie. I'm just nervous."

He patted her back as gently as he was capable. "We'll be just fine, lass. Let us take up our journey and see what the forest has done with us."

Jamie saddled their mounts and then put out the fire. Elizabeth looked up frequently at the sky above them as they traveled, just waiting to see the first jet pass overhead. Maybe they were too far north for jets.

Or maybe they were too far back in time for jets.

It seemed as though hours passed before the forest ended and Jamie reined in his horse. He looked at Elizabeth, and his expression was grim.

"What think you? Dare we go on?"

"Do we have any other choice?"

He put his hand on the hilt of his sword. "I can only hope we don't find ourselves riding into a band of ruffians who are so intent on killing us that they don't have the patience for a polite bit of talk."

She smiled at his dry tone and followed him from the forest.

Nightfall came early this far north. It was soon twilight, and she struggled to see what was ahead of them. She could have sworn she saw little fires in the distance. Was it too much to hope for that those fires would actually be lights?

Then she gasped. In front of them, not twenty yards away, was a road. Not a dirt road, nor a cobblestone road, but a paved road, with dashes separating the lanes. She heard the sound of a car before it whizzed by them. Jamie's horse reared at the noise, and it was all Jamie could do to quiet the beast. He slowly turned his head to look at Elizabeth.

"I think, my love, that we are no longer in fourteenth-century Scotland."

Elizabeth let out her breath slowly.

"I don't think so either."

She felt such a rush of emotions that she had a hard time identifying them. First and foremost, though, there was apprehension. That was something that wouldn't go away until she knew exactly what year they had come to. And why they were still in Scotland. If she'd come to the forest from New York, why hadn't she and Jamie been sent back to New York from the forest?

"Perhaps we should find an inn," Jamie said, scanning the countryside for signs of life. "And soon. The sun sets already."

She nodded and followed his lead as he walked his horse toward the road.

"Look both ways before you cross the street," Elizabeth said, out of long-standing habit.

"Why?"

"A car might be coming. It would kill you before you knew it if it hit you."

Jamie pulled himself up a bit further in the saddle. "I see," he said wisely. He looked first to his left and then to his right. Then he looked at his wife. "What exactly is it I am looking for?"

"One of those wagons that moves by itself. And it moves very quickly."

He nodded and looked again. Seeing nothing, he urged his horse forward. Elizabeth heard a car coming and reached for Jamie's reins and jerked back, just before the car whizzed by, honking. Jamie was visibly shaken.

"Wow," he said, giving her a wide-eyed look.

"I'll keep an eye on the roads until you get the hang of it," she said, trying to reassure him.

They crossed the road, and it was all Elizabeth could do to keep her husband in the saddle. What he wanted to do was get off his horse in the middle of the road and see what the pavement felt like. She promised him he'd have a chance later, and he agreed reluctantly. They rode on, picking their way down through fields toward lights that twinkled in the distance. They were lights. Elizabeth ignored the possibility that they could actually be in a place in time before she had been born. Just thinking about the ramifications of that gave her a headache.

"Elizabeth," Jamie began gruffly, "there is aught I would speak of with you."

She lifted an eyebrow at his lordly tone. "Go ahead."

"It may take me a few hours to accustom myself to these possible future ways, but that does not mean I am weak nor stupid."

Hours? She smiled. "I know that, Jamie."

"Nor does that mean that I have ceased being your lord. You will obey me in all things, as always."

"Of course, Jamie," she said meekly. "And should you demand knowledge about this or that, I would give it to you because you required it, not because I thought you didn't know the answer already."

"Of course," Jamie said arrogantly. "There would be no other reason to question you."

Elizabeth suppressed her smile and was thankful she was riding behind him so he didn't see the twinkle in her eyes. Heavens, what an ego her husband had.

An hour later they reached a house on the outskirts of a small village. To Elizabeth's immense relief, it was an inn, and it looked to be empty of guests. Even better. The fewer people Jamie tried to order about his first few days in the future, the better off they'd both be.

They rode up to the front of the house. Jamie dismounted and wrapped his reins around a bit of railing. He held up his arms for Elizabeth and pulled her down to the ground. Before she knew what he had in mind, he had captured her mouth in a searing kiss. He lifted his head and smiled down at her grimly.

"For good fortune," he explained.

She smiled lazily up at him. "Find us a quiet room, my lord, and I'll give you more than just a kiss for good fortune."

Jamie smiled briefly, then released her and threw his saddlebags over his shoulder. After a deep breath, he took her hand and led her to the door.

It opened onto a cheery entryway, complete with pegs for coats and a mirror on the wall. The moment Jamie caught sight of his reflection, he gasped and made a beeline for it.

"Jamie," Elizabeth said softly. "Later."

It was with great reluctance that he pulled away and gave her a bewildered look. "So much clearer than ours," he whispered reverently.

"There'll be plenty of time to gape at yourself once we have a chamber. And we need a chamber with a telephone, if possible."

"Telephone?" he echoed.

"Just ask for it."

He put his shoulders back and strode purposefully to a registration desk at the far end of the hallway. A short, red-haired man stood up instantly as they approached. He took one look at Jamie, then a long look at Elizabeth, then returned his gaze to Jamie. His mouth hung open, and his eyes looked as if they just might fall from his head.

"Your name?" Jamie demanded.

"Roddy MacLeod," the poor man squeaked.

"We've need of a chamber, kinsman, and stabling of our horses. Can you see to that?"

"Aye," Roddy squeaked again, then he cleared his throat nervously. "Right away, sir."

"A telephone," Elizabeth whispered, elbowing Jamie in the ribs.

"What? Oh, aye. We've need of a telephone also. We'll wish for a bath to be sent up shortly. And supper. Bring me plenty of ale. I've sore need of something to soothe my nerves."

"Of course, sir," Roddy said quickly, his eyes still huge in his face. "Will you be needing anything else?"

"You'll know when I do," Jamie said imperiously.

Roddy squirmed. "Will you be paying in cash?" he asked hesitantly.

"Cash?"

Elizabeth winced. Money was something she hadn't given any thought to. She tugged on Jamie's sleeve. "He wishes gold for the chamber."

Jamie slapped a saddlebag on the counter and rummaged around in it for a moment. He produced a slim card and handed it to Roddy. "Will this do?"

"Jamie!" Elizabeth gasped. "Where did you get my American Express card?"

He winked down at her. "I thought it might serve us eventually."

Roddy looked miserably apologetic. "Forgive me, but we don't take credit cards."

"Indeed," Jamie rumbled. "Then can you make do with a piece of gold?" He threw the American Express card back into the bag and pulled forth a coin.

Roddy accepted it with reverence. "Aye," he said quickly. "This will more than cover the room and your beasts. I'll see to things immediately. If you'll just sign here," he said, indicating the register.

Jamie hefted his saddlebag over his shoulder again and scrawled his bold signature in the appropriate place.

"I have to know the date," Elizabeth whispered to Jamie. She crossed her fingers behind her back.

Jamie nodded. "Give us the date, kinsman, if you will."

Roddy looked like he wanted to either weep or faint. " 'Tis the first of December, my lord."

Jamie waited.

"1996," Roddy added, his voice nothing but a whisper.

Jamie's arm suddenly around her shoulders was all that kept Elizabeth from falling. She clung to him. 1996. And they were in Scotland. Elizabeth felt a bubble of hysterical laughter well up.

"Oh, Jamie, 1996," she laughed. "I can't believe it!" Then she started to shake. "Jamie, it's been almost three months! My parents will be frantic!"

He held her close and bent his head to whisper in her ear. "Hush, Beth, and do not fret. We'll find them as soon as we can. Think on the joy they'll have seeing you again. Their pain is almost over." He kissed her hair. "Courage, my lady. We've things to see to this eve. You've no time for tears just yet."

Elizabeth nodded and let Jamie sit her down in a chair next to Roddy's counter. She waited while he and Roddy stabled the horses. There were so many different emotions running through her, she hardly knew where to start in identifying them. But tops on her list was relief. She was home. She and Jamie both were in her time. She wouldn't have to worry about losing him to a minor infection. She wouldn't have to worry about them both starving to death because the crops hadn't come through. Even getting pregnant had suddenly become an appealing thought. Oh, blessed anesthetic!

She looked up as Jamie came through the door, carrying their gear. Poor Roddy seemed completely overwhelmed by Jamie as he followed her husband into the entry hall. Elizabeth didn't miss the way he had taken to calling Jamie "my lord" and the way he jumped each time Jamie spoke. Jamie seemed to find this nothing but appropriate, which didn't surprise her either.

Roddy led them down a hallway and into a large, comfortable room. She immediately noted the bathroom and was grateful; theirs was surely the only room in the inn with its own private garderobe. A telephone rested on a dresser, and she stared at it for a moment in wonder. How strange it was to see something she thought she would never see again.

But Jamie obviously wasn't finding his surroundings as wonderful as she did. He stood at the far side of the room, wearing a stricken look. Elizabeth hurriedly ushered Roddy to the door before Jamie lost it completely.

"I'll be back right quick with your supper, Mrs. MacLeod," Roddy said with a nervous little bow. "It won't be but a minute."

"We appreciate your fine care," she said with a nod, then shut the door. She turned around and looked at Jamie who stood in the same place, clutching their saddlebags as if they were all that kept him from being swept off into nothingness.

"Jamie?"

"How did he kindle those fires?" he rasped. He looked at the lamps over the headboard of the bed. "How was that done?"

"There's a little switch over here by the door," she said. "Watch."

She reached for the light switch and flicked the lights off and then back on again. Jamie gasped, dropped the saddle bags and did something she never thought he'd ever do.

He crossed himself against her.

The wild look in his eye made her heart stop. For the first time since she had arrived in Scotland, she was afraid of him. She whirled around and grabbed the handle of the door. Then she shrieked as Jamie's arms went around her.

"My sweet Beth, I didn't mean it! 'Twas my hand that made the motion without my giving it leave! I vow it!"

"I'm not a witch!"

"By all the saints above, I know that!" He turned her around and clutched her to him. "Merciful God, I know that!" He buried his face in her hair and trembled. "Oh, Elizabeth, I can't bear this. Too many things I don't understand."

Elizabeth's heart broke at the way her gruff, courageous husband shook in her arms. She let out a slow breath of relief. Jamie was afraid of her time, not her. She brushed her hands over his back time and time again, trying to calm him.

"Jamie, it's all right," she said soothingly. "You'll do fine. You're just hungry. Roddy will come back with a meal in a few minutes, and then you'll eat and feel better."

Jamie said nothing, but continued to clutch her tightly. Elizabeth fought for air enough to soothe him some more.

"There's a logical explanation for everything," she said, patting his back. "Once you understand the reasons for what you see, you'll find you aren't troubled at all."

Jamie released her and let out a shuddering breath. "Merciful saints above, Elizabeth," he said, drawing his hand over his eyes, "I feel as if I'm dreaming and I can't wake up."

She reached up and pushed his bangs out of his eyes. "Now you know how I felt when I first arrived at your hall." She leaned up and kissed him. "Lucky for you I don't have a pit to throw you in, or I might. Just to get even."

" 'Tis only now I understand the fear you must have felt. Forgive me for what I did." He looked at her and his green eyes held a bit of telltale mistiness.

If there was one thing Elizabeth knew she couldn't see, it was her proud husband weeping. He'd wept the night before when he'd thought she was asleep, and it had broken her heart. He would miss Jesse and the rest of the clan so much. The very last thing he needed was to feel guilt over what he'd initially done to her.

She shook her head. "You've made up nicely for it since then, and you know I forgave you a long time ago." She smiled. "Let's go sit down. I think I hear your meal coming. I have the feeling Roddy's cook just might outdo Hugh tonight. I'm hungry enough to eat even haggis."

"You must be starved," he murmured.

Elizabeth steered him over to the little table in the corner of the room. Once he was seated, she put the saddlebags on the far side of the bed and went to open the door for the innkeeper.

Roddy carried in enough food and drink for half a dozen people. Elizabeth had hoped food would distract her husband, but she soon discovered it wasn't working. He merely watched what was set before him with a dazed look, as if food were a foreign substance he'd never partaken of before.

"Jamie?"

He looked up at her. He was still looking shell-shocked. For the first time, Elizabeth truly regretted having left the Middle Ages. If Jamie couldn't learn to adapt, he would never survive. What would happen the first time he saw a television? Or rode in a car? Or flew in a plane? Good grief, how else would they get to America? By boat? She closed her eyes briefly, praying for a miracle.

"Lady MacLeod? Do you require aught else?"

Elizabeth looked at the innkeeper and saw a miracle standing before her. If Jamie could see that men were still men, even though his surroundings had changed, then maybe it would ease the shock for him. And Roddy was the perfect guinea pig. He looked at Jamie as if he'd been a king. Surely a bit of deference would soothe her husband.

"Why don't you stay?" Elizabeth offered. "There's too much here for us to eat by ourselves."

"I wouldn't presume . . ."

"Stay," Elizabeth commanded, then gentled her command with a smile. "Stay and tell us a bit about the village. We've been . . . ah . . . away for a while. Jamie will want to hear the news."

Roddy sat and fidgeted.

"Roddy, tell us about your family," Elizabeth suggested, sitting next to Jamie and serving him enormous helpings of food. "Are you married? Do you have any children?"

"Aye, my lady, I'm wed. And my children are grown. Married and gone off to different parts. A pity children won't stay close to home. Always wanting adventure, they are."

Jamie grunted. "I understand that, kinsman. My son was forever wanting to ride off and stir up mischief."

"Aye, children need a tight rein," Roddy nodded wisely.

"Powerfully headstrong, they are. Especially the girls. My wee daughter caused me twice the grief my sons did. And then her wedding! I thought the cost would put me out of business. Keeping an inn isn't the best way to put food on the table, you know. Especially this far north. During the winter months, we eat what we've stored and no more."

"Indeed," Jamie said, lifting one eyebrow. "I can well understand your dilemma." He tore off a hunk of bread. "Tell me, how profitable is your hall, Roddy? I never could see how an innkeeper could feed his children, but perhaps things have changed."

And perhaps they hadn't. Elizabeth sat back slowly, afraid any sudden movement would break the spell. Jamie was eating. If nothing else, it was a sign that he wouldn't starve to death.

"Delicious," he said, through a mouthful of stew. "Now, kinsman, tell me more. I daresay I might have a suggestion or two for you about how to run your hall more efficiently. I've had much practice in feeding many on very little."

Elizabeth let out her breath quietly. Thank heavens for Roddy MacLeod and his inn. She ate a little, then sat back and listened. Whatever shock Jamie had felt was wearing off because he had assumed his most lordly tone and was questioning Roddy as closely as he would have one of his scouts.

Before Roddy knew it, he was divulging to Jamie his family history, his financial situation, and his hopes and dreams for the future. He also gave Jamie several of the more juicy tidbits of village gossip, as well as a complete rundown on the state of affairs in Scotland. Jamie listened to it all with great interest. And then he frowned.

"No king? What tale is this? Scotland has always had a king."

Roddy cleared his throat uncomfortably. "I regret to say, my lord, that Scotland is under English rule now."

"English rule!" Jamie bellowed, banging his fist on the table. "Impossible!"

Roddy winced. "And 'tis a queen who sits the throne, my lord."

Elizabeth knew trouble when she saw it coming. She could just imagine Jamie gathering up the villagers and marching them down to London to oust the supplanter. Or supplantress, as the case might be.

"Let's talk about something else," she suggested.

Jamie glared at her. "You never told me England had taken over my country. By the saints, Elizabeth, this is a disaster!"

"Well, there's nothing you can do about it. Learn to live with it."

"Perhaps we will move to this America of yours," Jamie rumbled. "I'll not be ruled by an Englishwoman!"

Elizabeth noticed Roddy only because his face was so white. He looked as if he'd seen a ghost. Elizabeth was about to suggest he go lie down, but Jamie beat her to the punch.

"Kinsman, I can plainly see there is aught that troubles you," he said, still frowning. "I would hear of it, so long as it has nothing to do with kings and queens."

Roddy moistened his lips nervously and tugged at the collar of his sweater.

" 'Tis nothing but idle fancy, but I'll tell it if you wish."

"I do," Jamie said imperiously. "Perhaps I can aid you."

Roddy clasped his hands around his mug so hard, his knuckles were white. "There is a legend in these parts, among the more romantic of us, of course, but a legend it is." He looked at Jamie and then looked back down at his mug. " 'Tis a tale told of the young Laird James and his beautiful wife, Elizabeth, who lived in the Bruce's day."

"Indeed," Jamie said, shooting a startled look at Elizabeth. "Go on."

Roddy squirmed. " 'Tis said that James loved his sweet bride so much that he found a way for them both to escape death. Every now and again someone will see them and be recipient of one of their good deeds. In fact, the tale is told that even Robin of Locksley, the Wolf's Head, allowed them to join his band of merry men in the fight against the Sheriff of Nottingham."

"Indeed," Jamie drawled.

Elizabeth met his eyes and saw the beginnings of amusement there. Well, at least he had given up the idea of anarchy.

"Know you who began this legend?" Jamie asked.

"I understand it originated with the wife of Jamie's son, Jesse. I believe her name was Megan."

Jamie snorted and looked at Elizabeth. "Somehow that doesn't surprise me in the least."

"It's romantic, isn't it?"

"As I said, I'm not surprised. 'Twas all those tales you told her at bedtime which confused her mind so."

"I think it's sweet."

Jamie leaned over to kiss her. "You've a tender heart, my Beth. And Megan certainly wasn't harmed by learning her ways from you."

The loud crack of crumbling crockery drew their attention. Roddy's mug had finally succumbed to the pressure of his hands and ceased to hold its form. He sat there, shards and dust from the stoneware covering his hands and lap, and looked as pale as death.

"Are you . . ." he trailed off, looking from Jamie to Elizabeth to Jamie again. "I mean to say, have you come . . ."

Immediately, a dozen ugly scenarios came to Elizabeth's mind. If anyone found out about this, they would treat Jamie like an alien. It was something she had never once considered while thinking of bringing him to her time.

Talk about a witch-hunt.

"Roddy," she said quickly, "can you trace your fathers back to this Jesse you speak of?"

"Aye, my lady," Roddy nodded slowly, "I can. Directly."

She chose her words carefully. Roddy seemed like a good sort, and he was certainly taken with Jamie. Perhaps if he understood the dangers, he would understand why he had to keep his mouth shut.

"If you can trace your line back to Jesse, then you can go back one step further to Jesse's father." She inclined her head just the slightest bit in Jamie's direction, then looked directly into Roddy's startled blue eyes.

"If people knew the truth that you now know, he would never know a day's peace in his life. First the newspapers would come, then the scientists, then the government. He would be interrogated, poked, prodded, put on display as a freak of nature.

Is that the fate to which you would sentence the fiercest laird the Highlands have ever seen?"

Bless his heart, poor Roddy looked as though he wanted to weep.

"Of course not, my lady."

"Then you tell me, Roddy MacLeod, how it is you can best serve the man to whom you owe your very existence?"

Roddy gulped. "I can find you clothes. Aye, and I can claim you're my kin, come to visit. I've kin all over Scotland, so it wouldn't be hard for the village gossips to believe." He smiled, almost proudly. "And it wouldn't exactly be a lie, would it?"

"No, kinsman, it wouldn't," Jamie said quietly, his deep voice echoing in the stillness of the room. "And we'd be grateful for your aid. Should I ever regain my hall, its doors will always be open to you. Of course, we will pay you well for your trouble."

"I couldn't accept anything," Roddy gushed, obviously overcome by what he had learned that evening. " 'Twould be an honor to serve you, Laird Jamie. And I'll keep your secret well, you'll see." He rose suddenly. "You both must be tired from your journey. The telephone's there, Lady Elizabeth, if you want it. We've running water for your bath, and I'll see that the rest of the house keeps quiet in the morning, so as to not disturb you. I'll see what clothes I can find in the morning."

With that, he scurried to the door, bellowed for his help and had the table cleaned off before Elizabeth could blink twice. After the chamber was put to rights, he made them both a low bow and backed out of the room respectfully. Once the door closed, Elizabeth looked at Jamie with raised eyebrows.

"I would say, my laird, that you have yourself a loyal kinsman there."

"I fear he has me confused with the king, what with all his bowing and such. As if we still had a king," he grumbled.

"He admires you greatly," she said gently. "And he recognizes what a fine laird you are. Though how anyone could help but see that, I surely don't know."

Jamie pulled her around the table and down onto his lap. "I will take that as a compliment."

"As it was meant."

He buried his face against her neck and sighed deeply.

"Thank you, Beth."

Elizabeth didn't have to ask for what. She wrapped her arms around Jamie's shoulders and rested her cheek against the top of his head.

"Sweet Jamie," she whispered, "how I love you. You're dealing with this so well. You'll get used to things, you'll see."

"Of course," he mumbled against her hair. "I *am* still laird."

"That you are, my love."

Jamie held her for several moments in silence, then pulled back and looked at her.

"What were you thinking about last night in the forest?" he asked.

"That I wanted nothing more than to stay with you," she said with a smile. "Which was exactly what I was thinking the first time I tried to go back."

"Truly?" he asked, surprised. "And that first time I was thinking I didn't want to let you go." He sat back and looked at her thoughtfully. "And yestereve I was thinking that instead of seeing your land, I wanted to see my Scotland in your time."

"Strange," she murmured.

He nodded. "Very." He pulled her close and gave her a gentle squeeze. "We're here together. Nothing else matters."

She couldn't have agreed more.

Chapter 25

ELIZABETH RESTED IN Jamie's arms until he finally stirred.

"Show me how the lights are kindled," he said, "then I will find a way to send word to your parents. But I must know the meaning of this other mystery first."

She nodded and rose. She led him over to the door and pointed to the light switch. "To extinguish them, you push down. To kindle them, you push up."

He reached out hesitantly and touched the lever. When he found it cool to the touch, he pushed down and plunged them into darkness. There was a long pause before he spoke.

"Elizabeth?"

"Yes, Jamie."

"Did I do that?"

"Yes, Jamie, you did that."

He grunted, though it was a grunt of awe if ever she'd heard one. Suddenly the lights went back on and Jamie gasped. Elizabeth caught sight of his grin the instant before the room was plunged back into darkness. He flicked the lights on and off half a dozen more times before Elizabeth begged him to stop.

He hauled her into his arms and hugged her tightly. "Perhaps I will find your time to my liking after all."

"I think you will, my lord," she said with a smile. "Let's call my parents, and then I'll show you a few more miracles."

Elizabeth dragged the phone over to the bed and sat down, staring at it. If she called her mother, her mother would probably faint. Even worse, the shock just might give her father a heart attack. Of all her brothers, she was closest to Alex and Zachary. She had no clue as to where to reach Zachary. His addresses changed as often as his girlfriends. Alex would still be in New York, and he was by far the most level-headed of the bunch.

"How much longer must we stare at it before it begins to work?" Jamie asked.

She looked up to find Jamie staring energetically at the phone, as if he were willing it to jump up and do something. She laughed as she realized she had been staring at it in the same manner.

"I was just thinking. Sorry. Actually when you pick it up, it starts working on its own." She picked up the receiver and put it to her ear. Once she heard the dial tone, she held the receiver to Jamie's ear.

"What a noise," he said, wrinkling his nose.

She put it to her own ear and had to agree with him. A dial tone was not the most dulcet sound ever to grace a person's ear.

"It is a bit harsh," she agreed. "Now, what happens is that I speak into this, and my voice goes down this cord," she indicated the black cord snaking across the floor to the wall, "and all the way to my parents' house. They'll pick up a phone just like this and talk back to me."

"Nay." Jamie's expression was one of disbelief.

"It's a bit more complicated than that, but that's the basic idea. I don't think we'll call my parents, though. We'll call Alex. He's more liable to react calmly."

"Call? How will you call to him? Is he nearby?"

"That's how you describe this talking on the telephone. He's in America."

"Ah," Jamie nodded wisely. "Very well, then. Call him. And let us hope we don't disturb his supper. His wife will likely be mightily displeased with us."

"He's not married, Jamie. The only thing we might disturb is his putting the moves on some poor debutante. Don't ask," she said, holding up her hand to stave off the inevitable question. "And besides, the time is different in America. It's still afternoon there."

She watched her husband digest that, then shake his head, as if it were just too much effort to deal with it. She completely understood. Time zones were too much math for her to face at the moment.

She called the international operator and placed a call to the brother she hadn't seen in almost four months. The phone rang easily a dozen times before Alex came on the line, sounding only partially awake. Maybe he was having an afternoon nap.

"Alex? It's Beth."

"Oh, hi, Beth," Alex murmured sleepily. Then his gasp came clearly over the phone. "Good grief, Beth, is that really you?"

She laughed at his stunned tone. Oh, it was so good to hear his voice!

"It's me, Alex."

There was a loud crash, sounding faintly like everything on his nightstand taking a dive to the floor, then several choice swear words, then Alex again on the line. "Honey, tell me I'm not dreaming!"

"No, you're not dreaming," she said, clutching the phone with both hands and smiling at Jamie. He smiled back. "How are Mom and Dad?"

"Frantic. They've torn the East Coast apart looking for you. By the way, where in the *hell* are you? This sounds long distance." He gasped again and began to speak so rapidly she could hardly understand him. "Were you kidnapped? Tell me where you are, and I'll be there on the next plane. Have they hurt you? Do you need to hang up? Do you need money?"

She laughed happily. "Alex, I've missed you so much. I've forgotten how nice it is to have my big brother looking out for me."

"Damn it, Beth, where the *hell* are you?"

She winced. "Scotland."

"And just how the *hell* did you get over there?"

"You wouldn't believe me if I told you. Besides it's not the kind of thing you want to talk about over the phone. When can you come over?"

"I want details, Beth."

Always the lawyer. "Well, you can't have them."

"Hmmm, I don't like the sound of this."

"I don't care. Oh, and I'm married."

"To whom?" he yelled. "The King of England?"

She laughed and put her hand over the phone. "He wants to know if I married the King of England."

Jamie snorted. "Tell him your aim was higher than that."

"A much finer man than any king, Alex," Elizabeth said with a smile. "And you can meet him if you'd be willing to loan me some money."

"No problem. Give me your address."

Elizabeth gave him the address off one of Roddy's travel brochures and then sighed. "Maybe you should call Mom and Dad and prepare them. I'd hate to give Dad a heart attack."

"I'll call them and then hook you both up. And I'll wire you some cash first thing to whatever bank is closest to your hotel."

"Thanks, Alex. You're a doll."

"I've missed you, Beth," he said. He paused again. "You're sure you're okay?"

"I've never been better."

"Well, you sound it. I'll be over with Mom and Dad as soon as we can get flights out."

"Really?" she asked. "You can come too?"

"To tell you the truth, tomorrow's my first day of vacation. I was going to make reservations for St. Croix, but I haven't done anything yet. Getting rained on in Scotland sounds much more fun than lounging on a white beach gawking at bikini-clad women all day."

"Gee, thanks Alex," she said, with a laugh. "I appreciate the sacrifice."

"Yeah, well, don't thank me yet. Zachary's been sleeping on my couch for a week, so you're going to get him as part of the package. I don't dare leave him behind. There'd be nothing left of my condo otherwise."

"Did he lose another girlfriend?"

"And his job, all in one day, if you can believe it. You can baby-sit him for a while."

Elizabeth smiled. "I've missed him enough to put up with him for a while. Bring him along. And thanks for coming. I'm going to need some legal help."

Alex paused. "I don't like the sound of that."

"It's nothing serious. Just get over here."

"All right. Hold on a sec, and I'll call Mom."

Within moments, Elizabeth heard her mother's voice. And from nowhere came tears she couldn't stop. She sobbed so hard while she was talking that she could barely breathe. Jamie put his arm around her to comfort her. Finally his hand stroking her hair helped her regain a semblance of control. And once she had regained control, her father began voicing his questions. Loudly.

"How in the *hell* did you get all the way to Scotland without any money and without a passport?" he shouted.

Elizabeth held the phone away. "Daddy, it would be better not to discuss this over the phone."

"And what is this I hear about you being married?" he bellowed. "Elizabeth Anne Smith, what in heaven's name were you thinking?"

Elizabeth winced. Her father was sort of a cross between Ward Cleaver and Bubba Smith. He'd played college football and had a tendency to coach his family as he would have coached a team. He was probably the most unlikely person ever created to have chosen to be a pediatrician, but the kids absolutely adored his willingness to drop his stethoscope and wrestle with any and all comers in his waiting room. On a more personal note, she knew his bellows were nothing but bluster, but they made her cringe just the same.

"Daddy, please just be patient. You'll meet Jamie when you come over, and then we'll explain everything. But you have to come with an open mind."

"Why?" he demanded. "Alex said you needed legal help. Is he a criminal?"

Elizabeth laughed in spite of herself. "Daddy, you'll be so pleased with my husband, your buttons will burst. He's just the kind of son-in-law you've always wanted."

Jamie tugged on her skirt. "Tell him I'm no wimp," he said haughtily.

"Daddy, he says to tell you he's no wimp. In fact, I think he'd even make a great football player."

Her father grunted, only somewhat appeased.

"He could probably take on all five of the boys at once."

Robert Smith grunted again. "Well, I'll get on the mobile and get us a pair of tickets. Don't you hang up before I get back, Mary. I think I may want to call a huddle with this man of Elizabeth's before things go too much further."

"Of course, dear," Mary said demurely. Once the extension had clicked off, she bombarded Elizabeth with questions. "Honey, how did you meet him? How old is he? What does he look like? How long have you been married? Can we expect grandchildren soon?"

Elizabeth lay back on the bed and laughed at her mother's barrage of questions. "I'll give you all the details when you get here, Mom."

"At least tell me what he looks like."

Elizabeth looked up at Jamie who sat on the side of the bed, smiling down at her.

"Well, he's taller than Daddy, but leaner. He has dark hair and dark green eyes and a beautiful smile."

Jamie flashed her a beautiful smile, just to prove the truth of her words.

"He's very sweet, unless he's grumbling at me, then he is most unreasonable and pig-headed."

"That sounds familiar," Mary said dryly. "Let me talk to him, honey."

Elizabeth put her hand over the receiver and looked up at Jamie. "She wants to talk to you."

Jamie paled. "She does?"

"She does. 'Tis a simple thing, my laird, surely too far beneath you for concern. Just ignore her Americanisms and you'll do fine. Your English is wonderful."

Jamie put his shoulders back. "Of course, I will speak with her immediately."

Elizabeth handed Jamie the phone, and he put it to his ear hesitantly.

"Aye?" he said, uncertainly. Then her mother must have replied because a look of complete wonder crossed his face.

"Lady Smith?" he inquired. He waited. "Aye, 'tis a pleasure to talk with you also," he said.

Now this was a picture for the history books: a Scottish laird in full dress, sword lying on the bed next to him, the huge aquamarine ring on his hand flashing in the light from the lamps above his head, chatting on the phone as though he had done it all his life. Elizabeth felt a deep sense of relief steal over her. Seeing Jamie relax at the table had been great, but it could have been a fluke. Watching him charm her mother over the telephone was undeniable proof that he could accept something he never would have imagined in his wildest nightmares and adjust to it without trouble. And Jamie certainly seemed to be adjusting without trouble. Not only was he carrying on an involved conversation with her mother, he was examining the phone, as if by looking at it he could uncover just where Mary Smith was hiding inside it.

Then he paled suddenly and held the phone away. "She's gone to fetch your father."

"Good luck," Elizabeth said cheerfully. Jamie wearing a look of trepidation was something she'd never seen before.

"Sir Smith?" Jamie listened for several minutes. "I know, my lord," he said quickly. "And I did want to ask you before I wed her, but 'twas impossible." He winced and Elizabeth could just imagine what her father was saying to him. "I know," he said again and then listened some more. "Aye, I know that too." He covered the phone as he had seen her do and whispered, "Beth, I can't understand half of what he's saying. Too many words I don't know."

"Get him to shut up or he'll go on all night."

Her laird took a deep breath and spoke into the mouthpiece. "Sir Smith . . . my lord . . . Lord Smith!" he finished at a half roar. That must have done the trick, for a look of satisfaction crossed his face. "I cannot answer all your questions now. All I can tell you is that I love your daughter more than my own life. And I would like to have your blessing." He waited. "If you wish to challenge me, I will understand. But consider this: if we fight, one of us will lose, and I can guarantee it will not be me.

You might give more thought to whether or not you want to put Elizabeth through that." And with that he handed her back the phone.

Elizabeth held it to her ear. There was silence on the other end.

"Daddy?"

"Good grief," Robert bellowed. "Elizabeth Anne, where in the *hell* did you find that guy? His English is practically unintelligible! And what is this challenge business all about? Is he going to shoot me when I get off the plane?"

"He would rather hack at you with a sword, I'm sure."

"Well, tell him I'm not about to fight—a *what*?"

"Daddy, trust me. Now when are you coming?"

Her father hrumphed, obviously displeased with her change of subject. "Our plane leaves in two hours. Alex is meeting us in New York, and then we'll fly out on the first flight we can get." He paused. "Baby, are you all right?"

"Daddy, I couldn't be better," she said.

He sighed. "If you say so. I can only assume you are safe. With the way that man talks, I'm not too sure."

"He loves me, Daddy. He would never hurt me."

"I'll take your word for it." He paused. "You don't know how frightened we were."

"I know, Daddy, and I'm sorry. I love you."

"I love you, too. I'll see you soon."

She hung up the phone and looked at Jamie. "He's not such a bad sort."

Jamie shook his head. "I would have felt the same way if my wee lass had come home wed and not told me. He's a father, and he loves you. But I will fight him for you if that is how he wishes it."

Elizabeth put her arms around his neck and held onto him tightly. "It won't come to that, Jamie. He'll like you very much."

"Because I lord over you so well?"

"Yes. It will please him greatly to know that there is actually a man I do not control."

"Ah, but you do control me. More than you know."

"And more than you'll own up to, no doubt."

"Of course."

Elizabeth yawned. "I'm exhausted, Jamie. Let's go get ready for bed. I think you'll like the bathroom."

"Bathroom?"

"It's a very luxurious garderobe."

She led him to the bathroom and turned on the light. The room had a deep bathtub, a toilet, a bidet and a freestanding sink. And a small mirror. Jamie ignored everything else and went straight to the mirror. He looked at his reflection and reached out to touch it. He looked back at her in wonder.

"This is so much clearer than ours."

She shrugged. "I prefer yours." And she did. A fourteenth-century polished silver platter was less harsh than a twentieth-century mirror. "That isn't the surprise," she smiled. She walked over to where he stood before the sink. She pointed to the faucets. " 'C' is for cold and 'H' is for hot." He looked at her, puzzled.

"Water," she clarified. She turned the cold water on and he jumped. He put his hand under it and then laughed. He cupped his hands and tasted it. She turned it off. "You turn on the hot," she urged.

He turned the faucet gingerly and then put his hand under the water. He looked at her incredulously. "Who boils this?"

"There is a machine that does it."

"And I can have this water whenever I want it by just turning this handle?"

She nodded.

"Och, what a fine idea!" he exclaimed. He looked behind him at the bathtub. He looked at her with raised eyebrows, and she shrugged with a small smile. He turned on the hot water there and positively chortled with delight. "If Angus could see this . . ." he trailed off, grinning. He watched as the water ran down the drain, and then looked for something to stop it up with. He found the rubber drain cover and set it over the hole. When he had filled up the tub a bit, he took away the drain cover and watched the water drain out. He fiddled more with the faucets until he realized he could turn on both at the same time. He adjusted the temperature of the water and then looked at her with a twinkle in his eye.

"A bath, Lady MacLeod?"

"I may fall asleep in it."

"I will take care of you." He looked at the toilet behind her. "And what, pray tell, is that?"

"The chamber pot." She flushed it, and he watched in wonder as the water disappeared and came back. He helped himself to its use and then flushed it himself. If the running water had delighted him, this absolutely sent him into fits. She had to clap her hand over his mouth to stifle his laughter.

"People are asleep, you bellowing bear!"

He removed her hand and grinned. "I can't help myself. Angus would keel right over if he could see this." He looked down at it. "But 'tis a waste of water."

"Then it's up to you to figure out how to improve it."

He started to take it apart but she stopped him.

"Tomorrow, Jamie. Let's have our bath and then go to bed. I'm exhausted."

They bathed together, and she almost fell asleep as she lay on her husband's broad chest. There really wasn't enough room for them in that tiny tub, but they managed. Elizabeth hardly woke as Jamie carried her to the bed and tucked her in.

Her family and her husband, both in the same century.

Life just didn't get any better than that.

Chapter 26

JAMIE WOKE WITH a gasp, his head still full of the dream he'd been having. He'd been in his own hall, kindling fires with a flick of his wrist, commanding boiling water to flow from spouts and, the most preposterous of all, talking to Andrew MacAllister on the telephone.

He looked next to him to find his wife smiling as she slept. He couldn't blame her. Seeing her family again was a joy she thought she'd never have. He was almost as excited as she, save for the slight anxiousness he felt about meeting her father. Surely the man would not take her away.

Well, kin or no kin, her father would find himself skewered on the end of a very sharp sword if he tried the like. Jamie hadn't risked life and limb to bring Elizabeth back to her time just to lose her. And the sooner he found a way to feed his wife, the less Robert Smith would have to say about it. It was most likely impossible to learn everything about her world before her kin came, but he'd master most of it. At least his English had been passable enough over the phone the day before. Learning a bit of it when he could had been a very wise thing to do. He would, however, need to acquire a few more words before Elizabeth's kin arrived.

He rolled lightly from the bed and padded across the floor to the privy closet. He flipped on the lights, then walked over to the mirror again. Aye, that was his face that stared back at him. He rubbed his hand over his unshaven jaw, then peered closely at the small scar near his ear. Angus had done a fine job sewing that one.

He looked at his eyes and actually found them to be a pleasing color. He'd suspected that before, but seeing them in a perfect reflection confirmed it. It pleased him that his eyes pleased Elizabeth. After all, she was the one who had to stare in them at all times. He next examined his teeth and found them to be rather fine, though not as white as Elizabeth's. Perhaps these future lads had a way to correct that flaw.

His hair, though, was surely something to be proud of. He gave it a thorough brushing. Aye, all in all, there wasn't too much lacking in his appearance. He wouldn't shame his lady.

As he used the chamber pot, Jamie shook his head in wonder. How strange it was to find the room actually smelling good. In fact, Roddy's entire house smelled good. Jamie hadn't been blind to the lack of rushes on the floor. Perhaps that had a bit to do with it.

He extinguished the lights in the garderobe, then returned to the main chamber. He walked to the bed and stared intently at the lamps that hung on the wall. Turning all the lamps on would disturb his wife, and he wanted to let her sleep a bit longer. He had a mind to have a few things under control before she woke.

It took him only minutes to discover that the little lamps could be turned off and on at the bed, but only if they had been lit from the lever by the doorway first. He smiled smugly to himself. Life was not so complex after all. He felt the lamps and found them to be warm to the touch. He tried to look closely at what lit them from within, but it burned his eyes and he had to turn away. Those fires were powerfully bright.

He gathered up all the thin manuscripts he'd seen the night before next to the phone, then went back to bed, sitting up against the headboard. He opened the first manuscript and found it to be full of people captured on the pages, just as Elizabeth had been captured on her driver's license. The sight stunned him so that he could only gape at them, fearing they would begin to move at any moment. He peered closely at them and saw that though they were indeed people, they certainly weren't real.

The plain script was easy enough to read, and he spent a few minutes puzzling out some of the words he didn't know. Future words, by the look of them. Ah, well, it was to be expected that man would have invented a few new words in honor of the things he had discovered.

Elizabeth stirred in her sleep, and Jamie put his hand on her shoulder to quiet her. He wasn't ready for her to rise yet. He had study to accomplish. He fully intended to have mastered at least a pair of the manuscripts so he wouldn't look the fool. Elizabeth wouldn't wake and find him wanting.

Elizabeth snuggled closer to him and Jamie gritted his teeth. She had chosen his hip to press her cheek against, and her warm breath caressed something that certainly didn't need any help in rising.

Och, but this was a dilemma. He looked at the sheaf of papers in his hand and frowned. Did he put aside his reading and give in to his body's clamoring for joining, or did he persevere?

He did his damnedest to ignore his wife. They could indulge each other in an hour or so. Perhaps he would woo her with a few future words while he was at it.

Elizabeth woke to the ringing of the phone. Oh no, not the phone. She reached for Jamie, just to make sure she hadn't dreamed him, then sighed in relief. Then she sat up, bleary-eyed, and tried to get out of bed.

"Stay," Jamie hissed, pushing her down. "I will see to this."

"Jamie, it's the phone. That noise means someone's trying to call you."

He grasped his sword and approached the phone stealthily. If Elizabeth hadn't known he would have been terribly offended, she would have burst out laughing at the adorable picture he made. Here was a naked man brandishing a sword, stalking a hapless telephone with every intention of killing it if necessary. He reached the phone and grabbed the receiver. The ringing stopped immediately, and he lowered his sword in surprise. Elizabeth watched her husband put the phone to his ear.

"Aye?" he said gruffly. When he actually got an answer, his

face lit up as if he'd just discovered a priceless new treasure. "Why, Lord Smith, 'tis you. A very fine morning to you, my lord."

Elizabeth grinned as she watched her husband listen to her father. Evidently he was getting quite the lecture because his face registered deeper and deeper confusion. Finally he shook his head.

"My lord, I fear I didn't understand a word of what you just said. Allow me to fetch Elizabeth for you."

Elizabeth sat up as Jamie dragged the phone across the room to her.

"Daddy?"

"Why does he keep calling me 'Lord Smith'?" her father asked suspiciously.

"Oh, Daddy, that's just his way. Isn't he wonderful?"

"I'll reserve judgment. We're about to take the plane from New York. We'll stay in Glasgow tonight, then come up tomorrow."

"No, we'll rent a car and come get you."

"You stay put, young lady, and we'll see you tomorrow. And don't have any of that haggis stuff waiting. I want a steak."

"All right, Daddy," she said with a smile. "See you soon."

She hung up and handed the phone back to Jamie. He returned it to its place, then sauntered back to bed. He slid in underneath the covers and reached for her.

"You look pleased with yourself," she noted.

He shrugged nonchalantly. "I thought perhaps we'd go down to the village and do a bit of shopping. I'll need a watch and perhaps some athletic shoes. A tour on the bus might be nice, but only after a hearty lunch at the local pub. What say you?"

Elizabeth laughed. "I'd say, my laird, that you'd been doing a bit of travel-brochure reading while I slept."

"A bit," he said, giving her a depreciating smile. "And there are a few questions I have for you. After."

"After?"

"After," he confirmed, pulling her closer to him. "I've a mind to show you that a seven-hundred-year-old man still is able to love you breathless."

She laughed and wrapped her arms around him. "Jamie, you ancient bear, I never doubted it."

"But, just in case you did . . ." he said, closing his mouth over hers.

Elizabeth closed her eyes and gave herself up to the magic of Jamie's touch. A few months of wedded bliss had turned him into a patient, wonderful lover. She shivered as he caressed her with his calloused hands, torn between wanting to weep over his gentleness and wanting to moan at the sensations he was arousing.

He had discovered rather ordinary places on her body that, when given closer scrutiny, almost sent her over the edge. Who would have thought the inside of her elbow would make her so crazy? She nodded to herself over that thought as Jamie kissed his way down her arm.

"Oh, my," she gasped, as he touched her skin with his tongue.

His only response was a knowing chuckle.

After a while Elizabeth lost track of where she began and Jamie ended. And, as Jamie had predicted, spent passion left her breathless. She didn't even have the strength to untangle her limbs from his.

"Shall I bathe while you recover?" he asked politely.

All she could do was stick her tongue out at him in response.

His walk was a swagger as he made his way to the bathroom. Elizabeth closed her eyes. She *was* breathless. Jamie's loving was just as wonderful as it had been seven hundred years ago.

She smiled, content.

Jamie rubbed his temples as he walked with his wife in Roddy's garden. It was all too much. He'd spent the day before down in the village with Roddy and Elizabeth trying to understand the world he was now a part of. It had been overwhelming, from the glass on the shop windows to the strange new sounds that continuously startled him.

He adjusted the plaid he wore, which was certainly different than the comfortable one in his chamber, the one Elizabeth said would make him too conspicuous. He didn't care for the colors and had thought them to look suspiciously like something he'd once seen a Fergusson wear. Roddy had assured him the colors were what all MacLeods wore, but Jamie would have to see a few of his kinsmen parading about in them before he believed it.

He looked down at his lady and frowned. The skirts of her dress barely reached her knees, and he was none too pleased with that, for it showed far too much of her legs. Just the day before he'd almost been forced to kill a man because he'd leered at Elizabeth. Aye, he might have, had Elizabeth not begged him so fervently to let the slight pass. It seemed that killing to defend your lady's honor thusly was frowned upon in the future. Jamie couldn't understand that but knew he had no choice but to accept it.

"You look tired," Elizabeth said. "Want to sit down?"

Jamie considered. "Will you comb my hair with your fingers?"

"If it will make you stop frowning."

He smiled wearily as she sat down with her back against a tree. "Ah, Elizabeth, you know my frowns are nothing." He stretched out with his head in her lap. " 'Tis only that I have information overload."

She laughed softly and began to drag her fingers through his long locks. "What you have, Jamie my love, is a television hangover. It's far worse than too much ale."

"Aye," he agreed. "But I find I cannot help myself. Though I begin to wonder if I will ever lose the look of amazement I'm sure is still fixed firmly to my face."

She leaned down and kissed him. "Jamie, you're handling this wonderfully. There wasn't another from your day who could have adapted so well."

"Of course there wasn't," he said gruffly. "You've much to be grateful for."

She only smiled, as if she knew it.

Jamie closed his eyes and immediately images appeared, things he had seen on the television last night. Now, that was an invention that he never would have dreamed of. He'd sat before the box for hours, touching the glass surface of it again and again just to assure himself there really weren't people inside, teasing him. Roddy had been completely inadequate to the task of explaining how the bloody thing worked, and Elizabeth had been no better. Roddy had begged off early in the evening, and Elizabeth had pleaded a headache around midnight. Jamie had been left alone in Roddy's solar with the television. He'd watched the events in several beings' lives be played out like a jongleur's act.

And then he'd seen a killing with a weapon he couldn't for the life of him understand. It had terrified him. He'd gone and fetched Elizabeth out of bed, then demanded that she explain what he was seeing. She'd called it a gun and told him it was a very dangerous thing indeed, and he would never get close enough to even touch one. Then she'd turned off the television and pulled him from the room. Jamie had been shaken enough to allow it.

A gun. The thought of killing a man so quickly and cleanly with something so powerful unnerved him greatly. And because it frightened him, he knew he had to find the weapon and master it. Unless he had mastered it, he couldn't protect Elizabeth from it.

"Lady MacLeod, your kin are here!" Roddy shouted from the gate. "Just getting out of the car right now, they are!"

Elizabeth jumped up, almost snapping Jamie's neck in the process.

"Oh, Jamie, I'm so sorry," she said, covering her mouth with her hand. She reached down and helped him up, then brushed him off.

Jamie scowled when she arranged his hair to her liking. "I'm not a bairn," he grumbled.

Elizabeth laughed and leaned up to kiss him. "Oh, Jamie, I can hardly believe this is happening. My family is going to adore you."

Jamie pasted a smile on his face, trying to look enthusiastic. In reality, he was more nervous than he had ever been in his life. This wasn't an earl, or even a king he prepared to meet: it was his wife's sire. Och, and what if the man didn't care for him? At that moment Jamie had a very hard time remembering he was, or had been, laird of the most feared clan in the Highlands. He suddenly felt like a young lad who was still holding onto his mother's skirts for protection.

There was a fairly large automobile standing in front of the inn, and people were crawling from it in a rush. Jamie hardly had the nerve to attempt to put names to faces. He released his wife's hand and patted her back gently, urging her forward. Too late he realized he had almost toppled her over. She only laughed and kissed him before she darted away to throw herself into the arms of a woman who could only have been her mother.

Mary Smith was indeed a beautiful woman. As Jamie looked at her, he lifted one eyebrow with a bit of smugness. So his Elizabeth would retain her beauty far into her older years. That was a boon indeed.

A long, wide, powerful shape unfolded itself from the opposite side of the car, and Jamie suppressed a gulp at the sight of Elizabeth's father. Merciful heavens, the man was enormous. Perhaps he was not as tall as Jamie himself was, but it seemed that Robert Smith was a wee bit broader through the chest and perhaps even a bit beefier in the arms. Aye, and he was wearing an intimidating frown. He only gave Jamie a curt nod before he snatched his daughter away and hugged her. Jamie was surprised at the gentleness with which he did it, but here was a man used to tending sick children. He'd obviously learned to control his strength quite well.

Two more men emerged from the metal box and took their turns hugging Elizabeth numb. Brothers, Jamie deduced with a thoughtful nod. Just as big and intimidating as their sire. The knowledge actually pleased him. Should he and Elizabeth ever fashion a son together, the lad would be sturdy and tall. Aye, that was a fine thing to know.

"You must be Jamie."

Jamie looked down and found Elizabeth's mother taking his hands. "Aye," he managed, feeling a bit awkward. What would Elizabeth's mother expect from him?

Before he could answer his own question, she leaned up on her toes and kissed him softly on the cheek. "Thank you," she whispered, her eyes swimming with tears. "You've taken very good care of my baby girl."

"I did what I could, my lady," he said, feeling himself begin to redden under her frank approval. "She's a fine lass."

"And you seem to be a fine young man. Let's get these introductions over with and then go inside and chat." She kept hold of Jamie's hand as she called to Elizabeth's two brothers. "Boys, come over and meet your brother-in-law."

"That remains to be seen," Robert threw over his shoulder.

"Oh, Rob, hush up," Mary chided. She smiled up at Jamie. "He's just upset because he wasn't consulted. He'll get over it."

Jamie soon found himself looking from one brother to the other and back again, trying to understand their questions.

"Wait," he finally said, exasperated. "I'm not sure who is who yet." Alex he knew to be somewhere near his own age of a score and ten. He looked at the older one. "You're Alex?"

Alex nodded and shook Jamie's hand.

"I'm Zachary, Beth's favorite," the second boasted. "But you knew that already."

Jamie smiled. Zachary was, from what Elizabeth had told him, the baby of the family. Aye, the lad showed that well enough. "Actually," Jamie said, "she named you 'Zachary the Brat,' whatever *brat* means. I came to understand it was not a complimentary term."

Alex laughed, and Zachary shoved him.

Mary rolled her eyes heavenward. "Boys, go play somewhere else. You'll have Jamie thinking we're barbarians with the way you two fight."

Actually, Jamie was vastly relieved. A good wrestle among family was something he was sure he'd never have the pleasure of again. Knowing Elizabeth's brothers were as ready with their fists as he was eased his mind greatly.

Jamie was soon face-to-face with his love's sire. On closer inspection, the man was not as tall as he had seemed at first. What he lacked in size, he more than made up for in the fierceness of his frown. Jamie slowly folded his arms over his chest and frowned right back. There was no sense in having the man think he was trembling from head to toe. Of course he wasn't. There was simply a bit of chill in the air that had slipped up his plaid and sent a shiver down his spine.

"So," Robert said, folding his own arms and jutting his chin forward stubbornly, "you're Elizabeth's young man."

"I am Elizabeth's *husband*," Jamie corrected.

Robert grunted. "That remains to be seen."

"I think not. I wed her when there was no hope of my ever seeing you to ask for her. Now the deed's done, I'd like your blessing, but I'll not beg for it. Elizabeth's my wife now, and you'll take her away over my dead body."

Robert Smith pulled his chin back and stroked it. Jamie could have sworn he saw a flicker of admiration light in the man's eyes.

"How old are you?"

"A score and ten, my lord." Plus a few hundred, he added silently.

"What do you do for a living?"

"Daddy," Elizabeth interrupted, "let's go inside."

"Elizabeth," Jamie said sternly, "come over here and be silent." He held out his hand and pulled her behind him. "I can speak for myself."

"I know that, Jamie, it's just—"

Just the slightest pressure on her hand silenced her. He forced back his smile at her sigh of resignation and surrender. She knew he was right. If he didn't stand up for himself now, he'd never have the chance again. It was best Robert saw from the beginning who was laird.

"What do you do for a living?" Robert asked sharply. "How is it you intend to see to my daughter? Support her? Put food on the table?"

Jamie grunted. That was a question to be answered if ever there was one.

"At the moment, Lord Smith, I cannot say. I have gold and jewels aplenty that will serve us for now."

"What did you do before?" Robert asked, his frown deepening. "How did you feed and clothe my baby girl?"

"I was the MacLeod," Jamie said simply. "I cared for her in the same way I cared for my kinsmen. Life in the Highlands is never easy, but there was never a night she didn't have food on the table or a warm place to sleep."

Robert looked at him blankly. "I beg your pardon?"

Elizabeth poked her head around him and glared at her father before Jamie could stop her.

"Daddy, Jamie just happened to be the most powerful laird in the Highlands during the fourteenth century. He earned his gold the way every other laird did, by raising crops and cattle and raiding the other clans. There was not a man who did not know him and fear him. You can interrogate him all you want, but don't you dare imply that he wasn't capable of caring for me or for the innumerable people who depended on him for protection, guidance and sustenance. I simply won't stand for it."

Robert Smith's eyes had taken on a decidedly glazed appearance. "Fourteenth century?" he rumbled, skepticism dripping from his words. "What kind of cockamamy horse manure has this man been feeding you?"

Elizabeth shoved her wedding ring at her father. "Take a look at this. Jamie, show him your wedding ring."

Robert looked at the rings closely and then looked at Jamie with a no less formidable frown. "That proves only that you're rich. What sort of story is it you've been feeding my daughter?"

" 'Tis no story. Elizabeth lived it with me."

"I don't believe it," Robert said flatly. "I don't like this one bit. Listen, whoever you are, I hope to hell you've got a good lawyer because you're—"

"Robert Alan Smith, that is enough," his wife said distinctly. "Jamie, take Elizabeth back in the house. Boys, get the bags. Robert, you come with me inside where we can talk in peace."

Elizabeth shot her father a murderous look before Jamie pulled her away. He put his arm around her shoulders and led her back into the house.

"I don't blame him for not believing. I wouldn't have believed it either if it hadn't happened to me."

"My father can be very unreasonable sometimes," Elizabeth said apologetically.

He gave her a gentle squeeze. "Beth, he's just protecting his daughter. I would be doing the same thing in his place. In time he'll either accept the truth or he won't. You can't make a man believe what he doesn't want to."

"I suppose," she sighed. "Perhaps if we show him a few of the things from our saddlebags. He can look over my journal if he wants."

"You've read my thoughts. Roddy," Jamie called.

Roddy scurried into the entry hall, all smiles. "Aye, my lord Jamie?"

"Might we use your solar to speak together for a time? We've a long tale to tell Elizabeth's kin."

"Of course, my lord. Call me if you've need of assistance."

"Chambers for my lady's kin and time in the solar will suffice at the moment. Perhaps a small snack if the labor becomes too heavy."

Roddy bowed and began issuing orders to his lads about providing for the laird's comfort. Jamie ignored Robert's skeptical mutter and headed back toward his temporary bedchamber to fetch his saddlebags. The man was a healer, and healers were known to have odd ideas about how the world worked. Well, he and Elizabeth had nothing to tell but the truth. Robert Smith would believe it or not in his own good time.

Elizabeth stood with her back to the fireplace and looked at her husband, who sat facing off with her father. They'd been talking for four hours, though it seemed more like four years. Jamie was hungry. She could see that by the hunger frown that sat on his brow. It was a very different frown from his intimidation frown or his I'm-just-frowning-to-remind-you-I'm-still-laird-here frown. She left the room, intent on finding him something to eat before he decided to gnaw on her father.

"Where're you off to, sis?" Alex said, following her from the room. "Aren't you afraid Jamie'll chop Dad in two with his sword if you don't stay and keep an eye on him?"

"He just might," Elizabeth said. "He's one grumpy Highlander if he doesn't get fed regularly."

Alex put his arm around her shoulders and walked with her to the kitchen. "Beth, this is the most incredible story I've ever heard."

Elizabeth looked up at him. They'd always been close growing up, and being in New York together had brought them even closer. Elizabeth felt as if she knew Alex better than even her parents did. She knew what to look for when she looked up at him; she saw no doubt in his eyes.

"You believe us?"

"Beth, I've been in that room for the last four hours too, you know," he said gently. "Jamie's not capable of lying. Did you see him break out into a cold sweat when he tried to avoid discussing where he'd put you when you first arrived?" He reached out and ruffled her hair. "Never thought I'd have myself an honest-to-goodness medieval laird as a brother-in-law, but I think I'll like it. What kind of bribe will it take for him to teach me how to use a sword?"

"He'd be more flattered than you could imagine if you just asked him. But be forewarned; he's merciless. You'll probably wish you were dead after the first couple of days when your muscles get sore. I know I did."

Alex opened his mouth and then shut it. "I won't ask the details."

"I certainly didn't get these calluses on my hands from scrubbing floors," she said haughtily. "Just remember who you're talking to, buddy. I'm Elizabeth MacLeod. That may not mean much to you, but it sure did to a lot of others."

"My sister the witch," he laughed.

"Yeah, well, before I put a hex on your lovelife, help me carry back a snack. Jamie's hunger frown may be a full-blown starvation scowl if we don't hurry."

"He suits you. You would never have been happy with a wimp like Stanley."

Elizabeth stopped at the door to the kitchen and looked up at her brother. "Can you do it, Alex? Get him a birth certificate and all that?"

"I'll do my best. If not, we'll just all move to Scotland and become part of Jamie's new clan. I can think of worse ways to live than raiding other people's property and wenching at all hours."

Elizabeth continued on into the kitchen. Maybe separating Alex and Jamie would be the best thing for everyone; she shuddered to think the mischief they would stir up together.

A quarter of an hour later, she and Alex reentered the study with a quick meal intended to tide Jamie over until supper. Elizabeth slapped the food down in front of her husband.

"Eat," she commanded.

He flashed her a grateful look before he reached for a cold mutton leg and practically inhaled it. Even her father couldn't keep up with Jamie's rate of consumption. They kept up their discussion for another hour before Roddy called them all to supper. Robert sat back and shook his head.

"This is the most unbelievable thing I've ever heard. If one of you had come to me with these hallucinations, I would have said you were crazy." He met Elizabeth's eyes as she stood behind Jamie's chair with her hands on his shoulders. "But there are two of you. That makes it harder to discount."

"It's the truth, Daddy," she said softly.

Robert pursed his lips. "Aren't you a little old for my baby?" he asked Jamie.

Jamie smiled for the first time that afternoon. "She was a bit young for me a week ago. 'Tis simply repayment."

"I suppose," Robert said. He looked at Jamie seriously. "I would prefer to see you marry her again. I'd counted on giving her away."

Jamie inclined his head just the slightest bit. "I will wed her again, if it pleases you, but you'll not take her from my bed before that time."

Robert sighed. "All right, Jamie. I'll give you that concession."

"Concession?"

"Compromise," Robert clarified.

"Ah," Jamie said wisely. "Then I accept it." He rose and waited for Elizabeth's father to rise before he put a hand on Robert's shoulder and walked with him to the dining room. "Now that we have that behind us, there are questions I would ask of you. Elizabeth is pitifully unable to explain several things that puzzle me deeply. You, as a healer, may be able to answer them to my satisfaction."

By midnight, Robert was begging to be excused from Jamie's questioning. Alex and Zachary had already taken refuge in their room, and Mary was sound asleep in her chair. Elizabeth finally convinced her husband to take pity on her father and allow him to go to bed. Jamie did, only after extracting a promise from his father-in-law that the questions could begin again early the next morning.

Elizabeth tugged and pulled until she had Jamie at least

going in the right direction. Once they were in their own bathroom, he dutifully used the toothbrush she gave him. Then he watched her as she did the same.

"You are very beautiful," he remarked.

"And you're very handsome."

He leaned back against the door frame. "I am going on a journey tomorrow with your sire."

Elizabeth frowned. "Where?"

"Wherever the road takes us. I wish to see this new Scotland of mine."

"But, Jamie," she said, uneasily, "I don't know that you should so soon."

He looked ready to simply issue an order, but then his expression softened. "If not now, Beth, then when? The sooner I am accustomed to your world, the sooner I will be able to care for you as I wish. Can you fault me for that?"

There was little use in trying to argue with him, especially when he was right.

"All right, Jamie. Just be careful. And don't get lost."

"I will be careful, and I will not become lost."

"You can't take your sword."

He frowned. "My dirk then."

"You'll have to leave it in the car."

"Am I at least allowed to take you to my bed this eve?"

"To sleep?"

"After," he said solemnly.

She put her arms around his neck. "Well, you *are* laird. I suppose I have little choice but to oblige you."

"At least someone remembers," he grumbled.

Elizabeth smiled as he led her back to the bedroom. She had the feeling his being laird was something no one, including her family, would ever forget.

Chapter 27

JAMIE EYED THE car before him with a narrow look. It was the same one he'd ridden in the day before with Robert Smith. Well, perhaps he would be more accustomed to the noise today. It was either that or walk to his keep, and he knew that would take too long, especially since the rest of the wedding guests were driving.

He steeled himself and crawled into the front seat. He arranged himself so Elizabeth could sit on his lap. His finest plaid had been put in the trunk in preparation for wedding Elizabeth again. In truth, the ceremony wasn't what Jamie was thinking about. Seeing his hall was the thought that consumed him. He'd seen remains of castles yesterday as he traveled with Elizabeth's sire, buildings that had been built long after his time. Unless his offspring through the centuries had been exceedingly careful, there would be little left of his keep.

Robert turned the car on, and Jamie forced himself to relax. The noise of the car still unnerved him, but it was definitely less unsettling than it had been the day before. He was certain he'd left permanent marks in the arm rest from where he'd clutched it. Robert had finally pulled over to give Jamie a look under the hood. That had eased his mind some, but he still preferred the whicker of a horse to the whine of an engine. Perhaps modern man wasn't that much better off.

Elizabeth's sire was quiet as they drove, following Roddy's directions. A road now led almost to the meadow. Jamie waited until the car had stopped before he opened the door and eased Elizabeth off his lap. He pulled himself out of the car after her and reached for her hand. He looked down at her and saw his own apprehension mirrored in her eyes. Taking a deep breath, he walked with her through the remaining bit of forest and out onto the meadow.

All his forewarnings to himself didn't prepare him for what he saw.

Or, rather, didn't see.

The village was gone. The wall surrounding the keep still stood, though it was crumbling in numerous places. Jamie took Elizabeth's hand and clutched it tightly as they made their way up the meadow, then through the twisted iron gates. Jamie stopped before the remains of his hall and stood there, speechless.

Elizabeth turned toward him and threw her arms around him. He gathered her close and rested his cheek on her head. Both the massive wooden doors were gone, doors that had once kept the night and enemies at bay. The walls were decaying, some covered with moss, most looking so unstable that he feared to enter. The roof was entirely gone. It looked as though some giant monster had stooped down and bitten off the top half of the keep, leaving the jagged walls behind as testimony to his hunger. Jamie couldn't believe this was the same place he'd left but a few days earlier. It was a sure sign of the centuries he and Elizabeth had passed through to come to her time.

"Can we rebuild it?"

Jamie looked down at his wife and was surprised by the grief in her eyes. So she had come to love the pile of stones as deeply as he. Well, if she wanted it rebuilt, he'd see it done.

"Of course we can, love," he said, wiping a few stray tears from her cheeks gently with his thumbs.

"Could we live here again?"

"You don't wish to return to America?"

She paused, then shook her head. "Maybe to visit now and then, but not to live. A week ago, I thought Scotland would be my home for the rest of my life." She smiled up at him, a small smile. "I still feel the same way. Only the century has changed, Jamie."

"Truly?" he asked, loving her all the more for her unselfishness. Though he desired to see the wonders of her land, the thought of never seeing his again had left a darkness over his heart.

"Jamie, I love Scotland as much as you do. I want our children to know what heather smells like when carried by a warm breeze, what the first snowfall looks like on our mountains, how it feels to sit in the great hall in the evenings and listen to the sound of a lute and feel the fire on their faces. How could we deny our children those pleasures?"

"But what of your storytelling? Do you not need to be in America for that?"

"Not with Her Majesty's Postal Service at my disposal."

Jamie frowned. "There's that business of a queen again. I don't know that we'll be using any of an Englishwoman's services."

Elizabeth only smiled. "Then we'll get a fax machine. No," she said, holding up her hand, "I don't want to explain it. Ask my dad later."

Jamie shut his mouth on the question she'd just avoided answering and shook his head. He was beginning to wonder if he would ever master all the things Elizabeth took for granted.

"Well, then, my lady," he said, "I will build you another hall just as it was in the fourteenth century, down to the smallest detail. And if you must use Her Majesty's services for your tales, I won't complain overmuch—"

"Jamie, listen," Elizabeth interrupted him. "Don't you hear it?"

"Hear what?"

"The lute," she said, her eyes wide with wonder.

"Elizabeth, the shock of seeing the keep in such poor shape has addled your wits. I hear nothing. Now let us speak about this wedding we will have again for your sire. I daresay the chapel—"

"Don't you hear the voice?" she interrupted again. She whirled around to face the hall. "Joshua?" she called.

The music stopped abruptly. Jamie's eyes widened as his former minstrel appeared in the doorway, looking as shocked as Jamie felt. Joshua looked from Jamie to Elizabeth to her family and back to Jamie again. Then he threw himself down the stairs and skidded to a halt on his knees in front of Elizabeth. He wrapped his arms around her legs and held on.

"Merciful heavens," Elizabeth said, looking up at Jamie with wide eyes.

"Aye," Jamie said, stunned. He put his hand on Joshua's shoulder. "Minstrel, are you alone?"

"Aye, m-my lord," Joshua said, his teeth chattering.

"Release your lady, Joshua," Jamie said sternly. "You're going to break her."

Joshua released Elizabeth only to turn and cling to Jamie.

"There, there, lad," Jamie said, patting Joshua on the back. "There's no reason to be in such a state."

"But the hall, my lord," Joshua said weakly. " 'Tis not as I left it yestereve."

"Up on your feet like a man," Jamie said, "and give me this tale. Have you forgotten who is your laird?"

Joshua rose obligingly, though he was none too steady on his feet.

"You've filled out a bit," Jamie noted. "Been training with Jesse?"

"Aye, my lord," Joshua nodded. He looked at Elizabeth and gave her a tremulous smile. "You're just as lovely as I remembered, my lady. I had wondered why my poor life had become so dark. Now I see that 'twas because I lacked the brightness of your beauty to give me sight."

Jamie sighed in exasperation. "I see you've lost none of your glibness, Joshua. Now, tell me how you came here."

"My mount threw me yesterday in the forest, and I hit my head. I dreamed so strongly of my lady Elizabeth, I was certain she had come home. I hastened back to the keep only to find it in this sorry shape. I was sure I was dead. Am I?"

"You're not dead," Jamie said, feeling very much the authority on the subject. "You're in the future. When we've time, you can take off your shoes and use both your fingers and your toes to count up all the centuries you've passed to come to this spot. Now, give me news of my son. He is well? What of Megan?"

"Both well and happy when I left them, my lord. With a fine new babe also—"

Joshua shrank back suddenly. Jamie heard the crunch of gravel behind him and rightly assumed that his father-in-law had just joined them.

"Aye?" Jamie asked, looking over his shoulder at Elizabeth's sire.

"Who is this?" Robert demanded. "And why was he mauling my baby girl?"

Jamie suppressed his smile at Robert's intimidating frown. 'Twas no wonder Elizabeth had known so well how to handle him, having grown up in a houseful of bears.

"This is my minstrel, Joshua of Sedgwick. Joshua, this is Lord Robert, Elizabeth's sire."

"Greetings to you, my lord," Joshua said, making Robert a shaky bow.

Robert looked at Jamie with raised eyebrows. "A minstrel? How did he arrive here?"

"Through the forest," Jamie said, feeling an unpleasant tingle go down his spine. The forest—a place to be reckoned with, to be sure. He would have to come to terms with it sooner or later.

But not today. He would take time enough to get settled. Then he would turn his mind to that other mystery.

He turned to his minstrel abruptly. "Joshua, run have yourself a bath and take a comb to those tangles. Elizabeth and I will wed today."

"Again?"

"Aye, to humor her sire. As you can see, Lord Robert is not a man you wish to anger."

"Aye, my lord." Joshua nodded vigorously. "I see that plainly. I'll return with all due haste."

Elizabeth reached out and put her hand on his arm. "I'm glad you're here, Joshua. Will you play for us tonight?"

"Aye, my lady," he said, drawing himself up suddenly and trying to look confident. " 'Twould be an honor."

"A bath first," Jamie reminded him.

Joshua nodded and practically fled for what used to be the garden. Jamie beckoned to Alex. "Come with me, brother, and aid me while I dress. Zachary, you will watch over your sister." He looked behind them and then back at Robert. "My lord, perhaps Roddy could use assistance in rousing the friar he procured for us. The man of the cloth looks to have fainted."

Elizabeth looked up at her father once Jamie and Alex had gone inside the keep. "You'll notice he didn't dare order you around," she remarked.

"Of course not," her father said, his eyes twinkling. "After all, I am Lord Smith, your sire."

Elizabeth reached for her mother's hand. "Mom, let's go check on Joshua before he drowns. He's not a very good swimmer. I'll show you the garden where Jamie picked all those flowers for me."

The garden was overgrown, and there was surely no sign of Malcolm's tenderly cared-for plants, but Elizabeth didn't notice. All she saw was the place where Jamie had crawled on his hands and knees time after time to find weeds to please her.

Joshua was just emerging from the lake when they arrived, shivering and shaking the water from his hair like a puppy.

"Elizabeth," Mary exclaimed, her hand to her throat. "Turn around!"

Elizabeth looked at her, puzzled. "Why?"

"He's naked!"

Elizabeth laughed. "Mom, they have a very different concept of privacy in the Middle Ages. Joshua would think I'd lost my mind if I turned away."

Joshua proved her point quite nicely by not even bothering to cover himself. He shook out his hair and dried off as best he could with his old clothes.

"Here's an extra plaid of Jamie's," Elizabeth said, handing him the clothing. She stopped as she caught sight of the long scar across his chest. "Joshua," she gasped, "how did you get this?"

"An ally of Nolan's, my lady," he said with a wince. "After Laird Jamie vanquished the Fergussons, Nolan took to roaming with whatever enemies we had. I earned this in a battle we fought for the McKinnon." He shuddered. "Perhaps the worst has been the last few months. Nolan's been spotted haunting the woods about the keep, as if he waited for something—"

"Or some*one*," Elizabeth finished for him. Not only was Nolan corrupt; he was cunning and probably smarter than any of them had given him credit for. He'd seen her come out of the forest; she wouldn't have put it past him to try a bit of time traveling.

Out of the corner of her eye, she caught a flash of red. She whirled around, her heart in her throat.

She looked intently at the trees surrounding them but could detect no sign of anything strange. Well, Nolan might have been smart, but she seriously doubted he was smart enough to figure out how the forest worked. Not even she and Jamie were sure of the specifics.

Joshua finished making himself presentable, and they returned to the keep just in time to have Jamie emerge, dressed in his finest plaid, with his bright sword hanging by his side. Elizabeth looked around to find her family all wearing expressions of incredulity. An anguished groan let her know the poor priest had fainted again. No doubt the man would think twice before he did another wedding for any of Roddy's guests.

She smiled as she realized why her family had been struck so speechless. They knew Jamie, but they'd never seen the MacLeod before. He looked every inch the proud Highland laird. He nodded briefly to her before he gathered up the priest and ushered the poor man to the remains of the chapel. Her family followed, all but her father, who stayed behind with her. He wiped mock sweat from his brow.

"Did I actually ever cross that man? What was I thinking?"

Elizabeth grinned. "Pretty impressive, isn't he? Now you see why the MacLeods were so feared in his day. Believe me, he's even more intimidating when he's coming at you full gallop on his horse, brandishing his sword and giving his battle cry."

Robert drew his daughter into a fierce hug. "I'm just glad you wound up with Jamie. He loves you very much."

"You believe us now?"

"I don't have much of a choice," he admitted, with a smile. "If watching Jamie come unglued in the car yesterday hadn't convinced me, seeing your minstrel would have. Young Joshua looks at Jamie like he's a king." He shook his head with a wry smile. "If I'm not careful, I'll be calling your husband 'my lord' just as easily as you do. And I'll be just as ready to hear it said to me." He shook his head again. "Your grandmother will croak the first time she hears Jamie call me Lord Smith."

"Don't get delusions of grandeur, Dad," she teased.

"Your mother won't let me," he grumbled. "Just last night she let me know in no uncertain terms that though my son-in-law might find my words just as sacred as gospel, she certainly didn't."

"Leave it to Mom to be practical," Elizabeth said, with a smile.

Robert put his arm around her shoulders. "Let's get going, baby. I can hear Jamie pacing from here."

After a simple, beautiful reaffirmation of their vows, the indisposed priest was hustled away by Roddy. Elizabeth walked with Jamie as he gave her family a tour of the keep. There wasn't much to see on the inside except the sky, thanks to the lack of a roof.

"Tell me it wasn't this cold even with the place in one piece," Mary said, rubbing her arms vigorously.

Jamie smiled. "My lady Mary, 'twas far colder, I fear. I would not be lying to say the only time Elizabeth's feet were warm was when we were abed, and they were pressed against my calves. I will have a fire prepared for your comfort posthaste. Joshua, fetch us some wood. Zachary, aid him in his task."

"Hey," Zachary said, "how did I get demoted to slave?"

Jamie looked at him with raised eyebrows. "Since you are such a wee lad, 'tis fitting you do the bidding of your betters."

"I'm almost as tall as you are," Zachary retorted. "And I'm sure I'm as strong."

"Indeed?" Jamie said, beginning to grin. "Perhaps you would care to step out into the garden for a wrestle? That would certainly give you opportunity to prove your words."

Elizabeth laughed at the hopeful gleam in her husband's eye. "Zach, I guarantee you getting wood will be much less painful than a thrashing from Jamie. You two can play tomorrow in Roddy's garden if your feelings still smart."

"Do the bidding of my betters," Zachary grumbled as he trudged to the door. "Come on, Joshua. Beats the hell out of me where we're supposed to find wood up here."

"I will help you, young Zachary," Joshua said with a wink thrown Elizabeth's way. " 'Tis a simple thing my lord asks of us. Be you instead grateful that he does not require we clean the stables or dig out the cesspit."

"Huh?" Zachary asked, his eyes wide. "How was that?"

"A minstrel's lot is a harsh one at times, my young friend. I will tell you of it as we gather the wood, and it will cause you to appreciate the ease of your life."

Robert pursed his lips as the two left the hall. "I don't think I'm quite up to any of Joshua's stories tonight. Yours were bad enough, Jamie."

"Indeed." Jamie smiled, then stiffened. He rose, his sword coming from its scabbard with a soft hiss. He cast his eyes about and then tossed the knife from his belt to Elizabeth. Putting his finger to his lips, he motioned for her to protect her mother. He crept stealthily into what had previously been the kitchen and disappeared into the darkness. Elizabeth held her breath until he reemerged, a deep frown on his features. He came across the grassy floor, resheathing his sword. He took his knife from his wife and put it back in his belt.

"Well?" Elizabeth prompted.

"My clothes are gone," he said, with a shrug. "And I thought I heard a noise in the kitchens; yet I saw nothing." He forced a smile. "It was no doubt the echo of Zachary's grumbles that has made me daft."

Elizabeth wasn't fooled for a moment. "Clothes just don't disappear, Jamie. You know, Joshua said something about Nolan—"

Jamie's hand over her mouth cut off the rest of her words. "I saw nothing," he repeated, giving her a warning look. "Elizabeth, I no doubt misplaced my garments. Let us hear a melody or two from Joshua, and then we will return to the inn. Tomorrow perhaps I will return and search with the full light to aid me."

The wood gatherers returned before Elizabeth could even begin her protests. She hadn't fallen for Jamie's line, but there was probably a good explanation for the entire affair. Roddy might have taken Jamie's clothes with him, thinking he was doing his laird a favor.

She watched as Joshua stacked the wood strategically on the hearth. He reached for flint and tinder, but Zachary shook his head and pulled a lighter out of his pocket. When the flame appeared, Joshua crossed himself. Zachary laughed.

"It's a lighter, Joshua. Here, you do it."

Joshua lit the flame as Zachary showed him and then dropped it in his surprise. Jamie chuckled, as he had already had that experience the day before.

"Pick it back up again, lad, lest you set the hall on fire. If my keep burns to cinders, I'll hold you blamed for it."

Once the fire was lit, Joshua stripped off his sword, picked up his lute and sat down near the hearth. Elizabeth sat on the ground and leaned back against Jamie's knees, relishing the sounds she had thought to never hear again.

He leaned down and put his mouth against her ear. "Shall we keep him?"

"We may have to fight my mother for him."

It was true. Mary clapped and gushed over everything Joshua sang, leaving Joshua blushing clear to the roots of his hair.

"Lady Mary," Jamie chuckled, "you praise my minstrel overmuch. He will think it a sorry thing indeed when he is forced to sing at my hall and receive only his supper as praise for his talent." Jamie rose and pulled Elizabeth to her feet. "And 'tis no doubt time we departed though, Joshua, I would have you sing all night before I fed you if it pleased me."

"Of course, Laird Jamie," Joshua said, making Jamie a bow. He straightened, then clapped his hand to his forehead. "My lord, Lady Elizabeth's beauty has driven all rational thoughts from my mind, and 'tis only now I remember what Laird Jesse said he would do before he passed on."

"And that was?"

"He planned to leave you a message behind the stone."

"The stone?" Jamie stood there for several minutes, alter-

nately stroking his chin and rubbing his neck. Elizabeth had no
idea what Jesse had meant and could only wait until Jamie figured it out. Suddenly Jamie strode to the mantel. He drew his
knife and began to dig away at the mortar around one of the
stones. Alex pulled a sharp stone from the hearth and began to
dig too.

After perhaps a half hour of steady digging, the rock began
to move. Within minutes, they had it dislodged. It took three of
them to lower it to the floor. Then Jamie thrust his hand in the
opening and began to grin. He pulled out several bags, followed by a wooden box. Opening it revealed a rolled piece of
parchment. Jamie handed it to Elizabeth. She unrolled it and
began to read.

Dearest Mother and Father,

*I pray you will someday read this and know that we are
well. At this moment I am in Father's thinking room,
watching Megan put our newborn babe down in the cradle. This will be our last bairn, I think, as we are both too
tired to chase little ones. The lass is a sweet thing with
Megan's beauty already. I only wish you both could see
her.*

*Life is as ever; hard, dangerous and full of struggles,
but perhaps that is best. We would not appreciate the
beauties otherwise. Of our wars and strifes, you will read
much in your books. Nolan has stirred up mischiefs that
were indeed grievous, but you will read of those too, so I
will not waste ink on them.*

*One thing you will perhaps not read is about the love
that we've kept in our hearts for you both since you left.
God willing, we'll meet again in heaven and recount earlier times when we were together.*

*The gold is what I've acquired in your honor, Father,
over the years, in hopes that you would someday have a
use for it. I know we often spoke of the loose stone in the
hearth as a fine place for secrets. I'm pleased it serves its
purpose after all. There are a few gems also in the bags,
but no emeralds, I fear. Megan has this idea that they re-
semble my eyes and she snatched out every last one be-*

*fore I could seal these things up in the hearth. I found my-
self completely unable to rebuke her for it. Father, I'm
sure you can sympathize with my plight.*

*May your lives be long and happy, beloved Mother and
Father, and may you always remember those in the past
who love you.*

> *Your son,*
> *Jesse MacLeod*

"The lad's gone daft," Jamie grumbled as he pulled forth a handful of gold coins and jewels. "And I'm quite sure *acquired* is a pretty way of saying *stole*. As if he didn't have better things to do than think of me."

Elizabeth blinked back tears at the news of Jesse and Megan's happiness and tried not to smile at Jamie's gruffness. That Jesse had given him so much thought obviously touched her husband deeply.

Alex gasped as he finally got hold of a coin. "Jamie, this is worth a fortune!"

Jamie shrugged. " 'Twould buy a few mares, or ore for many blades. Or a few wooing trinkets," he said, flashing Elizabeth a teasing smile.

Alex put his hand on Jamie's shoulder. "Maybe that's all it would buy in your century, but not in mine. Even if you only sold half of this, it'd put you in the top half of the Forbes Four Hundred. You'll never have to work a day in your life with the cash you could get from this!"

"Forbesfourhundred?" Jamie echoed. "What is that?"

"Never mind," Robert said dryly, giving Alex a shake. "Alex always has had dollar signs in his eyes."

"Let's put it this way," Alex said, tossing his father a scowl. "You'll have enough gold to rebuild your hall and support Elizabeth without lifting a finger."

Jamie nodded. "Then let us seek out masons as soon as may be. I don't fancy digging snow out of the great hall because we lacked a roof."

The only damper on the day was what Jamie learned when he returned to Roddy's and sent the innkeeper down to the local pub to round up men to see to the rebuilding. Poor Roddy came back home, bearing tidings that the land no longer belonged to the MacLeods. When Jamie demanded to know who had possessed the cheek to acquire it, he was informed in trembling tones that the land now belonged to a man named Ryan Fergusson.

Jamie, Alex, Joshua and Zachary paid a visit to Ryan Fergusson the next day and found him to be more than willing to sell in the face of four such intimidating frowns. Elizabeth was relieved to learn that the land was once again in her family. Jamie looked rather smug at the lowness of the price he paid for the land. And Joshua, having found frowning to be a most satisfactory activity, frowned often from then on.

It was another gruffly successful day on MacLeod soil.

Chapter 28

ELIZABETH SAT IN Roddy's parlor near the fire, turning the pages of her journal and smiling at the memories. It would make an incredibly accurate historical romance. On second thought, maybe leaving out some of the more earthy details, such as the stench of an uncleaned great hall or the adventure of braving a chilly stone garderobe on a winter's morning, might save her future readers the willies. They were certainly things she hadn't been sorry to leave behind.

She looked at the little group clustered around the table and smiled. She'd brought with her what was most important. She still couldn't quite get over having Jamie and her family in one place. It was almost too good to be true.

Jamie and Zachary were discussing plans for the new keep. Elizabeth had her doubts Zachary had planned on a medieval hall being his first project after getting his degree in architecture, but he seemed to be holding up fairly well. Jamie had insisted on hiring him, once he'd learned Zachary had lost his job and his woman within hours of each other. "Och, the poor lad," had been his comment. Elizabeth shook her head as she listened to her husband and her younger brother hash out the details. Jamie was getting quite the education in the intricacies of modern plumbing and electrical wiring.

Alex sat on the other side of the table, keeping track of the costs. He freely admitted he wasn't much of an accountant, but all his legal work was done, and he was keeping himself busy. Elizabeth didn't ask where he'd come by birth certificates and passports for Jamie and Joshua, and Alex certainly hadn't volunteered the information. His secretary had done the honors of searching through Elizabeth's apartment for her passport.

Elizabeth had the feeling Alex was toying with the idea of staying with them. He'd said more than once over the past three weeks that he'd about had it with the corporate rat race. Jamie had offered him a job as clan legal adviser (a term he'd made up and was very proud of), but Alex hadn't given him an answer yet. If Alex wanted to become an attorney in Scotland, he would have to start over again with law school, and she had the feeling he wasn't up to that. For that matter, she wondered how he'd made it through law school in the first place. He'd majored in history in college, but he'd decided teaching wasn't lucrative enough for him.

Secretly she thought he would much rather have been chasing down archaeological finds in a leather jacket and beat-up fedora. She laughed to herself over the thought. Alex was a knight in shining armor trapped in a gabardine business suit. Maybe traipsing around Scotland in a kilt for a few years was just the thing to cure his corporate blues. If nothing else, he could offer Jamie what legal advice he could, then spend the rest of his time turning Jamie's memoirs into a mighty interesting history test.

Her parents had gone back to the States the week before. Her dad had stretched his time off as much as he could, then relented when he thought the partners in his practice might have changed the locks on the doors. Elizabeth suspected it was really because he couldn't handle giving Jamie any more driving lessons. He swore he came home with a few new gray hairs after each experience.

"Och, but I've had enough for the morning," Jamie said, standing up and stretching. "Building a keep was much simpler in my day, Zachary lad."

"I imagine the building codes weren't quite so clear-cut," Zachary said, with a laugh.

Elizabeth smiled as her husband came and hunkered down in front of her.

"How goes your reading, my love?" he asked.

"Entertaining, as always," she said, with a smile.

He scowled. "I'm half afeared I'll find my most intimate secrets popping up in one of your manuscripts."

"You have given me lots of good material," she agreed, "but I'll try not to use too much of it."

Jamie grunted. "My thanks, my lady. Now, are you packed to leave?"

"I have been for days. You're the one I'm worried about. Will you be done with your plans in time for our flight?"

He nodded. "Enough that the workers can make a good start. Young Zachary will stay behind and see to it."

She reached out and smoothed his hair back from his face. "Thank you for coming with me back to the States."

He shook his head. "There's no need. You need to gather your things and fetch your other books. I for one would like to meet Stanley." He flashed her a sweet smile. "Just to apologize for stealing his bride, of course."

"Of course," she said dryly.

"Then you can show me those books on Scotland you read. I would like to see what happened to my clan after we left."

Elizabeth nodded, though she was sure she wasn't as enthusiastic about the idea as Jamie was. She'd already had one bad experience with a book on the Clan MacLeod. All she needed was to have Jamie vanish into thin air beside her while he was reading.

"Jamie, your hall is going to cost a fortune."

Elizabeth looked up to see Alex shoving a stack of papers at her husband.

"It's a good thing you've got it to spend," Alex added.

Jamie shrugged. "What else have I to buy with it? Elizabeth needs a home, and I will provide it. The more quickly, the better, as I see it."

"Money talks," Alex offered.

"So I'm learning."

Alex smiled. "I'm going to go pack, and then I think I'll have a nap. I don't want to be running us off the road tomorrow."

Jamie frowned up at him. "I will drive to Glasgow."

"What you'll do is drive us into a ditch," Alex said, with a grin. "I'll just keep the keys."

Jamie rose and folded his arms across his chest. "Perhaps we should settle this with a wrestle."

Elizabeth rolled her eyes as Alex readily agreed and followed Jamie out into the garden. She put her book away and walked to the door. No sense in not being there to administer first aid to her brother when Jamie was through with him.

"Jamie, stop in the village just for a minute, would you?" Elizabeth said as Jamie pulled the car away from Roddy's inn.

"Again?" Jamie sighed, rolling his eyes heavenward dramatically. "Elizabeth, you used the closet not three minutes ago."

"For your information, Laird MacLeod," Elizabeth said haughtily, "there's a sweet little figurine in the shop next to the pub that I wanted to get for Mom."

Jamie stopped in front of the shop. "Five minutes, or I'll leave you here. Heed this, Alex," he said as Elizabeth got out of the car, "you must show them from the beginning who is laird, and then they will never forget it."

"I couldn't agree more," Alex said, with a laugh.

Elizabeth slammed the door. She was locked in the same car with two chauvinists of the first water, doomed to endure their presence for at least ten more hours. Her only satisfaction came from knowing Jamie was suffering from bruised ribs, and Alex was sporting a huge black eye from their wrestling match the day before. Maybe their injuries would keep them quiet on the flight over.

The figurine was purchased in three minutes flat, and Elizabeth hurried from the store. She lifted her eyes to the far side of the street and froze.

It was Nolan. He was dressed in modern clothing, but it was him, just as surely as she lived and breathed. She couldn't tear her horrified gaze from him. He lifted one eyebrow in challenge, then gave her a mocking smile.

"Elizabeth!"

She was turned abruptly to face the worried frown of her

love. Only then did she realize that the figurine had slipped from her trembling fingers and smashed against the pavement.

"Jamie, I saw Nolan!" she exclaimed, looking back across the street. He was gone. She looked around frantically, stepping out into the street to see more clearly. Jamie jerked her out of the way of an oncoming car and gathered her close.

"Love, you're imagining things," Jamie said soothingly. "And you've dropped your gift. Let's go find another. Your mother will be pleased with it, I'm sure."

"Jamie—"

He put his finger to her lips. "Beth, listen to reason. Joshua came to us by sheer luck. All he remembers is dreaming about you and then waking to find the hall in ruins. He saw no one when he woke. Nolan is not quick-witted enough to learn the secret of the forest. How could he be when we have yet to truly understand it ourselves? Now, come, love, and let us see if the shop has another little statue."

Elizabeth allowed him to lead her back into the store, but she wasn't convinced for a minute. She'd seen what she'd seen, and that was that.

Jamie lay on his back and stared up at the ceiling of Elizabeth's New York apartment. The entire apartment was not much larger than his bedchamber had been. It was certainly far noisier. He hadn't slept a wink the night before, and that hadn't been by choice. It was a wonder anyone slept, what with the televisions going, the people fighting and trucks rumbling along the streets all night long. He'd never felt homesick before, but he found himself indulging in that sensation fully and not regretting it a bit. It was no wonder Elizabeth had found his time so peaceful.

He winced as the bed poked him in the back with some sort of metal object. No doubt something had come loose while they tugged the bed down from its place inside the wall the night before. Jamie was exceedingly grateful he was far wealthier in this century than he had been in his former one. He would certainly buy a decent bed to sleep in when they returned home.

He rolled from the bed with a groan and stumbled to the bathroom. He turned on the shower and stepped under it by reflex. It was amazing how easily one became accustomed to the comforts of modern life.

The door opened and shut softly, startling him.

"Beth?"

"You were expecting someone else?" she asked sleepily.

He reached around the curtain and pulled her into the tub, clothes and all, before she could even squeak in protest. Once he had tossed her soggy pajamas over the curtain rod, he pulled her close and kissed her.

"Saucy wench," he grumbled.

"Didn't you sleep again?" she asked with a yawn.

"Not at all."

She pulled her head back and looked up at him apologetically. "I just need a couple more days to pack; then we can go home."

"Tonight we will stay in an inn," he said decidedly. "I cannot believe you slept in that poor excuse for a bed all those months."

"All right," she said, yawning. "Jamie, you get up too darn early."

"Some things never change," he sighed, reaching for the shampoo and pouring a bit on her hair. He hurriedly washed the rest of her, then shooed her from the shower so he could concentrate on his own bathing. Foolish as it might have been, he had the most ridiculous desire to make a good impression on Elizabeth's former fiancé.

He was finally to see Elizabeth's house of books. She had hoped the ones he wanted to see would have still been in her little apartment, but Alex had informed her that Stanley had wanted the manuscripts returned. Something about astronomical fines. Jamie hadn't asked the details. All he knew was that such fines meant he would see Stanley in the flesh, and he couldn't have been more pleased about that.

He dressed with special care, choosing his favorite pair of jeans, his most stylish pair of cowboy boots and his finest denim shirt. He liked the jeans. He wore them, of course, to tempt his wife. He'd bought a pair when they'd first arrived in New York a se'nnight past, and Elizabeth had taken them off him before he could even admire himself in the mirror. She said she found them sexy. That, and their comfort and warmth, was reason enough for him to purchase a few more sets. He topped off his outfit with the leather jacket Elizabeth had given him for Christmas. Zachary had told him it made him look "exceedingly bad," which had offended him greatly until he learned that it was a compliment. Americans and their strange terms.

He shoved his hands into his pockets and swaggered over to the bathroom, where Elizabeth was brushing her hair. He leaned casually against the door frame and looked at his wife.

"Well?"

"Well, what?" she asked, not sparing him a glance.

"Elizabeth!"

Damn her if she wasn't teasing him. He could tell she was purposely ignoring him. Another growl at least earned him a look.

"Well?" he repeated.

She gave him the once-over. Her eyes traveled from his head to his toes and back again, lingering just a bit somewhere in between.

"Very nice."

"And?"

"Intimidating. Big. Awe-inspiring."

That was the look he was going for. "Bad?"

"Exceptionally." She grinned.

He grunted. "Hurry. I'm anxious to see this wimp you almost wed."

"You hurry while I'll still let you get away," she said meaningfully.

He gave her a lazy smile. "I like to be chased."

"So I've noticed," she said dryly. She set her brush down and pushed him back into the chamber. "Let's go."

He locked up the apartment, wondering why he bothered, and led Elizabeth down to the street. He flagged down one of the little yellow cars and ushered his wife inside.

"I'm impressed," she whispered after she gave the driver their destination. "I never could get them to stop like that."

He snorted. "I intimidate cab drivers, my enemies, my wife's family and her New York neighbors. The only woman I really want to intimidate ignores me when I try, or makes me blush when I succeed. My lot in life is a sorry one."

She laughed. "Why don't I pity you?"

"Because you're a heartless wench," he grumbled. "You love to see me suffer."

He lost the thread of the conversation at that point, because the traffic began to bother him. It seemed that every possible bit of space in New York City was covered by either a building, a car or a body. He wondered how people bore being in such close confines. Quarters had been close in his hall, but at least he'd had the freedom of escaping to the vastness of his land when he became restless. Saints above, he never could have lived here.

He followed Elizabeth into the library, trying not to look as overwhelmed as he felt. He doubted he would ever get used to the richness of the buildings.

"We're going to the reading room," Elizabeth whispered. "Just follow me."

Jamie did. And he waited while Elizabeth flipped through long boxes of little cards, found which manuscripts she wanted and wrote down information about them. He sat with her while she waited for the books to be sought out and brought to her. And, for some unaccountable reason, he was nervous. He wasn't sure if it was because he might soon see Stanley or because he would see his name linked to events that had taken place seven hundred years earlier.

It was enough to give him gray hairs.

Elizabeth poked him in the ribs with her elbow and stood up. "Hi, Stanley."

A thin, balding man was walking toward them, books in his hands. Jamie hid a most smug smile. So this was Stanley the Wimp. Jamie knew he could have intimidated this man if he'd been wearing a dress and sporting ribbons in his hair.

"Elizabeth," Stanley said weakly. "Alex told me you'd been found, but I hardly believed it could be true." He turned his quavering gaze on Jamie. "And this is your husband?"

Jamie kept the conversation short, fearing Stanley would break down and weep if they stayed and talked much longer. He offered to pay Stanley back for the betrothal ring he'd given

Elizabeth, but Stanley wouldn't hear of it. Jamie excused them and led Elizabeth away, feeling very sorry for the little man who had so little hair left on top of his head and so little courage in his soul. He smiled down at Elizabeth.

"I think you married well, Lady MacLeod."

"Don't I know it," she agreed, giving his hand a squeeze.

"Now you will show me those books on Scotland you read that fateful day?"

She nodded, then handed him the books Stanley had shoved into her arms. Jamie followed her to one of the nearby tables, then sat and spread out the books. A tingle went down his spine as Elizabeth handed him one thick volume.

"This is it?" he whispered.

She nodded solemnly.

He opened the book and scanned the first few pages for the name MacLeod. It was there, and he turned to the section on his clan. Much as he looked, he simply didn't see a drawing of his forest. He pointed that out gently to his wife, not wishing to have her look the fool.

Elizabeth dived into the book with a vengeance. She flipped from the front of the book to the back several times. Finally she looked at him, clearly dumbfounded.

"This is the book, but the drawing of the forest isn't here."

"Maybe you have this one confused with another," he suggested.

"I don't," she said firmly. "It was called *Scottish Lairds and Their Clans*, by Stephen McAfee."

Jamie looked at the book. That was indeed the title, and that certainly was the author's name.

"It's been several months, Beth," he ventured.

"But I'm positive this is it," she said. She put the book down, picked up another and flipped through it, still wearing the same look of puzzlement.

Jamie reached for another of the books on Scottish history. He caught sight of a map as he was thumbing through the pages. He studied it closely, recognizing the branches of MacLeods he knew existed. A frown crossed his brow as he saw another grouping marked. When Elizabeth had drawn him a map of clan territories just before they left his time, she had specifically drawn the ones he recognized. Even if Elizabeth's wits were somewhat addled from all their traveling, his weren't.

He turned back to the beginning of the book and identified where the sections on his kin were. He scanned the text, noting the rulers listed from the time of Kenneth MacAlpin. He felt odd as he saw his name listed during the Bruce's time. A shiver went down his spine as he looked at Jesse's name, followed by James, then several other of his descendants.

After tracing that branch down a few hundred years, he turned to the other group of MacLeods. That yielded nothing surprising. He stumbled upon the new clan and felt the hair on the back of his neck stand up. Forcing down the premonition of dread, he started to read.

> *The battle for the lairdship of the clan McAfee is likely one of the bloodiest in the history of the Highlands, though it is the one we know the least about. Daniel and Dougan McAfee, twin brothers, were brilliant strategists, skilled warriors and magnificent leaders. The clan was cleanly divided down the middle by conflicting loyalties to the brothers. Perhaps the struggle to claim the chieftainship would have gone on indefinitely if it had not been for the intervention of the MacLeod clansman discussed earlier.*
>
> *His strategy consisted of nothing more than pitting one brother against the other in a conflict that escalated to all-out destruction within a matter of weeks. Once both sides were reduced to almost nothing and both the brothers lay dead in the hall, the laird of the new clan MacLeod stepped into the chieftainship as if he'd been born to do so. What follows is forty bloody years in which the former clan McAfee, joined by the MacLeod clansman's ruffian allies, made war against any MacLeod they could find. The bloodshed ended only with the chieftain's death.*

Chills went down Jamie's spine, and he hardly had the courage to look at the previous page to find out who the bloodthirsty MacLeod clansman had been. He had the terrible feeling he knew already.

In 1450 A.D. Nolan MacLeod appears in the annals of history. It is odd to note that this fifteenth-century Nolan MacLeod's namesake lived during the fourteenth-century, with just as devastating results. The later individual is credited with spawning evil the western Highlands will never forget. It is that Nolan who concerns us here, as he was the one to wipe out most all traces of the northern branch of the clan McAfee and replace it with a branch of the clan MacLeod.

The battle for the lairdship of the clan McAfee is likely one of the bloodiest in the history of the Highlands, though . . .

"Jamie, you're pale as a sheet," Elizabeth whispered, startling him from his reverie.

Jamie closed the book with a snap and fixed a smile to his face. "I'm hungry. What say you we find one of those wiener merchants and have ourselves a dog or two?"

He rose and pulled her to her feet before she could protest. Though what he wanted to do was bolt from the building, he forced himself to walk calmly and look unconcerned. He even managed to banter with Elizabeth, though he was certain she thought him daft. No doubt his responses made little sense at all.

He doubted he would ever forget the horror of what he'd just read or the sickening feeling it had given him. He should have killed Nolan the night he tried to rape Elizabeth. Casting him from the hall had been far too lenient a punishment.

Jamie now had no doubts that Elizabeth hadn't been imagining things when she'd seen Nolan in the village that day. He'd likely followed Joshua forward to the present day, then learned the secret of the forest and gone back in time. Jamie shuddered at the very thought. Such knowledge in the hands of such an unscrupulous man was enough to give any man the shakes. But that wasn't the worst of it. The saints only knew what Nolan would do if he managed to catch Elizabeth by herself and unawares.

They returned to Elizabeth's apartment and Jamie bade her hasten her packing. After dropping off several boxes at Alex's apartment, they checked into the most luxurious inn Alex could find them.

Jamie was too distraught that evening for play, despite the temptation of his wife's sweet body. She curled up in bed with a book, and he sat in front of the television with a bottle of whiskey, determined to erase the vision of the haunting words he'd read that day.

He couldn't stomach more than a sip. It was still very late by the time he forced himself to rise. He slipped under the sheets next to Elizabeth. She wasn't asleep and immediately drew him into her arms. He laid his head on her shoulder, threw an arm and leg over her and released a great, heavy sigh.

"Jamie, love, what's bothering you?" she asked softly.

He was tempted to unburden his soul, but to what end? There was no sense in upsetting her unless he had to. Nay, he would keep the knowledge to himself until he had a plan formulated. Perhaps he would keep silent even then. He would go back in time, right the wrong Nolan had done, then come home to Elizabeth safe and sound.

"Jamie?"

He sighed and pressed his lips against her neck. " 'Tis nothing, love. I am only weary from lack of sleep."

"I don't believe you."

He lifted his head and silenced her with one hard kiss. "I am your lord, wench. If I say there is nothing amiss, there is nothing amiss. Take your rest as you may. I think I will wish to be chased long and hard tomorrow, and you're just the lass to do it."

She muttered a few uncomplimentary adjectives under her breath but relaxed just the same. Jamie sighed as he felt the tension drain out of his beloved wife. She would thank him one day for having kept his mouth shut.

Chapter 29

JAMIE WALKED DOWN the path to Roddy MacLeod's inn.
He'd been walking the whole of the day, first up to his hall,
then down the meadow again. He'd roamed trails he had
roamed as a youth and a young man. He'd relived skirmishes
fought. He'd even examined old escape routes he'd taken in the
past after lifting cattle from neighboring clans. He had been
sure such wanderings would ease his restlessness. Indeed, he'd
expected to feel a good deal more relaxed once he was on na-
tive soil again. Somehow, it hadn't happened.

He hadn't slept well since he'd been to the library. He'd tried
to wear himself out by packing up Elizabeth's belongings and
seeing them sent to Scotland. He'd tried to distract himself by
visiting what Elizabeth called tourist attractions. He'd been
overwhelmed by the symphony, left lukewarm by Broadway
and petrified by his trip to the top of the Empire State Building.

But he hadn't slept any better.

Seattle had been rainy, and that had made him homesick.
He'd met Jared and Stephen and their families. He'd even been
allowed to observe a surgery at the hospital. The sight of blood
and innards had made him homesick too, but he'd been less
than impressed that the wounded one had been asleep during
the operation. He'd felt every bloody stitch Angus had ever

taken in his poor flesh. Aye, he could have used some anesthetic for a few of those wounds.

But none of his traveling, none of the delightful family gatherings with children scampering about and adults laughing and talking had eased his mind any. Nolan MacLeod was still alive, and it was his fault.

He walked into Roddy's house, then locked the door behind him. The place seemed to be put to bed for the night. He knew he'd missed supper, but somehow that didn't trouble him. That was a sure sign he was more stressed out than was good for him. *Stressed* was a term Alex had used repeatedly in connection with his labors in New York. Jamie was coming to understand the meaning all too well.

He turned into Roddy's solar. Perhaps a few minutes warming up in front of the fire would take the chill off his heart.

Alex was occupying one of the chairs. He looked up as Jamie entered.

"Hey," he said, with a smile. "How's it going?"

Jamie only shook his head and sat down in the chair opposite. It was going more poorly than he could attempt to say.

"Jamie, what's up?"

Jamie looked at Alex, his clan legal counsel. Jamie had been very happy when Elizabeth's older brother had decided to move to Scotland with them. Even though Alex said the subtleties of American law were different than Scottish, he knew enough to muddle through whatever Jamie might need. Jamie knew Alex would eventually find something to keep himself busy. For now, it was enough to have a brother again. Perhaps Alex could be persuaded to keep Elizabeth under control while Jamie did what he must.

At the moment, his wife's brother was looking at him with such an assessing gaze, Jamie wanted to squirm. Perhaps the man should seek to become a Scottish attorney. His piercing gazes would go to waste otherwise.

Jamie wiped his hands on his jeans, then tugged at his watchband. When that gave him no relief, he worried his wedding ring. And still Alex waited. Well, there was surely no man Jamie trusted more than Alex, and Alex was a clear thinker.

There was no harm in discussing the subject with him. Jamie met Alex's aqua eyes unflinchingly.

"I have to kill a man," he said, without preamble.

"Really," Alex said, his voice completely without any inflection of surprise or disdain.

"Aye. My cousin."

"Why do I have the feeling this cousin isn't living in the twentieth century?"

Jamie smiled, in spite of himself. "Because you're very wise, Alex."

"Give me the whole story," Alex urged. At Jamie's hesitation, his look sobered. "It will go no further than me unless you want it to."

Jamie looked around the solar. Elizabeth had surely gone to bed hours before. Zachary was only heaven knew where. Joshua was no doubt sleeping outside Elizabeth's door, as was his wont when Jamie was away. Aye, there was privacy enough for the telling of the tale.

So he did. He told Alex everything, starting with Nolan's original desire for Elizabeth and ending with what he had read at the library. Once he was finished laying the story before his brother-in-law, he sat back and waited, wanting to see whether or not Alex would come to the same conclusion he had.

Alex stared off into space thoughtfully for several minutes. Then he looked at Jamie.

"You're certain you know how the forest works?"

"Aye, certain enough for my purposes. I've questioned Elizabeth thoroughly about her experiences with it. When she first tried to go back to her time, she was thinking she wished she could stay with me." Jamie didn't bother to hide the smugness in his voice. "And then this time, we were both wishing to see Scotland in the future. 'Tis my theory that once the proper place in the forest has been reached, your innermost desires are what directs the power of it."

"Great. When do we leave?"

Jamie's jaw hung slack. That was the last thing he'd expected his wife's brother to say. "We?" he echoed. "Alex, I must go alone!"

"And leave me behind to face Elizabeth?" He smiled. "Forget it. I'll be much safer with you. Besides, you can't go by yourself. I'm not the best swordsman to hit the lists, but I'll do in guarding your back."

"Alex, I couldn't ask you to . . ."

"You didn't and you wouldn't have had to anyway. That's the end of this tale, Laird MacLeod," Alex added, cutting off Jamie's protests. "Instead of wasting your breath on changing my mind, spend your energy making plans. At first glance I would have said we had all the time in the world, but the more time that passes, the more centuries Nolan could foul up. The sooner he's taken care of, the better."

Jamie didn't argue further. Having a brother to count on would be a fine thing indeed.

"Aye," he agreed. "Nolan must be stopped before he wreaks more havoc. But I wish this to remain between you and me. Zachary will stay behind, as will Joshua. I would not be surprised in the least to have Elizabeth try to follow us. I daresay she thinks me barely able to use the privy closet on my own," he said, disgruntled.

Alex chuckled. "I don't think it's quite that bad, but I wouldn't doubt her wanting to come along for the ride." His smile faded. "She'd die if she lost you, Jamie. You'd better be damn sure you'll come back to the right place in time."

"I will," Jamie said.

Alex rose. "We'd better spend the next few days training. And you can teach me a few of those choice swear words I never understand. My Gaelic is getting pretty good, but I still think I curse like a woman."

Jamie smiled weakly at Alex's jest as he rose, then reached out and pulled his brother-in-law into a fierce embrace.

"Thank you, Alex."

Alex slapped him on the back with a few hearty blows. "It's nothing I wouldn't do for a brother, Jamie."

Jamie closed his eyes and gave thanks for his newly acquired family. He pulled away, took Alex by the shoulders and shook him roughly.

"I feel the same way."

"Good. You never know when I'll get lost in the Middle

Ages and need you to rescue me from too much beer and wenching."

"Ale, Alex. It's *ale* and wenching."

Alex merely smiled. They left the solar to find Zachary standing in the entryway, trying to look innocent.

Alex exchanged a glance with Jamie. "I'll leave you to deal with this one. 'Night."

Jamie watched him go, then turned to look at Elizabeth's brother.

"Nothing good ever comes of eavesdropping," he remarked casually.

Zachary looked guilty as hell, only confirming Jamie's suspicions. Zachary stuck his hands in his pockets.

"Sometimes it's hard to avoid."

"Sometimes it's best to forget what you've heard," Jamie countered.

"Then again," Zachary said, looking Jamie square in the eye, "sometimes it's not."

Jamie straightened and glared the younger man down. "I'll tell you this for nothing," he said rapidly in Gaelic. "You wouldn't last the space of two breaths without knowing a thing or two more than you do now. Your swordplay is sloppy, and you're far too hotheaded for this kind of business. I need no lackwits aiding me in this cause."

Zachary returned his glare and strode across the kitchen to stand toe to toe with Jamie. "My swordplay, *my lord*," he returned, also in Gaelic, "is much better than my brother's, and I'm not a lackwit!" He got so close that their noses were almost touching. "And I may be hotheaded, but I love my sister. If all I do is keep you alive for her, then maybe my hotheadedness isn't such a bad thing after all!"

Jamie had a hard time not showing his astonishment. Obviously Joshua had been teaching young Zachary quite a bit of Gaelic over the winter. Jamie was very pleased, but he frowned anyway. No sense in encouraging the lad.

"You'll get yourself killed if you don't learn to control your temper. Losing your head is the easiest way to truly lose it."

Zachary nodded and did it, amazingly enough, silently.

Jamie grunted. "I don't like this much."

"I never expected you would, but I'm coming whether you like it or not."

Jamie clapped his hands heavily on Zachary's shoulders and gripped him roughly. "Hear me, little one, and hear me well. I will take you along only because I believe you are foolish enough to follow if I do not. But," he added quickly at the hopeful light that sprang instantly into Zachary's eyes, "on one condition."

"That is?" Zachary asked carefully.

"That you obey me without question. I have not survived countless battles because I was stupid, nor because I did not know what was best for my men. If you cannot obey me instantly and without hesitation, I will see you sent to Seattle, where your parents can keep you prisoner until the tale is finished."

"Of course, Jamie."

That promise was given too easily. "Zach," Jamie said, his voice suddenly soft, "this is no amusing adventure. This is riding into certain war. Many men will die by your hand. You yourself may not escape unscathed. You vowed to come when your blood was heated. Think on what it is you promise. I have no choice in the matter, for 'tis my fault I let Nolan live in the first place. You are not caught up in this tangle."

"You are my brother," Zachary said simply. He put his hand briefly on Jamie's shoulder before he moved past him. "Get some sleep, Jamie. You'll wish you had once we start practicing swordplay tomorrow morning in Roddy's garden."

Jamie sighed deeply. Well, there was no point in trying to convince Zachary otherwise. The lad was as stubborn as his sister.

Jamie wandered back to Roddy's kitchen. Perhaps a small snack was called for. He sat down at the table to contemplate what would please him the most. Before he had the time to gather his thoughts, the chair across from him was pulled out, and a long form settled down into it. Jamie smiled wearily at his minstrel.

"I take it you were eavesdropping also?"

"I learned the habit from you."

Jamie smiled wearily. "Ah, Joshua, what a fine family we have acquired here."

"Aye, they are fine, loyal lads, my lord."

"You need not call me that."

"I do it to humor you," Joshua said, with a half smile. "And to let you know I will do your bidding."

"Even if it means staying behind?"

"You trust me with what means the most to you. I would count it an honor, not a slight."

Jamie rubbed his forehead tiredly with one hand. "Is it possible she slept through all tonight's goings-on, or have I much explaining to do?"

"I looked in on her once I heard young Zachary begin to bellow. She sleeps soundly. I only pray the lads can keep silent about this. Elizabeth will be furious. I daresay keeping her from following you will be the most difficult task of all."

"I daresay you're right." He sighed. "Let us drink a cup or two together, my friend. To good fortune."

"And a safe journey," Joshua added. "That more than anything is what should be wished for."

An hour later Jamie checked the locks on Roddy's doors and walked back to his chamber. Elizabeth was indeed asleep but stirred and reached for him the moment he slipped into bed beside her. He held her close and closed his eyes, offering up a heartfelt prayer. There were many things he prayed for that night, and that his wife would have the good sense to stay home was not the least of them.

It was another fortnight before he could bring himself to leave. He and Elizabeth had been up to the keep several times to see the progress the workers were making. The floor was down, and the roof was on. Great strides had been made toward restoring the chambers. Elizabeth had teased him that his thinking chamber would be restored to its former state of glorious disarray. Jamie had chuckled with her, thinking silently that he hoped he would be there to enjoy the mess.

He knew that the time had come to leave. He simply couldn't wait any longer.

He dressed just before dawn, praying Elizabeth wouldn't wake and see him clothed in his medieval garb. After putting his weapons outside the bedchamber door, he knelt down by their bed and smoothed the hair back from his lady's face. He hadn't meant to touch her but found he couldn't help himself.

She opened her eyes and smiled sleepily. "Howdy, lover," she said softly.

"Howdy to you too, beautiful one," he whispered, bending to press a gentle kiss against her forehead.

"Come back to bed, Jamie."

"I will in a bit, Beth," he said softly. "I'll be back before you'll even miss me."

"I'll miss you even in my dreams," she murmured, her eyelids closing relentlessly.

He waited until he felt her drift off, then blinked back his tears and rose. With any luck at all, he would take care of his affairs and be home before she woke up. That was surely the beauty of time travel.

He smiled grimly as he fastened his sword about his hips, slipped one dirk in his left boot and another into his belt. Had he possessed any sense at all, he would have brought along a gun or two. That would have made short work of Nolan's minions.

By the time he reached Roddy's kitchen, his frown had become forbidding. There was no time for tears. As in the past, what served him best was cold detachment. He would find Nolan, slay him and return home. There would be ample opportunity later to think on what he risked. It would be a fine distraction while he listened to a well-deserved tongue-lashing from his wife.

Alex, Zachary and Joshua were waiting for him at the table, already eating. Roddy cooked in silence. The only explanation Jamie had offered him the night before was that they were off to take care of a few things and would hopefully be back before nightfall, and would Roddy mind cooking them something tasty before they left? Roddy had taken a long look at Jamie's blade, one of his eyebrows had disappeared into his hairline, and then he'd gone quite pale in the face. But he'd nodded readily enough. Jamie had the feeling Roddy was mentally rehearsing that legend of the young laird Jamie and his beautiful wife Elizabeth who had lived in the Bruce's day . . . Heaven only knew what new adventures the innkeeper would add to the tale.

Jamie wolfed down a hearty meal without speaking. When he rose, his kin rose with him and followed him out to Roddy's stables. Mounts were saddled in silence. Jamie sent his brothers-in-law on ahead and remained for a quiet word with Joshua.

"She'll be furious when she wakes," Jamie warned, "but hopefully I will be back before dark."

"Better furious than frightened," Joshua said grimly. "I daresay she'll be both, but I will keep her here if I have to tie her up." He laid his hand on Jamie's shoulder. "Good fortune to you, my lord. We'll have supper on for your return."

Jamie mounted and hurried from the stables. He caught up with Alex and Zachary at the road he and Elizabeth had crossed that first night in her time. Alex looked resigned; Zachary looked like a lad trying to pretend he wasn't frightened witless.

"Zachary . . ." Jamie began.

"I'm ready," Zachary said sharply. "I don't go back on my word."

Good enough. Without another word, Jamie took the lead into the forest. There was no need for speaking, as they had gone over their plans time and time again over the past few days. Jamie took a last critical look at his comrades before they entered the forest. The clothing suited the brothers well, and they carried themselves arrogantly. Well, Alex carried himself arrogantly; Jamie had no worries about him. Zachary was nervous, and that was plain to the eye, but there was little to be done about it. He would either lose his head or keep it; Jamie could only protect him so far before he was on his own. He said a quick prayer that Zachary would make a good showing.

As they rode, he let his only thought be of Nolan. He pictured his cousin in his mind's eye with a singleness of thought he never knew he possessed. He could almost see the sun glinting off his kinsman's beard. It would work. It *had* to work.

Jamie called a halt at midday. They stood in a circle and munched on a bit of bread and jerky. They spoke only in Gaelic and only of inconsequential matters.

*   *   *

As the sun was setting, Jamie spotted the faint light of a fire in the distance. He hissed a warning to his brothers, for brothers they would pretend to be until the deed was done, then continued on, praying he would reach the fire before he was set upon.

He and the lads were allowed in, then found themselves encompassed by a goodly number of rough-looking clansmen. *Medieval* clansmen. Jamie identified the leader, then dismounted slowly, keeping his hands in plain sight. The leader, a lad not more than a score and five, stepped forward and looked Jamie over thoroughly.

"Your name?" he demanded.

"My name is my own to give or keep, as I wish it," Jamie said calmly.

The man's dirk was out and the tip pressed under Jamie's chin in the blink of an eye. Jamie could have deflected it easily but chose not to. Let the lad talk for a few more moments.

"You look like a bloody MacLeod," the younger man snarled, "and I've seen more MacLeods than I care to remember roaming on my land."

"Daniel or Dougan?" Jamie inquired politely.

The lad's eyes narrowed. "I might be or I might not—"

"Dougan," Jamie guessed, and correctly, if the further narrowing of the lad's eyes was any indication. So, he had successfully reached Dougan's time. Young Angus the womanizer ruled the Clan MacLeod. It would be easy enough to pass himself off as one of his descendant's bastards. "We have a common enemy."

"That remains to be seen. Your name," he demanded again.

"James MacLeod, bastard—"

"Whoreson," Dougan McAfee finished for him. "Aye, I'm sure of that."

Before Jamie realized what his fist intended, it had smashed into the young McAfee's face. It was a hopeless fight, but Jamie gave quite a few of Dougan's men tokens to remember him by before he succumbed to the relentless darkness that fell.

He'd arrived in hell, and it certainly looked as if the inhabitants planned on him staying.

Chapter 30

ELIZABETH WOKE AND snuggled closer to Jamie's place. It was cold. She sat up with a start, then sighed in relief when she realized where she was. She'd had a terrible dream about being back in the Middle Ages. It would have been just plain ugly, especially in her condition.

"A good time will be had by us both, my little one," she said softly, patting her belly. Thank heavens for spinal blocks. She lay back with a smile and gave herself up to the sweet contemplation of how she would tell Jamie about his coming child. Perhaps it would be a boy. Jamie missed Jesse deeply; it would be good for him to have another son to raise. Then a daughter and then a few more boys. She'd have to give birth to enough for at least a skeleton football squad. Jamie would probably rent other boys from the village if she didn't.

She rose, then hummed to herself as she showered and dressed. Perhaps a picnic would be the proper setting for her revelation. No, March was not the time for that. Perhaps they would have lunch in front of the fire in Roddy's solar. She bounded down the hallway, already itching to put something in the picnic basket and steal her husband away.

She walked into the parlor to find Joshua sitting in one of the chairs before the hearth, tossing twigs onto the roaring fire.

"Where's Jamie?" she asked.

"Out," Joshua said.

"Out where? Riding?"

"Aye."

"I'll go find him." She smiled. For a moment there, she'd had the most terrible premonition.

Joshua was on his feet and stopping her before she took two steps. "He'll be back soon enough, Elizabeth. I think you should wait for him."

She looked up at him in surprise. "Why?"

"Because I think it best," Joshua said. A muscle in his cheek twitched.

"I am perfectly capable of making up my own mind," she said tartly.

"In this instance, I will choose your actions for you," he said, his face taking on a decidedly Jamie-like frown. "You will remain in this inn until they return."

"They?" she echoed. The feeling of dread hit her right behind the knees, and her legs buckled. "No," she said, shaking her head in denial. "They didn't go into the forest." She looked up at him and read her answer in his eyes. "They didn't go into the forest!" she shouted.

"They'll be back before you know—"

"Let go of me!" she shrieked, trying to pull away from him. "Damn you to hell, Joshua!"

"My lady—"

She managed to get one arm free, and that was all she needed. She hauled back and slugged Joshua as hard as she could in the face. She shook her throbbing hand as she fled for the entry hall. Joshua bellowed a foul oath and thumped after her. He caught her before she had the chance to wrench open the door. He spun her around and took hold of her shoulders.

Elizabeth shook with violent tremors. "W-why?" she managed, wanting to break down and weep. "Oh, Joshua, why did he go?"

Joshua released her hands and gathered her close. "It was Nolan, Elizabeth. He found a way through the forest and has been wreaking havoc through the centuries. Jamie went back to kill him."

"Oh, please, no," Elizabeth said, shaking her head. She was dreaming; that was it. Jamie couldn't have been so stupid.

"Elizabeth, he did what he had to do to right Nolan's wrong. He left you behind because he loves you and wished to keep you from harm. Surely you realize that."

"That doesn't make it any easier!"

Joshua slipped his arm around her shoulders and led her over to the chair in front of the fire. He pushed her down gently, then knelt before her and took her hands.

"My lady, he will come back," he said earnestly. "I'm sure of it."

Joshua patted her hands, trying to soothe her. He felt as effective as a candle trying to melt a mountain of snow. Before he could think of anything else intelligent to say, Elizabeth had sunk to her knees before him and was sobbing against his shoulder. With a sigh and a prayer that Jamie wouldn't beat him senseless for taking such liberties, he put his arms around his lady and rocked her gently.

"There, there now, love," he said softly, "hush with these tears. Jamie's going to come back through that door in the next few hours, and he'll hold me responsible for your weeping. Doesn't it pain you to think of me maimed? Or worse?"

Humor was definitely not working. Elizabeth only sobbed harder. Joshua gave up on trying to talk and simply gave her the comfort of his arms. He loved Elizabeth deeply, and even doing her such a small service was a joy to his heart. He only regretted that she suffered so gravely, and there seemed to be little he could do to ease it.

It was a very long time before she pulled back. He winced at the determined look in her eye.

"My lady . . ."

"He'll need help."

"Elizabeth, I will not let you go," Joshua said, dredging up every ounce of sternness he possessed. "Even if Jamie had been uncertain about the matter, I would say you nay. As it is, Jamie specifically instructed me to keep you here, and keep you here I shall if I have to throw you into the dungeon to do it."

"Roddy doesn't have a dungeon," she shot back.

"I'll dig one, just for you," he growled.

To his surprise, she smiled. "Joshua, you're turning into quite the grumbly bear."

"Flattery will not work with me, Lady MacLeod. Your husband's fists would hurt much more than yours, and I guarantee you I would feel them repeatedly if I gave in."

Her fingers on his rapidly swelling eye made him wince, despite her featherlight touch. "Forgive me."

"Behave, and I might think about it." He reached out and brushed the tears gently from her cheeks. "Come, light of my heart, and let us go bake some cookies."

"It's not even lunchtime yet."

"It will take your mind off my dungeon threat." He rose and offered her his hand.

She accepted his help, then stopped and smiled at him wearily. "Thank you, Joshua."

"No need," he said, with an attempt at cheerfulness. "Keep in mind I will be watching you and will know if you put something foul in these treats."

"You're too sly for me," she said, giving him a grudging smile. "Maybe we'll make some fudge while we're at it."

His ears perked up. "It sounds sinful."

"It is. Let's go see what a mess we can make of Roddy's kitchen. When Jamie gets back, I'll make him clean the whole damn thing up as penance for ruining my morning."

Joshua escorted her into the kitchen, sincerely hoping it was only her morning that was ruined.

Elizabeth pulled up to the gates and turned the car off. It was Jamie's new toy, a dark green Jaguar. Alex had cried when Jamie had bought it, presumably because he was sure Jamie would total it within days. Elizabeth herself had almost plowed into a few things herself on the way to the keep. It was that wrong-side-of-the-road business.

"I don't like this," Joshua said, as they got out.

Elizabeth sighed. "I just want to sit up here for a while, Joshua. Give me that much, won't you?"

He nodded, then put his hand to his head and groaned. Elizabeth smiled in spite of herself. He was looking very green around the gills.

"Poor boy," she said, taking his arm. "You didn't have to eat both pans of fudge."

"I was powerless to help myself."

"Well, Roddy will cook us something healthy for dinner. That will balance out your sugar overdose nicely."

Joshua's only response was a whimper as she led him up the steps to the hall.

He did, however, manage to get a fire going in the hearth. Elizabeth rubbed her arms as she sat on the stone floor nearby. The workers had been *too* good at reproducing the bone-numbing chill of a great hall.

The outer walls were up, as was the ceiling. Work was progressing well on the bedrooms, but it would be a few months still, despite the staggering sum Jamie was forking out to get things done in a hurry. Elizabeth inched toward the fire, forcing herself not to give in to the panic that threatened to choke her. Jamie would be back. They would live out their lives in the most boring of ways in modern Scotland. No cattle raids. No swordfights. No neighbors bent on murder. Hopefully the worst they would run into would be a few skirmishes with the local PTA.

Elizabeth looked at their minstrel. He closed his eyes, likely to recover, when a knock sounded. Elizabeth jumped up and ran to the front door. She almost had it opened, but Joshua was too quick for her. He gave her a glare and gently pushed her aside. He drew his sword and opened the door slowly.

Twilight silhouetted a tall, broad man. His dark hair was long, and his unruly bangs hung with casual abandon into emerald green eyes. Elizabeth shoved Joshua aside and threw herself into the man's arms.

"You're home!" she cried, but then she stiffened and pulled away. The man could have been her husband's twin, yet it was not Jamie.

The man grinned, and Elizabeth wanted to weep out loud at the little dimple that appeared in his cheek.

"I don't think so, but I wish to hell I were." He held out his hand and smiled. "Patrick MacLeod."

Elizabeth felt her mouth drop open of its own accord. "*You're* Jamie's brother?"

Patrick MacLeod blinked. "I'm sure we could not possibly be talking about the same man, miss."

"Mrs.," Elizabeth corrected automatically.

"*Lady* MacLeod," Joshua corrected. He resheathed his sword and stood back, gesturing for Patrick to enter. "Please come in, my lord."

Patrick froze halfway across the threshold, his gaze glued to the hilt of Joshua's sword.

"You're taking this medieval craze a little too seriously, old man, don't you think?" he asked. His eyes flicked from Joshua to Elizabeth, and back.

"There is no other way to take it, my lord." Joshua made him a small bow. "Joshua of Sedgwick," he said respectfully. "Minstrel to Laird James MacLeod, at your service."

The blood drained from Patrick's face. Elizabeth caught him around the waist, then she and Joshua helped him over to the fire. He slid to the floor with a thump.

"I think I need a drink," Patrick said thickly. "I've come to this keep time and time again over the past few years but never seen it restored until this winter. I had only come to see who'd bought the place." He rubbed his eyes and looked around the room. "I'm quite sure I'm either hallucinating or dreaming. I'm positive I'm hearing things." He nodded. "Yes, that's it. I'm hearing things." He looked up at her. "I really do need a drink. A stiff one."

Elizabeth looked at him and marveled. So close, yet so unalike. Where Jamie's face was stern, Patrick's was relaxed and gentle. He had little laugh lines around his eyes and his mouth, lines Jamie had only recently begun to acquire.

"We didn't bring anything strong," Elizabeth apologized, when Patrick's color didn't change from pasty white. Jamie had had people out looking for Patrick for three months, and now his brother showed up during the one time Jamie wasn't around. Somehow, it just figured.

Patrick waved aside her words and simply put his face in his hands for several moments. Then he looked up and gave Elizabeth a shaky smile. "I'm a poor guest. Allow me to reintroduce myself. I'm Patrick MacLeod—"

"Of the Clan MacLeod, born, I believe, in the year 1285 near

Benmore forest to the laird, Douglas. Bane of your brother's existence, pest extraordinaire, womanizer of the most impressive of reputations . . ." She paused. "Am I missing anything?"

"Did not Ian refer to him as 'possibly the poorest swordsman the clan MacLeod ever saw,' my lady?" Joshua asked politely.

Patrick looked even paler, if possible, than before. "How did you know all that?" he whispered.

"I'm Jamie's wife, Elizabeth," she said simply. "I found myself in fourteenth-century Scotland a few months back. In Jamie's forest, to be exact. From there it was a small matter to wind up in your brother's hall."

"He allowed you to stay?" Patrick asked incredulously.

Elizabeth laughed. "You have no problem believing I traveled through time, but you can't buy that Jamie let me in the front door?"

"Right now, I'd believe just about anything," Patrick said, drawing his hand over his eyes. "So, tell me how you accomplished this feat."

"A lot of time, patience and spending days on end listening to Jamie grumble and complain," Elizabeth said with a deep smile.

"Things didn't change, I see." He looked at her closely. "Jamie didn't come with you?"

"Oh, he did," she said. "He's just off roaming through the centuries trying to find Nolan and kill him. We really had expected him back in time for supper."

Patrick looked as if he just couldn't handle too many more shocks that day. He started to laugh, but it was laughter tinged with hysteria. Elizabeth understood completely.

"My lady," Joshua said sternly, "I think it time we returned to the inn. Your brother-in-law looks to need sustenance worse than I do. Come," he said, motioning for her to rise.

She could hardly believe her ears. "Joshua, you're beginning to sound disturbingly like my laird with your orders."

Patrick lifted his head and looked at her. "You actually know my brother, don't you? You actually married that foul-tempered, impossible, overbearing oaf."

"He's mellowed," Elizabeth said. She looked at him and

shook her head, with a smile. "I have so many questions I want to ask you."

"Such as, what was it like to stumble into the twentieth century in nothing, and I mean nothing," he added with a grin, "but a plaid, carrying a broadsword?"

She laughed. "Something like that. But I think I'll wait until after dinner. Then you'll have to repeat it all for Jamie when he gets home. He'll want to hear too. You know, he's had people out looking for you since we got back to my time."

Patrick smiled sadly. "My wife died in childbirth a few months ago. I've been moving around a bit since then."

"That must have been hard," she said softly.

"Aye, it was," he nodded. "Somehow I think finding my family again will ease my pain greatly."

"I'm glad to hear it."

She rose and walked with Joshua and Patrick outside. How happy her husband would be to see his brother again. And she was going to make sure he'd have that chance.

Elizabeth peeked out the door and scanned the hallway for bodies. Noting that there were none, she slipped out the door and closed it softly behind her. Joshua had been standing guard at the end of the corridor when she'd gone to bed; obviously he had tired of his vigil. She crept down the hall, pleased there were no creaking floorboards to give her away. She was even more pleased with her outfit. A pair of her dark leggings and an oversized tunic of Joshua's snatched from his closet while he wasn't looking made the perfect disguise. A knife in either boot, another up her sleeve and her sword at her side made her feel infinitely secretive. As long as her hair stayed under her hood, she was a sure success.

She'd spent most of the night talking to Patrick and comparing notes about the twentieth century, Jamie and the forest. It was his thoughts on the forest that had intrigued her the most. She hadn't talked with Jamie about it much, but she'd been fairly sure that the gate worked based on the destination the traveler filled his mind with. Or her mind, as the case was. Elizabeth could vouch for that. Hadn't she been thinking intensely of the forest after she'd seen the pen-and-ink plate in that book on the clan MacLeod? Then hadn't she been wishing to stay with Jamie the first time she'd tried to go back?

And then coming back to her time, hadn't she wished only to go where Jamie went? He'd been wanting to see Scotland in his own time. Joshua had come forward because he'd been wishing with all his heart to see her again. She smiled when she thought of the sweet ballad he'd composed around that very tale.

Patrick had gone back to see Jamie, then returned to his wife the same way. Elizabeth was sure that if she just concentrated hard enough on Jamie, she would find him. She just wouldn't give the forest any other choice. She continued toward the entry hall, already formulating in her mind what she would take in her saddlebags to appease her husband's humor, as she had the feeling it might not be too sunny when he saw her.

She hadn't taken ten steps across Roddy's polished stone floor before she found herself dangling half a foot off the ground, held up by the back of her cloak and tunic.

"Put me down," she squeaked, finding her air supply cut off by the shirt caught at her throat.

"Didn't Jamie tell you to stay home?"

Of course it had to have been Patrick to catch her so neatly. She had told herself she wouldn't think twice about kneeing Joshua in the groin to escape; doing the like to Jamie's intimidating brother gave her pause.

"Patrick, put me down!"

He set her gently on her feet and turned her around, clucking his tongue. "Shame on you, Elizabeth. You know Jamie likes his kin to be obedient."

Before he could blink, she had her knife down from her sleeve and pressed against his throat.

"I am going to get Jamie, and damn you and Joshua both if either of you thinks to stop me," she said tightly. "If he hadn't needed help, he would have been home long before now."

"I'm not going to let you be the one to rescue him," Patrick said placidly. "And I'm just as stubborn as Jamie. Learn that right now, little sister."

"I'll slit your throat if you hinder me," she warned.

Patrick's eyes flicked above her head, then back down while

a mocking smile formed on his face. Elizabeth whirled around, fully expecting to see Joshua sneaking up behind her. The next thing she knew, Patrick had her divested of all three knives and her sword.

"Off to bed," he said pleasantly.

"Patrick, please," she pleaded, clutching the front of his shirt. "Jamie *needs* me. I know it."

Patrick hesitated. Before Elizabeth knew what her knee was thinking, it had connected solidly with his family jewels and he was crashing to the floor. She knelt with her shin across his neck and rested the tip of her recovered knife over his heart.

"You think I can't take care of myself?" she asked archly. "I took MacLeod Survival 101. Now," she said, robbing him of a bit more breath, "I *am* going to get my husband, and you're not going to stand in my way. Is that understood?"

Patrick closed his eyes in surrender. "All right."

She released him and stood, taking back her weapons. Patrick rose to his feet slowly, then put his hand on her shoulder and leaned heavily on her for several moments.

"I'll come with you. That way once Jamie finds out I let you lead me about like a docile lamb, he'll at least thank me for escorting you before he carves my heart out with his dullest blade."

Elizabeth smiled up at him. "You're very much like your brother."

Patrick snorted. "I don't grumble nearly as much, nor as loudly."

"But you're just as sweet."

He looked at her sharply. "Are we talking about the same James MacLeod? Since when did my brother become sweet?"

Elizabeth smiled. "I'll give you a list of his newly acquired traits while we ride. Go get dressed and bring Joshua. He won't want to miss out on this."

"If he has any sense, he certainly will," Patrick groused as he stomped across the floor. "Don't you dare move a muscle, Elizabeth MacLeod, or I'll beat you black and blue. Don't think to test me on that because I'm in earnest."

She waved him away. "I'll go get the car warmed up. At least we can drive as far as the hall."

She opened the front door and looked out into the dawn sky.

"Hold on, Jamie," she whispered. "We'll be there as soon as we can."

Chapter 31

JAMIE SQUATTED DOWN in front of the fire and tortured a twig between his fingers. Time was moving too slowly. Already he had been in the fifteenth century a month. Who knew how many days had passed in his own time by now? Elizabeth would be frantic with worry. He was almost surprised not to have seen her wicked aqua eyes peeking out from a hood. Perhaps Joshua was doing a better job controlling her than Jamie had dared hope.

He looked up as Dougan McAfee came toward him, frowning.

"Any word?"

"It doesn't look good for my brother," Dougan said grimly. "Nolan is a cunning bastard, and Daniel is gullible enough to believe your cousin's pleas for peace. He's already let the whoreson inside the gates. If what you say is true, Daniel won't see spring."

"You've no wish to aid your brother?"

"None at all. If you'd been witness to what Daniel did to our sister, you'd not wish to aid him either. I'll never forget the sight of him tearing off her shift—"

"Enough," Jamie said sharply. "I've no desire to hear your family's tales of incest. I'm only interested in your loyalties."

"They are to myself and none other."

"Fair enough. Any thoughts on how long it will be before Nolan finishes off your brother and his lads?"

"I'm thinking not longer than a week. Daniel didn't have that many followers left after our last battle. And once he's removed from my path, Nolan will have his turn."

"Nolan is mine," Jamie said curtly. "I have waited many months for this, and I'll not have my revenge taken away."

"Aye, I know," Dougan grumbled. "He is yours to slay at your leisure."

"See that your men know it. I'd be tempted to repay whoever ruins my pleasure."

Dougan's eyes widened, and he nodded with a convulsive swallow. Jamie smiled to himself. How sweet it was still to intimidate a soul or two. Dougan scampered off with as much dignity as he could muster to once again remind his men of his bargain with "that fiercesome MacLeod bastard." Jamie had heard himself called that so many times over the past weeks, he'd almost come to like the term. Though he was hardly a bastard in the truest sense of the word, fiercesome was indeed pleasing against the ear.

The first few days had been touch and go, but Dougan was just as intelligent as the history books had indicated. Even though Jamie had been a bit vague about his origins, he hadn't been vague at all about his purpose, and Dougan had grasped that immediately. He'd swallowed the lie about Jamie's being Angus MacLeod's bastard son without trouble and soon had promoted Jamie from prisoner to top adviser. Jamie was reluctant to interfere too much, not knowing the effect his actions would have on the course of history, but he interfered enough to make sure he had a good chance of removing Nolan from the picture entirely.

Now his only problem was helping events move along with greater haste. He found himself missing his wife with a longing that made his chest ache almost continuously. Aye, she had him wrapped around her little finger, all right. He'd be sure to grumble about it loudly when he returned.

He lifted his eyes in time to see Zachary coming to him. His youngest brother-in-law strolled over casually and squatted down next to him.

"Brother."

Jamie smiled dryly at him. "Aye, little one? Still reeling from too much wenching last night?"

"I shudder to think of the diseases I've caught."

"Dougan said the girl was clean."

"I fear the diseases Dougan left behind," Zachary grumbled. "It's surprising how low a man will sink when desperate." He looked at Jamie sideways. "You're not feeling a bit desperate?"

"If you knew the kind of sweet fire that awaits me at home, you'd not have to ask that question," Jamie said, amused at Zachary's lack of subtlety. "I'd not betray her."

Zachary had the grace to redden. "Just checking."

Jamie cuffed him lightly on the side of the head. "I know, brat, and I know why."

Zachary continued to look uncomfortable. "You know, Jamie, you could come with us some night and . . . well . . . you know, pretend to wench a bit if you wanted. You know . . . to save your," he swallowed with a gulp, "reputation."

Jamie threw back his head and laughed. "How very thoughtful of you to think on my poor reputation, tattered and shred though it is."

"I think the lads are beginning to wonder," Zachary said miserably. "You claim not to have a wife, then, well . . ." He shrugged helplessly.

"Zachary, you don't listen well enough," Jamie smiled, not offended in the least. "I've laid claim to half of Angus's bastards and not been questioned about it as the bairns have the great fortune to have my black hair and bewitching green eyes. Dougan thinks I pine for a Lowland lass. That is fodder enough for talk in the evenings."

"If you say so," Zachary said with a relieved sigh. "Maybe it's just as well. Beth would probably take a knife to you if she heard even rumors of your being with anyone else."

"My thoughts exactly, and your sister is mightily skilled with a blade." He looked around the glen. "Where is Alex?"

"Off telling battle stories. Lying through his teeth," Zachary clarified. "Last I heard he was boasting of his lack of scars, saying he was so skilled that no one could touch him. The guys were extremely impressed."

"Let's hope he doesn't boast too much," Jamie said darkly. "I daresay all the thrashings he's given that loudmouthed cousin of Dougan's have gone to his head."

"Yeah," Zachary agreed with a grin. "He's almost as arrogant as you are, Jamie, and that's saying something."

Jamie was contemplating the merits of beating Elizabeth's youngest brother senseless when there was an enormous commotion to his left. He stood immediately, his sword already in his hand.

Then he heard the unmistakable sound of his wife swearing like a seasoned mercenary.

Zachary leaped forward, but Jamie pulled him back by his hair.

"Carefully," Jamie said sharply. "We dare not acknowledge her. Feign ignorance." Zachary looked ready to protest until Jamie favored him with the blackest look he could muster. Zachary gulped and turned his eyes forward, struggling to keep his expression neutral.

Elizabeth was, of course, dressed like a boy. Jamie groaned silently as she was dragged into camp, cursing with oaths he hesitated to use himself. Dougan appeared and came to stand next to Jamie. Elizabeth's hood was ripped back, and every last soul in the hastily formed circle gasped when they caught sight of her face.

"Jamie!" she cried gladly, trying to shake off her captors' hands.

Dougan turned to him. "You know this wench?"

"He's my husband!" Elizabeth exclaimed.

Jamie glared at her briefly before he gave Dougan a bored look. "I told you I have no wife."

Elizabeth looked as though she'd been slapped. She called to Zachary, who gave her the same bored look. Alex came up behind Jamie and put his hand on his shoulder.

"This is interesting," he said dryly.

Elizabeth looked like she either wanted to burst into tears or kill the three of them. Jamie didn't doubt for a moment that the latter appealed to her more.

"If she's not yours, then I'll have her," Dougan said, looking at Elizabeth with undisguised lust.

"I don't think so," a voice said from the far side of the glen.

Jamie looked up and met a pair of deep green eyes in a face which resembled his own so strongly, he could have been looking into a mirror. He would have fainted had Zachary not jabbed him so sharply in the ribs. By all the saints, that was Patrick!

His brother strode across the forest floor, tossed Elizabeth's captors from her as if they'd been bairns and pulled her against his side with his arm protectively around her shoulders.

"Beloved, I thought I told you not to stray too far from camp," he said, giving Elizabeth a reproving look. He lifted his eyes and pinned Dougan to the spot where he stood some three paces from them. "She is mine, and I would suggest you take that knowledge to heart. I've killed many a man to win her, and I'll continue to kill to keep her near me. Though she has been known to lust after Jamie, she'll remain with me should I have to chain her to me."

"Ah," Dougan said wisely, "so she wishes to roam. Well, I daresay I understand why you would keep her in spite of it. A more beautiful face I've never seen, though I care not for the sharpness of her tongue. Now, who are you? I daresay I should know you for a MacLeod and doubtless kin of Jamie's. You look to be twins."

"Brothers," Jamie said quietly, when in reality he wanted to leap across the fire and hug Patrick senseless. "This is my younger brother, Patrick. It has been many a year since we last broke bread together."

"Aye," Patrick said, giving Jamie a nod. "Many years." He looked over his shoulder and beckoned with his hand.

Jamie's eyes widened as Joshua approached. Joshua flashed him an apologetic smile before he came to stand next to Patrick.

"My wife's brother, Joshua," Patrick said to Dougan. "I give him food and clothing to keep watch over his sister. Obviously he hasn't done a very good job of late."

"Obviously," Jamie muttered. Dougan threw him an amused smile before he welcomed Patrick to their camp, then moved off to see to his affairs. Jamie took stock of the situation quickly. Elizabeth was resigned but furious; Joshua was resigned and obviously sure Jamie would kill him; Patrick was fighting a grin that surely would have split his face in two. Jamie ignored his wife and his minstrel in favor of his brother. He strode forward and pulled his younger brother into a fierce hug. Patrick's return embrace almost broke his back.

"I've missed you, Patty," Jamie said hoarsely.

"Aye," Patrick whispered, just as hoarsely. "So have I."

There was too much to be said, too much to be learned and no time to spare for it. Jamie pulled back and slapped his brother's cheek affectionately. "You've grown a bit."

"So have you. Especially around the middle," Patrick said with a mischievous grin.

Brother or no brother, that was an insult that couldn't go by unnoticed. Patrick landed on his back in a cloud of dust, and Jamie followed, showing his younger brother just how much middle had been acquired.

"Jamie, get off me," Patrick wheezed. " 'Tis only muscle you wear, I vow it."

Jamie got up, then hauled Patrick to his feet. The insult was forgotten, but there was yet a matter to be settled. He put his face in his brother's.

"You had to bring her?"

"First she fair ruined my chances of ever fathering any children, then she tried to slit my throat. I had little choice in the matter."

"Little choice?" Jamie said incredulously, knowing he was very close to shouting. "You're twice her size and at least four times as strong! You're such a woman you couldn't subdue one simple-minded, headstrong wench?"

"You can't seem to. Why should I be any different?"

Too much time travel had obviously reduced his brother's common sense greatly. He gave Patrick a glare that should have made him back up a pace or two and whimper. Instead, his fool brother only chuckled. Jamie was not amused.

"I control her well enough," Jamie snapped. "Never does she forget who is laird in my hall. 'Tis only when I leave her with my *lackwit minstrel*," he threw Joshua's way with an accompanying scowl, "does she allow her foolish notions to run rampant. Damnation, but I did not need this distraction!" The more he thought about it, the more irritated he became. He poked his brother in the chest. "You keep your *wife* out of any more trouble." He whipped his head around to lock gazes with Joshua. "You keep your neck out of reach of my blade, or your head's the forfeit. And you," he growled, turning a black look on Elizabeth, "you stay out of trouble, or I'll beat you, and I vow this time I'll do it."

With that, he stomped away. He had no destination in mind, but just the stomping was satisfying. On a whim, he grabbed the front of Zachary's tunic.

"Follow me. I feel the need to train."

"Oh, no," Zachary groaned.

Jamie ignored Zachary's pleas for mercy. Anger was his only refuge. After Nolan was dead, he would take the time to rejoice over the fact that his brother was again his and that his wife was easily the most stunningly beautiful, spirited, courageous, *stubborn* woman he had ever met. Aye, 'twas a fine life he led, and he vowed to be grateful for it in due time. But gratitude now would only distract him, and he could not allow himself to be distracted at any cost. Nay, anger served him best.

As he took out his frustrations on his wife's brother, another thought occurred to him.

If Elizabeth pretended to be Patrick's wife, they would likely sleep on the same side of camp, perhaps even within shouting distance.

Zachary watched with open mouth as his volatile brother-in-law suddenly stomped back to camp, then heaved a huge sigh of relief that his turn as torturee was over.

"Eat up, lover."

Elizabeth gave Patrick a glare before she accepted a bowl of something she didn't even try to identify. "You're pushing it, Pat."

He chuckled. "And enjoying myself immensely, thank you. It's been years since I've been such a thorn in my brother's side. I daresay I'd best savor the pleasure while I may."

"You should," Elizabeth agreed darkly, "because Jamie and I will fight for the privilege of torturing you once we're back home."

Patrick put his arm around her shoulders and gave her a gentle squeeze. "Couldn't you at least try to pretend I'm Jamie? We could even exchange a few chaste kisses. Just for appearances sake," he added. He ducked as a clod of dirt went sailing past his ear. "See? Jamie no doubt finds the idea highly satisfactory."

Elizabeth tried to frown but couldn't manage it. The fact that her husband was sitting across the glade from them with a clod or two more at his elbow only added to her amusement. She smiled and leaned back against the tree, the bowl of indescribables next to her forgotten.

"Patrick, you are far too sweet for me to ever mistake you for my beloved laird."

"Perhaps if I grumbled a bit more?" He gave her an exaggerated frown. "Is this better?"

Elizabeth was showered by the spray of dirt a juicy clod released as it exploded against the side of Patrick's head. She put her hand over her mouth to hide her grin.

"He's really going to hurt you if you don't stop."

Patrick rubbed his head and threw his brother an annoyed look. "About the time I go deaf from too much dirt in my ear, *he'll* be the one who's truly hurt."

Elizabeth smiled as she listened to her brother-in-law go on about all the times he had thrashed Jamie when they were younger. That he was exaggerating the truth greatly and now and then telling an outright lie didn't bother her in the least. She was simply grateful for the diversion.

It was amazing how much Jamie and Patrick resembled each other and yet how unalike their personalities were. Patrick was carefree and happy-go-lucky, in direct contrast with Jamie's constant obsession with being in control. Perhaps it came from Jamie's always having known he would be laird and Patrick's having had the freedom to do as he pleased. Yet even so, she could clearly see the deep love between the two men. Once they returned home, she had the feeling it would be days before she saw her husband again; he would no doubt be spending all his time catching up with Patrick. Though at the moment Jamie looked like he'd sooner kill his brother than chat peaceably with him.

Of course, Jamie would not look at her. She had given up the idea of catching her husband's eye already, as he had not spared her even a glance. So he hadn't needed a rescue; how was she to know? He could have been at least a bit grateful for her efforts.

She slept between Joshua and Patrick that night. Well, perhaps *slept* wasn't the right word. She was *crushed* between Joshua and Patrick that night, as they seemed determined to keep her protected.

The feel of a hard hand over her mouth startled her to wakefulness and she immediately began to thrash, trying to get her mouth free to scream. The fact that her idiot protectors didn't stir through the entire affair made her panic even more. She would be raped before they were the wiser.

Her knee connected with her abductor's groin as he struggled to drag her from the camp. The grunt and particular swear word uttered made her groan in misery. Of all people to have wounded, her husband was her very last choice. She relaxed as he swung her up into his arms effortlessly and strode deeper into the forest.

Before she could even think up an opener for a bit of polite conversation, he had laid her down in a bed of soft leaves and was leaving her breathless with his kiss. His kiss was anything but timid, and she groaned as he forced his stiff tongue in her mouth over and over again until she was tugging at his clothes as frantically as he was tugging at hers. He jerked her leggings down and took her immediately, not even bothering to do more than push his plaid out of his way. Had she not been aching for him so painfully, she might have thought to chastise him for his lack of foreplay.

A lifetime later, she realized that that first bit of passion was all the foreplay she was going to get. Jamie loved her over and over again until she began to wonder if she would ever walk again, much less move.

"You missed me," she murmured, eventually.

He groaned. "I don't think that describes it."

"You ached for me, then."

"I ache for you still. It will take me the rest of my life to have you enough to make up for the past month. Resign yourself to a lifetime of very little rest at night."

"I'll take naps."

He snuggled even closer to her. "Aye, you'll have to do that."

She sighed, relishing the feel of her husband's hard body pressing her against the ground and regretting the fact that the sun would be up soon, and they would have to hurry back to camp before any of the others were awake. It might just be the last time she'd have the chance to talk to Jamie in private. Well, there was no time like the present.

"Jamie?"

"Aye, love."

"I'm pregnant."

His gasp no doubt woke every last Highlander in Scotland. He jumped to his feet.

"You're *what*!"

She sat up, rearranged her clothing, then smiled up at him. "We're going to have a baby."

She wasn't sure if he was going to cry or throttle her. He looked infinitely capable of doing either. Before she had much time to wonder what his choice would be, he had her flat on her back and was looming over her menacingly.

"You mean to tell me," he began in a low, gravely voice, "that you were feeble-minded enough to travel back through the centuries on a whim when you knew you were carrying my child?"

"I'm only a few months—"

"How many?" he demanded.

"A few," she answered hesitantly. "Maybe three." So it would be a throttling. She really couldn't blame him.

"By all the saints above!" he thundered. "Elizabeth, have you lost your mind?"

She clapped her hand over his mouth. "Be silent, you bellowing bear!"

"How could you have been so witless!" he hissed. "What if you miscarry? In case you had not marked this, there is no hospital down the road! You would bleed to death before I had the time to carry you home."

"Jamie," she said gently, "the baby will be fine—"

" 'Tis not the babe I'm worried about, you foolish girl!"

"Oh," she said in a small voice. A smile that began in the tenderest place in her soul crept out onto her face. She put her arms around her husband and held him tightly. "There is no other man alive or dead I could ever love as much as I love you," she whispered. "You have no idea what you mean to me."

With a gruffly muttered oath, Jamie dropped to his side and pulled her close to him, almost crushing her ribs with his embrace.

"I'll cherish your sweet words, but don't think they excuse you from the thrashing you'll get after this babe is born. I doubt you'll sit for at least a fortnight. I did not need your aid."

"You don't know that," she protested.

"Aye, I do," he growled. "If I had the time, I'd take you back home right now."

"Don't worry about me, Jamie. I'll just make myself scarce until you're through, then meekly follow you back home."

He grunted. "That I'll believe when I see it."

Elizabeth lifted her face for his kiss, then suddenly found him not there. He stood over her with his sword drawn, waiting for whatever was crashing through the undergrowth to cease its crashing. She lurched to her feet, pulling up her leggings in the process. Zachary stumbled through the trees, panting hard.

"Daniel's dead. Dougan's ready to take the keep, and he's prepared to go alone."

Jamie swore. "Zachary, see your sister back to camp." He turned, stooped and kissed Elizabeth hard on the mouth. "Behave and keep your wits about you. I'll see this finished quickly." With that, he was gone.

Elizabeth crawled to her feet, took Zachary's hand and pulled him toward camp.

"Beth, there's no hurry—"

"I want to know their plans."

"Beth," Zachary groaned, "please don't get involved—"

She ignored her brother and tromped back doggedly toward the camp. She was there; she might as well be of some use. If nothing else, she'd be there to wait until Jamie came back.

*   *   *

Plans were made quickly, and a small force set out for the keep, intending to take it by surprise. Elizabeth watched her husband and Alex leave, praying it wouldn't be the last time she'd see them. Dougan seemed supremely confident in their ability to sneak inside the hall. He had boasted of the secret passageways hidden in the walls which would allow them to penetrate the inner chambers of the keep with no trouble. If only it could be that easy.

Zachary, Patrick and Joshua did their best to entertain her, but she wasn't in the mood to be humored. What she wanted was her husband back in one piece.

Hours passed without word. Elizabeth sat by the fire far into the night, praying for the sound of a certain footfall. It didn't come.

By morning she was frantic. Even Patrick was grim-faced as they made a poor breakfast of stale bread and dried meat. It took little effort on his part to round up a few lads itching to be stirring up some trouble. Before Elizabeth could stop him, Zachary had joined the band of rabble-rousers and was following his brother-in-law into the forest. Elizabeth sighed as she looked at Joshua.

"It looks like we're left behind to hold down the fort again."

"It looks that way," he agreed. He tried to put on a cheerful face. "They'll be back soon, my lady. I'm sure of it."

He was so sure of it that he took to sharpening his sword. Elizabeth already knew her blade was sharp enough, so, for lack of anything productive to do, she began to pace.

By the time she'd worn a groove near the fire, another day had passed. Questioning what scouts had returned revealed only that the keep looked still as death and that they had seen men go in but not return.

Elizabeth didn't have to hear more. It was obvious her men were either taken prisoner or dead already. She prayed she wouldn't rescue them just in time to bury them. After considering the factors, she formulated a quick plan and presented it to Joshua.

"Absolutely not," he said firmly.

"It's the only way. Joshua, surely you see that."

He gave her a dark look. "Have you any idea what will happen when Jamie learns of this? He will never forgive me for taking such a foolish chance with your life."

"You're right," she returned hotly. "He won't forgive you because he won't be alive to do it! If he'd been successful, he would be back by now. It's obvious something has happened to him. This is the perfect plan, Joshua, and you know it. Nolan never met you. He might have seen you from a distance, but he won't recognize either you or me if we do this right. It won't take long to figure out what's happened to the men. Then we'll get them out and go home."

"I don't like this."

"That's why it will work," she retorted.

An hour later, Lord Joshua of Fenwyck, an obscure but important Lowland keep, set out for the ancestral home of the Clan McAfee, accompanied by his faithful, aqua-eyed squire.

Chapter 32

JAMIE SHIELDED HIS eyes from the light as the dungeon door was lifted and the ladder was let down. Even the faint light of a torch was like the blinding sun after two days spent in darkness. Several bodies were urged ungently down the ladder, finally being shaken off the rickety steps like fleas being flung off a twitching hound. One of the bodies landed hard in the ooze. Jamie had no trouble recognizing the user of such colorful American obscenities.

"Zachary?"

His brother-in-law groaned as he crawled across the pit.

"I think the bastards broke my ribs," he moaned.

"Carefully!" Jamie exclaimed, wincing at Zachary's innocent grazing of his back. The open wounds left by the whip were far from healed. Alex's wounds were even worse, if possible, and had rendered him mercifully unconscious.

"Jamie?"

Oh, merciful saints, that was Patrick's voice.

"Pat, come give me the news," Jamie said, trying to sound gruff and in control. In reality he was trembling with fear. Now only Joshua was left to guard Elizabeth, and he was surely not strong-willed enough to keep her out of trouble. Jamie forced himself not to think of what sort of mischief the two of them would combine when left on their own.

"What'd they do to you?" Patrick asked, groaning as he settled himself next to Jamie in the slime.

"A token or two of Nolan's affection," Jamie said. "Nothing I won't enjoy paying him back for later. Have you seen Dougan?"

"Outside, tied to a whipping post. I wouldn't be surprised to learn he's bled to death."

"Guards about the dungeon?"

"Numerous."

"In the hall?"

"Nary a one. It seems our beloved cousin knows from whence his main troubles would spring if allowed," Patrick said, his tone dry. "He has all his men down here guarding you."

"I'm flattered."

"You should be. You should have seen Nolan's face when he caught sight of me. I vow he came close to soiling his plaid." He laughed softly. "Ah, Jamie, 'twas the sweetest moment of my life, seeing him look at me as if I'd been a ghost."

"Soon he'll be seeing ghosts in truth," Jamie growled. "Give me news of my lady. You left her only after ordering her to remain behind, aye?"

"Of course."

"And she will immediately ignore your words," Jamie added darkly.

"Of course."

"Wipe off that smirk, Patty. There is nothing humorous about this."

"I'm simply envious. She loves you deeply to risk so much coming after you."

Jamie sighed and tried to drag his fingers through his hair. It was too matted with filth and blood for him to have much success.

"And now she will have the pleasure of trying to rescue me only to face rape at Nolan's hands," he said. "If I didn't know it was a sin, I'd think about taking my own life simply not to have to hear her screams."

The flat of Patrick's hand against his ear made his ear ring.

"She's more clever than you give her credit for being," Patrick snapped. "I'll vouch for her ability to protect herself."

"Against half a keepful of men?"

"All the men are here watching over you. She'll make it past Nolan easily enough."

Jamie paused. "Think you she'll come?"

"Dolt, of course she will!" This was accompanied by another sharp cuff on the side of the head.

"When my back heals, you'll regret that abuse."

"I'm retaliating for all the dirt still in my ear."

"I've a thing or two to say to you about pawing my wife, too," Jamie growled.

"Concentrate on a plan, brother. If you get us out alive, I just might listen to your tirade with a straight face."

Jamie growled again, when in reality he was almost smiling in the darkness. How he had missed bantering with his brother! God willing, they would be doing it far into their old age. During the days, of course.

The nights were most certainly reserved for the courageous woman somewhere outside the keep. Saints, but he was fair frantic at the thought of her coming inside the gates. He had no doubts she would. What she would do then was anyone's guess. He didn't want to think the worst, but he sincerely hoped Nolan would mistake her for a lad and toss her straight into the dungeon. At least then they could starve to death together.

He didn't want to think about what would happen if Nolan found her out before she reached the pit.

Elizabeth sat in the corner and stewed. She'd been stewing for two days, keeping herself hidden in Joshua's room except for meals. At least she'd made it past Nolan. She'd felt his eyes boring into the shadows of her hood often, but he hadn't recognized her.

Or so she hoped.

Nolan had looked at Joshua closely a time or two, but Joshua had done such a caricature of an effeminate lord that Nolan had left him alone, likely out of a sense of self-preservation. She was counting on the fact that Nolan had never met Joshua personally. Joshua said he thought Nolan was suspicious, but Elizabeth had the feeling Nolan had come that way from the womb.

A splash and a deep, throaty laugh drew her attention. Joshua was such a resourceful lad. He'd managed to wangle a bath from a man who had obviously not bathed in years. Nolan never had been one for personal hygiene. Now Joshua sat in a large, comfortable tub, teasing a witless girl into telling him more than she should have.

"You, lovely maid, are easily the sweetest morsel I've seen in years," Joshua said, leaning back and allowing the wench to wash his chest. "Tell me there is no member of the keep who binds you to him already."

"No one of consequence," the girl said softly.

"Perhaps it is because you have so few to choose from?"

"Nay, my lord, there are lads aplenty here."

"There are many, in truth?" Joshua asked, trying to sound surprised. "Where do they hide? I saw only two in the hall."

The girl cast a furtive look behind her, as if she thought the very walls would overhear her words. Elizabeth had to lean forward to catch what she was saying.

"Most of the men are below, guarding the prisoner."

"How many men must it take to guard a simple captive in a dungeon?"

"But 'tis not a simple man Laird Nolan keeps. I hear this prisoner is powerfully handsome, with hair as black as the Devil's and a temper to match. He has a brother who looks just like him and a few more bastard brothers to aid him in his cause." The girl sighed and pulled away from Joshua. " 'Tis a pity, I say, that they weren't able to defeat the new laird. Dougan cared for his kin. This other man kills who displeases him for any reason, however slight."

Elizabeth fought the panic that rose again in her throat. Whatever she did to trick Nolan, she had to do it soon. There would be no help from Dougan; he was now lying in the great hall, more dead than alive from the wounds inflicted by Nolan's whip. Jamie, Patrick and her brothers were probably in just as bad shape, and time wouldn't help them. If something were to be done, it would have to be done that night.

And then inspiration hit.

She rose and crossed the room, then knelt down behind Joshua. She put her arms around his neck and kept her face in the shadows of her hood as she spoke to the serving girl.

"You'll have to go," Elizabeth said. "My lord will be wanting me now."

The serving girl paled and backed away so quickly, Elizabeth almost smiled.

"Young Geoffrey, you cease with your mischief," Joshua warned.

Elizabeth plunged ahead. " 'Tis always how my lord does it. First a bath, then a lad, then," she paused and made sure she had the girl's full attention, "then a man. Know you of any men my lord could have?"

"Geoffrey!"

"Make haste, girl," Elizabeth said quickly, "before he loses his temper!"

"Several members of the guard," the girl blurted out. "Any number of them."

"Bring him one. The most handsome and the tallest. Someone who matches my lord in size." Elizabeth leaned forward and pressed her lips against Joshua's cheek. "In a half hour, girl. And come back with him. If my lord's humor is fine, he just might bed you both."

The girl fled. Elizabeth rose and bolted the door behind her, then turned and leaned back against it, waiting for Joshua to explode. He rose from the tub, dried himself off, then dressed. He turned slowly and gave her a frown Jamie would have been impressed with.

"I hope to the Blessed Virgin you had a reason for that."

"I've got a plan."

"I cannot wait to hear it."

She smiled grimly. "This is what we'll do. I'll steal the girl's clothes, and you take the guardsman's. We'll dress up and go down to the dungeon. While I'm distracting the men, you toss a ladder down into the dungeon and help the prisoners up."

"Distracting the men?" he echoed. "Elizabeth Anne MacLeod, you're almost four months along! Think you I would be daft enough to agree to such a thing? Jamie would geld me!"

"Then *you* distract the men, and I'll throw the ladder down."

"El-iz-a-beth," Joshua groaned, dragging her name out into all the possible syllables.

"Do you have a better idea?"

He bent his head and rubbed the back of his neck. Elizabeth smiled at the sight. It was Jamie's gesture, and she knew Joshua must have loved him to watch him closely enough to mimic his movements. She crossed the room and put her arms around him. She hugged him tightly.

"I'm so glad you're here, Joshua. You've been a wonderful friend."

He kissed her on the forehead. "And you've been my inspiration, fair one. Very well. Let us rescue this grumbly lord of ours and head home. And then you will spend the next year baking me all manner of chocolate creations for what I'm about to do below. God help me." He shivered. "Distraction I can do, but I will not go so far as to kiss one."

She smiled and released him. "Jamie will appreciate the sacrifice."

"He will owe me much repayment for this deed."

"You bet he will."

A knock sounded on the door and Elizabeth took a deep breath. "Can you take care of the man?"

"I can."

Elizabeth nodded and went to open the door. She stayed behind it until two bodies had entered, then she shut it and bolted it.

She gasped. It was the serving wench again, all right, along with possibly the widest, burliest, roughest man she had ever seen. And the man was blushing. He made Joshua a low bow.

"My lord."

Joshua reached for his sword and sighed deeply. "Come closer, lad, and let me have a look at you."

Elizabeth snuck up behind the serving girl and grabbed her, holding her still by means of a knife across her throat.

"Move and you're dead," Elizabeth said quietly.

The girl went still as a statue.

"You're a girl," she whispered. "But why—"

"You're better off not knowing. Now, please just be quiet."

Elizabeth watched as the burly guardsman came to stand in front of Joshua.

"Kneel," Joshua commanded, "and bend your head."

The man obeyed. Joshua brought the hilt of his sword down on the base of the man's skull. The man slumped over with a groan. Joshua leaned down and felt for a pulse.

"He'll live. Tie up the wench, Beth, and let's be about this business."

Elizabeth looked around for something to use as a rope. "It's too bad we couldn't sound an alarm or something. It would certainly clear out the guardroom."

"That would be a great help," Joshua said, stripping the man's clothes from him.

"Think they have some kind of bell?" Elizabeth asked conversationally. She took one of Joshua's wet towels to tie it around the servant's wrists.

"There is," the girl whispered.

Joshua stopped the donning of his tunic and looked at her. "There is?"

"Don't believe her, Joshua," Elizabeth said, throwing him an exaggerated wink. "She'd probably lie just to get us in trouble." *Please be telling the truth!*

"'Tis true," the girl said, beginning to tremble. "And I woulda rung it, but there was no one to come to Dougan's aid."

"And what care you for Dougan?" Joshua asked, pulling the tunic down over his head and crossing the room to stand before the girl.

"I carry his babe."

Ah, now this was convenient. There was very little a woman wouldn't do for the man she loved.

Elizabeth had firsthand knowledge of that.

She tossed the wet towel across the room and turned the girl around. She put her hands on the young woman's shoulders.

"Why should we believe you?"

"Because 'tis true," the girl blurted out. Then she started to weep, great wrenching sobs. "And now that Nolan MacLeod has likely killed him! I'd kill Nolan myself if I dared. Dougan was good and kind, nothing like Daniel. If Danny hadn't been such a fool an' started this war, Dougan and I'd be wed, and he'd have all his lads still alive. Then they coulda kept Nolan without the gates. Damn that bloody MacLeod bastard!"

Well, that was all she needed to hear. Elizabeth shook her gently.

"Enough tears, girl. We'll save your Dougan and finish Nolan, but you have to help us. My husband's in the pit, and we'll never manage this without him." She dried the girl's cheeks with the hem of her sleeve. "Once we free the men from the dungeon, they'll take care of the rest. Now, can you ring the bell for us?"

The girl nodded, sniffing loudly.

"A pity we don't know the secrets of the passageways in the walls," Joshua said with a frown. "Dougan certainly knew them well enough."

The girl smiled. "Aye, as do I. That's how I came to him always," she said, blushing.

"Then show us," Joshua commanded. "Let's finish this while we still can."

Ten minutes later Elizabeth was following Joshua down a claustrophobic flight of stairs inside the walls of the castle. The girl certainly seemed to know her way around, and Elizabeth only prayed she hadn't led them into a trap. If the wench had, she and Joshua could kiss any hope of escape good-bye.

The passageway widened at the bottom of the steps. The air was dank and musty, and the humidity of it seeped right through Elizabeth's heavy cloak. She huddled against Joshua's back and closed her eyes, listening as the girl described the layout of the cellar. Then Joshua sent the girl back up the stairs to sound the alarm.

"Think this will work?" Elizabeth whispered, once the girl was gone.

" 'Twas your idea, not mine. How would I know if it will work? Just draw your blade, and try not to get yourself killed."

Elizabeth took her knife in her left hand and her sword in her right. And to calm herself, she thought back to the hours she had practiced with Ian in the garden, learning to fight like a Scot. She smiled when she remembered how well her street-mugging defenses had worked against Jamie's cousin. Hopefully they would work again today.

The sound of a bell in the distance made her jump. Joshua muttered a hasty prayer and set his shoulder against the stone. Elizabeth moved to stand next to him and put her ear against the wall. It was much thinner than she had expected, and she clearly heard the curses and the sounds of men rushing from the room.

"Now," Joshua barked, and they both shoved at the doorway.

It swung open easily, and they fell out into the chamber. Four guards remained, and they whirled around in surprise. Joshua snatched up a crossbow and unloaded it into two of the men. Elizabeth followed his lead and shot the third man in the arm. It was as close as she could come to killing him.

Joshua had no such qualms. He silenced the wounded man and his remaining comrade with two swift thrusts of his blade.

"Gather the weapons while I release Jamie and the lads. We'll have one bloody furious fight on our hands when the guards return."

Elizabeth gathered up discarded bows and relieved the dead guardsmen of their weapons. She spotted Jamie's sword on a table along with several other weapons that possibly belonged to Dougan's men.

"Elizabeth . . ."

Elizabeth whirled around at the sound of Jamie's voice, then gasped at the sight of him. He was half-dressed and covered with blood and bruises. She rushed to him and threw her arms around him. He gasped out a curse, and she hastily released him. Her hands came away bloody.

"Oh, Jamie—"

"Later," he growled. He turned to help others out of the pit, and she clapped her hand over her mouth to silence the yell that surely would have brought the walls down. His back was covered with open wounds from a whip.

"I'll kill him myself!" she shouted, snatching up a crossbow. Mercy? No, she'd never felt such a thing. Nolan would pay. And then she would find the specific man who had done this to her husband and kill him too. And probably take a good deal of pleasure in it.

The rest of the men, including Patrick and her brothers, were in no better shape than Jamie. But they were angry. Weapons were distributed quickly, and none too soon. Men came thumping back down the steps before the last of Dougan's kinsmen had climbed from the pit.

The first of Nolan's henchmen met his end with an arrow in his throat. The man behind him set up a cry before he died in a like manner. After that, Elizabeth lost track of the men who died on their way down the stairs. When the stock of arrows was depleted, swords were used. One thing she could say about Dougan's men, they were fine warriors. And with Jamie to lead them, they were invincible.

A hand closed over Elizabeth's mouth suddenly, and she was pulled backward.

She struggled, but her captor had her in a grip that wouldn't allow for it. She was pulled back into the hidden passageway and dragged up the steps. Struggling had been her plan until she felt a blade across her throat. After that, she went quietly, forcing herself to think calmly. Jamie would come for her. He wasn't outnumbered downstairs. Eventually he would realize she was gone; then he would figure out where she had disappeared to and follow her. And then Nolan would get his just desserts. She had no doubts it was Nolan who held her. The smell was a dead giveaway.

She was released when they reached a chamber, but it wasn't the chamber she'd been in before. She spun around as Nolan closed the secret passageway door. He turned to face her and smiled, very unpleasantly.

"Cousin."

"You're no kin of mine," she spat. "You just wait until Jamie gets here."

"It will be too late, Elizabeth. After I finish beating you, you won't have the strength to scream while I rape you. Jamie won't hear a thing." Nolan laughed, showing his rotting teeth to their full advantage. "Ah, how I do love traveling through the centuries and tormenting my cousin. Think you we'll spend eternity doing the like? I will stir up mischief, and he will follow to right it. Only you won't be there to save him. Perhaps

I'll merely let him follow me through a few more adventures before I finally finish him. What think you?"

"How did you learn about the forest?" Elizabeth asked. Jamie would come for her, if he had enough time to do so.

Nolan smiled again, a gruesome baring of his teeth. "Dear cousin Ian boasted of it. I visited the Fergusson during a time Ian happened to be rotting in the laird's dungeon, near death. He boasted he would escape and come to your time, now that he was so close to dying and wouldn't mar the fabric of time. He babbled some nonsense about a gate in the forest." Nolan laughed. "Ah, what a pitiful mind he had. He had no idea of what could be done with the forest."

"Is he dead?"

Nolan shrugged. "I left him dying. If he escaped, I know nothing of it."

"But surely you don't understand how the forest works." *Please hurry, Jamie!*

Nolan huffed and puffed. "I certainly do. You and your kin were too foolish to realize that I overheard your conversations at the keep the day you and Jamie found your minstrel. Jamie and one of your bastard brothers discussed it at length that afternoon. But I'd known before, of course. 'Tis the only reason your pitiful minstrel came forward. He never could have come here on his own."

"Gosh, you're pretty smart, Nolan." She didn't buy a word of him having known before, but eavesdropping was certainly something she could credit him with. So he *had* been lurking around the keep that day, and she had seen him in the forest near the pool.

"You're very fetching, Elizabeth. A pity you'll be dead so soon."

"Not if I have aught to say about it," a deep voice growled from behind Nolan.

Elizabeth cast her eyes heavenward and sighed in relief. Jamie's timing was perfect.

Her husband clutched his bloody sword, looking more fierce than she'd ever seen him. He was past angry. He was cold, as cold as steel and just that unyielding. If Nolan had possessed a grain of common sense, he would have thrown himself on his own sword.

But Nolan was Nolan, and he was a fool. He turned around to face Jamie, then drew his own sword and backed up a pace or two.

"Welcome, cousin," he sneered. "Now, you'll watch me as I rape your woman and slay her once I'm finished."

"In hell," Jamie said, his tone icy. "I've several marks to repay you for, cousin. Believe me when I say I'll relish the deed. But not in this chamber. 'Tis too small, lest you feel the need to flee. I daresay I'd enjoy the chase greatly. Elizabeth, open the door."

Elizabeth did, then heaved another sigh of relief at the grim-faced warriors who entered the room. Dougan's men. And each of them had a big axe to grind with a certain Nolan MacLeod.

"Help him down to the hall," Jamie commanded. "Dougan will want to see this. Joshua, see to my lady."

Elizabeth watched her husband leave, then took Joshua's arm as they descended the steps to the great hall. Her heart caught in her throat when she saw how her husband swayed as he walked down the stairs. He was weak. Nolan was well-rested.

The fight had already begun by the time she reached the great hall. Elizabeth stood near the hearth, surrounded by her brothers and Joshua and Patrick. It didn't comfort her. Jamie was weary from the harm that had been done to his body. Nolan took advantage of it to the fullest. Elizabeth gasped the first time Nolan's blade found its mark on Jamie's arm. The very last thing he needed was to lose more blood.

But that cut seemed to be the last straw, if the turn of events was any indication. Jamie's swordplay showed that he had dredged up strength from some hidden source. Nolan looked like a child in comparison. Jamie came at him, his sword thrusting as quickly and accurately as a striking snake. He cut Nolan a dozen times before he finally stepped in close and buried his sword up to the hilt in Nolan's chest. He lifted his cousin off the ground and looked at him, his face as hard as granite.

"For what you have done to me. And to my lady. Die and may you go to hell."

Nolan gurgled out a curse, then went limp. Jamie shoved him off his blade, then resheathed his sword. Elizabeth didn't wait for him to call her; she ran straight into his arms. He winced when her arms came in contact with his back, but he didn't pull away.

"Och, my bonny Elizabeth," he said hoarsely.

She couldn't speak. All she could do was hold him and shake.

It was over.

She spent the rest of the afternoon sitting on a stool near the hearth, waiting while her weary husband cleaned up the rest of the mess Nolan had made. She rested her forehead on her knees and let the tension ease from her. Around her she heard the sounds of victory: the weak congratulations a very battered Dougan gave his men, Alex's boasts, Patrick's laughter, a now-familiar serving wench's tears. It was all good and fine, but what she really wanted to do was go home.

And once they got back, she was never going to travel through time again.

"Elizabeth."

She looked up and took the hand Jamie offered her. She rose and went into his arms.

"Jamie, let's go home."

"You don't wish to stay the night?"

She shook her head. "I want to leave now. You need to get to a doctor."

"Perhaps I should bathe first."

She looked up and smiled in spite of herself. "You *are* rather fragrant. But you're also very sweet, James MacLeod. Have I told you lately how much I love you?"

"Nay, not recently, but I will hear it repeatedly once I am better rested. Come, love. Let me take you home."

If we can get there, Elizabeth added silently.

She stood by herself in the middle of the hall and watched Jamie have a final few words with Dougan. It was a very odd scene. Jamie was shaking hands with a man he would leave behind him several centuries in time. Zachary and Alex were exchanging parting words with men who had no idea her brothers would go back home and drive cars and fly planes. Then she thought of Roddy's legend that said she and Jamie were always popping up in different times to right wrongs.

Heaven help her.

No, it just wasn't going to happen. She would put her foot down on that, and Jamie would listen. No more wrong rightings. Robin Hood would survive without their help.

But as she saw Jamie's look of satisfaction as he came toward her, she had the feeling it might not be as easy as she hoped.

A half an hour later, they were riding through the gates. Elizabeth rode Jamie's horse with him, enjoying the saddle while he enjoyed Astronaut's rump. She wasn't about to ask him if he'd like her to move. She wanted his arms around her, and she didn't care what she had to do to have them that way.

And while they rode, she dreamed of home. She longed for their modern keep as she'd longed for nothing before. First their keep, then a trip in the car to Roddy's, then a long bath. And then a huge batch of Toll House cookies. She had to have some reward for surviving a trip to hell.

They might have ridden for hours, they might have ridden for days. Elizabeth wasn't sure, though she had the feeling she'd spent a great deal of time dozing in Jamie's arms.

They left the forest at sunrise. Jamie reined in Astronaut. Elizabeth hardly dared look, on the off chance they'd come back to the wrong place.

She took a deep breath and opened her eyes.

And there, at the base of a craggy mountain, sat a castle. Not an elegant castle like Versailles, nor even a comfortable English castle like Buckingham Palace, but a medieval castle in perfect condition.

With Jamie's dark green Jag parked outside the gates.

Elizabeth closed her eyes and let the tears trickle out from under her eyelids unchecked.

They were home.

Epilogue

JAMIE SAT IN his great chair at the head of his long table and sighed in satisfaction. It had been a fine Christmas feast, made even more so by the company that had joined him in Scotland for the holidays.

To his right sat his lady. Once again he looked at her beauty by light of the fire in the enormous hearth of the great hall. Ah, but it brought back such sweet memories. Elizabeth was just as lovely as she had been the first time she'd sat at his long table in the fourteenth century.

Motherhood suited her. She held their wee bairn in her arms, cooing over him with purely maternal noises. Jamie had done his best to imitate her noises, but young Ian seemed to prefer it when his father growled at him gently, so Jamie stopped fighting it. Go with the flow, as Zachary always said. At three months, Ian already showed signs of MacLeod grumbles, and Jamie couldn't have been more pleased about it. And how could Ian help but grow up strong and manly, with so many uncles about who were as fierce as his father?

Jamie was favored with a sweet smile from his wife and he made himself a mental note to take her upstairs as soon as was polite and show her just how pleased he was with her. Though they had taken care of Nolan several months earlier, Jamie still couldn't hold his wife enough. The thought of being without her was the one and only thing that could make him weep, and it always did when he thought about it too long.

He looked to his left and smiled at his brother. Ah, now this had been an unexpected joy. Patrick had taken up residence with him along with Zachary, Alex and Joshua. Jamie had been enormously pleased by it. Having kin about to wrestle and tease with had taken him back to his earliest years, before the heavy weight of responsibility had descended and turned him into a very young laird. He and Patrick spent hours roaming over their land, reminiscing about times past, speculating on the fate of friends and foes. And it was a pleasure to hone his skills with his brother. Patrick's swordplay had certainly improved with time.

All things considered, the forest had turned out not to be such a bad place after all. Indeed, Jamie had begun to look on it with a friendlier eye. After all, it had given him his brother back. And it had brought him his love.

"Jamie, I'm going to put young Ian to bed," Elizabeth said, rising. "I'll see you later?"

"I'll be there immediately."

He watched her walk away and smiled to himself.

"You're drooling, brother," Patrick teased. "Follow her, if you like. I'll see to your guests."

The guests were actually Elizabeth's family, and Roddy and his family. Jamie looked over the long table, liking how it felt to have kin close. Elizabeth's brothers had all come over with their wives and their children, and the hall was filled with sounds of merrymaking. Patrick continually teased Jamie that he'd gone soft to allow so many women in his hall, but Jamie only smiled. He liked walking into the kitchen and eavesdropping as Elizabeth and her sisters-in-law cooked up desserts for a very demanding Joshua of Sedgwick. He liked to watch Elizabeth's mother as she shepherded the children into his thinking room to tell them stories. There was a warmth of spirit that permeated his home, a warmth that hadn't been there before Elizabeth first came. Her women kinfolk only added to that sweetness.

Of course, the lads balanced that out nicely enough. The hall floor saw many wrestling matches. Jamie's thinking room was more often than not used for the watching of television and the consumption of ale. Having so many people about reminded Jamie of the confusion and lack of privacy he had enjoyed in the fourteenth century. Aye, it was a fine life.

But it would be just as fine when everyone left, and it was back to the few who made up his new clan. He would once again boot the lads outside and make love to Elizabeth before the fire in the great hall. He wouldn't blush because her father clucked his tongue in a purely paternal way when Jamie chased Elizabeth up the stairs. Her brothers and Patrick were used to that by now.

"Jamie, go," Patrick ordered. "I'll see to your hall well enough."

Jamie didn't have to hear that twice. He slipped out of his chair and walked toward the stairs. Elizabeth's father cleared his throat pointedly, and Jamie quickened his pace, feeling a blush color his cheeks. No sense in having a lecture until after the fact.

Elizabeth smiled at him when he walked into their bedchamber.

"Did my dad tease you again?"

Jamie walked over to her. "Aye, he did. By St. Michael's knees, Elizabeth, we're properly wed! When will he cease to make me feel guilty about bedding you?"

Elizabeth laughed. "He's just showing you how you'll act when you have a daughter of your own. Take notes, Jamie. I'm sure they'll come in handy."

"Aye, and I'll likely be as irritating as your sire."

She smiled. "Probably so. Let's go have a bath. It will soothe that infamous temper of yours quite well, I think."

Jamie allowed her to lead him into the marvelous bathing chamber off their bedchamber, then sat on the sink while Elizabeth prepared their bath. Then he graciously allowed her to make love to him and held his hand over her mouth while she found pleasure. After all, they had guests downstairs.

He leaned back against the side of the Jacuzzi tub, held his wife close and let his thoughts wander. And they wandered right to the forest. Perhaps a bit of time travel wasn't completely out of the question, now that they seemed to have gotten the hang of working the forest. There was something exciting about the thought of sailing on a seventeenth-century pirate ship. Jamie could see himself at the helm, brandishing his saber and hoisting the skull and crossbones as cannons belched balls and smoke against his enemies; aye, he could see them turning tail and fleeing . . .

"Jamie, what are you thinking about?" Elizabeth lifted her head and looked at him suspiciously.

"Nothing." He affected a look of innocence.

"No time traveling. I won't let you out of the house again if you don't promise me that."

Och, what a dilemma.

"Jamie," Elizabeth warned.

"What if I promise that I'll do none unless I take you along?"

"No. Ian needs both his parents. And he doesn't need to come along with us and learn history firsthand. He'll do just fine learning it from a book. Now, promise me."

Jamie kissed her. And when she tried to speak, he kissed her some more. One thing led to another, and soon he was carrying her to his bed. He loved her sweetly, then passionately, then slowly and powerfully. And once he thought she just might be asleep, he put his hands behind his head and let his imagination run away with him again.

"I don't distract that easily," Elizabeth murmured. "Promise me, Jamie."

Jamie sighed. "I promise. No time traveling."

Elizabeth's sigh of relief was so audible, her sire likely heard it. Jamie smiled and kissed the top of her head. After all, what did he need back in the past that he didn't have right there in his arms?

Aye, time had already given him gifts he could never repay.

It was enough.